Chained by Fear

LOST AND FOUND DUET

HARLIE KAY

For permissions or inquiries, please contact:
whisperedwordspress.com

ISBN: 978-1-966611-03-5
Published by: Independently Published
Cover Design by: K.B. Barrett Designs
Editing by: Independently Edited

Printed in the United States of America
2025

To the ones who believed in me when I forgot how—thank you for holding me together when I wanted to fall apart.

To the friends and family who endured every chaotic meltdown, mood swing, and late-night rant—you deserve a trophy (or at least a stiff drink).

To the English teacher who kept confiscating my notebooks because my stories were "too graphic" for school: I turned them into a career. No hard feelings... but you were kind of a buzzkill.

And to the dark romance lovers—the ones who spot a red flag and lean in closer—this one's for you.

Check Out My Playlists

Music fuels emotion, and this story was written with loud and honest songs playing in the background.

Scan the QR code below to listen on Spotify.

Tracklist Includes These and More:
1 *“Angry”* – Paravi
2 *“Sabotage”* – Bebe Rexha
3 *“Lovely”* – Billie Eilish
4 *“Hurt”* – Johnny Cash
5 *“Paint it, Black”* – Ciara
6 *“The Devil Within“* – Digital Daggers
7 *“Animals”* – Architects
8 *“Take Me to Church”* – Hozier
9 *“Runaway”* – AURORA
10 *“Survivor”* – 2WEI
11 *“What Was I Made For?”* – Billie Eilish
12 *“Declined”* – Britton
13 *“Burning Down”* – Alex Warren
14 *“A Little Death”* - The Neighbourhood
15 *“DROWN (tie me up)”* - Layto

This playlist captures the emotional chaos, haunting memories, and fleeting moments of hope woven into every chapter.

Trigger Warning

Before diving in, please take a moment to review the following content warnings. This book contains dark, emotional, and potentially distressing material. Everyone processes trauma differently, and your well-being always comes first.

This story features:

- Present-time sexual assault
- Childhood sexual, physical, and psychological abuse
- Physical and emotional abuse toward adults and children
- Gaslighting and manipulation
- Psychological torment
- Betrayal by loved ones
- Captivity / confinement
- Torture (both physical and emotional)
- PTSD, trauma flashbacks, and dissociation
- Suicidal ideation
- Panic attacks and emotional breakdowns
- Alcohol abuse
- Drug use
- Coercion and power imbalance
- Dominant/submissive dynamics (non-kink, trauma-related)

- Verbal degradation
- Characters with explosive anger and violent tendencies
- Lying and withholding of the truth
- Revenge themes
- Complicated and morally gray relationships
- Emotional whiplash, instability, and grief
- Mental health struggles, including depression and hopelessness
- Human Trafficking

This story also involves deeply flawed male characters who do not make the best choices for themselves or the female main character. Their growth is slow, messy, and often painful, mirroring the healing journey of our female main character.

If any of these topics are harmful or triggering for you, please consider reading with caution or skipping this book altogether. Your mental and emotional safety is more important than any story.

PART ONE

Lost

"I like to think that our story
isn't over just yet,
that someday we'll meet again
and finally get it right."

- faraway

CHAPTER 1

Ember Rose

APRIL 25TH, 2019

"This is the *worst* idea you've ever had," I groan while Marissa grins with manic glee. She smooths her tight dress, the material hugging like a second skin. I envy her confidence as she tugs on the fabric, trying but failing to cover the curve of her right buttcheek.

"No, my sweet Em." She winks, gripping my hand. The pungent smell of alcohol on her breath makes me wince. "This is a brilliant idea." Giggling, she pulls me from my hiding place behind a rust-covered stack of aluminum scaffolding, dragging me into the wild west of the unknown.

My gaze sweeps over the horde of watchers—it's... a lot. People drink, laugh, dance, and smoke what I can only assume are less-than-legal substances. Despite this being a legitimate racing circuit, the presence of illicit drugs doesn't come as too much of a shock. Marissa claims cops rarely patrol this far out of the city; I've even spotted some off-duty officers joining the fun. Showcasing New York's finest.

"It's *my* duty as *your* best friend to get you out of the house, *especially* for your birthday."

"And you thought bringing me to a place where I have to do a powder check on the toilet seat is something I'd like?" She smirks a wildcat grin in response as I roll my eyes. "You're the absolute worst friend," I grumble, though there's no spice to my words. Unlike me,

Marissa isn't afraid of pushing boundaries, especially mine, taking personal offense to my desire for a quiet night at home with a book in my lap and hot tea on the stove.

"No." She drags out the *O* in a sing-song sound before finishing her statement. "I'm the best."

She drags me through the spectators, weaving us between drunken dancers, if grinding pelvises together can be called that. I've read about dry humping in books and thought it was sexy. But it's really not when witnessing it. Put that on the list of things I don't wanna read about anymore.

Marissa scans the horde of party-goers, and we dart under a set of rusted bleachers, their metal frame seeming just a few pounds away from collapsing. Just keep my hefty butt off it, and we should be safe. The urge to wrap my arms around my torso to shield myself from wandering eyes is tempting, but I force myself to stop. No one is paying attention. I'm not that important.

A group of tatted, leather-clad men leers at us while we hurry past. I tug on my blouse, trying to cover up, hyper-aware of their eyes on the low cut of my shirt. Unease crawls up my back beneath their salacious stares.

"Babe!" Marissa shrieks, causing me to jump like a frightened cat. Jesus, she has a scream on her.

She tears away from me, rocketing herself into Jason's arms. A contented sigh escapes as she buries her face in his neck. His fingers tangle in her blonde strands. Watching him inhale her scent, holding her like she's the first and last thing on his mind, leaves me feeling like an intruder. I stand there, arms wrapped around myself, the only embrace I can count on. *Morbid much?*

"Happy Birthday, *Rosie*," Jason says, setting Marissa down before helping to adjust her dress. "I'm surprised she got you to come out tonight. This doesn't seem like your kind of...scene."

"And what exactly is my kind of scene, *Jasey*?" I sass, satisfied when his eyes narrow at the nickname. Smirking, I cross my arms in a challenge. If he wants to throw out old nicknames, I can match him. Being called Rosie dredges up pain I've worked hard to bury. Like carpet burning across my entire body, it stings with a rawness that drags me back in time. Suddenly, I'm twelve. Terrified. Hurt. Vulnerable. And I swore to myself a long time ago that I'd never be that scared little girl again. So if he wants to play that game, *Jasey,* it is.

"He didn't mean anything by it, Em." Marissa frowns, observing us.

The corner of my mouth twitches with how forced my smile is. I know he didn't *mean* anything by it. Bullies *never* see themselves as bullies. With my best friend dating the man who tortured me through high school, he'd suddenly sweetened up to me. However, that doesn't erase the fact that he'd used family privilege to make high school unbearable. Being the dean's son guaranteed the teachers looked the other way. When Marissa introduced me to the dreamy guy she couldn't stop raving about, imagine my surprise when the reason I ate lunch under the stairwell extended a hand like we were old buddies. So, of course, for Marissa's sake, I plaster on a smile.

"Sorry, Jason. Just a little on edge tonight," I apologize. He nods, sliding his hand to rest on Marissa's *tiny* waist. *I wonder what it would be like to have a guy want to touch me like that?* My heart sinks as I shake my head to rid myself of the intruding thoughts.

"No problem. Maybe you got a little dose of the good stuff walking through the bustle."

I snort, cringing at the skunk-weed smoke as it mixes with the scent of BO. "Or maybe I'm high from toilet seat cocaine."

Marissa rolls her eyes while Jason bellows. "Right on, that's the spirit, Emmy."

He leans into Marissa for a kiss, which she eagerly accepts, and I turn away, already over my lovey-dovey capacity. *Yuck.* The race track looms nearby, a so-called venue that's just a circle of dirt littered with cigarette butts and either strangely shaped balloons or used condoms. Despite the grimness and lack of basic hygiene, a line of pristine cars is lit by giant stadium lights, every inch gleaming with polish. From the hood to the tires, they are utter perfection.

I truthfully don't know much about cars, especially the level of customization these metal monsters have undergone. There is no way these prized hunks of tin are road-legal. But, being miles from the nearest town, far from any police station, no one seems concerned. The whole thing feels ripped straight from a *Fast and Furious* movie—fun to watch, sure. From the comfort of my couch. Wrapped in a fluffy blanket. Sipping black tea. At least through a screen, I don't have to deal with this appalling smell.

"For what it's worth, you're doing a bang-up job blending in," Jason remarks, much to Marissa's delight.

My outfit is all her doing—Jason probably picked up on that right away. The mom jeans and fitted tees I usually live in are long gone, swapped for distressed denim that rides dangerously high on my thighs and flares out more than I'd prefer. At least my ass isn't exposed. Because my top doesn't offer the same grace, it's barely more than a strip of fabric diving between my breasts, putting my not-so-average cleavage front and center. The open back lets the breeze rob me of any warmth, making it obvious I've got no bra on. Marissa made that call, relying instead on enough boob tape to hoist the girls to runway standards. Six-inch stilettos were never happening, since I drew the line there—my toes are thankfully toasty in my beat-up black Vans.

"Do a twirl for us, Em," Marissa demands, spinning her finger in a circle for emphasis, thrilled with her work. Rolling my eyes once again, I humor her with a quick spin. "So adorbs. I can't get enough of that fiery hair. I wonder if I could pull that off as nicely."

Said hair sits in a relaxed ponytail, which is a complete lie considering that straightening my stubborn curls took over an hour. And having someone yank at your hair for an hour is not fun.

The so-called "casual makeup" feels just as deceptive. Marissa labeled it a "she woke up like this" look, yet half a bottle of concealer tells a different story. None of it matters in the dead of night, illuminated only by headlights and the white beams on the track.

A car horn sounding draws everyone's attention, the thrum of bass-heavy music lowers, and I watch as a woman scrambles onto the hood of a car, wearing the skimpiest outfit I've ever seen. It appears to be made entirely of cheerleader pom-poms, sparkling like the prize car she's perched on.

She spreads her arms wide, commanding attention. "Hello, Little Racers!" she shouts, words soaring above the restless energy. "Tonight's a night to remember! And you know we've got your favorite—Killer Thorne on the docket today! Though he is more like a thorn in my side.

If you know, you know." She winks at a nearby group of ladies, and they giggle, turning toward each other to gossip.

The crowd laughs, morphing into cheers, forming a chaotic symphony of hoarse shouts and sharp whistles, soaring above the rumble of motors revving mixed with the stench of exhaust. Voices clash, overlapping like thunder cracking through the grimy, oil-streaked racetrack. The sound courses through me, pulling me into madness—the sheer energy of it all—wild, messy, maybe even a little exciting.

Pom-pom's voice rises above the chatter. "Now, let's go over the rules!" she declares, silencing the stragglers' murmurs. "One: No tampering with vehicles. If you're caught, you're out!"

A ripple of groans spreads through the gathering, laced with sarcastic shouts of "Well, duh!" and "Of course!" *Do people actually do that? I didn't think it was that serious. What did Marissa get me into?*

"Two: No reckless driving that leads to, you guessed it, crashes—I'm not in the mood to call emergency services *again* because some of you don't know how to control your cars."

Scattered laughter mixes with exaggerated sighs, but Pom-pom continues, her grin growing. "Three: All bets close before the motors rev. Don't come crying to us if you're late; time management is key here."

She stops, eyeing the crowd, "And Four!" She continues with a playful edge, swishing her pom-pom skirt. Heads snap up, faces tense. "This one's new." Her expression gleams with mischief. "If there's a tie, racers, you take the back seat, and your romantic partner takes the wheel."

The air erupts. Pom-pom observes like the queen of mayhem, smirking, daring anyone to challenge her. Unease moves through those already calculating how this twist impacts their bets.

Marissa groans, tugging at the delicate strands of her hair as she paces in circles. Her heels grind on the gravel, the sound scratching at my ears. She stops abruptly, fixing Jason with a look of pure rage.

"Did you know about this?" Her fingertips dig into her temples as she shakes her head. "Unreal."

With a quick pivot, she closes the distance between them in two strides, jabbing a finger into his pec. "You *know* exactly what will happen if I get behind the wheel."

Her focus drifts to the gleaming car before returning to him; she bats her lashes, a slow, mischievous smirk tugging at her lips. "What are you going to do if I crash it? Hmm?—because it will happen—don't act surprised, you know I can't drive stick," she grumbles, her bottom lip jutting out.

Jason runs his hands down his face. "Mare..." She folds her arms, tilting her head, sizing him up—the energy between them is laced with mild amusement rather than real anger. He looks at his car, and I instantly recognize his expression—admiration mixed with some mild obsession. His lips pinch, and his nose wrinkles; his shoulders square like he's trying to shield the vehicle from her physically.

Marissa snorts. "Unbelievable," she huffs. "That damn car is all you think about. Admit it—you love it more than me." Her tone dips into a mock pout, playful but still laced with just enough accusation to make him squirm. It's kinda fun to watch, honestly; he always loved to make cruel, teasing comments to me that made me feel the same. And what's worse, he doesn't deny it—a subtle wince, a slight tilt of his head toward the car—confirmation enough for Marissa.

He leans in. "Trust me, Baby. I'll do everything possible to make sure that doesn't happen."

I roll my eyes at their theatrics. Once he's done whispering sweet nothings, Jason steps back, scanning the other drivers—or, more likely, sizing up his chances. His jaw locks, betraying his usual confidence.

"LET THE RACES BEGIN!"

The words ignite the frenzy, a bomb of booze, drugs, and adrenaline detonating. Bodies surge forward, desperate for the best view. I try standing on my toes to see over the crowd, but my five-foot-three self doesn't have much luck.

"Come on, Shorty." Jason teases, his firm hand finding my back as he guides Marissa and me through the throng.

Drunk bidders sway, their laughter drowned out by the loud flirtations of drivers looming over the women who hang on the powerful machines. Jason steers us from the frenzy, and I catch little snippets of the vehicles lining up. I can see a towering man standing next to a maroon vehicle, and I strain to see more, but Jason pulls away.

"Where are we going?" I shout, the deafening beat of the music swallowing my words.

Jason flashes all his teeth, his hands gripping my hips as he lifts me with surprising ease into the back of a black truck. "Up you go!" *How the hell did he lift me so easily?* Jason is like a twig, similar to Marissa in that aspect. But, I guess they are both tiny when comparing them to me.

"Let's see who's got balls and who's just bark!" Marissa hollers, perched on the edge of the truck.

"Is this Jason's truck?"

"No, it is one of the other racers; they just let me use it when I come to the races, so Jason doesn't need to worry about where I am," Marissa yells. I nod as if this all makes sense, but truthfully, this is all a little overwhelming.

Leaning over the side of the truck, the engines roar, vibrating through the ground, rattling my insides.

It's straight out of a movie as a woman commands the front, a scarf snapping like a ringmaster's whip. Each movement drips with intention—her body a carnal temptation swaying in the smoky haze from the exhaust. Her skirt hangs low, inching toward the edge of indecency, while her top barely qualifies as clothing. Every seductive sway of her hips taunts—a dare, a silent promise. Heat creeps up my cheeks, a slow flush rolling through me.

"On. Your. Marks..." She lifts the scarf high, the fabric catching in the headlights. The ground vibrates, sending birds into flight. Excitement boils like lava through my veins, every muscle wound in expectation.

"Get set...GO!"

She folds her body forward, the scarf whipping behind her in a flash of red lightning. Cars explode off the line, tires grinding against gravel, kicking up a dust storm. The engines scream, speed taking over, the race shifting into high gear.

I watch the cars streak across the track, my gaze following their rapid sprint. "Breathe, Em." The tightness relaxes as I release the air I'd been holding.

The distant hum from the vehicles fades into the background, swallowed by the steady thump of bass vibrating through the crowd.

Bouncing on my toes, I keep my eyes on the disappearing tail lights. They vanish behind the sea of bodies.

Before I know it, they are racing back toward the starting line. A shudder rolls through me, excitement swooping in my ribcage as they round the final curve and barrel toward the finish. The tires scrape against the dirt as the drivers slam on the brakes, the cars skidding to a halt, dust dancing in their wake, and the crowd goes wild.

The driver of a sleek white car throws his arm out the window, grinning. I smile as the masses swarm around him—a frenzy of dancers, bidders, racers—clamoring to celebrate his win.

"First race winner is Tristan Devereux!" Pom-pom booms over the loudspeakers. Electricity hums as if the whole damn place just erupted in flames.

"Next racers, take your mark!"

"I need you both to stay here until I get back, okay?" Jason pleads, and for the second time tonight, hesitation creeps in. *What could happen here?*

We nod. Satisfied with our response, Jason wastes no time, moving through the mob. I track his path as he shoulders his way through to get to his car.

Engines rev, a mechanical symphony echoing through the night. Jason moves with practiced precision, hands gliding over his car, ensuring every part functions flawlessly. His focus is razor-sharp, but there's a gnawing unease in my gut. The air feels wrong—like the calm before a storm.

The horn blares, warning of the start of the next race. Jason slips into his car, and the sleek machine purrs as he rolls toward the starting line. The engine growls—a mighty rumble and a ripple of excitement moves through the crowd.

Two vehicles pull up beside him, their drivers hidden behind tinted windshields, keeping them from view. "Jason! If you finish first, you'd better know how to finish me next!"

I quake, "Marissa!"

"What? He needs a reason to win, well, I just gave him one."

"I think everything will be just fine without your motivation," I mutter, squeezing her hand. She doesn't look at me, but her fingers curl into mine.

"I'm not worried," Marissa grumbles. Though she tries to tug away from me, I hold firm, keeping her hand entangled with mine. Her eyes narrow, watching Jason's car. "I'm just worried he'll end up in a tie. This stupid rule's going to be the death of me, I swear. If I have to drive that damn thing, he won't be getting any blow jobs for a month."

A chuckle bubbles out of me at her bluntness. "Dang, Mare, don't punish the poor guy."

The same woman from before returns, twirling her scarf in the air as she starts her countdown. As she finishes her show, the racers launch forward. "Hope your brakes are better than your pullout game!" Marissa taunts, her eyes fused to the action like she's willing Jason's car to fly faster.

As he rounds one of the bends, his sleek black Charger comes neck-and-neck with a Dodge Challenger. Both vehicles are pushing their limits, their engines screaming in competition. "I swear to god, Jason, if you don't win this..." Marissa yells as they round the final bend, dust and debris spitting from their wheels while the cars fight to take control. The crowd screams, shaking the night as the race hurtles toward an explosive finish.

"No... NONONO!" Marissa's screeches as they cross the finish line... at the same time. The tires grind to a stop, and her hands fly to her face. "Fuck, no."

"Well, well, everyone!" Pom-pom's voice rises above the buzz. "Looks like the first tie of the night just happened!"

Shouts fill the air, and excitement crackles as everyone waits for what's next.

Marissa sinks behind me, face pale. "I can't drive his car, Em," she hisses, eyes attempting to find an escape. "I was joking about crashing it, but if I get behind the wheel, that's exactly what'll happen. It's a stick shift, for crying out loud! I don't know how to drive that—I'll humiliate myself... Jason, too."

For a moment, I toy with the idea of stepping in and giving her an easy out. But the memory of how she dragged me into this mess stops me. Watching her squirm proves too satisfying to resist. A tiny grin threatening to surface.

"Well, Marissa, what's the plan?" I ask with faux sweetness as I flutter my caked eyelashes.

Her mouth opens, but before she can protest further, I grip her hand, tugging her to the end of the truck bed. Her heels scrape against the aluminum.

"Hey! Wait—" she sputters.

"Too late!" I sing over my shoulder, grinning as she stumbles along. "Come on, you wanted me to experience excitement for my birthday, didn't you? What is more exciting than this?" I tease, shooting her a mischievous grin.

"Ember, let me go!"

I laugh, ignoring her. The more she resists, the more amused I get. Talk about Karma being a bitch.

Jason pushes his way through the mob, his jaw tight. He locks onto Marissa, the silent plea clear. *Please don't destroy my car.*

The sight fuels my giddy feeling, and a grin spreads across my face. This night is shaping up to be far more entertaining than I expected. The thought of Marissa behind the wheel of Jason's beloved car feels almost too good to be true.

Jason stops at the foot of the truck. "Babe..." he drawls, his tone carrying a soft whine as he stretches a hand toward her.

"No!" Marissa snaps. "I warned you, Jason. Put me behind that wheel, and your precious car will look like it's been through a tornado, rolled off a cliff, and dragged through a scrapyard by the time I'm done with it."

Jason's big brown eyes go full puppy-dog mode as he looks up at her, complete with a jutting bottom lip. *Gag.* It's enough to make me cringe, but apparently, it works like a charm on Marissa.

"Ugh," she groans, letting Jason help her down from the truck. The moment her feet hit the ground, she spins toward me, her grip like iron as she grabs my arm. "You're coming with me, bitch," she hisses.

"Why am I being dragged into this? I didn't sign up for it!" I laugh as she moves, letting Jason help me to the ground.

"Because if I go down in a fiery car crash, you're coming with me," she huffs as she pushes past the pack of onlookers, not bothering to hide her exasperation. She doesn't bother apologizing when she bumps into someone—instead, silencing them with a glare over her shoulder before firing another barb at Jason. "You had *one* job, Jason—*win* or keep it in your pants. Now I've gotta hump gears like a virgin on prom night and you're definitely not getting any blow jobs tonight."

A disbelieving laugh bursts from me as she pulls me along in her wake. Marissa moves with the grace of a big cat on the prowl. While I'm breathless, struggling to keep pace, she never slows, never looks back as we weave through tipsy fans, bidders flashing wads of cash, and the air heavy with gas fumes, sweat, and cheap perfume. Chaos swirls, but nothing slows her. She continues to move like a woman possessed.

I start to relax, but a chill snakes up my spine, cold fingers trailing the back of my neck. Long since buried instincts flare. I scan the crowded scene. Faces blurring, a sea of strangers. Yet I see... nothing. Not a hint of anything out of place. The laughter, the shouting, and the thrum of engines continue as if the world's spinning fine. But that uneasy tickle refuses to go away. It gnaws at me.

Shoving the discomfort aside, I toss Jason a forced grin. "This is all your fault, you know!" Jason scrambles to keep up, a touch frantic. The tension in his jaw betrays his calm, only fueling my amusement.

"Shut up, Emmy," he grumbles. His gaze moving to Marissa. "You don't mean that, babe. I tried! I didn't know that I would be racing Thorne, or I would've signed up for a different race."

Marissa stops dead in her tracks, whirling on him with a glare that could peel chrome off a bumper.

"Oh, *you tried*?" she spits, one brow arched high. "That's what you're going with? You *tried*? What, did your balls shrivel the second you saw Thorne's name on the roster?"

Jason opens his mouth, but Marissa steamrolls over him.

"Next time, *don't sign up at all* if you're gonna fold faster than your dick on a cold night. I told you—I don't do gears, I do lip gloss and threats. And now I'm about to stall out on the starting line and get smoked by a guy named after a villain in a bad erotica."

Jason tries to laugh it off, but it comes out shaky. "Come on, babe, you've watched me do it a hundred times—"

"That's not how learning works, dumbass!"

Another laugh escapes me, more out of disbelief than amusement. People are watching now, snickering behind their hands and phones as Marissa yanks the driver's side door open and stares at the stick like it personally insulted her.

She mutters under her breath, "Okay, clutch is... whatever. This bitch better pray I don't grind her into dust."

Jason clears his throat behind her. "Technically, *you* are the bitch in this scenario—"

Her head snaps around like something out of a horror movie.

"Finish that sentence and I swear to God, Jason, I'll leave your body in the trunk and *still* come in second place."

He wisely shuts up.

I glance back toward the crowd. The unease returns—slithering like smoke under my skin. I don't see anything, but it's *there*. Watching. Waiting.

A group of men stands off to the side, movements clipped, their hands cutting through the air as they argue. I can't hear a damn word over the pounding bass and growl of engines, but it's obvious—they're pissed, and they're hunting for someone. The way their attention darts between the car lineup and the crowd's edge has my skin crawling.

"Yikes," I mutter, shifting toward Jason. "You might be broody, but at least you're not *that* kind of disaster."

He doesn't respond. Doesn't even blink. Just tracks the men like he's trying to figure out if he should throw punches or run.

"Come on, Speed Racer." I bump his elbow. "We've got a problem to prep for before Marissa launches your car into orbit."

Still nothing. His jaw clenches hard enough to creak.

I press against the side of his car, and the chill hits me like I slammed into a block of ice. The shiver that rips through me could register on the Richter scale. "Next time, I'm wearing a damn coat. Screw aesthetics."

No response. He's somewhere else entirely.

Across the lot, the argument continues. Their body language is loud—urgent, not even pretending to stay cool. It hits me with a weird familiarity I don't ask for. That kind of fury... I've seen it before. In a kitchen too small for everyone's egos. In the hallway outside my childhood bedroom. That same barely-held-together chaos pretending to function.

I shake it off like a bad dream.

Jason and Marissa are going at it beside me. She's in the car, attempting to adjust mirrors and mumbling threats while Jason tries to explain which button not to press if she doesn't want to eject herself into the stratosphere.

"Seriously," I say under my breath, folding my arms tighter across my chest, "how did I end up in the middle of all this?"

A familiar shout slices through the noise.

"Do we have our tiebreakers?"

Jason reacts like she fired a gun. His head snaps toward the commotion.

"We don't have partners, Charlie," one of the arguing men calls out, frustration dripping from every syllable. "Unless you've got a better plan—"

Charlie doesn't miss a beat. She lets out a sound that could peel paint. "Pick someone. I don't care if it's your ex, your mom, or a drunk girl with a learner's permit. Just find someone who won't crash."

That's the match to the powder keg.

Suddenly, women are on their feet. A few wave their arms. Others strike poses like they're auditioning for centerfolds. One hikes her dress up her thigh and winks at the crowd.

I drop my head, kicking a line in the dirt with my Vans. Dust floats up and settles on my shoes. The cold's working its way through the seams of my jeans now like teeth gnashing at skin.

Jason's still rattling off a tutorial like his car's the crown jewel of the damn race scene. I tune him out.

Then—

"You."

Everything stills.

My head jerks up. Heat crawls across my neck as I register what's happening.

Every person in the area has turned toward me.

And the man's hand?

It's pointing straight at my chest.

My voice catches before it fully forms. "M-me?"

CHAPTER 2

Ember Rose

My head jerks between the pointed finger and the sea of watchers, disbelief churning in my chest. One hand rises to my collarbone. "I'm sorry—are you serious?" My brow arches, every word dry. I offer an empty smile. "Yeah, that's gonna be a no from me."

The man leaning against the fender doesn't react. Arms folded, muscles stretching the sleeves of his shirt, he watches like he's already made up his mind. No urgency. No hurry. Just a silent command as he crooks a finger.

A summons.

"I don't think you have a choice, Princess."

The words barely register before hands clamp around my waist and force me forward.

My shoes scrape against the dirt, kicking up dust as I'm pushed toward him. No grip. No footing. Just motion I didn't ask for.

"What the fuck do you think you're doing?" I snap, my nails raking across the skin over his knuckles. He huffs a low laugh, like I'm a fly buzzing too close to his drink.

"They can't just *grab* her!" Marissa calls out, but Jason holds her back.

Another man closes in, an arm slung across my shoulders like a noose made of charm.

"Aww, don't want to help us out, Sweetheart?" His grin is lazy, all teeth. He's taller than the other, and his blue-brown stare doesn't waver, studying me like he already knows how this ends.

The space around me disappears as they herd me forward—my pulse surges, thudding in my ears like war drums. Every direction feels blocked, like I've walked straight into a trap, and the walls are already in place.

I rear back and slam my elbow into the stomach behind me. Bone meets muscle, and pain bursts up through my arm like fire. *Ouch!*

A groan confirms the hit landed.

"Goddamn," he wheezes. "What are you made of?"

His buddy doubles over laughing, hands on his knees, shaking as if he can't believe it.

That's my moment.

I break from the group, sprinting between bodies and shouts, breath burning in my lungs. Dirt flies beneath my feet, the air cooler now.

I almost get away.

Before a hand snaps around my throat and yanks me off course.

I collide with a solid chest, the force stealing whatever air I had left. The zipper of his jacket grazes my skin, cold and biting. Heat radiates off him like a furnace, and the scent that clings to his shirt curls into me—smoke, cedar, leather, and control.

"Where do you think you're going, Red?"

The words wrap around my skull like velvet dipped in gasoline.

His hold tightens, not enough to choke, but enough to remind me who's in control.

A whimper escapes, barely audible. Not fear. Not defiance. Just raw confusion at how badly my body reacts.

I lean in. Not on purpose. Not really.

He notices.

And pulls me closer.

Like I belong there.

"I—I was..." The words evaporate as the trio crowds in. The one with eyes like waves battering cliffs focuses on me, and everything inside me answers with an involuntary yes.

Beside him, the man with moss-colored irises lingers in his wake, wild and unreadable. Their presence envelops me, and I can't tell if it's fear, curiosity, or a strange sense of security wrapping around me.

"We need you to race."

Goosebumps rise across my arms. If it weren't for the pasties holding everything in place, this cold would've made a spectacle out of me—mental note: next time, screw Marissa's wardrobe choices.

"I... I don't know how to drive a stick," I murmur, eyes darting between them. His grip tightens at my throat, just enough to steal air. Part of me hopes that confession makes them reconsider. The other part? The twisted one? Prays it doesn't.

They move in unison. Not rushed. Not frantic. Just methodical. Wolves circling their mark. My nerves spark, but no alarm follows. I'm not frozen in fear—I'm suspended in the kind of anticipation that steals common sense.

Heat creeps down my spine. Twenty-five years untouched, still technically innocent... and yet I'm standing here, pulse thudding hard, a truth blooming inside me that I can't smother: I want them.

"Well, Red?" He murmurs in my ear.

I jerk upward, fast enough that our noses brush. Air whooshes out of my lungs. He doesn't miss a beat. He dips forward and grazes the tip of my nose with his teeth. Barely a nip. But it's electric.

A slow grin pulls at his mouth. His eyes—rich, burnished, impossible to pin down—roam over me like he's already mapped out every inch.

"I'll ride with you," he says, warm breath brushing my skin. "But you'll need one more. Who's it gonna be?"

His hand slips from my throat, the loss hitting harder than it should.

"What?" The word scrapes from my throat as I stumble backward. Metal bites into my back, the chill biting through my skin. He smirks, too damn confident, too damn sure.

A sound rumbles from him—half chuckle, half warning. My gaze drops on instinct—to his chest, arms, the curve of muscle under that shirt, the way his jeans cling just right. It's... a lot.

"Red?"

My attention snaps back up. His grin widens, all heat and arrogance.

One hand runs through his hair, tousling it in a way that feels effortless and practiced, like he knows the damage it does.

I chew on my lip, scrambling for words. "I… um… I can't—"

A throat clears beside me.

Blue Eyes leans on the fender, arms folded, hair a dark mess over his brow. Scruff shades his jaw, giving him the kind of edge you only earn from bad decisions and good lighting.

"So, who do you choose, Princess?" The third steps forward. Matcha-green eyes drag over me like velvet and nails. He adjusts himself without shame, and I make a slight noise—half shock, half intrigue. His hair's pulled back, jaw locked in an angle that dares me to look away.

My attention wanders too long. He notices. Of course he does.

Fingers wrap around my chin, steering me back to him. Lava simmers behind his stare.

"Pick one," he growls. "You know you want to."

Everything around me falls away. I stand there, rooted, torn, pulsing with indecision. I must resemble a deer in headlights—except the car is hot, and the drivers are devils.

"Drivers, are you ready?"

Pom-Pom's shout slices through the haze. But the man doesn't move.

He slides me off the car, his palm dragging across my waist like a spark trail left by fire. The driver's door swings open. With a motion that feels rehearsed, he settles me inside like I'm not going anywhere.

Leather meets my back. Cold. Slick. And his scent—cigarettes, leather, cedar—floods my head. A whimper sneaks out before I can stop it. His head dips closer, drawing a deep breath like he memorizes me.

He stares, gaze molten. The kind that makes you feel bare.

I reach for the seatbelt with trembling hands, sinking deeper into the seat. His knuckles graze my shoulder as he fastens it for me, a satisfied lift tugging at his mouth before he slams the door shut, sealing in heat, sealing out sense.

Grabby rounds the front, yanks the passenger door open, and climbs in like he owns the space. Confidence oozes from him, casual and unbothered. The man watches through the windshield, silent and unmoving.

Whatever passes between them is unspoken—but not unreadable.

Before I can blink, Grabby's ripped from the seat. A yelp slips from me as the man claims the spot beside me, low words falling under his breath.

The rear door creaks open.

Grabby slides in behind us, like none of it mattered.

"What the hell are you doing?" He growls at him.

I shrink against the door, fingers fumbling at the handle.

"I want in," Grabby whines, burying his nose in my neck. A ripple courses through me. "She's soft. Smells amazing, J."

Every part of me stiffens. My brain screams to get out. My body? Traitorous. Still. Caught.

This isn't real. It can't be. I'm the girl who reads about this kind of chaos, not the one it happens to.

Yet here I am. In a car with two men who could ruin me in every possible way—and I don't move.

"If Kill gets to go, so do I," Blue Eyes snaps. *I guess, make that three.* Blue Eyes shoves his way in beside Grabby—Kill, apparently— which is a stupid fucking name by the way.

"Red, start the car," J commands.

"What?" My hand finds the wheel. Knuckles white. Breath shaky. My brain tries to latch onto logic. Fails.

He holds the keys out.

"Start the car," J says again, quieter now. But it's not a suggestion.

I fumble the key into the ignition. It catches on the first try—then sputters, groans, and finally growls to life like it resents the effort.

From the backseat, someone snorts.

"Aw, listen to her," Grabby says, tapping the back of my seat. "She's a little temperamental. Just like you."

My cheeks light up. "Are you talking about me or the car?"

"Why not both?" Blue Eyes mutters, settling an elbow on the console and peering at me from between the seats like this is a joyride, not a crisis.

Outside, a cluster of women eye the car with the kind of hostility usually reserved for cheating exes. Arms crossed. Faces pinched. I swear one of them mouths *lucky bitch.*

"Remind me," I mumble, "who do I sue for getting roped into this? Because I didn't sign up for fast cars and faster egos."

"Marissa," all three of them say in unison.

I groan, wiping my hands down my thighs. "Of course."

The engine idles under me, waiting. Judging. I stare at the pedals, willing them to be less... complicated.

Blue Eyes leans in slightly, tapping the side of my shoulder. "Left pedal. That's the clutch."

"Right," I say. "So I just... do car things."

"Exactly that," he replies, all fake encouragement and a smug grin. "Do the car things, Sweetness."

I clap my hands once. "Okay. I've never done this before. I might throw up. Or win. There is no in-between."

"Hot," Grabby deadpans. "She's feral *and* unstable. J, can we keep her?"

"She's not a stray," J mutters, one hand resting on the gearstick. "She's the driver. Focus."

My heart thrums as J reaches out, guiding my fingers to the gearshift—his hand slides over mine.

Electricity shoots straight to my core.

I suck in a sound before it slips out, then turn my head toward J, needing a distraction from how touch-starved I feel under their hands.

J's stare pins me in place—quiet, deep, unreadable. If he's worried, he doesn't show it. If he's turned on... well, that's a different problem entirely.

"J will call the gears," Blue Eyes says, calm as ever. "Clutch in, gear, gas. You'll feel it."

"I won't," I admit. "But let's pretend I will. Maybe the car won't notice."

"Fake it till you make it," Grabby chimes in. "Or crash dramatically. Either way, it'll be a show."

I narrow my eyes at the rearview mirror. "You're incredibly unhelpful."

"You're welcome."

The woman in red steps forward. Scarf raised. The world holds its breath.

"On your mark..."

My hands grip the wheel.

"Get set...GO!"

J shifts forward. "First gear. Clutch in. Now."

My body moves on instinct, following their directions like my survival depends on it. Which, let's be honest, it probably does.

"And, Red?" J murmurs, fingers brushing my wrist as he guides me through the gears.

"Y-yeah?"

"Don't stall. We're not walking back."

"Wow. So supportive," I mutter, slamming the pedal like it insulted my mother.

The wheels kick up dirt in a furious spray, and we lurch forward—violent, fast, perfect.

"Second!" J barks.

Our hands collide, then move in sync as the gear clicks into place.

"Third!"

The car surges beneath us, roaring with new life.

Laughter bursts from me—loud, wild, completely real. It spills out of my chest like it's been trapped there for years.

"She's unhinged," Grabby calls from the back. "I think I'm in love."

"You're in the backseat," I fire over my shoulder. "Pipe down, back there."

"You're doing great, Sweetness," Blue Eyes adds, unbothered. "Remind me to never bet against you again."

"Remind me to start charging for rides," I shoot back, still grinning.

Marissa's headlights fade farther behind us with every second. She's nowhere close. My grip tightens. The wind howls past the open windows. The night feels electric, wild, mine.

And when the finish line rushes up, I don't hesitate.

We fly across.

The engine groans as we coast to a stop, the tires skimming the gravel. Dust curls in thick spirals around us, wrapping the car in haze like a well-earned exhale.

The passenger and rear doors fling open. Grabby and Blue Eyes spill into the crowd like chaos set free.

They're yelling something—probably cocky and unearned—but it fades beneath the blood rushing in my ears.

J doesn't move.

Neither do I.

The silence between us crackles.

My tongue slips over my lips, nervous and unsure, but ready.

I turn to him, but he's already watching me.

His hand lifts—rough, warm fingers brushing the side of my neck before settling there like he belongs.

Then he leans in.

The kiss hits different. It's not hurried, not hungry. It's worse than that.

It's careful.

Deliberate.

The kind of kiss that peels you open instead of setting you on fire.

His lips trace mine once, twice, then linger there, waiting for me to pull away.

I don't.

I can't.

My whole body leans toward him, craving more contact than the console will allow. My fingers twitch at my sides, aching to grab on. To hold. To be held.

His mouth moves slowly—no urgency, no agenda—like he's offering instead of taking.

It wrecks me.

The soft drag of his lips. The brush of his stubble along my skin. His fingers slip into my hair, gentle at the roots, anchoring me to this moment without caging me in.

When his teeth scrape my bottom lip, I gasp.

It isn't loud. Isn't dramatic.

It's the sound of a girl starved for touch—of someone who didn't realize how badly they needed this until now.

His tongue teases mine, coaxing, not demanding. Every sweep sends a pulse through my limbs, melting the steel I've wrapped around my heart for years.

My hand finally finds his shirt, clutching the fabric like it's the only thing keeping me from dissolving entirely. I don't even remember moving.

And I don't care.

He kisses me again—slower this time. Deeper.

Somewhere inside, I know I should be scared.

But I'm not.

Because this doesn't feel dangerous.

It feels like mine.

Then—

From outside the car: "You two done sucking face in there, or should we get a hose?"

Grabby.

Of course.

I start to pull away, but J's hand slides to my jaw, holding me there for one last brush of his lips. He pulls back just enough to murmur, "Let him wait."

I blink up at him, dazed. "Are you always like this?"

"Only when I'm winning."

"Cocky," I mutter, but my cheeks are burning. I don't even try to hide the smile stretching across my face.

"Confident," he corrects, sitting back with a smirk.

The rear door flies open again. Blue Eyes pops his head in. "We're placing bets back there on whether Red's gonna marry you or murder you."

"Both," J says, without missing a beat.

I groan. "Can I crash this thing now and blame it on peer pressure?"

Grabby's voice rings out from somewhere nearby. "We'll call it a draw if you take us all out at once!"

I'm still trying to catch my breath—not from the race, but from the way J kissed me like he was trying to unravel all the parts of me I've spent years holding together.

Blue Eyes swings the rear door open wider, sticking his head in again. "Seriously, though—if you two are gonna keep playing house here, we're heading to get drinks. Try not to fog up the windows."

"They already did that," Grabby calls from somewhere behind him. "I saw it. I feel like I need a cigarette, and I wasn't even involved."

I flip them off without turning. "You're both dramatic."

Blue Eyes grins, clearly enjoying every second. "Enjoy your afterglow, Red." His eyes flick to J "Try not to get too handsy. The car's got feelings."

"I make no promises," J says without looking at him.

Grabby cackles, then slams the back door. "Don't forget who wants you when we're not in motion, Princess," he calls through the window.

I scoff. But the way my stomach flips says something else.

Then it's quiet.

Their footsteps fade into the thrum of the crowd. Just us now. Me. J. The car. And the echo of that kiss is still pulsing in my skin.

I shift in the seat—awkward, uncertain, very aware of every inch of space between us... and every inch that isn't.

J doesn't speak right away. He just watches me. Not intense. Not heavy. Just... there.

Present in a way most people aren't.

"You gonna run now?" he asks eventually, voice low, like he already knows the answer.

I shake my head. "Should I?"

He leans back, arm draped across the headrest. "If you were going to, it would've been before you kissed me like that."

I scoff, heat crawling up my neck. "*You* kissed *me* like that."

His lips twitch, not quite a smile. "And you didn't stop me."

"You act like I had a choice," I murmur, eyes fixed on the smudged windshield. "You kiss like a trap."

J hums. "Is that a complaint?"

"No. It's a warning."

He turns slightly, his thigh brushing mine. "Then let me be clear." His hand finds my knee, slow and easy. "I'm not sorry."

My breath hitches—but I recover quickly, smirking. "You say that now. Wait till you realize I talk during movies and eat fries out of the bag before we're home."

"Cute. You think that's a dealbreaker." His fingers move, barely grazing the inside of my thigh. "I'm already past the point of making good decisions."

My skin sparks under his touch, but I pretend I'm unaffected. "So this is a bad decision?"

"No," he says without hesitation. "This is the first good one I've made in a long time."

That silence settles in again—comfortable and terrifying all at once.

"I haven't..." I start, then stop.

He waits.

I try again. "It's been a while since someone touched me and didn't want to break something."

J's hand curls tighter around my knee.

"Then let's start over," he murmurs. "No damage. No rush. Just this."

My chest aches. The kind of ache that has nothing to do with pain.

"I don't know how to do this," I admit, fingers twisting in the fabric of my shirt.

"You don't have to," he replies. "I'll go slow. You tell me when to stop."

"I won't."

He nods once. "Then I won't either."

Another long pause. This one quieter. Heavier. But not in a way that scares me.

"You're dangerous," I whisper.

He finally smiles—full, slow, unbothered. "Sweetheart... you haven't seen dangerous yet." Then he pulls me toward him.

CHAPTER 3

Ember Rose

"You did so well, Red," J murmurs against my mouth, low and gravelly, like smoke curling into velvet. The words slide over me, slow and deliberate, melting past my skin before I catch my next thought.

Leather. Sandalwood. Heat.

He smells like every reckless decision I've never been brave enough to make.

"Th-thank you." It falls out broken. My throat knots up, and my brain forgets how to function under the weight of his attention. His thumb drags along my cheek, then dips to trace the edge of my bottom lip. The touch is barely there, but it scatters through me like lightning.

"Who are you, Red?"

I can't answer. Not with sense, anyway. I feel hollow and heavy all at once. My chest threatens to split open under the weight of how long it's been since someone made me feel seen—wanted.

"I don't know," I whisper. "Who do you want me to be?"

His hand moves behind my neck, fingers threading through my hair. He tugs me toward him—not rough, just sure like this is a promise, not a question.

I fold toward him, knees digging into the seat, body stretched across the console. When our mouths meet, the world drops away.

No crowd. No chaos. No fear.

Just this.

He kisses me like he has time to savor it. Like, he wants every second to ruin me.

His lips part mine in a slow tease, tongue sweeping forward with just enough hunger to make me ache. My hands hover in my lap, useless, until I can't stand it anymore. I grab the hem of his shirt, curling my fingers tight like I need proof he's real.

I lean farther. My chest brushes his. The console jabs into my ribs, but I couldn't care less. I'd crawl over it if that's what it took to get closer.

A sound escapes my throat—soft, needy, helpless.

He drinks it in with another kiss, slower this time. More heat than oxygen. More ache than restraint.

His hand trails down my back, steady and warm. When it reaches my waist, he tugs—drawing me closer until I'm molded to the lines of his body. I shift without thinking, hips rolling forward to chase the friction I shouldn't be craving.

He breaks away, just enough for his forehead to graze mine.

"Red," he murmurs, rough and frayed. "You make me want shit I swore I buried."

I lift my head, our mouths still a breath apart. "Then stop pretending it's dead."

The words hang there. Bold. Stupid. True.

A slow grin curls at the corner of his mouth—sharp, unrepentant. His hand tilts my chin, thumb brushing over the corner of my lip again.

But before he can close the gap between us, the driver's door rips open. A fist knots in the front of my shirt and yanks me out of the car.

I cry out. Not loud. Just startled.

Air hits my skin like a slap. Hands grab. Boots skid across dirt. My body is no longer mine as I'm dragged into a crowd that doesn't care who I am.

"That was some impressive driving, Little Dove."

The man who's got me smells like cheap liquor and ego. Gray streaks his hair, but there's nothing soft about him. His fingers clamp down on my shoulders like he's already claimed me.

"Um... thanks?" I manage, trying to move back.

His grip tightens.

"Maybe I'll take you for a spin next."

My stomach churns. My skin crawls.

Then—he's gone.

Grabby slams into him, all fury and heat. The older man stumbles, snarling under his breath.

"Don't touch her," Grabby snaps, stepping between us like a wall made of muscle and murder.

"I didn't know she was claimed," the man sneers, adjusting his coat like he's owed something.

Grabby doesn't even blink. He slides a hand to my waist, solid and grounding.

"She is now."

Another figure moves in beside me. J. Calm, lethal. His hand covers Grabby's, sealing me between them.

I don't flinch.

I don't pull away.

I lean into the heat of their hands like I've earned it.

The older man scoffs. "I bet neither of you even knows her name."

My face burns. Shame flares hot, and my eyes fall to the dirt.

But J doesn't waver.

His hand slips from mine to my chin, lifting it with gentle insistence. Not to silence me—but to remind me I don't have to hide.

"She's not yours to name," J says, calm as a loaded gun.

"Emmy!" Jason's shout cuts through the chaos.

I spot him weaving through the crowd, waving his arms. I try to move toward him, but Grabby won't let go.

"Where do you think you're going, Princess?" he hums near my ear, his lips grazing the edge of my hair.

"My friends are waiting," I say, forcing my head high. "They're my ride."

A hand slips between us. Blue Eyes. Quiet, steady, and somehow already there.

"Come on. I'll take you."

I don't question it. I slip my hand into his.

He moves like he's done this before—guiding me through the crowd with ease, his arm resting around my waist like I belong there. Every bump, every body, every misstep is cleared before it can reach me.

"Th-thank you," I manage, barely above a whisper.

He smirks, like he's been waiting for me to say it. "You won us that race."

"Then I deserve a cut," I fire back, trying to keep up the game even though my heart's still racing from everything—and him.

He stops.

Turns.

And moves in closer.

"How much?" The words skim against my ear, low and too close for comfort. Or maybe too close in exactly the right way.

My stomach flips. "What?"

"How much do you want, Sweetness?" he repeats, all tease, no shame.

My throat tightens. " I-I was kidding. J did most of it. I just... didn't stall."

"Didn't stall, didn't crash, didn't flinch," he says, brushing his fingers beneath my chin. He lifts it slowly, eyes locked on mine. "Sounds like you did more than enough."

We're close. One wrong breath and our mouths would meet.

My knees wobble.

His mouth tips into a grin like he knows I'm seconds away from folding.

And then—

Marissa barrels into me from the side, arms slung around my shoulders like a tactical strike. "There you are, you slippery brat," she huffs. "You *disappeared.* Jason and I thought someone dragged you off to sell your organs."

"In their defense," Blue Eyes cuts in, tone too casual, "I only wanted one."

Marissa throws him a side-eye so deadly it could scorch the earth. "Not helping."

"I tried to find Jason," I mutter, pulling away from her just enough to find Blue Eyes again. I don't know why. Maybe to prove I'm still okay. Maybe to prove he didn't break me open.

He doesn't say anything. He just stands there. Still. Waiting.

Marissa's grip tightens. "You can't just wander off with random hot guys, Emmy. That's how horror movies start."

"Technically," Blue Eyes muses, "this would be act two. She already raced."

Before I can respond, J appears behind me—silent, solid. His hand lands at the base of my back, grounding me in a way that shouldn't feel as good as it does. "Every okay, Red? You look cold." He shrugs off his jacket and drapes it over my shoulders like it's second nature.

The warmth sinks in immediately, but the scent hits harder—leather, something woodsy, and the exact kind of danger I'd convinced myself I'd sworn off.

"Thanks," I whisper, pulling the sleeves over my hands.

Marissa raises a brow. "Red?"

"I'm fine," I say quickly, trying not to sound too fine. J's hand slides higher along my spine, steady and sure.

Blue Eyes hums like this is all playing out exactly as expected. "Told her to name her cut," he says, casually folding his arms.

J chuckles. "Did she?"

"I told him I didn't need one," I blurt. "I had fun. That's enough."

Marissa levels both of them with a glare that could peel paint. "You and I need to talk."

I nod, but my feet stay planted.

Because even as the world pulls me back into reality—into the noise, dust, and chaos—I'm still in that car. Still tangled up in a kiss I didn't see coming and never wanted to end.

CHAPTER 4

Ember Rose

"How about we talk about it in the parking lot in about an hour?" Blue Eyes drawls, velvet-smooth with a grin that should come with a warning label. "We'll know our winnings by then, split it up. Sound good, Sweetness?"

"U-uh, sure? But I was kidding," I stammer, dragging my fingertips over the cracked seams in the leather jacket sleeves. Do they think I hung around just for cash? The heat crawling up my neck makes me want to melt into the pavement.

"I guess I should give this back," I murmur, fumbling with the collar. No way am I meeting them later. Better to make a clean exit before this spirals into something I'm not equipped to handle.

Before I can shrug it off, Blue Eyes tugs the jacket firmly back onto my shoulders. "Keep it," he says, cockiness curling his mouth. "It looks better on you than it ever did on him."

Over his shoulder, Marissa appears with a smug arch of her brow and a smirk that practically screams *I told you so.*

The parking lot stretches under the fluorescents, chrome catching every twitch of neon like it's showing off. The air is mixed with burnt rubber and engine heat. This place doesn't just pulse—it growls.

I cinch the jacket tighter around me, unsure what the hell I've just walked into, but one thing's clear: backing out isn't going to be as easy as I thought.

J appears beside me like he's always been there. "Mind if I walk with you?"

"I'm here with Marissa and Jason," I say, trying for disinterest.

He shrugs. "Doesn't mean I can't walk you, does it?" His smirk is lethal. That scent—leather and spice—wraps around me like a well-worn memory I can't remember.

"I g-guess not," I mutter, catching Marissa's look. She rolls her eyes but nudges Jason forward with a sigh.

J falls into step beside me. Every brush of our shoulders might as well be a live wire. My nerves are fried, skin buzzing, blood rushing loud enough to drown out the idling engines.

He drags a hand through his messy hair. "Listen," he starts, voice low, hesitant. "I know you're not interested in the money. But maybe there's something else..."

He trails off. The pause stretches.

"Like?" I ask, heart stammering like it's got its own engine.

He steps in, close enough that I catch every fleck of midnight in his eyes. "Maybe we could create our own kind of prize," he murmurs. "Something worth more than a payout."

My back bumps against a car, cold metal biting through the heat he's radiating. His fingers sweep a stray strand from my face, knuckles grazing skin like a dare.

Then his lips crash into mine.

My grip fists the front of his shirt. I don't mean to pull him closer, but my body's already working on impulse, chasing the fire he lit with a single touch. He tastes like danger wrapped in comfort, and I can't breathe through the want clawing at my chest.

"W-what kind of reward are we talking about?" I manage, lips brushing his.

His chuckle vibrates against my mouth. "Something you'll think about every time you look at that jacket."

Then I'm lifted, his hands strong, and my legs wrap around his waist before I can second-guess the move. I'm all heat and friction, pressed against him in a way that should be illegal in public.

Except doubt creeps in. The tight fit of my thighs, the way his hands settle like they belong there—what if this is a joke? What if I'm the punchline?

His hand cups my jaw, gently turning my face. "What's wrong, Red?"

"You could have anyone here," I whisper, tears threatening to sting. "Why me?"

His voice drops. "Open those eyes."

I try. I really do.

"Look at me," he says again, firmer this time. When I do, there's no pity, no hesitation—just hunger. Real, staggering hunger.

"Do you really think I don't want you?"

Then his lips crash into mine again. This time, there's no hesitation —just fire.

His mouth moves with a hunger that undoes me—my fingers thread through his hair, anchoring myself to him.

He drags us into the backseat of a truck—his, I assume, from the lazy click of the lock and the way he moves like he owns it. I land hard, breath knocked from my lungs.

"This yours?" I ask.

"Any car is mine if I ask nicely," he purrs.

"You didn't ask me nicely," I sass back, breath catching.

He leans in, lips grazing my ear. "Can I pretty please peel off these jeans and bury my face in your pussy?"

My laugh chokes out in a gasp. "Do lines like that actually work?"

He grins like the cat that just knocked over a priceless vase and blamed the dog. "Red, I usually don't have to ask," he murmurs, dragging his nose along the waistband of my jeans like he's savoring the anticipation.

"Wow," I breathe, half-laugh, half-gasp. "You say that like it's a badge of honor."

"Just letting you know what league you're in now."

His fingers toy with the top button, taking his sweet time like he's unwrapping a present he's waited all year to open. His eyes stay locked on mine—a silent, smoldering dare. One nod is all he needs.

I give it.

And his smirk turns into a predator, and I'm the prey. The zipper slides down with a low purr, and he peels my jeans off like he's done it a thousand times, though we both know he hasn't. My breath catches as the cooler air brushes over newly exposed skin, heightening everything.

He whistles low. "Red... you've been hiding all this under denim? Tragic."

"Not all of us are out here trying to seduce people with our skin on display," I shoot back, though my voice wobbles.

"Maybe not on purpose," he mutters, then lifts my legs with infuriating ease, draping them over his shoulders like he has the right.

He presses a kiss to the inside of my thigh, and I shudder. Then his teeth graze the same spot, and I jolt, nerves lighting up like a struck match. My thighs twitch, clenching on instinct.

"Careful," he chuckles darkly. "I bite back."

The next kiss lands dangerously close to my center. My fingers dive into his hair, desperate, needy. I'm barely hanging on.

"J..." I whisper, and the sound is already half a plea.

He hums against me, vibration like static. The moment he slips his fingers under the edge of my panties, he pauses.

"Say the word, and I'll stop."

I don't. I can't.

He doesn't need further convincing. The snap of stretched fabric fills the car, followed by a soft thud as ruined lace hits the floor.

"Seriously?" I hiss. "Those were expensive."

"Consider it a sacrifice to the cause," he replies, voice unapologetically wicked. "Besides, you won't need them where I'm going."

Heat scorches through me.

Then he's between my thighs, tongue replacing breath, worship replacing words. His mouth moves with lazy expertise, dragging noises from me I didn't know I could make. My back arches, heels digging into his shoulders as he pins me in place.

"Trying to give me a black eye?" he asks, voice muffled.

"Maybe if you'd slow down—oh god, never mind."

He doesn't slow down. He doubles down.

His grip strengthens, lips working me with an intensity that borders on reverence. Every swipe of his tongue has me unwinding, piece by piece, until I'm a mess of trembling limbs and broken moans.

"Please," I beg, not sure what I'm even asking for—just more, always more.

"Say less," he murmurs.

And then—fire.

The release slams into me like a wave I never saw coming. I shatter, breath stalling, world tilting, stars behind my eyes. My thighs snap shut around him as aftershocks ripple through me. He hums again, riding every quake with sinful satisfaction.

When I finally collapse, boneless and dazed, he peppers soft kisses against my skin.

"Told you I wanted a taste," he murmurs, smug and...glistening.

I drag him up to me, needing his mouth, needing him close, grounding. He kisses me like he means it—like he's claiming a victory he's not ready to share.

"Don't think this makes us even," I whisper.

"Didn't plan on stopping yet."

He peels off his shirt, muscles flexing, and my breath hitches. Scars lace down his arms—silent stories I'm not ready to ask about. It's not my business.

"You okay?" he asks.

"I will be," I whisper, reaching for him.

His hand finds the back of my knee, hitching my leg higher as he nudges against me. My skin burns where we touch, nerves pulsing in sync with the teasing shift of his hips.

"Ready?"

"I'm not made of glass."

He groans at that, pushing forward, stretching me open with a care that contrasts with everything else about him.

His lips brush mine. "I'm going to wreck you, Red."

"Good," I gasp.

And then he moves.

There's nothing gentle in the way our bodies collide. Every inch he drives into me is a full-body confession. The slow drag, the twist of his hips, the slight grind that sends white sparks ricocheting through my skull.

"J," I gasp, clutching his arms. "You—God, you feel—"

"Say it," he pants, voice frayed.

"Perfect."

That single word turns him feral.

His rhythm deepens, turns into something that steals the breath from my lungs. I meet him thrust for thrust, not just taking—giving. Demanding. Our mouths meet again, desperate and searching, tongues tangling in a battle of who can break first.

His teeth catch my bottom lip. I answer with a roll of my hips that drags a growl from him so deep it vibrates against my chest.

He rears back, propping himself up so he can watch as he drives into me. His eyes blaze. My body moves beneath him like it was made to.

"You're mine like this," he murmurs, almost reverent. "All mine."

I grab his wrist and bite the edge of his thumb. "Then stop talking and take me like it." *Whoa, who is this bold lady?*

He shifts, flipping me over with fluid control. The press of leather against my chest, the sudden tug at my hips—he doesn't miss a beat—one arm snakes beneath me, the other slides under my waist, guiding me to my knees.

He slides back in, and the angle is so much deeper that I forget to breathe. My hands scramble for traction, nails dragging along the seat.

"Still want more?" he rasps.

"Hope you a-aren't close to being finished."

"Not. Even. Close." He punctuates each word with a slam of his hips against mine.

His thrusts build, harder, deeper—deliciously punishing. Each one lands like a promise he intends to keep.

His fingers find me, circling where I'm already so sensitive. The pressure coaxes that familiar climb, tighter and tighter, until I'm quaking.

"J—" I whine, back arching as I meet his movements.

"That's it," he growls. "Let go for me again."

I do.

The second release crashes into me with brutal force, a shockwave that steals the ground out from under me. I collapse into the leather, a mess of sound and sensation. My face squished into the tacky leather.

He keeps moving, dragging out every last spark until I'm clenching around him, wrung out and wrecked.

Then he finally allows himself to let go, a strangled groan tumbling from his lips as he pushes deep, hips locking, body jerking as his release takes him.

We stay like that—sweaty and tangled.

He lifts his head and grins like he just stole a crown jewel. "Still think I'm a two-pump chump?"

I snort. "Might need a third to make a final call."

His laugh is low and wicked. "You're going to kill me."

"Only if you're lucky."

His arms circle me, his thumb stroking slow, lazy circles over my hip. For the first time in what feels like forever, I let myself find comfort in someone, the quiet aftermath, and the sensation of being completely, thoroughly ruined by him.

And I never want to leave.

J kisses my forehead, his fingers tracing lazy, soothing patterns along my back. "You're something else, Red," he whispers, sending a wave of tenderness flooding through me.

I roll over, cuddling into him. Looking up, I drink him in, the rest of the world blurring into nothing. Only the intensity in his gaze remains, the echo of our racing heartbeats thrumming like a distant drum. A smile tugs at my lips, a sense of belonging settling over me. Melting into his hold, I absorb every part of him, engraving this moment into my soul.

A knock taps against the window like karma has come to collect. Whatever spell I was under shatters, and I bolt upright like I've been caught doing something I definitely *was*. J mutters a low curse and pushes the door open with a scowl sharp enough to draw blood.

"What the hell, Kill?"

Kill doesn't blink. Doesn't stutter. Just stares straight at the scene like a nosy raccoon at a crime scene. "Uh... dude. Is that blood?"

And there it is—the shame. It doesn't creep in. It *detonates*.

Blood.

From *me*.

Because I just lost my virginity. In the back of a truck. With a man whose real name might not even be J. I don't know his last name. I don't even know if he *has* a last name. Hell, I don't even know if this truck is his. I could be bleeding on a borrowed seat.

Scrambling, I hunt for my underwear like it might fix any of this—what's left of it, anyway. All I find is a destroyed tangle of lace and elastic, courtesy of J's *very eager* hands. Great. Love that for me.

My jeans are halfway up when the chafing starts, and that's when it hits—I am not built for one-night stands, especially ones that involve denim aftermath and zero aftercare snacks.

"Where are you going?" J snaps, slamming the door to block Kill out like it might also block out the humiliation clinging to me like a second skin.

"I have to go," I mutter, blinking hard. "Marissa and Jason are probably wondering where I disappeared to."

"I'll drive you."

"No!" The panic in my voice is immediate, embarrassing, and louder than I intended. I force a breath. "I mean... It's fine. You don't have to."

He stares, like he's trying to read between the lines, like there's a version of this where I don't regret every choice that led to me being half-dressed and emotionally unhinged.

His hand lifts to my cheek. Gentle. Careful. And somehow that's worse. I feel like I might cry again, which is *super* fun and not at all on-brand for the girl who just threw away her virginity like a lit match.

A tear slips loose. Because, of course, it does. His thumb swipes it away like he's allowed to still touch me.

"Red..." he says softly. "You don't have to run."

"I'm not," I lie, pulling out a brittle smile that feels like it might crack my face. "I just... need a minute. Or like, twenty years."

His brow twitches like he wants to stop me, hoping I'll say this meant *something*. And maybe it did. For him. For a second. But for me? Right now, it just feels like shame and denim burn.

"I get it," he says finally. But he doesn't. The edge in his voice says he *doesn't get it at all.*

I nod and slide out of the truck, the air hitting me like cold guilt. I move to shrug off his jacket, but his hand catches mine.

"Keep it," he says, giving me a crooked, almost-smile that lands between hopeful and hurt. "That way I know you'll come back."

My throat tightens. He leans in, kissing my forehead like this was tender. Like it wasn't rushed and reckless and happening between strangers who never asked for names.

Outside, Kill shuffles by the tailgate, blinking like he walked in on the world's worst porno.

"So... did I interrupt, or...?"

"Nothing," J bites out, brushing past him like the night didn't just fall apart in his hands.

Blue Eyes lingers for half a second longer, giving me a slight nod—maybe understanding, maybe judgment. I can't tell. Then he's gone too.

And I'm left standing alone, bruised pride wrapped in J's jacket, with a ruined thong in my pocket and a thousand questions I'm too ashamed to ask.

The air outside sucker-punches me, slicing through J's jacket and straight into my skin. I wrap my arms around myself like that'll help, trudging toward the chaos where Marissa and Jason are waiting. Every step feels like I'm dragging my shame behind me on a leash, still wearing a stranger's clothes and some deeply questionable decisions.

My brain? A blender of bad choices and delicious kisses. That shouldn't coexist. But here we are.

And just when I think I might slip away unnoticed, Marissa comes skipping up like she's been waiting to pounce.

"What the hell was *that*?" she exclaims, eyes wide, voice high, and oh-so-judgy.

I freeze mid-step. "I... I don't know," I manage to croak out, because the truth sounds even worse out loud. Saying it louder won't make it less tragic.

"You were gone forever, then came stumbling out of his truck looking like..." She waves her hand at me, as if my mess speaks for itself.

Jason stands beside her, silent. Watching. Definitely judging. Fabulous.

I glance down. Yep. Jeans barely buttoned, shirt twisted, hair that screams *wild night or wind tunnel?* And my face? Still lit up like a neon sign flashing **DEFLOWERED.**

"I'm fine," I mutter, which might be the biggest lie I've ever told. "Just... need to go home."

Marissa narrows her eyes. "Fine?" Her sass wavers as worry creeps in. "Did he hurt you?"

"What? No! God, no," I rush out, shaking my head so fast I might give myself whiplash. "It's not like that. It's just..." I bite down on the words. "It was my first time. And I didn't exactly plan for it to happen in the back of a pickup like a deleted scene from Fast & Reckless."

Her expression melts instantly. She hugs me like she's trying to stuff me back into a cocoon.

"Oh my God," she whispers. "Are you okay?"

"I don't know," I whisper back. "I think I need a reset button. Or a coma."

She pulls back, brushing my hair out of my face with the tenderness of someone who's seen me ugly-cry over a broken nail. "Let's get you home. And if you want to talk about it later, I'll bring the ice cream and zero judgment."

I nod, grateful she's not pushing. But inside? It's a category-five hurricane of feelings. I glance over my shoulder, half-expecting to see J standing there watching me walk away. But the spot is empty. Of course it is.

Jason finally speaks. "We'll get you home. Don't worry about anything else."

I nod again, exhausted, but his calm helps. Until—

"Did they give you that money?" Marissa asks.

"What money?" Jason cuts in, eyes narrowing like this just got interesting.

"The drivers," she says, giving me a sideways glance. "They offered her a cut for helping them out."

Jason's eyebrows shoot up. "Wait... Jake, Ash, and Killian offered you *money*?"

"Wh-who?" I blink at him. That name combo punches me in the gut like a twisted déjà vu. My brain fumbles through mental files, attempting to connect the dots.

Jason lights up like he just discovered a cheat code. "The guys you helped? They're the Thornes'. Like, *the* Thornes'."

"Why do you sound like you're about to pee yourself over it?" I ask, scanning the lot for any sign of them.

"Because they're *legends,*" he says. "Top racers in the circuit. Tied to the black market. Real-life ghosts. And Jake—J—is the ringleader. He's got a thing for sharp objects."

My mouth opens, closes, then opens again. "What kind of sharp objects are we talking about here? Chefs knives? Serial killer chic?"

Jason shrugs. "Wouldn't be surprised if he kept one in his sock. Then there's Kill. Killian. He's batshit. Will throw himself off a bridge if it gets a win. He once punched a cop and still somehow walked."

"And Asher?" I ask, my voice a little too small.

Jason doesn't notice my slip-up, how I could possibly know his full name without being told."Ah, the calm one. Quiet, smart, deadly. They're not brothers, but they'd die for each other. No joke."

My stomach twists into a pretzel. Suddenly, everything makes way too much sense.

Jason keeps going, way too into the lore. "Last race, Kill was drunk and started rambling about 'finding her.' Jake and Ash shut it down fast, but I remember it. I haven't figured out who yet, though."

Ice snakes through me. That pull I felt... it wasn't nothing. It was real. Familiar.

I stop walking, knees locking as my breath catches. My fists clench, nails biting into my palms. The pieces are sliding into place like a puzzle I didn't know I was solving.

"Em? Are you okay?" Marissa says. "What is it?"

"I have to go back." The words rush out. "I need to find them."

"What? *Why*?" she asks, grabbing my shoulders. "What's going on?"

"I don't know!" I cry. "But I *need* to. Mare—it's them. It's really them."

Her eyes go wide. "Like... *them*, them?"

"Yes!" I spin toward the crowd, already moving. "Come on—"

Screech.

A white van barrels in, tires screaming as it jerks to a stop in front of us. The doors swing open.

"What the—"

Two men jump out. Before I can react, one of them grabs me.

"Let me go!" I shout, thrashing like a rabid raccoon.

Marissa lunges for me, but the other man shoves her so hard her head slams into a car. She crumples. Doesn't move.

"Mare!" My scream tears out of me as I claw at the man holding me. My limbs are on fire, panic burning through every nerve.

"Em!"

Jason's voice cuts through—he's running toward us.

Bang.

Jason stumbles, a red bloom spreading across his chest. He hits the ground hard.

"NO!"

A scream rips from me as the masked men drag me closer to the van. I twist, flail, strike—anything. One breaks skin under my nails. *Good. Bleed, bastard.*

"ROSIE!" Jason yells, the sound slamming into me.

Then I see them—Jake, Killian, Ash—charging through the crowd like gods of vengeance.

"Red!" Jake's voice hits me like a lifeline.

"Jakey! HELP!"

I land a hit. The guy yells and loosens his grip. I drop to the pavement, gravel biting my knees as I crawl away. But another set of hands snatches me up.

"Ash! Killian!" I scream, fingers clawing, feet kicking. I draw blood. I don't stop.

"Get her!" Jason gasps.

They're so close.

But it's too late.

The van door slams. A cloth covers my face. Chemicals burn my lungs. I choke, thrash—until my body betrays me and everything starts to blur.

Through the back window, I see them.

Jake's fist hammers the glass. Killian's green eyes blaze. Ash's lips form my name, his breath fogging the glass. Their desperation is a brand on my soul.

Then the engine roars, and I'm gone.

"ROSIE!"

Their voices follow me into the dark—but I can't hold on.

The last thing I heard was the driver.

"Yeah. We've got her."

Like I'm cargo.

A prize.

And then—

Nothing.

My head throbs. Each pulse drills deeper, making it impossible to think, let alone move. I can't tell if it's blood pounding in my skull or just the overhead light digging into me like punishment. Every time I try to open my eyes, the glare burns through my lids like it's trying to carve its way in.

Metal digs into my ankles and wrists. Cold. Heavy. Unforgiving. I pull instinctively—dumb, really—and the chains rattle loud enough to echo. The sound bounces off stone and slams right back into me, a cruel reminder that I'm not going anywhere.

Then comes the voice. Too smooth. Too sweet.

"How much do you want for her?"

It floats in like a casual offer over coffee. My stomach twists. My limbs go still. The words take a second to sink in, but when they do, they hit like a punch to the gut. I flinch. Not that it gets me far—metal bites harder when you fight it.

A low groan slips out as I lift my arm to shield my face. No use. The chains yank back.

"Well, look who's finally awake," another voice cuts in. This one I know.

I swallow a curse as my head turns, nausea tagging along for the ride. Through the fluorescent assault above, I manage to make out the outline of a man.

That smirk. I remember it. Less nightmare, more party trick—until now.

Tristan. Devereux. I think that's what they called him.

"What...?" My throat feels like it's been sandpapered. "Where am I?"

I know the answer. I hate it.

Tristan steps forward, shadow stretching across the floor like it's proud to follow him.

"Exactly where I wanted you," he says, grin wide enough to show too many teeth.

I yank at the chains again, harder this time. The sound scrapes at my ears. It's useless, but I can't stop. "Don't touch me."

He doesn't. Not yet. Just hovers like he's savoring the lead-up.

"Oh, I won't," he says, tone dipping low. "I'm not the one who paid."

He steps aside, like this is some twisted reveal on a game show, and there's the prize: a man emerging from the shadows, adjusting his pants like he's late to something.

The bile hits my throat so fast I nearly choke on it.

"She's a fighter," the stranger says, smiling like he just discovered a new toy. "I love a fighter."

He peels a wad of cash from his pocket. Tosses it to Tristan without blinking.

Tristan counts each bill like he's unwrapping candy. The more he flips, the wider his grin stretches. Greed shines on him like sweat.

The air thickens. My chest tightens. It feels like the room's caving in, like the walls are inching closer to watch me fall apart.

"You don't have to do this," I manage, barely holding back the crack in my words. "Whatever you think this is... it doesn't have to be."

The stranger steps closer.

"Oh, Kitten," he purrs, like he's amused. "You're adorable."

His hand darts out and clamps around my neck.

My body jerks. The chain around my wrists catches hard. My lungs scream, desperate for relief.

I claw at him—my nails digging in deep—but he doesn't flinch. I thrash. Panic flares so fast my muscles go tight, useless. I can't get air in. The corners of the room swim and smear together like wet ink.

He leans in close. His breath is hot, his words worse.

"You'll be at your new home soon."

The sentence slices through me like a blade. I stop struggling. Not because I give up—but because everything inside me locks up at once.

That's the promise, then.

This doesn't end here.

It starts.

My ribs tighten—my mind races—tripping over dark corners, hiding behind locked doors.

He releases me with a shove, and I crumple back onto the cot. My chest heaves. My limbs scream. I want to vomit.

But I don't.

I stay there, the silence thick, except for the sound of my heartbeat thundering against my ribs, loud and erratic like it's trying to escape from me.

No one moves.

No one speaks.

And I finally understand what they mean when they say a moment can split you wide open.

Because mine just did.

The world tilts sideways—slow, uneven, like it's deciding whether to let me fall or make me wait for it.

Everything inside me drags.

My arms won't listen. My legs feel like sandbags. My heartbeat stumbles and stutters. The pounding in my skull dulls, then fades, then—

Nothing.

Cold punches through my clothes. Not the kind that wakes you up. The kind that settles deep, like it belongs under your skin.

Something drips nearby.

I peel my eyes open and regret it instantly.

The air is damp. Stale. Each inhale feels stolen. The walls are slick with moisture. Black spots bloom across the ceiling. It smells like wet dirt and rust.

I'm not on the cot anymore. Just tile—cracked, uneven. My cheek sticks to it when I try to sit up. My clothes are damp. My wrists sting.

No chains. Not yet.

A bare bulb swings from above, sputtering like it's choking on its own light. It barely touches the corners of the room. Most of it stays swallowed in shadow.

This place doesn't want to be seen.

There's a drain in the floor.

It isn't empty.

Red smears lead to it. Some dry. Some not.

A camera watches from above, blinking in slow, taunting pulses. It is not high-tech or clean. It is just there, patient and waiting.

I turn my head and freeze.

A metal table. Streaked and stained, covered in what might be a tarp. The shape underneath it isn't moving. But the outline is too defined. Too human.

Hooks line the walls.

Some hang bare. Others don't.

My pulse skips. Then spikes.

I start crawling.

The floor scrapes at my knees, grime coating my palms. I don't care. I need distance—from the table, the drain, whatever waited for me to wake up.

There's no door.

No way out.

Just more tile. More rust. The table again, now on my left instead of my right. Like it's following me.

I curl into a corner, back against the wall. My limbs tremble.

The bulb swings once, then settles.

I raise my head. *Fake it till you make it, right?*

Doing the only thing I can think of that might unsettle them.

And smile at the camera.

It's not brave. Not really.

But it's the only thing I have.

If they want to watch me fall apart, they're going to have to work harder.

CHAPTER 6

Ember Rose

TEN MONTHS LATER...

Pain splits me in half.

No warning. No relief. Just wave after wave of raw agony tearing through my lower belly and straight into my spine. My back arches, every nerve screaming, my hands clutching at the thin mattress beneath me as if it might anchor me to something solid.

It doesn't.

Nothing does.

The muscles in my abdomen seize again, harder this time, and my body convulses with the force of it. The scream never makes it past my throat. It dies there—crushed beneath the weight of the pain and the hands digging into my thighs.

“Push, you stupid slut,” the woman snarls, her tone soaked in disgust. Her voice slices through the haze like a whip.

I try to yell back. Try to tell her to go to hell. But my mouth only opens for a sob that sounds more like a dying animal. My jaw aches from clenching. Tears streak down my cheeks, mixing with the sweat that’s soaked into my hairline. Everything blurs. Everything burns.

Another contraction rolls in.

I brace.

No—it braces me. Slams into me.

I cry out, a hoarse, ragged sound that tears at my throat. My legs tremble. My arms shake. My body is giving everything it has, and still, it's not enough.

"Push!" she snaps again, louder this time.

I bear down.

My body curls on instinct, the pain barreling through me like broken glass grinding against bone. The pressure is unbearable, a ripping sensation that sends me right to the edge. My mouth opens, and this time, the scream comes. Raw. Guttural. Terrified.

Then it happens.

A tear. A rush. My hips jolt.

The cry that follows doesn't come from me.

It cuts through the air—sharp, wild, alive.

A baby.

Mine.

I collapse back, arms useless at my sides as the woman lifts him, his tiny limbs flailing, skin flushed purple and covered in vernix.

She slaps him into my arms like he's cargo. Her lip curls. "Congratulations, whore," she sneers. "You've got yourself a bastard."

The words cut deep—but not deep enough to reach what I'm feeling.

I can't stop staring.

His mouth opens in a wail, his fists clenched in protest at being born into hell. He's beautiful. Terrifyingly small. Furious and loud.

Perfect.

My arms curl around him automatically, muscles trembling under his weight. "H-hi, Baby Boy," I whisper, voice cracking like old paper. Tears fall onto his forehead, tracing tiny rivers down his soft, wrinkled skin.

"I'm your mommy."

The words don't sound real. They feel like something out of a dream I never dared let myself have.

But he's real.

He's warm.

He's mine.

The woman watches from the corner, her shadow stretching across the floor like a stain. Her eyes narrow, but she says nothing. Maybe she's waiting for me to fall apart.

I don't.

I rock him, barely moving. My muscles scream with every twitch, but I need him close. The room around me is cold and wet, the air thick with old blood and fresh cruelty, but none touches the space between us.

My fingers trail over his cheek. He's stopped crying. His mouth stays open like he might try again, but he rests his face against my chest instead. His skin is still damp, but warm enough to pull a sob from me.

Everything hurts. My body feels broken in places I didn't know could break.

But I'm here.

He's here.

And we are still breathing.

I don't know how long I have. Minutes. Seconds. Maybe she'll take him from me next. Perhaps she won't. But I know this:

I will not die here.

I will not let *him* grow up here.

I hold him tighter, the pain still roaring inside me, and whisper words that are a promise to my newborn son.

"I'll get us out. I swear to you, baby... I'll burn this place down if I have to."

CHAPTER 7

Ember Rose

TWO YEARS LATER...

The cake is a mess. Lopsided and too sweet, made with powdered milk and crushed-up chocolate bars I'd been hoarding for weeks. I scraped together the ingredients like they were gold, using a metal cup and my hands since my captor refuses to leave me anything that could double as a weapon.

He only allowed me to make it because I'd been "good"—his words, not mine. Because I hadn't fought back. Hadn't screamed. Hadn't cried. That was the reward: a few supplies, a few hours of pretending I was a mother in a real home, not a prisoner in a concrete cage.

Atlas doesn't care. He squeals when he sees the sad excuse for frosting, tiny fingers grabbing at the uneven surface before I can even light the candle. There's only one—hidden away from his birthday last year. He thinks it's magic. I let him.

"Make a wish," I whisper, holding the candle upright while he huffs a little too hard, nearly sending the whole cake toppling. His cheeks puff out, excitement sparking across his face. The candle goes dark in one strong breath.

He claps, chocolate already smeared across his chin, his grin wide and sticky. I laugh—a sound that feels unfamiliar, a little jagged. But it bubbles up anyway.

Because he's happy. And for a few minutes, this place doesn't feel like a prison. It feels like a sliver of something good—a moment truly ours.

"Did you wish for a pony?" I tease, nudging his knee with mine. "Or maybe a rocket ship? A mountain of peanut butter cups big enough to climb?"

He nods with full seriousness. "A big one," he says, then shoves another bite into his mouth, chocolate smearing across his lip.

I reach over and swipe my thumb across his chin. "Good choice."

I want to give him more than stale air and shadows. More than whisper-sung lullabies and make-believe stories. I want him to have sunlight, fresh fruit, and swings that creak from joy instead of rust. I want him to have a real birthday—friends, noise, cake from a box with his name scribbled in bright blue icing.

But we're still here.

And today is all I can manage.

The silence above us stretches. No footsteps. No keys. That silence terrifies me more than shouting. More than the beat of boots on the stairs. Because silence means he could be listening.

I keep glancing at the ceiling, scanning for changes in the quiet. The pressure coils beneath my skin, a hum I've learned to live with.

Atlas hums to himself, oblivious. He eats like it's the best thing he's ever tasted, crumbs everywhere, his cheeks round with satisfaction. I let him. I don't tell him to slow down. I don't take the food from his hand, even though part of me wants to save what's left.

Because today, he turns two. And he deserves more than rationed joy.

I made a crown out of construction paper—red, his favorite. It took hours. I used bits of old magazines to rip shapes: stars, planets, a sun with a jagged yellow edge. I told him he's the king of the basement today. He paraded around like it meant something. Like it gave him power.

I envied that.

I tuck the rest of the cake into a cracked Tupperware container and shove it under the blanket we use as a tablecloth. My captor purchased the ingredients, the only contribution to Atlas's big day. But, he still wants no trace that the celebration happened.

Atlas crawls into my lap without a word. He does that—just climbs up, burrows into me like I'm still the safest place in his world. I wrap my arms around him, hold him close, breathe in the scent of chocolate and dust and that faint sweetness that clings to his skin.

He doesn't ask questions yet. Doesn't wonder why we're always inside. Why do we whisper? Why can't I go up the stairs with him?

But he will.

And I don't know what I'll tell him.

"Happy birthday, baby," I murmur, my lips pressed to the top of his head.

He hums, and my chest aches. I close my eyes, imagining we're anywhere else.

A park. A kitchen with real sunlight. A room that doesn't smell like mold and fear.

His breathing slows. He's dozing off, warm and trusting against me.

I shift us both to the mattress, curling around him as gently as possible. The lights above buzz faintly. The cold concrete wall presses against my back. I ignore the ache in my joints, the pinched feeling in my lower spine.

I can live with discomfort. I can't live with losing him.

I stare at the door, counting the seconds.

I used to track them obsessively, keeping tallies in the dust. I marked time in candle drips and sleep cycles. I gave that up months ago, but it didn't help.

But today, I feel every minute.

Because every birthday is a reminder that time is passing. That he's growing up in a place where he shouldn't have to. That if I don't find a way out soon, he'll stop being a baby and start asking why I can't make it stop.

Why did I let this happen?

I bite down on the inside of my cheek to keep from sobbing. The pain is grounding. Familiar.

Atlas stirs in his sleep and mumbles nonsense. I smooth a hand through his curls, whispering a song I remember from somewhere distant. My mother, maybe. A childhood I barely believe was real anymore.

When the last note fades, I listen.

Still no sound above.

That should comfort me. It doesn't.

I pull the blanket higher over Atlas and slide from the bed. My legs protest, but I move anyway. I kneel beside our pretend castle—and pull free the hollowed-out dictionary I've been using to stash what little I can hide.

A spoon. A scrap of wire. A single key I haven't dared test.

And a folded paper: a list of every day since his birth. Little notes. His first word. His first step. The day he laughed for the first time. The day he saw a bug and screamed as if it were trying to kill him.

I read through the list like a prayer.

This is how I stay sane.

Atlas shifts again, letting out a little sigh. I return the book to its spot, brush my palms over my pants, and cross to the other side of the room.

The mirror is small, cracked, barely reflective. My face looks older. Not in the way of time, but in the way of survival. The kind of aging that doesn't touch everyone. Just the ones who've had to claw their way through every day.

I pull my hair into a knot and wipe the chocolate from my cheek. I don't want *him* seeing anything that might give away how good today was.

How much we needed it.

Atlas turns on the bed, one foot kicking free of the blanket. He mumbles again, this time something closer to words.

I cross back, kneel, and pull the cover up around him. I kiss his temple and whisper the same phrase I do every night.

"I'll keep you safe. I swear it."

He won't remember today. Not all of it.

But I will.

And someday, when we're free—because we will be free—I'll bake him a real cake. One that doesn't taste like desperation. I'll buy candles that don't come from stolen drawers. I'll give him a birthday he won't forget.

Until then, this has to be enough.

I sink beside the bed and watch over him as he sleeps, listening to the sound of nothing from above.

Waiting for whatever comes next.

CHAPTER 8

Ember Rose

PRESENT TIME...

"Ember," my voice shakes as I struggle to inhale. "My name is Ember Rose Abbott." The name feels foreign, a distant reminder of who I used to be.

A deep breath fills my lungs, and I release it with a hiss as I grasp the small truth. "You are Ember Rose. And you are Atlas's mother."

The mantra is a lifeline, a delicate thread connecting me to my identity as the years blur into one another, each chipping away at the person I used to be. The more he calls me *kitten,* degrading me with every nickname, the harder it becomes to hold on. But I must. "You are Ember Rose Abbott," I whisper. "And you cannot break."

The metallic grind of the lock on a metal door snaps me out of my thoughts. It's a sound I know all too well that signals *his* arrival. A wave of dread sinks into my bones. I roll toward a wooden door that will draw him nearer and pull the collar taut, the chain sinks into my neck, stealing the air from my lungs. Fire spreads through my lungs as I cough, and the sound weakens as I increase the restriction. The room begins to spin, black spots dancing at the edges of my vision as my body protests, desperate for air.

The pressure is overwhelming; the choking sensation pulls me back into the present. If I can push just a little further, I might gain a small sliver of control I so desperately crave in a world where I have none.

The thought tempts me, a dark whisper in my mind. *I could hang myself. End this nightmare once and for all.* It isn't the first time I've thought about it. Giving up has been haunting me more often, but I cling to life for *him*, my son.

Someday, we will escape. I don't know when or how, but if I endure the degradation and keep my head down, I believe I'll find a way out. For Atlas, I'll hold on. I have to.

The thud of his loafers echoes on the concrete stairs. My pulse races, and I scan the small, barren room, my fingers closing around the crude, handmade weapon I'm hiding.

The makeshift shank, whittled down from a toothbrush, feels light but sturdy. Typically, he replaces these items too frequently for me to use them, but it's been weeks since his last visit. Weeks since he's checked on me.

I slip the weapon into my sweatshirt sleeve, hugging it close to my wrist. *It might work if there's a chance to get close enough to catch him off guard. But he has to be holding the keys.*

Escape—find Atlas—get out. The thought burns, a beacon of hope in the darkness. His footsteps grow closer.

A deep inhale, a slow, measured exhale. "Deep breaths, Ember."

Moving into a sitting position against the headboard, I scan the space I've grown to call home. The entire cell is concrete, smooth, and utterly isolating. Down here, no one can hear me scream. I've tried. I've cried, shouted until my voice gave out, my throat raw as I coughed up blood. All of it in vain. There was no one to hear my desperate pleas.

"Kitten," he sings, the sound muffled through the thick door, sending a shudder down my spine. The key slides into the lock with a soft *click,* the sound reverberating in the empty space like a cruel reminder of how close freedom is—and how unattainable.

The other barrier is the solid metal door at the top of the staircase. I reached it once, my fingertips brushing the cold steel, before he dragged me back down. It feels like a lifetime ago, but I'd been so close.

The door creaks open, and the hinges desperately need WD-40. Stepping into my cell, his eyes have a familiar glint. The keys dangling from his finger in a taunting, hypnotic sway. "I'm sorry I haven't been around much lately," he coos, "so much planning for the party, and you know how the wife gets about these things."

His chuckles are unsettling; they echo in the stifling space as he strolls toward me. The keys keep spinning, a cruel tease of the freedom they represent.

My hand grips the toothbrush handle, the plastic rough in my palm as I fight to calm my nerves. My eyes stray to the keys. They're my way out, my only hope of saving Atlas and finally getting us somewhere safe.

Two years ago, I tried, and it backfired.

"What were you trying to do, Pet?" He spits, his hot saliva hitting my face. My knees crack against the floor as he forces me to my knees. Ripping my head back, I wince, feeling threads of my hair being yanked from my skull.

"I-I'm sorry," I cry, grasping his wrist, trying to relieve the pain. "I w-won't do it again." Tears stream down my face, snot running like a faucet.

"Crawl to the bed, like the worthless pet you are," he growls, and I do. Shame floods me hot, and I wish I had the strength to fight back, but I'd been too eager. Desperation clouded my judgment as I launched for the keys to my escape. I just wanted to get Atty out. "You can be such a good girl when you listen."

"Y-yes, sir."

"Now lean over the side of the bed, it's time for your punishment." The first strike of his belt on my back was blazing, the next strike was like lava on my spine, and by strike three, I felt numb. The pain was there, but I couldn't comprehend it. "I don't think this is punishment enough, Pet. Seems too easy."

"Of c-course, Sir. Whatever you deem worthy." I force the words out, trying to breathe through the pain.

"Three days without food or water, and you won't see your son for a month."

"Wait! No, please, sir. Anything but that," I beg, turning to face him and clasping my hands together. My whole body quakes from the aftermath of the whipping, but I will do anything for him not to keep Atlas from me.

"Hmm, then I guess you'll learn never to try to escape again." His laugh was so cruel, and as he left. I lay there curled up on the cold floor.

I shake my head, trying to rid myself of the memory. The bruises, the three days spent without food or water, the humiliation of his laughter as I lay helpless on the cold floor—it claws at me, leaving a bitter taste in my mouth. But, it was the month without Atlas that was true torture, not seeing him, or getting to hear his laughter, was a cruelty I didn't know could break me.

And for the first time in my captivity, I'd thought about giving up. Letting him break me the way I know he wanted to.

And I know if I try again and fail today, it won't end with bruises and starvation. He'll make sure I don't survive the consequences. Or worse—he'll let me live just long enough to endure a punishment far more brutal.

Loosening my grip on my weapon, I slip it back into the pillowcase I'd kept it hidden in, the scratchy fabric grating against my fingers. *Don't repeat the same mistake,* Marissa's voice echoes, a faint reminder of my promises to survive—for myself, for Atlas.

But I'm unable to protect myself, let alone my son. Not yet.

"Did you miss me?" he purrs, his hand cupping my cheek with tenderness. His touch is revolting, but I suppress a shudder. Angering him will only bring more pain, more chances for him to strip away what little strength I have left. I won't give him any gratification.

Tipping my head, I force myself to meet his gaze. My lashes lower as I whisper, "Yes." The word tastes like ash, but I keep my face neutral, masking my disgust.

His lips curl into a smile as he stands, his fingers brushing my skin again before he steps away. He hangs the keys by the door, the metal glinting in the low light, far enough out of my reach to taunt me.

My *room*, if it could even be called that, is a stark fifteen-foot square of concrete. The chain around my neck allows me a mere ten-foot radius, tethering me like an animal. The collar's weight is a constant reminder of my imprisonment.

Against the far wall sits a mattress on a rickety bedframe. I only ever use it when he's here, its presence as restricting as the space itself. Beside it, a small side table holds a meager pile of clothes and one battered relic of a life that feels more like a distant dream. The worn leather is cracked and fading, but its weight is comfortable. Every night, I clutch it close, fingers curled into the material as it holds the last remnants of who I used to be—a lifeline to a world beyond these walls, to a time before chains, before *him*.

To the right, a tiny bathroom houses a sink, toilet, and shower. My first failed escape attempt was born here. I'd used soap to try slipping out of the collar. The punishment had been brutal, his cruelty a calculated effort to crush my spirit. But I refused to be broken.

Next to the bathroom, a kitchenette sits unused, another failed attempt. This one is hard for me not to smile at. This one scarred him more than it scarred me.

The pot has been sitting on the stove for a long time since it started to boil. The water rolls, bubbling rapidly, as I sit at the small kitchen table, waiting for his return. It shouldn't be long now.

"Kitten," Ahh, right on time. I plaster a fake smile on, my hands folded politely in front of me. "Oh, look at you, my precious." He purrs, shoving the keys in his pocket before gracing me with his presence. "What are you making?"

"Have a seat, Sir. I thought you might be hungry after a long day at work." I stand, making my way over to the stove, mixing the plain water. "You take such good care of me and Atlas, I thought I should surprise you."

He eyes me, eyebrow raised. "Oh, really?" I feel him step up behind me. "What the—?" Grabbing the pot, I turn, dumping the boiling liquid onto him. The scream he releases splits my ears, and as he writhes in pain. The scent of cooked flesh fills the room, clogging my senses as I shove my hands into different pockets.

When the cold metal brushes against my fingers, my blood sings. I might actually get us out of here. Tugging the keys out, I unlatch the collar, sprinting toward the door. I know he left it unlocked, but I can't reach it, so what would be the point?

What I hadn't expected was the solid, vault door at the top of the stairs... and it's closed. I pound on it, hoping that someone, anyone, can hear me. "Please! Help me! Is anyone there?" Red smudges across the door, my hands splitting open as I slam them into the metal.

"Stupid, fucking whore," I hear him growl, and I know I'm running out of time.

"P-please, if anyone is there, please help me," I beg, my strength ebbing away as I hear him getting closer.

"There's no one there, Pet." His good hand snags my hair, ripping me backward and sending me tumbling down the steps. My head cracks against

the bottom, and the room spins as I struggle to organize my thoughts. "Look what you fucking did!" He screams, slamming his foot into my stomach. I cough up blood, curling in on myself. "Did you really think you could get away from me?"

"I-I'm sorry!" I cry, trying to figure out if I should protect my stomach or my head more. "P-please, stop, I'm sorry!"

"You'll never see your son again, you ungrateful bitch."

"No!" I yell,

Then everything goes black as he slams his foot into my head.

Fuck, memories are hounding me today, I try to force them away, but I can't seem to focus on anything else. None of my escape attempts have done me any good. Including the time I tried to choke him with his own chain. But he'd overpowered me easily, throwing me to the floor. The pain from a knife sliding into my stomach had been shocking. Certain I was about to die. Instead, he called a doctor.

"Save her," he'd said, his tone indifferent, considering the pain. I'd begged the doctor to help me, but it was futile. He'd muttered apologies as he worked to stitch me back together, but made it clear there was nothing he could do for me.

It had just been another dead end.

And, through it all, I'd refused to break. I'd refused to let him win. As long as I breathe, as long as I fight, I can find a way. For Atlas.

"I have a present for you," he chimes, causing my stomach to churn. "But first, are you ready for some bonding time, Kitten?"

My nose wrinkles as he shrugs off his jacket and tosses it onto the table. His hands wrap around my ankles, and he yanks, causing me to lie flat and dragging me to the end of the bed. My legs dangle from the edge, and I clench my fists into thin sheets, forcing myself to remain still as he crawls over me.

The thought of his "bonding" time makes acid burn in my throat. He uses me in ways his wife would never permit, twisting intimacy into a weapon of cruelty. Every visit is a reminder of my reality. My fists strangle the sheets as I watch his movements, my skin crawling. Today feels different—his mood is darker, his movements restless.

"Y-you're upset," I squeak as I reach out. My hand brushes down his front toward his waistband. "Let me s-soothe you."

His smile stretches like a wolf baring its fangs, a glint in his eyes as he watches my hand glide over his bulge. He thrives on my submission, feeds off my fear, and uses every sign of resistance as an excuse for pain and punishment. Retreating to a safer place in my mind is the only way I've survived this. It's a coping mechanism I perfected long ago, a refuge that shields me from the worst of it.

His fingers dance across my stomach before slipping into my sweatpants, invading the space between my legs with an unfeeling touch. The intrusion is brutal, his finger thrusting inside me without care. My teeth sink into my bottom lip as I fight back a cry.

How does a body betray you like this? An unwanted response, a reaction I can't control, no matter how much I've tried. He's all my body has known, all it's been conditioned to understand, apart from that one night with Jake—a memory that feels like a lifetime ago.

"Always so eager and responsive for me, aren't you, Kitten?" He purrs, his praise oozing like honey. His fingers fumble with his belt like an eager teenager getting laid for the first time.

Swearing to himself, he yanks his hand free, tugging my sweatpants down my hips. I inhale as the cold air brushes over my exposed skin. There was a time when I would have given anything to be this skinny, to see my hips jutting out and my thighs a gap. But now, I long for the softness I once had—the extra protection that kept me alive in this freezing cell.

Every movement, every word he speaks, chips away at my resolve, but I hold on. I retreat further into my mind, to memories of Atlas and the hope that this nightmare will end soon. I won't let him take that from me. I won't let him destroy me.

Parting my legs with his knees, he thrusts inside me. I bite down harder on my lip, the taste of blood filling my mouth as I stifle a whimper. Tears gather in the corners of my eyes, blurring my vision. His voice grates against my ears. "That's right, Kitten. So tight... so wet."

Bile increases, but I swallow it down. Reacting, showing him anything, would only feed his sadistic pleasure. My only solace is knowing he doesn't last long.

Closing my eyes, I retreat into my mind, imagining every possible way I could make him suffer for what he's done. The fantasies bring no relief, only a bitter taste of strength I'll never have while I'm chained to this hell.

"Happy Birthday, Kitten," he grunts as he finishes, and the words hit like shards of glass, tearing through the fragile remains of what I thought I still had left. A part of me shatters, crumbling into pieces too small to mend, and the fire from his body wraps around me like a vice.

"Aww, why so sad?" he sneers, grinding against me a few more times, dragging out the moment. "Don't you enjoy our special time together?"

"O-of course," I stammer. Though the tremor betrays me as I try to keep it under control.

His mood changes. With a disgusted snarl, he shoves himself away from me, leaving me feeling exposed. I pull the sheet over my bare skin, clinging to the fabric as if it could shield me from the shame.

"You ungrateful slut," he spits, the word landing like a slap. Before I can react, he yanks the blanket from my hands, grabbing a fistful of my hair and dragging me to my feet.

I cry out, the pain sending fresh tears streaming down my face as he forces me to bend over the bed. Fear courses through me when I hear the unmistakable sound of his belt sliding from its loops.

"Don't I treat you well, pet?" he snaps, dripping with sarcasm. The first crack of the belt echoes through the air, the sting burning across my skin like searing fire, leaving a trail of lava in its wake.

The pain that claws its way out of my skin leaves a hot line of anguish in its wake. I cry out despite myself, as if my soul itself is being torn apart. The tears continue, spilling freely as though they are the remaining fractures of my shattered resolve.

"Don't I take care of you?" he snarls, punctuating the question with a strike.

My knees wobble, threatening to give out, but I force myself to stay upright. The embarrassment burns as hot as the pain, and every fiber of my being screams to fight back, to resist. But I can't.

"Yes!" The word ripped from me like a jagged wound. The sheets shred in my grip.

"Then why do you disrespect me at every turn?" he snarls, dripping with venom, a promise of pain as the belt cracks across my thighs once more. The blaze rips through me, searing into my flesh, and I cry out once again. A wetness trickling down my legs.

"Disgusting," he growls, sneering back at me.

Shame floods me as I peer down. The mixture of urine and semen puddles at my feet, and I can't stop the shaking in my legs. The cuts on my thighs sting, blood swirling into the mess on the floor. I collapse, my knees hitting the damp ground.

"Damn it," he spits, rising as he paces. "Why can't you be fucking grateful? You're just like her. Krystal doesn't want to go to the party anymore... she is such a frigid bitch!"

My body quakes as I drag my sweatpants back over my battered legs. Every motion sends a fresh wave of agony, but I bite it back, swallowing the pain. I won't give him the satisfaction. Won't let him see me break. Forcing my hands to keep moving, I steal a look over my shoulder. He doesn't even look at me—refastens his belt with a grunt, as if I were nothing more than an afterthought.

THE SWEATPANTS HUG my damp skin, fresh out of the icy shower I was forced to take. The harsh, chemical scent of the cheap three-in-one shampoo, conditioner, and body wash clings to me, a poor substitute for the cleansing I desperately need. It does nothing to erase his touch or the filth from under my skin.

Freshly dressed, I sit and fight to calm the jitters while huddling into myself. He continues to mutter comments about Krystal and the party they *were* planning. I attempt to blink back tears, refusing to let him see me cry.

He slumps onto the mattress, causing me to bounce. I pull my knees to my chest, circling my knees as he buries his face into his hands. "Krystal wants to throw this huge party to show off the *new* house, and now she doesn't even want to go." He pushes himself off the bed, pacing the space in front of me. His anger crackles like static. It's the same anger that's left me covered in cuts, welts, and bruises tonight. This is my punishment for not reacting the way he wanted, for not playing my role to perfection.

"She's pissed off because I'm not letting any of her little *brunch friends* come. But she doesn't understand—this party isn't about her or this fucking house." He stops, turning toward me, his smirk lifting as he steps closer. "I have a special surprise planned for my guests." He adds, his tone turning quieter, a more menacing edge. His eyes gleam as they rake over me.

I shrink back slightly as his smile widens. The chains rattle from the movement. I refuse to give him the pleasure of seeing my fear. I hold my ground as my mind races, grasping for a way out.

"Don't worry, Pet," he murmurs, belittling me. "You'll make this party unforgettable."

His hand slithers around the collar, using it like a noose, and yanking me forward. The chain digs into my skin, its cold metal biting, causing me to stumble to the end of the bed. My skin stings, the burn from his body searing through the thin fabric of my shirt. I wince, peeking up to meet his cold eyes, like ice.

"You'll be attending, Pet, that is part of your birthday present," he whispers, his hot breath sweeping across my face, "and you're the main event."

Stunned, I try to step back to look at him. "M-me?" I stammer. He nods, his fingers brushing my tangled, wet hair over my shoulder. He growls, yanking at my hair as he gets stuck in the snarls. Pain shoots through my scalp, and I hiss. Strands of my hair are ripped free, and I watch as he tosses them to the floor.

"Yes, my little pet. You."

I stare at him, speechless. The thought of being let out of this prison is unthinkable. This room has been my entire world for years—a place of unending torment. The walls of this house were built around my screams. Why would he consider letting me out now?

Unless... he's confident I have no chance of escaping. My mind reels at the possibilities. His "guests" could be as monstrous as he is—perhaps even worse. Suddenly, leaving my cage is more terrifying than staying within it. At least here, I know the devil I'm dealing with. Outside, there could be threats I can't predict or defend against.

"I've wanted to showcase my precious pet to my guests for some time," he continues, dripping with delight. "And now that the wife has decided not to attend, it's an even more perfect opportunity to display you at the party rather than keeping you as mere evening entertainment."

He pinches my chin, forcing my head back, compelling me to meet his gaze. My skin tingles where he touches, every part of me screaming to pull away.

"Don't disappoint me, Pet," he sneers, his lips curling into a sadistic grin. "You wouldn't want me to punish you in front of them, now would you? Although they enjoy our videos," he nods toward the mounted camera. I stare at it, watching the green light flash, a silent witness to every moment of my torment. He relishes filming our encounters, preserving his cruelty when he can't visit in person.

He once bragged that people paid well to see me break beneath him, but I haven't. He hasn't broken me yet.

I used to beg, plead for mercy. But my cries only excited him more, fueling his determination to document my suffering. Over time, I stopped begging. When he wasn't in the room and the green light switched on, I tried pleading with anyone watching. *Please help me. Please, someone save me.* But after a year and no sign of rescue, I knew the truth. The viewers were just like him, deriving pleasure from my pain.

"You're letting me out?" I gasp, unable to conceal the hope that bubbles.

His cruel grin widens. "Before you get any ideas about escaping," he observes the scars marring his arm, and a small sense of pride courses through me, "my friends would love the chance to punish someone like you. They'd relish it."

The fragile hope splinters like glass, and I recoil, my stomach knotting as his fingers tangle in my hair, dragging me closer. Tears sting my eyes as he leans in. "And since you have such a charming habit of trying to run, let me be clear—this house has automatic locks. All controlled from my phone. So there's no way out."

"Okay," I squeak as my scalp burns. Finally, he loosens his grip, and I collapse back onto the bed, hugging myself.

"Perfect," Clapping his hands together, the sudden sound making me flinch. He notices and chuckles. "Saturday morning, a team of stylists will prepare you. Until then, remember these three rules."

He raises a finger with each rule as he counts them off.

"One: Do not speak to anyone unless I am present."

Don't talk to anyone...

"Two: Only respond with 'Yes' or 'No.'"

Stick to yes or no answers...

"And three," his grin turns sadistic, his eyes glinting, "if you try to run, I won't punish you. I won't kill you."

He leans closer, dropping into a whisper. "I'll kill *our* son. But, as the second part of your present, I'll send Atlas down in the morning, and you can spend the day together."

His words crush what little strength I have left. "T-thank you, Sir," I respond as my tears flow freely.

A weight settles in my stomach. It's unlikely anyone at the party would help me; I gave up on the idea of saviors a long time ago. But being let out, even temporarily, offers a different kind of opportunity—a chance to assess the remaining obstacles, to piece together a more effective plan for our escape. I cling to that thin thread of purpose as he strides out of the room, the click of the lock sealing me in once again.

I make my way into the shower, my movements sluggish and mechanical. The hot water scalds my skin, but I don't flinch. I scrub until my flesh feels raw, desperate to erase the memory of his touch, but no amount of soap can reach where his presence buried itself.

Eventually, the water runs cold, but I don't move. Instead, I sit on the shower floor, letting the wet tiles cool my skin. The ground is unforgiving, but I don't care. Here, in the small confines of the shower, is the only place I feel even a semblance of safety. The tiles dry, sticking to my skin the longer I stay.

I force myself to get up, pull on a loose T-shirt, and grab a few supplies before returning to my safety net. Wrapping myself in a blanket with a pillow clutched to my front, I pull the worn leather jacket close, my fingers curling into the cracked seams; it's the only thing keeping me from falling apart. The scent has faded, but traces of him—of Jake, of safety—still linger in the aged leather, a cruel echo of a life stolen from me. My captor let me keep it, not out of mercy, but because he knew it would break me in ways shackles never could. A reminder of what I lost. A taunt disguised as a kindness. A tether to a past that feels more like a dream with every passing day.

Huddling into a ball, I bury my face into the pillow, the soft leather brushing my cheek. My wet hair clings to my face, my body shivering from the cold and the weight of exhaustion. The scent of Jake, faint as it is, gives me a weak sense of comfort. For a moment, I let myself pretend I'm not alone. Pretend the jacket wrapped around me is him, holding me, shielding me from the crushing nightmare.

It isn't real. I know that. But in the stillness of the shower, in the solace of this small space, I can hold onto the illusion for a little while.

CHAPTER 9

Jake

Ash slaps the invitation onto the table like a hand grenade, for which we should all thank him. "Patrick's a paranoid bastard, Jake. This might be the only shot we get to step foot inside his damn house."

His tone is clipped, sharper than usual. Ash doesn't push unless he's sure. He's the one who calculates odds and rarely raises his voice, so when he does, it means we're officially out of options.

"He's been in hiding for three years. Ever since we put a bullseye on his back."

I lean back, fingers twisting the hilt of my blade against my palm, welcoming the sting. It's either that or punching a hole through the wall. "So what? You want us to suit up, smile pretty, and play nice at a damn housewarming party?"

Ash is hunched over the invite, eyes scanning like the paper's going to start whispering secrets if he squints hard enough.

"What fresh hell is this about tuxes?" Killian's voice cuts in like a cleaver. He stalks into the room, drenched in someone else's blood—again. The stain across his shirt is loud, but not as loud as the snarl on his face.

Ash doesn't look up. "That poor bastard Tristian, the one you redecorated with, was supposed to be on the guest list."

Killian picks up the invite with two fingers, as if it might bite him. "And?"

"And this party's being hosted by Patrick St. John," Ash snaps, finally locking eyes with him.

Killian's smile isn't friendly. It's the kind of grin people pray never gets aimed their way. "Well, then. I guess I can tolerate playing dress-up if it gets us close enough to bury him."

"He took her from us," Killian says, quieter now. Dangerous. "And if he's stupid enough to parade around like he's untouchable, then we remind him he's not."

Ash, who always clings to logic like a lifeline, drops it now. "Do you think he'll admit anything? That she might still be alive? We found the other girls... but not her. Doesn't that mean something?"

Killian's hands hit the table with a crack. "She's gone. Accept it. I have. You want a miracle? This isn't it. This is revenge."

He shoves away from the table, the chair crashing backward. "And maybe if you'd gone after her the second you turned eighteen, we wouldn't be here now."

The door slams behind him.

Ash flinches. I pinch the bridge of my nose, the weight of everything pressing down like a steel boot. "None of the others made it more than a month..."

The words claw out of me, raw and awful.

Ash's fists slam down. "You think I don't know that?"

His voice splinters. Ash, the one who keeps his shit together, is unraveling right in front of me. His composure is a house of cards in a hurricane. And watching him crack? It guts me.

"I know she's probably gone," he bites out. "But so help me, I will burn that house to the ground before I give up without checking."

For four years, we've torn through the underworld, chased every ghost lead and fake whisper. Kicked in doors. Put bodies in the ground. And now, thanks to one sloppy mistake, we've got an in.

Ash straightens, brushing invisible lint off his blazer like it'll wipe away the emotion. "She's dead. And that's on us."

Then he walks out.

I stare at the blade, twisting it harder until blood pools in my palm. I swear I see her. The last time she smiled. The day she disappeared. The day we failed her.

The day we lost our Rose.

Fifteen years ago...

"Jake!"

I don't even get a warning before a blur of copper curls launches into me like a missile. Rose comes flying on rollerblades, arms flailing, zero control, zero apologies.

"Move your face!" she shouts—too late.

We collide hard. Her skates clip my shins, and I go down like a sack of bricks. My back smacks the dirt, breath knocked clean out of me.

She lands on top of me, limbs everywhere, curls in my mouth, laughter bubbling up like she hasn't just tried to end both our lives.

"Jesus, Rose," I wheeze. "Planning to kill me before lunch?"

"You lived," she grins, pushing herself up with her palms flat on my chest. "Barely."

Her cheeks are flushed, her hair a halo of chaos, and those eyes—always too bright, too knowing.

"Your idea of a thank-you is attempted manslaughter?" I mutter.

"Oh please," she says, smirking as she balances awkwardly on one knee. "You looked bored. Consider me your adrenaline shot."

"You're insane."

"And yet you let me near sharp objects."

I roll my eyes, but can't fight the smile pulling at my mouth. "One day I'm going to let you fall flat on your ass, and I won't feel guilty about it."

"You say that now," she says, sitting on my stomach like I'm not trying to breathe. "But we both know I'm your favorite disaster."

She is. God help me.

"Jake?" she says suddenly, quieter now. "Can I ask you something?"

"Only if you get off me first."

"No promises."

She leans in, her face close, too close, and something in her gaze shifts—playfulness dips into something deeper.

Her lips brush my cheek, featherlight, a whisper of a thing. My heart stutters.

Then a motorcycle roars in the distance, and I shove her off me like she's burned me.

"Jake—"

"You can't do that," I snap, scrambling to my feet.

Her smile drops. "Do what?"

"That. That thing with your face and... lips and proximity."

"I'm almost sixteen, not six," she argues, standing up and brushing off her knees. "You don't have to treat me like I'm made of glass."

"You're not glass. You're dynamite."

"So what, I'm dangerous now?"

"Yeah," I growl. "To me."

"Jake..."

"Don't."

The air snaps taut around us.

Then a new voice breaks it like a rock through glass.

"What's going on here?"

We both turn. A woman—rigid, prissy, and definitely not invited—stands at the end of the driveway, clipboard clutched like a weapon.

"Oh hell no," Rose mutters.

"Rose, dear, it's time to go," the woman says, already walking toward us like she owns the damn pavement.

"Who the hell are you?" I demand, stepping in front of Rose.

"Mrs. Langston. Social services."

Rose shrinks behind me.

"You're not taking her," I snap.

"This isn't your decision," she replies smoothly. "She's being transferred."

"Like hell she is."

Killian appears beside me, arms crossed, glare locked on the woman like he's choosing which bone to break first. Ash follows, oil-streaked and silent, assessing the situation like he's about to go full tactician.

"Paperwork," Ash says flatly.

Langston pulls out a folded document with the smugness of someone who thinks a stamp gives her power.

I yank it from her hand, scanning it. Court order. Signatures. All legit.

But too clean. Too convenient. Dated two days ago—no warning, no hearing. No one even contacted us.

My stomach drops.

"This was signed by the Fosters. Why would they do that?" Ash mutters, reading over my shoulder.

"That's not how this works," I snap at the woman. "What's really going on?"

"I'm just following orders," Langston chirps. "Now, Rose."

"No," Killian says, stepping forward. "You don't get to just show up out of nowhere with your fake-smile bullshit and take her like she's furniture. Where's your badge? Your ID? Anything that proves you're not some creep with a clipboard?"

Langston's smug expression falters. "I don't have to show you anything."

"Then you're not taking her," I growl.

Rose clutches my sleeve.

Ash shifts his stance. "You're bluffing. And if you aren't, you're involved. Either way, you're not leaving with her."

Langston's voice rises, brittle and strained. "Interfering with a legal removal—"

"Requires proof you're actually legal," Killian snarls, stepping in close, his voice low and lethal. "So where the hell is your backup? Your ID? Your state badge? Why are you the only one here, if this is so damn official?"

Rose's lip trembles. "Jake... I don't want to go."

"I'll come get you," I say, locking eyes with her. "Three months. I'll find you. If this is even legal."

Langston reaches out and grabs her arm.

Rose flinches, hard.

I'm moving before I know it, grabbing Langston's wrist with enough pressure to make her wince. "Touch her again, and I swear—one more finger, one more goddamn inch, and you'll leave here in pieces. Try me."

"Jake," Rose whispers, eyes wide, pleading.

Langston yanks away, snarling, "You're all going to regret this."

She grips Rose again, dragging her toward the car.

Killian starts forward, fury radiating off him in waves, but Ash throws an arm out, blocking him.

"Not like this," Ash mutters. "We can't fight paper with fists. We talk to the Fosters, or Jake will get her back in three months when he turns eighteen."

Rose stumbles once, her head snapping back to us just before the door closes. "D-don't forget."

And then she's gone.

CHAPTER 10

Killian

Memories of Rose rip through me like bullets, each one trailing smoke and blood. It's a fury I've carried for over a decade—an infection that never healed. We failed her. I failed her. When she needed us most, we froze. And when Jake finally decided to act, he was too damn late.

That hesitation? It cost everything.

Fifteen years of dragging this guilt behind us like a corpse. Every contact we pulled, every whisper we chased, every threat we made—all to make up for what we didn't do. And still, we've been two steps behind. Always too slow, too careful, too late.

I remember the way her face looked on the news. It wasn't a photo—it was a death sentence. Just another missing girl filed away and forgotten. The news anchor talked like she was already gone. And she was. The cops didn't care. Not about her. Not about us.

So I burned the rest of my life down and disappeared. I lived in the city's underbelly, hunting monsters in alleys and backrooms. I didn't sleep. Didn't eat unless I had to. And I heard her voice every time a lead ended with a body. Or worse, mine—telling her I'd keep her safe.

But I didn't.

And when I came back, everything had changed. The space between

Jake, me, and Ash was a canyon. I blamed them. I blamed myself more. The truth? I let her down. I let *him* have her.

So yeah, this mission? It's personal.

St. John's fortress gleams like a polished grave. All glass and chrome, like money can buy innocence, like security systems can keep ghosts out.

"These pants are cutting off circulation to my junk," I mutter, adjusting where the fabric's trying to neuter me. Tristian must've been built like a damn twig.

A woman in some bird-themed masquerade mask wrinkles her nose and turns away like my suffering offends her.

"Should've let me tailor them," Ash mutters beside me.

Jake doesn't say a word. Just walks forward like he's already got St. John's throat in his hands. Ash and I fall in step.

The doorman barely checks our invitation. Idiot. He deserves whatever mess we leave behind.

Inside, the place is all marble and ego. A house pretending to be a museum. Soulless.

"There he is," Ash hisses. He nods toward the stairs.

St. John stands there like a king surveying his kingdom. Arrogant. Polished. Dead man walking.

Then I see *her*.

Behind him. Half a step back, like she knows her place. Hair like fire, skin like porcelain, and a black lace mask that hides everything but her eyes. And God, those eyes—green and gold, haunted. Her dress clings to her body like it was sewn there. She moves like a whisper, and every man in the room watches her like they're starving.

But flinches when she catches their stare. She shrinks just a little—lip between her teeth. Head ducked. Trying to disappear in plain sight.

And something in me *cracks*.

She's too thin. Too polished. Too *perfect*. Patrick did that. Starved her down, pressed her into a mold. She chews her lip like Rose used to when trying not to cry.

She's not the woman we expected when describing his wife. She's a phantom. And when she walks, she does it like prey.

I watch as she vanishes into a side room.

"Kill, eyes on St. John," Ash orders. "We keep this clean. You hear me?"

"Yeah," I lie.

But I'm already drifting. Already moving. Already chasing the ghost.

She slips through the door. I follow.

The room is dim, draped in velvet and silence. She stands by the window, back to me. Small. Tense. Alone.

"You good?" I ask. My voice sounds wrong. Rough.

She turns slowly. Those eyes hit me like a punch to the ribs.

"No," she says. Voice low. Real. "Just needed a minute away."

That shouldn't undo me. But it does.

She's shaking. Not visibly. But I see it. In her hands. Her stance. She's bracing for impact. I know that posture. I've lived it.

And for a second, I forget the mission. Forget St. John. Forget everything but the girl in front of me, who looks like she's drowning and trying to smile through it.

"You shouldn't be alone," I mutter.

"I usually am."

She's not lying. I can hear the truth. Can see it.

I step closer.

And I *feel* it.

Something's off. Almost familiar.

She turns her head, and the light catches her jaw.

And I know.

This isn't just Patrick's wife. This is a thread—a loose string in a sweater we've been knitting for years.

I start to ask why she says. But I don't.

Because I already know.

And if I say it, everything changes.

So instead, I say nothing.

She leaves. Quiet as a breath.

And I stand there.

Shaking.

Because I've seen the monster.

And now I've seen the one thing that might still matter.

And we almost missed her.

CHAPTER 11

Asher

I take a champagne flute from the tray as it passes, the cool glass resting neatly between my fingers. A sip confirms what we suspected—cheap and acidic. The carbonation bites at my tongue, faintly metallic. Patrick's budget is bleeding somewhere, and he's hiding the cracks behind imported glass and artificial charm.

The gallery walls are cluttered with ornate frames. At a distance, the images mimic wealth and self-importance. But as I scan the details, the truth slips through.

They're all a woman.

One woman, in varying stages of undress. Her body twisted into poses that try too hard to be artistic. Her face is turned in most—strategically hidden or cropped out entirely—but the damage is visible. Bruises on her ribs. Marks along her thighs. The stark contrast of black and white photography only enhances the disfigurement.

This isn't art.

These are trophies.

My hand tightens around the stem of the glass. I take another sip, but the sting of the bubbles makes it worse, not better.

He displayed her pain.

He framed it.

I finish the drink, set the glass down, and adjust the line of my tie.

Control requires structure; right now, mine is the only one I can manage.

I turn into the first hallway, needing to move. The plan requires a clean exit—fast and undetected. Every door I open leads to a dead end: a cramped office filled to the brim with dusty canvas, an ornamental bathroom, a room overflowing with sculptures that shouldn't see daylight. I log each detail with practiced precision. Every light bulb that flickers. Every misplaced object. Every imperfect corner. But, there is no exit in sight.

I return to the main space and cross to the opposite hallway.

A woman blocks my path. "Hello there, handsome."

Her hand grabs my arm—nails sharp enough to leave indents but not to break skin. I stop. She wraps herself around me like a silk scarf, all expensive perfume and desperation. Her mask is black-and-gold with dangling butterflies that flutter as she talks.

"I've never seen you before. I'd remember seeing you at one of these," she purrs.

"I don't attend often," I answer flatly. Looking over her head at the hallway.

"Well, you should," she continues, unbothered. "Patrick always ends these parties with a bang. Something unforgettable."

The way she says it lands wrong.

I peel her fingers off my sleeve one by one. "I'll keep that in mind."

Her smile stretches wide. "Well, come find me after if you need some relief. I know I'll need it." I nod and keep walking.

Down the second hallway, I resume my search. Room after room, all smoke and mirrors: a study filled with untouched books, a lounge that feels more like a themed nightmare, a bedroom so pristine it looks like it's never been slept in. Nothing useful.

The last door on this side opens into a library. Aesthetically clean, but functionally irrelevant.

I smooth a hand over my hair.

Patrick built a fortress—every angle curated. Every corner is designed to display dominance. But perfection leaves trails. And trails can be followed. *So, why can't I find the trail?*

I circle back and pause near the refreshment table. Glasses have been replaced and refilled—new footprints on the floor. Patrick's people are organized, but not careful. I mark three directions they head in, mentally map the distance to each, and measure how many guests stand between me and the front drive. Then I breathe. Just once. Shallow. Then back to work.

"Hey," Jake calls as he intercepts me, his fingers catching my sleeve. "You good?"

"I can't find another exit," I snap. My hands fist and composure slip as I throw one at the wall. Jake blocks the hit, fingers wrapping around my wrist.

"There's one in the office," he says. "If we get him in there, we can vanish. You just need to handle the lock."

I exhale through my nose. "Another damn office. How many of these does one egomaniac need? Does he sign contracts in every room like he's running a Monopoly empire?"

As we walk, Jake adds, "Kill's flirting with that redhead."

"Of course he is," I mutter. "It's like trying to train a golden retriever who keeps finding new fire hydrants to pee on. Put a sexy dress on it and he'll follow it home."

Jake huffs a laugh, but the weight in the air returns as we reach the office. The lock confirms my suspicion—a digital overlay on a traditional structure. Expensive. Loud. But flawed.

While I examine it, Jake drags his fingers along one of the bookcases, stopping at a misaligned seam. He pushes. It clicks open.

Behind it—a vault door.

"Really?" he mutters. "Was he expecting a war?"

"More likely, he was hiding prisoners."

The wheel turns with little resistance, and the door groans. A stairwell leads down, narrow and concrete.

Each step echoes.

At the bottom: a single door. Plain. Wooden.

I test the knob.

Unlocked.

The air inside is humid. Stale. It clings to my skin, dense and unmoving. The space beyond is...sterile. No windows. No decor.

Just a bed, a kitchenette, and a chain bolted to the headboard.

The collar is intact.

The distance from the chain's end to the other areas—just enough for function. Bathroom. Kitchen. Bed. Nothing more.

The smell makes it worse. Not rot. Just... life forced into a box for too long.

Jake steps forward like he's underwater. He runs his fingers across the blanket, then the mattress. His throat works, but he doesn't speak.

"She was here," he mutters finally.

I nod, fingers tight at my sides. "Construction started last year. But this? This took longer."

He's still standing at the bed when - *crash.*

Wood splinters.

Jake swings again. A chair splits apart under the blow. Then the table. He's not stopping. Each hit lands with the fury of someone you don't walk away from.

He finally drops to his knees, panting, shoulders heaving.

His hands cradle something against his chest.

I kneel beside him.

It's a jacket. Leather. Large. His jacket.

"She was wearing this the day she disappeared," Jake says, his grip white-knuckled.

I can't speak. The room closes in, a box made of guilt.

Finally, I whisper, "Come on. We're not done."

He hesitates, then shoves the jacket inside his coat like it's sacred.

I stand. He follows. We leave the room behind. But the silence clings to us.

In the hallway, I pause long enough to realign a crooked frame. Jake watches me do it. Doesn't question it. He never does.

"We'll get her back," he says.

It doesn't feel like a promise, more like an apology. One that we can't afford to repeat.

The sound of laughter and champagne flutes returns. Guests continue to pretend they don't know what this place is.

But now we do.

And we can't forget.

CHAPTER 12

Ember Rose

In all my years of captivity, I've never felt like this—scrubbed clean, stripped bare, and polished until there's nothing left of me underneath. After being plucked, shaved, waxed, and coated in expensive creams, the woman in the mirror doesn't look back—she stares through me. Her skin shines with an unnatural glow, too smooth, too soft, like she might crack under pressure. The sting from the waxing remains, a quiet burn beneath the surface, proof of what was taken. My eyebrows are sculpted into perfection, framing wide eyes that don't recognize their reflection. Even my lips, slick with gloss, look like they belong to someone else.

I lift a hand, brushing trembling fingers along my jaw, desperate to find a trace of the girl who used to live in this skin. But she's gone, replaced by this version molded to please, obey, and disappear.

The stylists have transformed me into someone flawless. My makeup—a soft, smoky appearance in addition to the bold red lips—is perfect, designed to enhance features I barely recognize. The black lace mask perched over my face hides my identity, turning me into a caricature of elegance rather than a captive.

The lace dress clings to my body, highlighting my lack of curves, while the softness of the fabric glides like water under my fingers. After years of sweatpants and tank tops, the luxury only underscores the absurdity of my situation. Perfect. I need to be perfect tonight. If I follow all his rules, he'll let me see him. My ribs squeeze painfully like they're closing in—it's been weeks since I last saw my baby boy, still, the aching need to ensure he's safe is almost unbearable.

I turn toward the floor-to-ceiling windows, my reflection distorted by the dim light outside. For a fleeting moment, I could almost convince myself this is a dream—a masquerade where I'm simply another guest. The illusion shatters as quickly as it forms, replaced by the harsh truth of my reality. The mask may shield me from the guests' scrutiny, yet it doesn't protect me from what lies beneath.

"You look stunning, Miss," a gentleman remarks as he passes, raising his glass in a toast. His tone is polite, though his focus lingers too long. Forcing a tight smile, I dip my head in acknowledgment before moving through the room.

Deep breaths, Em. One foot in front of the other. Simply another performance. You've done it before; you'll do it again.

The man follows, his hand hovering at my lower back, nudging me through the guests as though he's presenting me for inspection. I move stiffly, discomfort showing with each step. He leans in and murmurs in my ear. "I'm sure Patrick won't mind if I steal a few moments of your time." His presence is hot against my skin, sending an unpleasant flutter coursing through me.

As we walk, he pauses occasionally to greet others, never straying far. Though his words are smooth and polite, his focus never leaves me for long, trailing me like a shadow. When the man stops to speak, his attention stays on me, hunger barely concealed in his expression. The women's expressions are more subtle but no less cutting, their disdain sharp enough to draw blood.

The lace bodice of my dress doesn't help, clinging to me like a second skin. It's an outfit designed to make me unforgettable, even as I pray to remain invisible. My captor chose it well—black lace that hides merely enough to maintain a facade of decency while ensuring every bone is accentuated. The mask covering the upper half of my face offers a semblance of anonymity, although I know better than to hope it will shield me from the attention of the partygoers.

I let my attention drift to the windows, calculating distances, memorizing exits. Even as the man herds me deeper into the throng of people, my mind churns, desperate to find a way out.

"Kitten?"

The word halts me mid-step, its chill crawling up my spine, familiar as a ghost. A vice-like grip around my core. Turning, I come face-to-face with Patrick St. John—my captor. His name has floated from the guests' mouths like a ghost; now his black orbs are locked on mine with a predator's intention.

"Yes, Sir?" I murmur, my voice a carefully controlled whisper. I stand frozen under his scrutiny, acutely aware of the man from before hovering directly behind me like an obedient dog—his hand twitches as though debating whether to reach out to me again.

Patrick's lips curl into a faint smile that doesn't reach his vacant stare. "Why don't you mingle with the other guests?" he says smoothly, his tone leaving no room for argument. "And remember what we discussed in your room." His glare sweeps to the man trailing me, a silent dismissal.

I force myself to nod, the movement stiff and unnatural. Patrick doesn't wait. He turns and slips back into his group, swallowed by the crowd like he was never here.

The other man pauses briefly, mutters a remark under his breath—low, but thick with contempt—then turns and storms off, leaving me with a prickle under my skin and a hollow settling in my chest.

The soft click of my heels against the polished marble floor is deafening amidst the low hum of conversation and clinking glasses. My fingers twitch at my sides, resisting the urge to pull the lace bodice higher, to shield more of myself from the predatory stares that pierce through the elaborate masks— the delicate black lace edging my vision. Every inhale is shallow, caught somewhere between dread and determination.

Patrick's parting words echo in my ears as I weave through the assembly, my movements stiff. Guests brush past me, their chortles too loud, their smiles too wide. A woman in an opulent gold gown bumps into me, her perfume overwhelming. She sneers, barely acknowledging my presence, before sweeping away, her mask glinting in the dim light. A pressure builds deep inside me, but I keep moving, head bowed, as though humility might render me invisible.

The large windows lining the walls draw my attention again. I drift closer, the glimmering cityscape beyond them almost taunting in its freedom. My reflection examines me, a stranger with a strikingly painted mask. The makeup is flawless, designed to captivate. However, the hollow look in my gaze betrays the truth. I reach up to touch my cheek, the smooth foundation an unfamiliar barrier against my skin.

A loud burst of laughter behind me makes me flinch. My attention jerks to the source, landing on a group of men gathered around a woman perched on a chaise. Her gown sparkles like starlight, her mask tilting as she throws her head back. They lean toward her, their attention ravenous, and I turn away before one of them notices.

A server approaches, balancing a silver tray laden with champagne glasses. His expression is neutral, his mask plain, a stark contrast to the garish display around him. I reach for a glass; my hand wobbles as I bring it to my lips. The bubbles prick my tongue, though I force myself to swallow, the taste souring in my mouth.

"Not much of a drinker, are you?" a low voice murmurs beside me.

I startle, nearly spilling the champagne as a man steps into my space, his presence cutting through the air like a blade. His mask is sleek, an elegant shadow that stands in stark contrast to the bright, gaudy spectacle of the room. It's almost too perfect, a reflection of mystery against the garish light. His focus swipes over me with a cold, casual interest, like a predator sizing up its prey, unreadable yet piercing, just long enough to unsettle.

"I'm sorry," I manage, my voice barely audible.

"Don't be." His lips quirk in a small smile, but there's still an edge to it. "You're new here, aren't you?"

A rapid beat races through me, each thump vibrating against my ribs like a wild drum echoing through my veins as I force myself to meet his stare. "I—" My voice falters, and I turn away, fixing my eyes on the champagne glass in my hand.

He chuckles softly. "Don't worry," he says, his tone dipping lower. "We all have to start somewhere."

Before I can respond, he steps back, his presence fading into the crowd as quickly as it appeared. I exhale, my fingers clenching the stem of the glass as I try to steady myself: the champagne sloshes, a small reminder of how off-balance I am.

The heavy thud of my pulse drowns out the noise around me as I turn back to the window, the city lights beyond a distant, unattainable dream. The room begins to close in on me, its opulence and pretense stifling. Still, I force myself to remain upright, keep moving, and endure. There's no other choice—not yet.

The air rushes from my body as I crash into what registers as a wall, except the strong arm around my waist tells me otherwise. My fingers clutch at the lace of my dress as I steady myself, my pulse racing. The embrace warms me through the thin fabric, grounding me despite the whirlwind of fear.

"Shit!" The word escapes my lips again, half-gasp, half-expletive, as I tilt my head back to see who—or what—I've collided with. I study the broad expanse of a chest clad in an ill-fitting suit, the fabric stretched tight over defined muscles.

"You okay there?" A deep voice rumbles from above me, like honey poured over gravel. It moves through the air and sinks into my skin, sending a slow ripple down my spine. The sound wraps around me, velvety but edged with a bite I can't quite name. My head snaps up, and I meet a pair of forest-green eyes flecked with gold. Long lashes cast faint shadows, but his gaze gleams—curious, amused, maybe both.

"I-I'm sorry," I stammer, trying to step back, yet his arm remains firm, keeping me close. My eyes flit anxiously to the rest of the room, scanning for Patrick or anyone else who might notice. The last thing I need is to draw more attention to myself.

"No harm done," he says, his lips curving into a slight smirk. His hand flexes briefly against my waist, and I perceive the strength behind the casual gesture. "Though you might want to watch where you're going."

I swallow hard, my cheeks flushing with embarrassment. "I wasn't—I mean, I didn't mean to—" I stammer, unable to form a coherent sentence. His focus holds mine, making my cheeks bloom with color.

"Relax," he murmurs, his tone softening as he releases me. I stagger back, smoothing the folds of my dress to compose myself. "I've got you."

"Th-thank you," I manage. My fingers fidget with the lace sleeves of my dress, and I feel the full force of his attention. It isn't the hungry, invasive stare I've come to expect from the men here; it carries a different kind of intensity—steady, unnerving, and hard to place. My thoughts scatter.

He tilts his head slightly, brows drawing together as if trying to figure me out. "You don't seem like the mingling type," he says.

I bite my lip, unsure how to answer. The truth—that I don't belong here, that I'm just a piece in Patrick's game—isn't safe to admit. "I'm just... not used to these kinds of events," I murmur, eyes drifting to the side.

"Hm," he hums, one brow arching like he's not entirely convinced. "What's your name?"

The question throws me. The air stills around me, my breath catching as panic builds. No one ever asks that. Not here. Patrick made sure I forgot who I was, reduced me to nothing but *Kitten* or *Pet*. I flounder for an answer, unsure of what I'm allowed to say—but he speaks again before I can.

"Scarlett," he says, a faint smile ghosting across his lips as his gaze lingers on my hair. "It suits you."

The name stirs a distant and unfamiliar feeling in me, like a thread tugging at a long-forgotten memory. I open my mouth to respond, but no words come. Instead, I nod, my fingers curling tighter into the fabric of my dress.

"Well, Scar," he says, stepping back. "Try not to knock anyone else over." His smirk softens, warmth flickering behind it, and then he turns, slipping into the crowd with a casual nod.

As he disappears from view, I let out an exhale. My body vibrates with the adrenaline of the encounter. My hands cup my cheeks, willing the glow to subside, peering around to ensure no one else noticed the exchange. For a fleeting moment, I encounter the strangest pang of regret as he vanishes into the sea of faces. Nevertheless, I quickly shove it aside—attachment, even curiosity, is a luxury I can't afford. Not here. Not now.

The swirl of snickers and clinking glasses grows faint as I move through the throng of bodies, each step sending a heavy thud reverberating through me, a force driving my every movement. A jolt runs through me when I glimpse over my shoulder and meet his gaze again. They don't simply watch; they bore into me, like a hand reaching out to pull me back. My stomach twists, forcing my stare forward as I weave through the gathering.

A voice snakes through the noise, sharp as a knife against my senses. "Who was that?" it murmurs. The words pierce me, freezing me midstep, my body tensing like prey caught in a spotlight. The pull to peer back claws at me, but I fight it, my fingers digging into the lace at my sides as I push forward. Keep moving, keep breathing.

"I'm not sure," Green Eyes replies, rougher, barely audible over the thrum of conversation. "But she reminds me of her."

The world tilts. A vise clamps down on me, making my steps falter. Their words hang in the air, wrapping around me like a noose. My legs carry me forward, though I experience it like I'm moving underwater. The hallway looms ahead, quieter, shadowed, a sliver of escape. I slip into the first door I find and collapse onto the edge of a leather sofa, the cold surface comforting me. My inhales come in short, ragged bursts; my hands fidget as I clench them together in my lap.

Deep breaths, Em. Deep breaths. The familiar cadence of Marissa's voice echoes in my mind, a whisper from a time that feels worlds away. Slowly, the tension in my back eases enough for me to unclench my fists. The weight of those stares, that voice—it stays in my mind.

Time drags, each second scraping against my nerves like a dull blade. I shift, exhaling through clenched teeth. How can a moment so painfully slow still feel like it's closing in on me? My fingers curl into fists again—restless, anxious. If I wait much longer, I might unravel completely.

I scan the dim room—a library, shadows cast by rows of books moving like restless ghosts. Eventually, I rise, shaking my hands as if I can fling off the unease crawling under my skin. Patrick will notice. If I don't return soon... the consequences hang over me like a stormcloud, unspoken but certain.

Just as I reach for the door, low murmurs stop me cold. The tones cut through the still air like blades. I lean in, ear near the wood.

"Did you see him?" a deep, gravel-coated tone rumbles, rattling the fragile calm I'd tried to hold. The sound sends a chill down my spine, my body going still, every nerve on high alert. "I swear I saw him come this way."

Another responds, smooth but lined with irritation. "Last I saw, he was near the stairs. Then he vanished." A pause follows, the next words quieter but no less pointed. "I got distracted by the redhead who ran into K."

A hard pull tightens deep in my gut, knocking the breath from my lungs. The air in the room feels thinner now, every word settling into me like ash. Me. Are they talking about me?

"There was something about her..." a third voice murmurs, so quiet I have to strain to hear it. It carries a weight, an uncertainty that prickles at my skin. "She seemed so similar to—"

"It's the red hair," the smooth voice interrupts, sharp now, almost dismissive. "They have similar hair. Apparently, *he* has a type."

The grains of wood dig into my forehead, a stark contrast to the frenzy spinning in my head. I push harder, like I could sink into its surface, vanishing from sight. My teeth sink into my lip. The words on the other side of the door twist the knot of unease, each syllable like a stone dropped into an already churning sea.

"What if she's being held captive?" A voice, reminiscent of Green Eye's, breaks through the silence, its unsteadiness slicing through the air like a razor. Each syllable echoes the cries I've buried deep within me for years—silent screams that claw at the walls of my insides. Yes. YES! The truth burns like a wildfire, desperate to escape, to tear through my lips. Even so, I clamp my mouth shut, the pressure building behind my teeth, unwilling to let it slip. Not yet. Not when I can't risk the consequences. Not while someone else's life hangs on my silence.

My hand finds the doorknob, the icy metal biting into my palm, though it anchors me. It's the only thing keeping me from collapsing under the weight of hope and terror warring within me. My fingers flutter, clinging to the cold, as I will myself to remain still.

"If we take him out, it'll help her too—if she's even a prisoner," a second voice cuts in, smooth as polished glass, carrying the sharp bite of a hidden blade. Frustration simmers beneath the silky tone. "You don't even know this girl. Don't lose focus now, not when we're this close, Ki—"

"You don't get to say that to me. Not after everything." The words rip from his throat like glass dragged across stone. The following snarl is volatile, snapping like a live wire. A sudden scuffle—boots scraping hard against the floor. "You don't get to tell us that."

The sound breaks through the stillness, layered with more than anger—grief, betrayal... the unraveling of someone barely holding it together.

Their voices fade, growing softer as they move further down the hallway. I lean harder against the door, straining to catch their words, my pulse hammering in my ears. A flutter of recognition stirs in my mind, a ghost of a memory barely out of reach, yet it slips away before I can grasp it.

"Help me... please, help me," I whisper, my words fogging against the wood. Forcing myself to calm, I grip the doorknob, willing the jitters in my body to subside.

With a cautious twist, I crack the door open, peering into the hallway. Empty. Adrenaline courses through me as I step out, smoothing shaky hands down the front of my dress, trying to calm the flame coursing through my veins.

"There you fucking are!" Patrick's furious growl shatters my brittle composure like glass. I whirl, startled, his hand clamping down on my arm before I can move. His grip is iron, fury radiates off him like fire.

"I was trying to find a restroom," I blurt, stumbling in my heels as he drags me back toward the party. My words tumble out in a panicked rush. "I tried to find you, I didn't know where you were."

"Then you hold it until you do!" he snaps, his fingers digging into my arm like claws. Pain shoots up to my shoulder, though I bite down on the whimper threatening to escape. His face inches closer, heavy against my ear. "You were trying to escape, weren't you?" he growls, a dangerous rasp.

"No! No, I would never try to escape!" I cry, my voice cracking as tears blur my vision. "You know that!" My eyes dart around, searching desperately for help, for a sympathetic face—anyone who might intervene. But the room spins with indifference. Every gaze glides past me, dismissing me as invisible, another accessory in Patrick's carefully crafted world.

The revelers swirl around us, chuckling and conversing, blending into an indistinct hum. I can only focus on him—the man with emeralds behind his mask. His stare meets mine, and for a fleeting moment, hope flares to life. "Please," my voice so faint it gets lost in the noise. "Help me."

The steel clamp of Patrick's fingers grind the delicate bones in my wrist. Pain spikes through me, wrenching a sharp cry from my lips. Green Eyes takes a step forward, his jaw ticking. I watch as a firm hand clamps down on his collarbone area, halting him. My faint hope shatters, scattering like shards of glass. His hesitation seals my fate.

Patrick yanks me toward the steel door looming ahead, its surface like the face of a tomb, offering nothing but the bitter taste of despair. The metallic scent of it fills my nose, the chill creeping into my bones. My legs betray me, buckling under the weight of dread, crashing over me like a tidal wave pulling me into the depths. *Not the cell. Not again. I won't survive it this time.*

"No. Please, Patrick!" My voice quivers, cracking with desperation, though it's useless. His hand shoots out, releasing my arm only to latch around my neck. The world tilts dangerously. A gasp escapes me as his fingers sink into my neck, the pressure stealing the sounds from my lips.

"What did you call me, Pet?" he hisses, a venomous whisper. I claw at his wrist, my nails scraping across flesh. The effort is futile, only serving to deepen his sadistic pleasure, a cruel smile twisting on his lips as I fight for air.

"I-I'll be good, Sir," I gasp as black spots bloom at the edges of my vision. "I promise."

Patrick's sneer deepens, his teeth bared. "You're just like the rest of them," he growls, his free hand tearing at the hem of my dress. Fabric rips, the sound slicing through my mounting panic. "Always thinking you can outsmart me, always thinking you're better than me." His words carry the weight of every cruel intention as he lifts me off the floor, his grip crushing what air remains in my lungs.

My vision narrows. My limbs grow heavy. My fingernails break against his skin, drawing thin lines of blood that do nothing to weaken his hold. *I can't let it end here. A* spark of defiance flickers beneath the encroaching darkness. *Not like this.*

My heel catches on the edge of the top stair, the space behind me a yawning abyss. The void churns my stomach, a sickening vertigo rising as Patrick's sneer burns into my skin. Suddenly, his hand shoves me, and the floor vanishes.

Weightlessness shatters into chaos. The first stair slams into my back like a brutal punch, sending a shockwave of pain tearing through my body. I twist mid-fall, instinctively trying to shield my head, even so, another jagged edge sinks into my ribs, ripping away my soul. The impacts come fast, each one compounding the agony, a symphony of sharp edges and blinding pain that echoes through me. My head strikes the cold stone floor at the bottom with a sickening thud, the sound reverberating in my skull. The world tilts violently, spinning out of control. A faint, broken whimper escapes my lips, the only sound left in the silence that follows.

Patrick's voice snakes through the haze. "Oh, don't worry, Kitten. You won't be in pain for much longer." His heavy footsteps echo down the staircase, each step belittling my futile struggle.

My arms throb, each muscle screaming in protest as I drag myself forward, fingers scraping desperately against the jagged floor. The coarse texture rips into my skin, the sensation as unforgiving as my efforts. Every inch I crawl feels insurmountable, as if the ground beneath me is pushing back, each movement tearing at what strength remains. The shredded remnants of my dress cling to my legs, the fabric twists, mocking my struggle, pulling me back with every agonizing tug. The door is so close—within reach—at the same time feeling like an eternity away, an unreachable promise that taunts me with its proximity.

"Poor little kitten," Patrick taunts, crouching beside me. His voice wraps around my quaking form like a noose. "Always trying to survive." I freeze as he leans closer, his exhale is hot against my cheek. "Tell me—what are you even surviving for?" His tone like a blade drawn across velvet, laced with cruelty. "Oh, that's right. Atlas."

A sob catches as his hollow cackle rings out through the air. He grips my chin, forcing me to meet his eye. "No matter how hard I tried, I could never break you," he murmurs, almost admiringly. "Was his life not worth behaving for?"

"P-please," I stammer, tears streaking down my face. "Don't... don't h-hurt him." Patrick's lips curl into a sadistic grin. His fingers trail down my cheek, deceptively gentle, before twisting cruelly into the shredded fabric of my dress. With one sharp tug, the delicate lace tears with a sound like a soft, broken whisper, filling the room with its unforgiving rip. Cold air rushes in, biting at my exposed skin, sending a chill skittering across my flesh like a thousand tiny needles.

"If I have to kill you," he whispers, "I'll make sure to use you one last time."

The sting of my tears mixes with the chill of the floor as they trail unchecked down my face, soaking into the grime. My body refuses to obey, my limbs useless, the fight drained from my marrow. I want to scream, to claw, to bite—anything—yet all I can do is lie there, broken.

"St. John!" A thunderous shout cracks like lightning and reverberates from the top of the stairs. Patrick freezes mid-motion, his hand slackening its brutal grip as he whirls toward the sound.

"What the fuck? How did you—" His words are drowned out by the cacophony of pounding footsteps—the brutal collision of bodies. The impact rattles the floor beneath me as Patrick is tackled, his grunt of surprise giving way to a guttural snarl. The room erupts into mayhem—curses spat through gritted teeth, the visceral thud of fists meeting flesh, the scrape of shoes struggling for traction on the floor.

The sounds around me blur, muffling into an indistinct hum as a new voice cuts through the haze. "Hey... can you hear me?" A hand cups my cheek, the touch like sunlight after a storm. It's the first kindness I've felt in so long—the contrast overwhelms me, a fresh tide of tears spilling down my face. "Look at me, Sweetness," the voice urges, its tenderness pulling me from the depths, a lifeline in the sea of my despair.

I blink sluggishly, my lashes sticky with tears and blood. The world tilts like a fractured painting, the edges smearing as I try to focus. A shadowy figure hovers above me, bluish gold flecks catching the dim light. His voice wraps around me like a balm against the rawness of my despair.

"Y-you have to s-save h-him," I stammer, my voice fragile like a dying bird's wings fluttering. My head lolls to the side, too heavy to lift. I fight against the pull of unconsciousness as the coppery tang of blood coats my tongue. "P-please..."

"Who?" the voice asks. A hand brushes against my forehead, sweeping away strands of matted hair. The tenderness in the action registers as foreign. It's as if a blade dipped in honey is digging into my skin, sharp yet sweet in its contradiction, stirring memories of every bruise, every wound, every broken promise. "Stay still, Sweetness," he urges. We're going to get you out of here."

My body jerks. "N-no... him," I choke out, forcing each syllable through the haze of exhaustion. The effort drains what strength I have left. "S-save him."

His hand pauses, comforting me against my clammy skin. "Who do you mean? Who is *he*?" he whispers, leaning closer. I want to respond; I open my mouth to try. But, nevertheless, the shadows creep closer, swallowing the edges of my vision. My lips part, though no more words come—only a faint gasp as the void takes hold.

The last thing I experience is the weight of his glare on me, his presence a fleeting anchor in a world slipping away.

They can save him. They have to.

The world fades completely, yet for the first time in years, peace flutters through my body like a dying ember, promising that maybe, just maybe, this nightmare is finally over.

CHAPTER 13

Asher

"Come on, Beautiful, open your eyes," I whisper, quieter than I've spoken in years. The girl in my arms remains still, her copper strands stuck to her cheeks with blood. She's too weightless—barely there. Holding her feels like cradling a ghost.

Warmth soaks through my shirt. Blood. I shift her, careful not to jostle her more than necessary, and straighten.

"We need to move," I say. The words come out too harsh, too sudden, but there's no room for hesitation.

Killian stands over St. John, his hands clenched around the man's throat. He doesn't stop until the body goes limp. When he finally lets go, the sound of Patrick hitting the concrete is louder than it should be.

Jake crouches, grabs a fistful of the bastard's shirt, then drops him again, this time face-first. The crunch echoes.

Jake lifts the limp frame like he's dragging a bag of trash. "Oops."

I glance down at the red spreading across my shirt. It clings to her skin. I'll burn every thread of these clothes when this is over.

"We take him with us," Killian mutters, already walking. "He doesn't die until we have answers."

Jake makes sure Patrick hits every corner on the way out.

We move fast, retracing the route we planned days ago. Each step feels like it's pulling something from me. Each breath tastes like metal.

The keypad gives. The hallway yawns open.

We didn't expect to find anyone, not like this. Not someone so broken, collapsed beside the man we came here to end—the woman we thought was his wife—the one no one had seen.

My jaw locks. I can still see how he dragged her through that party, how no one blinked.

A sound pulls me back. She shifts against me, her body curling in. A sudden inhale. Barely there.

"Stay with me, Beautiful." My thumb brushes a smear of blood from her temple. She doesn't respond. Her breaths are uneven, her skin cold beneath mine.

Jake throws Patrick into the trunk and slams it shut with enough force to shake the car.

"She needs a hospital," I tell Killian. "Now."

He nods, a second too late.

The back door swings open. I slide inside, careful with every movement. Her head rests against my chest—every inch of her screams broken.

She whimpers, and my stomach twists.

Killian climbs in front. Jake's already behind the wheel.

"How bad?" Jake asks, gaze locked on the road.

I look down at the red smearing across my arms. "Too much blood. I don't know how long she has."

Jake's hands freeze on the wheel. "Get in. Get out. No hesitation."

We speed through the dark. Tires hum. The inside of the SUV is filled with everything we can't say.

Hospital lights pierce the night. Jake only slows when he has to. Gravel crunches beneath the tires as we come to a stop.

"Cameras," Jake says. "No attention."

Killian nods. The back door flies open. He meets me halfway and helps lower her carefully. My chest aches. My arms don't want to let go.

Inside, the lights are too harsh. I find a gurney and set her down. Her blood stains the white like an accusation.

"She needs help!"

A nurse rushes over, her mouth flattening when she sees the mess. "What happened?"

"She fell. Stairs."

She doesn't believe me. Doesn't need to. She calls for a doctor.

More people crowd the gurney. Hands everywhere. Barked orders. The doors close behind them.

I step forward. A nurse stops me with a hand to my chest. "Wait here."

I don't respond. She's already gone.

Killian's grip finds my shoulder. "We have to move."

I let him guide me out, my arms still burning from holding her.

Jake glances at me through the mirror. "How bad?"

Killian answers. "They took her in. It's not good."

Jake curses, low.

I can't stop thinking about her hands, her ribs, her blood on my shirt.

I hit the car door. Hard. It's not enough.

"We get answers," I say.

Jake nods. "And then he dies."

As the hospital disappears behind us, I shut my thoughts off and make a promise.

Whoever she is, whatever hell she's been through—we won't fail this time.

THE ROOM IS STILL. Too still.

Killian paces like a caged animal. Jake leans against the wall, arms crossed, jaw working.

I stand near the sink, scrubbing until the blood's gone. I can't seem to stop. Need it gone.

"Tick-tock," Jake mutters. "He should be waking up."

Killian grunts. Doesn't slow.

My hands shake. I cycle through every worst-case possibility. "Let's get down there."

We enter the basement, the door slamming shut behind us, and I am greeted by Patrick, chained to the chair, slouched but smiling like he's at brunch.

"Took you long enough," he drawls. His busted lip stretches into a grin. "Miss me already?"

Killian walks in last, carrying a toolbox like it's dessert.

"Comfortable?" Jake asks.

"I've had worse dates."

Killian drops the box. The clang is satisfying.

Patrick chuckles. "Oh, don't look at me like that. You boys are so dramatic. It's almost romantic."

"You know what's not romantic?" Jake picks up a wrench and turns it slowly in his hand. "Kidnapping. Torture. Trafficking."

Patrick shrugs. "Details, details."

I step forward. "Start talking."

He looks me over like I'm a menu. "And you are?"

"The one who kept her alive."

Patrick snorts. "Her? You mean my pet?"

Killian's fist connects with his jaw. Patrick laughs through it, spitting blood on the floor.

"Still not scared?" Jake asks.

"Should I be?" Patrick smirks. "What are you gonna do, kill me? That's the easy way out. You want answers, not a corpse."

"Then give us some," I say.

He leans back—or tries to. "You've got nothing. You think I'm afraid of three boys with vendettas? Please. I eat men tougher than you for breakfast."

Killian grabs a blade and holds it over the light.

Patrick grins. "Oh, look. A prop. How very theatrical."

Jake steps closer. "Where is she?"

Patrick tilts his head. "You'll have to be more specific. I've had a lot of playthings."

Another punch. This time, he grunts.

"You talk now," I say, "or we start taking pieces."

Patrick lifts his head and smiles, blood on his teeth. "You can have whatever's left. She was never yours to begin with."

Killian moves, but I stop him with a hand.

"No," I say. "He wants to die. He thinks we'll give him the easy way out."

Patrick chuckles low. "Smart one, this guy. Shame you're all wasting your time."

Jake steps in, close enough to make him lean back. "You have no idea how much time we've already wasted."

"Then stop pretending this is about her," Patrick says. "It's about you. It's always been about you. You're just mad I beat you to it."

Killian moves again. No one stops him this time.

And the screaming finally starts.

Patrick's scream chokes off into a wet gasp as Killian pulls the blade back. Blood drips steadily onto the concrete, but the bastard still has that same smug curl to his lips, even as pain ripples through him.

"Is that it?" he croaks, coughing once. "Is that your big move? You wound me, gentlemen. Literally."

Jake wipes the blood from the blade on Patrick's shirt, disgust curling through him. "You keep flapping your mouth, and I'll make sure the next one cuts deeper."

"You think this is the first time someone's tried to make me talk?" Patrick wheezes a laugh. "Hell, I've paid for worse. You boys don't have the stomach for what it takes."

Killian's hand twitches toward the toolbox, but I hold up a palm.

"Let him keep talking," I say, stepping in closer. "Every word he spills makes tearing him apart easier."

Patrick leans forward as much as the restraints allow, blood seeping into his collar. "Oh, how noble. Big, bad boys come to save the girl. Too late, as usual. She was mine long before you ever showed up."

Jake's hand slams down on the table beside him, the metal tools jumping with the impact.

"You drugged her," he growls. "Starved her. Used her. That doesn't make her yours—it makes you a parasite."

"Careful, Blondie," Patrick taunts. "You're starting to sound emotional."

Killian crouches beside him, grabbing his chin hard enough to bruise. "Let's test your memory. Tell me about the others. The ones you buried. Maybe we'll start matching names."

Patrick just smirks. "Names blur together after a while. So many pretty little projects, all begging for someone to take control."

The words snap something in Jake. He drives his boot into Patrick's leg. There's a crack, a howl, and for the first time, that arrogant smirk falters.

"You're gonna run out of bones," Patrick spits through clenched teeth.

"And you're gonna run out of excuses," I reply, kneeling to meet him eye to eye. "We're not like the cops. We don't stop at paperwork. You talk, or we get creative."

"You think she wants to be saved?" he sneers. "She'd crawl back every time. Begged for it. Liked it."

Killian's fist crashes into his temple—blood sprays, and Patrick slumps, dazed but not out.

Jake leans in, his breath slow and controlled. "We're not here to save her. We're here to make sure you never touch another woman again."

Patrick laughs weakly. "Then you're gonna have to kill a lot of people. I'm just one branch of a very large tree."

My stomach knots. He's not bluffing. Not entirely.

I glance at Killian. "He's not alone."

"No," he agrees. "But he's going to be the first to fall."

Patrick wheezes. "If you kill me, you'll never find her."

Jake tilts his head. "Tell us where she's buried."

Silence. Just for a beat.

Then Patrick curses under his breath. The kind of slip that tells us everything.

Killian grabs the pliers. "You remember where Rose is."

Patrick snarls. "You're all dead men walking."

"Maybe," I say, grabbing the chair and yanking it forward, so he's face to face with me again. "But if you know where she is? You just gave us the one thing we needed—peace."

And this time, when the screaming starts, no one moves to stop it.

CHAPTER 14

Ember Rose

A dull throb hangs at the base of my skull, each wave building until the ache swells like a storm behind my forehead. The overhead lights burn with cruel force, washing everything in sterile white that stings even with my eyes closed—a constant beep drills through the silence, a metronome for the chaos inside my head. I inhale too fast, the sound scraping through a dry throat, memories dissolving before I can pin them down.

"Ah, you're awake!" A chipper tone snaps through the haze, jarring in the muted quiet. I tilt my head toward the sound, slow and unsteady. A woman stands near the bed in cotton-pink scrubs, tapping a pen against a clipboard. Her smile lands soft, but the brightness behind it feels too loud.

"How are you feeling, sweetheart?" she asks, lowering her voice. "I'm Samantha, your day nurse. Do you need anything?"

Her presence is gentle, calm in contrast to the harsh light and white walls. I try to respond, but the attempt drags through grit and dryness. Only a cracked rasp escapes. My tongue tastes like antiseptic and copper.

"Water... please?" I manage to whisper.

She nods without hesitation, setting her clipboard aside. The sound of pouring water echoes too loud, the rustle of packaging amplified in the quiet. She places a small plastic cup in my palm, guiding it into my grasp. I brace, moving slow as gravity fights every effort. She presses a button, lifting the upper half of the bed so I don't have to fight for leverage.

The first sip cools my throat like rain after drought. I exhale, barely audible, as the ache inside eases. She watches without speaking, letting the moment unfold.

"Would you like anything else?" she asks.

I drink again, trembling. A bit spills onto the blanket, soaking into the stiff fabric. My head thrums with fresh discomfort, and the fog doesn't clear.

"I... don't know," I whisper. Her expression doesn't falter.

I open my mouth, trying again. "W-where..."

Concern flashes across her face. "More water?" she offers. This time, a cup with a straw. I nod faintly, and the liquid slides down easier. Cool. Slightly metallic. But clean.

"Go slow," she murmurs, taking the cup gently away. Fatigue replaces thirst like a tide pulling back. I sink against the raised mattress.

"Where am I?" The question comes out wrong, muffled.

"Mount Sinai Hospital," she says. Her words are soaked in empathy.

Everything inside me goes still. Panic climbs fast, and the monitor quickens its pace. I try to sit up, but the agony in my head detonates into a fresh wave of pain. A groan escapes as I press my palms against my temples.

"Take it easy," she says, placing something cool against my neck. Even that simple gesture drains me. My limbs won't cooperate.

Somewhere beneath the pounding and the plastic tubing, fear writhes. I draw in air slowly, trying to keep control.

I meet her stare, grasping for answers. She doesn't rush me.

"How... did I end up here?"

She props the pillow higher behind my head. "I'll get the doctor. Try to rest."

"How long... how long have I been here?"

She checks the chart. "You were admitted July 16th."

I stop breathing. "What's today?"

Her hesitation splinters through me. "August 6th."

The cup slips from my grip. "Th-three weeks?" The words crumble, brittle, and thin.

A sound claws from my throat. The monitor blares louder. My vision blurs. Three weeks. My baby. Alone. Exposed.

"I need the police! Please, I need them!" The words collapse into sobs. "My son—he's alone! I wasn't there!"

She freezes, stunned by my outburst, and then bolts for the door. Scrubs flash like a warning light. The door slams shut behind her.

The room stills. Only the beep remains.

A ragged cry bursts from deep inside, splitting the silence. I curl, burying my face against the scratchy fabric. The blankets offer no comfort. Nothing could.

Three weeks. I press my arms over my ears, but the words won't stop.

Tears pour freely now, soaking the pillow. Each cry racks through me like a quake. The sound of the monitor pounds louder. Steady. Relentless.

I was gone.

He was alone.

And I don't know how to forgive myself.

A MUFFLED voice drifts into the haze clouding my thoughts. "Miss?" A faint brush grazes my arm. I blink, peeling myself back from the edge of unconsciousness. Samantha hovers nearby, brow furrowed in concern. Two officers stand behind her, both men carrying themselves with rigid authority and darting eyes.

"Hey there, ma'am," says the taller one, his tone businesslike with just a splash of boredom. "Your nurse said you asked for us?"

I nod and attempt to sit up, only for the room to tilt violently. My throat catches, scraping out a hoarse croak. "Water?"

Samantha is already moving, cup in hand, holding it steady while I sip. The liquid soothes the burn inside me, washing away some of the fog. I draw in another breath and grip the blanket for support.

"My name is Ember Abbott," I say, though it feels unreal, like I'm playing someone else's part in a play I never auditioned for. "I was kidnapped five years ago by a man named Patrick St. John and his wife, Krystal."

Silence answers. Samantha goes wide-eyed. The officers glance at one another, surprise flaring briefly before retreating behind their poker faces. The taller one steps closer.

"You're saying Patrick St. John—the guy with a security firm—abducted you? Held you for five years?" He studies me like he's deciding whether to believe a ghost.

"Yes," I say, teeth clenched against my frustration. "They locked me underground. There's a steel door in his office. They—"

I choke on the memory, barely stopping the tremble in my voice. "Why are you just standing there? Shouldn't one of you be writing this down?"

The shorter officer mutters, "Maybe she watched too many true crime shows."

The taller one holds up a hand like he's dealing with a fussy customer. "We're trying to understand the situation. You're claiming this man kidnapped you... and then what? Had a change of heart?"

The gall of his tone makes my skin crawl. Samantha bristles beside me, arms folded now.

"It wasn't like that," I snap. "I escaped. Barely. He hurt me. I had a baby. This isn't a fairy tale gone wrong. It's real."

Their silence only grows. The taller officer narrows his focus on me.

"How exactly did you escape?"

"I... I'm not sure." My thoughts reel. Cold air. Running. Blurred images like scenes from someone else's point of view. "It's scattered. But I got away."

His mouth twitches like he's already dismissed me. "You don't remember how, but you're sure you were abducted?"

Samantha's voice cuts in, dry and unimpressed. "She's been here three weeks. Showed up barely conscious. That's not enough for you?"

"Three weeks..." I repeat, disoriented.

The taller one sighs like I'm wasting his afternoon. "So you've got no memory of the escape, can't say how you ended up here, but you want us to believe a respected businessman did this to you?"

That word, *believe*, strikes something buried deep. I push past the knot of emotions rising.

"I was locked away, treated like trash, forced to give birth in that place," I say, heat rising under my skin. "Do you think I made that up? That I clawed my way out for fun?"

Samantha mutters, "Maybe they'd be more interested if she had a billionaire ex."

The shorter officer sighs and pulls out his phone. "Susan? Yeah, I need you to check for a missing person file. Name's Ember Abbott." He listens, nods, then pockets the phone. "If your name's in the database, we'll go from there."

A flash of hope dares to rise. "Thank you," I whisper, fingers curling into the blanket again. But the taller one still wears a smirk, like I'm a puzzle piece that doesn't quite fit.

The urge to scream crawls up my throat. "You can leave."

His head tilts. "Come again?"

"You heard me. You don't believe me. You've made that very clear. So go."

He folds his arms, planted and unbothered. Samantha stands taller beside me.

"She's been through hell," she says, steel lacing her words. "If you can't take her seriously, you're wasting space."

His lip twitches, ready to snap back, but the second officer's phone buzzing stops him. He answers, voice low.

"This is Grant... yeah. Alright. Thanks."

He ends the call and meets my eyes. "You were reported missing on July 12th, 2017. The report was filed by a woman named Marissa."

My stomach twists, too many emotions colliding all at once. Marissa. She searched for me. She didn't give up on me.

"Shall we start over?" he asks, this time with a shade more respect.

I breathe through the rising storm, wiping tears from my face. "Yeah," I say, quieter now. "Let's start from the beginning."

CHAPTER 15

Ember Rose

My morning with the police stretches like bad theater—boring script, wooden actors, zero depth. The air in the hospital room clings like glue, thick with the stink of recycled doubt and fluorescent apathy. The two men across from me wear their uniforms like armor and badges like they're owed applause.

"Run it by us one more time," the tall one drones, monotone as a vending machine. From what I can see, he clicks a pen against a notepad that might as well be blank.

I sigh, long and annoyed. "I was kidnapped. Bought by Patrick St. John like I was a discount item."

His face barely twitches, though I catch how his buddy squints like he's trying to see through me.

"And you just... walked out?" the second one says, flipping through a folder like he's skimming for headlines.

"Yes, because I figured a dramatic car chase wouldn't fit the mood," I snap. "There was chaos. I remember being thrown down the stairs, and someone showed up. I don't know who. Sorry if it doesn't come with a slow-mo montage."

They share a look. Not even subtle. It screams *waste of time*.

"Miss Abbott," the tall one says again, pretending to care, "you were reported missing... what year was that?"

"You've got the file. Don't play dumb."

He presses on, like I hadn't spoken. "And yet, not a single confirmed sighting from anyone else, why? No tip-offs. No leads."

"Yeah," I shoot back. "Almost like I was being *hidden.* Crazy concept, right?"

His buddy smirks behind his clipboard. "No proof. No names. Just your story. Reads like fiction."

"That 'fiction' includes being locked up, beaten, starved, and giving birth in captivity. So, unless you think I did all that for kicks, maybe stop acting like you're above this."

Standing off to the side, Samantha clears her throat with a pointed look. "Her records confirm injuries consistent with long-term trauma, childbirth complications, untreated wounds—"

"Appreciate the extra commentary, Nurse," Clipboard Guy interrupts, not even glancing at her.

I cut in before she can respond. "I told you who gave me to him. Tristan Devereux. Patrick's pet dealer. Dropped me off like I was an unwanted delivery."

"And your child?" the taller one asks, finally looking up. "Where is this kid now?"

"Still with them," I grind out. "Still trapped. Still waiting for someone to give a damn."

I shove both palms against the table, sending it screeching an inch forward—neither one flinches.

"Let me guess," I sneer. "Not enough *evidence* for you."

"Until we have more to go on," he says, tone flat, "there's not much we can do."

"Not much you *will* do," I correct. "Let me guess: You need a signed confession and GPS coordinates before you even bother calling it in."

He reaches into his coat and slides a card across the table like it's a favor. "Call us if you remember anything useful."

"Useful?" I echo, picking up the card with two fingers like it's coated in slime. "Here's useful: I survived. I'm sitting here, breathing, bleeding, missing pieces of myself you can't see—but that's still not enough for you."

Samantha steps in then, calm but firm. "She deserves more than this."

They ignore her.

"We'll follow up," Clipboard Guy mutters, already walking toward the door.

"Yeah, sure," I mumble. "Right after your donut break and paperwork nap."

The door clicks shut behind them. I stare at it, the rage in my chest too big to swallow.

Samantha touches my arm. "I'm sorry."

But "sorry" won't bring Atlas back. "Sorry" won't undo five years. "Sorry" won't find the man who still walks free.

Tears burn a path down my cheeks as the silence returns.

Let them doubt me.

I'll get my son back.

And when I do, Patrick St. John will learn what real fear feels like.

EXHAUSTION SETTLES over me like a heavy blanket as I struggle with the key in the lock. The metal resists, stiff from disuse, and I give it a frustrated jiggle. It finally gives, turning with a screech that sets my teeth on edge. The safety chain rattles free—evidence that the front desk had used their spare key to keep the place secured all this time. Thanks to Marissa, the bills stayed paid, and the utilities never shut off.

Stepping into my little studio—a space I once called my own—feels like walking into a stranger's home. Everything is dim and stiff, the scent of stale air clinging to every corner. The hush in the room weighs on me, too quiet, too still, as though it had been frozen in time while I was gone.

I pause in the entrance, staring at the cramped yet familiar layout. The memories of nights spent curled up here, my nose buried in books, rush back like a punch to the gut. It was my sanctuary once, a haven from a world I couldn't trust. Now, it simply stands... vacant.

With wavering hands, I peel off the worn hospital clothes and dump them into the trash. They land with a hollow thunk, a testament to the nightmare I can't quite leave behind. At least they're gone—like the final plastic wrapper on a gift nobody wanted.

I drift deeper, navigating furniture shrouded in a thin coat of dust. It's clear no one's been here for ages. Butterflies flutter inside me, knowing Marissa kept the rent paid and the lights on while I was gone. She never gave up, even as time moved on.

The narrow passageways lead me to the part of the apartment I've missed the most: my books. Floor-to-ceiling shelves sag under the weight of old favorites, stories that once gave me hope. Gently, I run my fingertips over the spines—titles half-obscured by delicate layers of dust. The musty smell is comforting in its own way, reminding me of nights when I believed escape could be found between the pages of a novel.

A small cloud puffs up as I drag out a chair, sinking into its worn plush. The seat cushion deflates beneath me, a sighing complaint at being disturbed. Dust motes dance in the sliver of midday light fluttering through the thick curtains, and I sneeze—a quick, painful reminder of my bruised ribs and aching muscles. My focus drifts across the walls, a room that once symbolized dreams and possibilities. Now, it's silent—like the apartment is relearning how to be inhabited. I inhale slowly, the air feeling tight and heavy, striving to reconcile the emptiness inside with the place I used to call home.

Home. What a loaded word. Despite the hollowness, dust, and memories weighing down on me, this is still mine. I'm here, in an apartment Marissa kept alive for me, opened with a key that the front desk kept for me, just in case. I'm not the same person who left, but I'm here—alive—and I have to figure out what that means now.

CHAPTER 16

Ember Rose

A low groan slips from my lips as the afternoon sun stabs through the curtains, searing into me the moment I pry my eyes open. My body protests even the slightest movement. I raise my arms above my head, stretching with a resounding yawn. *Too long in the same position,* my muscles complain, and the dull ache radiates from the bruises staining my skin a sickly yellow—a sharp pang spears through me, a cruel reminder of whose hands left those marks.

Oh, look how pretty you are, my little pet... so responsive to my touches.

The phantom sound slithers through my mind, an invisible hand wringing a feeling buried deep inside me. My fingers twitch as I shove it away, forcing it back into the shadows where it belongs. The next step pulls me out of the numbness, and I stumble toward the window. With my hands fisted in the old drapes, I rip them down in one furious yank, the metal rods crashing to the floor.

Years ago, I hung these curtains to keep the world out. Now I want the world to see me. I want *him* to see me, to witness that I'm alive—and to fear what comes next.

"I will find you...," I whisper, the vow scraping out like broken glass. The world tilts off-balance with the flood of light from the afternoon sun, a reminder of life and the child I lost to the shadows. Atlas. *He's out there, and he needs me.*

I rest my forehead against the window, my body tense. The glass is cold, easily clouding beneath my touch. Was he afraid? Did he cry for me? I clutch the sill, nails scraping the paint, the question grinding in my head until my vision blurs with tears.

Nothing in my old life feels safe anymore, but everything in me demands I fight. *I can't fail him.* My palms brace against the pane of glass as I let the sunlight wash over my battered body, fueling the anger that sparks in my veins. I survived the torture, but now I'm surviving for my son—and for the promise I made.

No more hiding. No more barriers. The only thing that matters is bringing Atlas home.

A sharp thud against the door shatters the hush, making me jolt so violently that I stumble backward. My foot snags on the fallen curtains, and I crash to the floor, a gasp of pain slipping past my lips.

A voice creeps through the wood like mist slipping through the cracks of dawn. It carries the jagged edge of fear, frayed at the seams as if chased by ghosts. The grain of the door hums with its vibrations, the sound threading through splinters and shadows, clinging to the silence like frost on glass.

"Em? Emmy, are you in there?"

The sound sends an electric zap through my body. I fight out of the tangled fabric, biting back the sharp sting of bruises with each strained movement. Every motion feels sluggish, muscles protesting the effort. I scramble upright, yanking the door open so forcefully it bounces off the wall with a crack. She appears.

Marissa.

Before I can speak, her arms encircle me in a fierce hug, squeezing me tight. Tears well up as we both sink to the floor in a messy heap, clinging to each other like we've been shipwrecked and found refuge at last. The sobs swell in me, and I bury my face in her neck, inhaling the faint scent of shampoo and salt tears.

"Is it you? Is it really you?" she whispers, thick like honey laced with shards of glass. She pulls back enough for the afternoon light to catch the fear swimming in her expression, searching my face as if it holds the answer to a question she's too afraid to ask. Her focus flits across my features—my hair, my cheeks, every detail—as if she can't believe they're real. A tear slips free, and she gently cups my face, tracing every inch of me for confirmation.

"Yes, it's me," I choke out, the words vanishing into a fresh wave of sobs. I collapse against her once more, my body taut as her fingers comb through my hair. Her presence is solid, steadying the quiver deep within, calming the restless tremor. We stay like that—on the threshold, knees fused to the cold floor—holding each other together in a way words could never manage.

"I looked everywhere, Emmy," Marissa whispers, voice hitching with emotion. "I never stopped looking."

Time slips by in quiet fragments after that. We remain on the floor, legs entangled, arms brushing lightly as if the separation might make one of us disappear. When we finally shift positions, lying against the cold, scuffed wall, our words are scarce—simple phrases traded in hushed voices. Each sentence weaves around the gaping holes of what we don't say, our shared silence heavy with unspoken grief.

"Em?" Marissa eventually murmurs, propping herself on an elbow. Her focus follows the shadows on my face. "What happened to you? Where were you?"

The question washes over me like a current. *Where was I?* My mind plunges into the depths—the place I've been trying so desperately to escape.

Well, look how pretty you are, my pet...

The memory sears my mind. I can practically feel his presence, hot against my neck, his hands roaming over my skin. My body fights, but the cold steel around my neck holds me in place.

Oh, little kitten, you can't move... you're mine...

The air stills in my body, the old terror morphing into a physical ache. I thrash inside my skull, desperate to break free from the memory's grip.

"Em?" Marissa's gentle voice reaches me, laced with urgency, its edges blurred and distant. "Ember!"

I gasp, yanking myself free of the past. I jerk away from her, my hands slamming against the floor as I scramble back. The wall stops me hard, the impact rattling my bones.

"Emmy?" she whispers, reaching a cautious hand toward me. But I flinch, huddling close to the wall. A frantic thrum echoes in my ears, every muscle drawn taut like I'm a cornered animal.

She sinks to her knees a few feet away, keeping her hands on her thighs, knuckles white. "I won't hurt you," she says softly, letting her palms open in surrender.

My body heaves, struggling to find calm, the images still filtering in my mind. I draw in air slowly, willing the panic to recede. "I... I'm sorry," I manage at last, the words splintered. I meet her stare, my cheeks burning with an apology.

"Please... don't apologize," Marissa says, cracking as tears slip freely down her cheeks. Each word wavers on her lips, and the deep half-moons her nails carved into her palms stand stark against her skin. Slowly, I set a hand over hers, coaxing her fists to unclench. My fingers trace the angry red marks left behind.

"A lot happened," I whisper, barely breaking the room's hush. "Things I don't want to talk about, not yet." I lift my head to meet hers, pleading. "Just... tell me about everything I missed while I was gone. Something normal. Please, Mar—I need it."

She gives a watery nod, and her words come out raspy.. "Yeah... yeah, okay."

With gentle care, we help each other to our feet, bodies still quivering from the aftershocks of my panic attack. I guide her to the couch, the one against the tall windows overlooking the city's neon glow. The sky outside bleeds deep blues and purples, punctuated by the glitter of distant buildings. Shadows move across the floor, dancing every time a car passes below.

We collapse onto the cushions, and Marissa pulls me between her legs, resting my back against her, the weight of her presence anchoring me. As her arms encircle me, she eases her fingers into my hair, combing through the tangled strands in a hypnotic rhythm. The simple, tender contact sends a sharp ache through me again.

For a moment, neither of us speaks, the only sound the faint hum of the city beyond the glass—distant sirens wailing, car horns blaring in sharp bursts, and the rhythmic thrum of tires against wet pavement, all weaving together in a restless New York lullaby. I exhale, barely above a whisper. "I really thought you were dead, Mar. The last time I saw you..." I swallow hard, the memory still sharp as a blade. "There was so much blood."

Her hand stills, and she goes completely still. She inhales, her fingers resuming their gentle path through my hair. "I was out of it for days," she admits, her words subdued. "Didn't even get to talk to the police until a week after. The hospital had me in a coma to stop the swelling in my brain."

A broken sound escapes her like glass shards scattering across a cold floor, its bitter edge slicing through the delicate silence. "Funny how everything feels so unreal when you wake up and half your life is turned inside out, right?" Her sad smile falters, and she quickly looks away.

"Mare?" I say softly, turning my head enough to glimpse the side of her face. Her presence behind me keeps me grounded in the present, but I can still sense the ghosts hiding in the corners.

"Hmm?" she replies, focusing on some invisible point beyond the windows.

I hesitate, nerves buzzing through my veins. Outside, a siren wails, muffled and far off, and everything around us pauses, waiting. We're safe right now—both of us alive, together—but underneath that uncertain security is an ocean of ache and questions we're still too scared to face.

"What happened to you? To Jason?" It sounds hollow, as if I'm afraid of the answer.

Marissa's expression flickers with pain, her body quivering. "He died," she says, her words cracking on the last syllable.

I whip around to face her, a roaring rush filling my ears. "What?"

"They shot him," she whispers, clutching her elbows as though she's trying to hold herself together. "He died before we could get him to the hospital."

Her words hang in the air, choking out the oxygen in the room. My tears threaten to blur the edges of my vision, the tortured grief etched across her face unmistakable. Without hesitation, I turn around, pulling her into my arms. She folds against me, sobbing into my shoulder, her tears hot against my skin.

"I'm sorry, Mare," I whisper, fingers threading through her hair in uneven strokes. "I'm so, so sorry."

We sink into the couch, bodies huddled together, the weight of loss and regret heavy in the space between us. At some point, exhaustion drapes over us like a worn blanket, and the world quietly fades away.

A gentle voice pulls me from the depths of sleep. "Hey, Princess," it coaxes, soft yet persistent. A cold touch brushes against my cheek, and the awkward angle of my neck sends a dull ache creeping through my muscles. My limbs resist movement, sluggish and weighed down like I've been sinking into damp sand.

"You can't sleep like this; you'll get a neck ache," the voice persists, coaxing me in that familiar, tender tone. A groan slips out as I stretch my arms overhead, catlike—a hand sweeps across my hair, brushing it from my face.

Blinking, I squint to find a man with striking green eyes gazing down at me—the same man from the party who seemed so different from everyone else.

"Come on, Princess," he whispers again, his thumb ghosting over my cheek. A familiar ease flutters through me, and I lean into him, grateful for the comfort. The scent of diesel and cedar fills my lungs, wrapping around me in a blanket of longing.

"Who are you?" I ask, still tangled in the remnants of sleep. A frown settles on my brow.

He only smiles, drawing back and leaving a chill in his wake. My skin pricks at the absence of his skin on mine. "Come on, Rosie," he teases, crouching at my side, dropping to a conspiratorial whisper in my ear. "Don't hurt my feelings like that. We told you long ago you'd never escape us."

A slither of cold snakes moves down my spine. That scent, so familiar, and a deep pang of longing swells within me. "Now it's time to take you home," he murmurs, but he's gone as I reach for him, desperate for any connection.

"No! Wait! Please!" I lunge forward, arms grasping at empty air. In the distance, three silhouettes appear, their backs turned. Killian, Jake, and Ash. I run, feet pounding against a black void, but the harder I push, the farther they drift. Their laughter—once my sanctuary—echoes in the emptiness, now hollow.

"No..." My plea rasps through clenched teeth. "No, no, no, it couldn't have been you," I whisper, the words tasting of denial. "Please don't leave me. I'm sorry I left... I'm sorry I disappeared..."

Staggering to my knees, I choke on sobs as I watch them slip further away, all color bleeding from the world around me. The three of them—once my protectors—vanish like ghosts, leaving me stranded in endless night.

Then a tiny, quaking voice shatters the silence. "Mommy, help me."

A small hand rests on my arm. I lower my head and see a boy, bruises scattered across his skin, copper curls tangled like a crown. His face is lost in shadow, but a deep pull rises in my chest when I see his eyes—deep brown, the same as his father's. Recognition crashes into me, leaving everything else distant.

Atlas.

"I'm coming back for you, baby," I whisper, the words slipping through broken sobs as tears spill down my cheeks. The sound escapes in fragments, fragile and uneven, as I cling to the fading image of the boy—my boy.

I turn, searching for the men who once meant everything. Killian, Jake, Ash—their figures blur at the edges of my vision, slipping into the formless dark. An ache builds, tangled in longing and loss. They had rescued me once... and then let me fall.

The social worker's cold words echo, saying that my behavior made the boys uncomfortable. That they went to the foster parents, that's why I was removed. Her pen tapping as she destroyed me like it was fact, like I was the problem all along.

I remember her expression, detached and distant, her attention fixed on the folder instead of me. My blood thundered in my ears, her words growing harder to follow. Uncomfortable? All I ever did was try to survive. She never explained—just scribbled in her notes and snapped the folder closed like I no longer mattered.

All I knew was one day I belonged—a bruised but hopeful kid, certain that "foster" meant "family"—and the next day, the front door slammed behind me for good.

Now, those silhouettes vanish, their figures melting into the shadows as if dragged away by the void they once shielded me from.

The boy disappears just as quickly, his small hand slipping from my body, leaving only emptiness that squeezes until it feels impossible to move, a hollow ache settling in my bones. I'm left alone, staring at the space where they all once stood.

A ragged sob escapes me, and the weight of that single promise—I'm coming back for you—burns in my mind, the only life raft in a sea of pain and turmoil.

A startled gasp tears through me, ripping me out of sleep. A strangled sob escapes me before a pair of gentle arms slip around me, pulling me against a body. The soft, reassuring murmur in my ear is the only thing that keeps me from spiraling.

"Breathe," the voice coaxes, low. "You're safe. You're not alone. You're here with me."

I steady myself, letting each repetition bring me back to my senses. Slowly, the terror recedes, replaced by awareness. Marissa's arms pull me closer, her fingers working through my hair, gathering it into a loose ponytail. I bury my face in her neck, letting her solid presence comfort me.

"They were there," I whisper, more to myself than to her, the nightmare's images still dancing behind my eyelids.

Marissa tilts her head, resting her chin on my shoulder. A subtle sheen catches the light, betraying the concern etched into her features. The tension in her brow and the parting of her lips speak volumes without a word. "Who was there?" she asks.

"Ash, Jake, and Killian," I whisper, catching on their names. "My family... at least, they were once." A hollow sound slips out, scraping against my heart. "They saved me, but of course, they left."

My cheeks flush as shame and grief intertwine until tears slip free, tracing uneven paths down my face. Marissa's hand moves in slow, tender circles across my back.

"You never talked about them much," she murmurs, her fingertips catching lightly on the fabric of my shirt. "I knew they hurt you... But you never told me how."

I inhale, the memories stirring. "I met them when I was eight," I begin quietly. "We ended up in the same foster home—a grim, toxic place. But the three of them... They made it bearable. They were everything to me, protected me, made me feel safe." My voice wavers, and I force myself to keep going. "I had a crush on all of them, really. I was so young, but... I believed they were mine."

The humiliation and sorrow tangle inside me, and Marissa's arm pulls me closer. "So when we ran from that group home..." she says carefully, "you were running from *them?*"

A ragged sigh leaves my lips, my limbs heavy. "Yes," I admit. "I couldn't bear it—they reported me to the foster parents, told them I was a problem. Said my 'behavior' made them uncomfortable. After all they promised, they...betrayed me. Instead of talking, they shoved me deeper into the system."

I bow my head, my face resting against Marissa's collarbone, drawing in the subtle scent of laundry detergent and faint perfume. The hurt in me throbs, old wounds laid bare. And yet, here we are—two damaged souls, clinging to each other in the aftermath.

Marissa's expression is gentle, and her features are easing. "Maybe they didn't realize it was you, you didn't recognize them, right?" she says gently, her fingertips resting on my arm. The following offer—*We can try to find them, Emmy, if that's what you want*—tangles every emotion inside me like threads in a knot. My reply catches, so I hide my face in her shoulder instead, letting the steady presence of her body answer for me.

"I'm so happy to be back here with you," I whisper.

Marissa's lips curve into a tentative smile, tears gathering at the edges, catching the light. "You have no idea how happy I am," she manages, steadying herself. "Alive. Breathing. *Here.*" She swallows hard, forcing a spark of cheer into her tone. "How about some two a.m. pizza? We need to get those gorgeous curves back on track."

A startled sound escapes me—small, but surprisingly welcome. My stomach grumbles noisily, as if echoing her words. "Pizza sounds perfect," I say, holding my hand against the rumbling. Yet the moment the lightness fades, reality tugs at the edge of my mind like a cold wind. "But first... I need you to help me."

Marissa stills, her brow pulling together. "With?"

I swallow. The name feels heavy on my tongue, but it's a weight I need to share. "I have a son," I whisper, gazing down at my lap, "his name is Atlas. I was hoping you could take me back to the house where I was being held. He's still there." The air thickens as Marissa stares at me.

CHAPTER 17

Ember Rose

The door crashes open with a hollow bang, the sound ricocheting through the empty house. I burst inside, my breath hitching as the air slaps me in the face—stale, heavy, laced with the acrid tang of cigarettes and spilled liquor. Dust clings to every surface, catching the fading light that streams through grimy windows, illuminating streaks of dirt on the floors and walls. The space is hollow and eerily quiet, the silence that makes you hold your breath—Patrick's house. Once filled with the sounds of my nightmares, now stripped bare, yet still suffocating in its emptiness.

I take the stairs two at a time, my footsteps pounding against the wooden boards, sending vibrations through the air. Dust particles dance from the disruption, there's broken glass under my feet, remnants of a rushed move-out. My hand grips the railing—it feels sticky and grimy—and I yank it away, forcing myself forward. The long and shadowed hallway stretches ahead of me, the door at the end standing closed like a cruel, silent dare.

As I push it open, my fingers tremble, the hinges groaning in protest. I step into the room, my stomach twisting into a knot. It's empty. Atlas's toys, the little clothes he used to tug on so proudly, the crayon scribbles he'd taped to the walls—all gone. The walls, now bare, taunt me with their emptiness. The faintest scent of peppermint sits in the air, so familiar it feels like a punch to the gut. My knees buckle, and I lean against the doorframe, a sharp cry tearing free from me.

"No!" The word echoes back at me, bouncing off the walls of the vacant room, as if mocking my despair. I slam the door shut, hoping it will change what I've seen, but it only amplifies the hollow ache clawing at my chest.

I stagger back down the stairs, the walls around me closing in as tears blur my vision. My breathing comes in ragged gasps, each inhale catching as panic takes hold.

Marissa's voice cuts through the haze, her hands gripping my arms. "Ember!" she shouts, her sharp tone edged with fear.

"It's gone!" I cry, cracking, my hands gesturing wildly at the devastation around us. "Everything's gone!"

My gaze darts around, landing on a jagged piece of debris. I grab it without thinking and hurl it at the nearest window. The rock bounces off with a dull thud, the glass refusing to give way. The failure sends a fresh wave of frustration surging through me. "He was here! He was right here!" I scream, breaking as I collapse to the floor.

The sobs come fast, shaking my entire body as I bury my face in my hands. The world feels like it's crumbling around me, the weight of it too much to bear.

Marissa drops to her knees beside me, her arms wrapping around my trembling form. "We'll find him, Em," she says, filled with conviction. "I swear to you, we'll find him." Her words are a fragile lifeline, a thin thread of hope I cling to with everything I have.

My fingers clutch at her shirt, my sobs muffled against her shoulder. "He must think I left him," I whisper, the words tasting bitter on my tongue.

"You didn't leave him," she replies fiercely, pulling me closer. "And we're going to get him back. I promise you, Ember. We will."

Weeks have passed, and the space between me and Atlas feels insurmountable with every second. The thought of him waiting, wondering why I haven't come—it's unbearable.

A spark ignites in the back of my mind. I jerk away from Marissa's grasp, the realization spilling from my lips in a desperate cry. "The basement!"

Her hand grabs for me again. "Ember, wait!" But I'm already moving, surging to my feet with adrenaline.

The sting of glass slicing into my palms barely registers as I stumble across the room, each step propelling me toward the heavy metal door at the back of the house. *They wouldn't leave him here, would they? What if he's dead? He can't be.*

I slam into the door with my shoulder, a grunt tearing from me as it groans and creaks under the pressure. The smell that hits me is instant and vile—a metallic, putrid stench that turns my stomach. My fingers scrape along the damp walls as I stumble down the narrow, uneven stairs, the cold concrete chilling me through my jeans. My foot slips, and I crash onto my knees, landing hard.

A strangled gasp escapes me as I look down. Blood...Dried Blood..

It pools around me, dark and thick, staining the floor. My stomach churns violently, the bile rising, but I force myself to move. My legs shake as I push off the floor, each step toward the wooden door at the end of the basement feeling heavier, slower, like I'm wading through tar.

Please. Please let him be here.

I reach the door and shove it open, my hands trembling, causing the handle to rattle against the wood. A jolt runs through me as I take in the room. Empty. A broken table lies overturned in the corner, a shredded mattress sagging against the far wall. The walls close in, and I collapse against the doorway, my breath rasping in shallow gasps. The despair is immediate and suffocating, the weight of it crushing me from the inside.

Then I hear it—a faint, rhythmic beeping.

My head snaps toward the sound, my body tense and braced as I move toward the ruined mattress. My pulse pounds in my ears as I spot it: a black phone lying on the torn fabric, its screen glowing with a flashing message. The faint light from the phone casts an eerie hue, cutting through the oppressive darkness of the basement.

Dread swarms me as I step closer, each word on the screen sinking into me like shards of glass.

Hello Ember...

My breath hitches as I read the message.

I'm sure you're shocked to find everything gone, but imagine my surprise when I returned from visiting my friends, only to find you had vanished. Poor little Atlas was left to suffer alone in his room for who knows how long before I got there. What an unfit mother you are for leaving him behind.

I choke on a gasp, my eyes landing on the camera still taunting me in the corner, the red light flashing. *So she can see me.*

What do you want?

Tell my stupid husband it's time to come home.

Confusion clouds my mind, my thoughts spinning as I type out a desperate response.

Patrick isn't with me… I thought he would be here with Atlas.

The reply comes almost instantly.

No one was here except your son when I returned, so where is he?!

My fingers fumble over the keys.

I don't know! I am just here for Atty.

The following message strikes like a blow.

Well, now we're at a standstill because I need to find my husband, and you want your son back.

What do you want from me, Krystal?

I type, my anger trembling beneath the surface, making my hands shake.

Her response is cruel.

> You are to find my stupid husband and bring him back to me. But there are a few rules to ensure your son's safety. I would hate to return him to you in worse condition than I found him.

The plastic cracks under my grip as rage simmers low in my gut. The sharp sound draws Marissa closer, her hand on my arm as she peers over my shoulder.

"Ember? Is everything okay?" Her gaze drops to the screen. Gasping, she covers her mouth with her hand. "Fuck."

The message continues, each word laced with venom.

> I'm glad you're willing to listen for once. My conditions should be simple enough to follow. First, find my husband and return him to me.

> Second, you cannot go to the police…again.

> Aren't you curious why they haven't tried working on your case? Why don't they seem to care about you or your son?

My stomach churns, my insides twisting like a cruel knot being pulled with every word. My gaze locks on the glowing screen, the weight of Krystal's insinuation closing in on me. The police—my lifeline, the people I should be able to trust with my life, with my son's life—they're working for her.

A cold chill creeps down my spine. *If I can't trust them, then who's left to help me? Who's left to help Atlas?*

The phone vibrates in my hand, drawing me back.

> Shall I continue?

I can almost see her smirk, the same scowl that was present at Atlas's birth. That condescending smile, the rise of her overly waxed brow, her icy blonde hair scraped into that painfully tight bun. I gnaw on my lip, my thumb hovering over the screen as hesitation takes root.

God, I am a *shitty* mother.

Every part of me screams to run, to leave this house that's soaked in my torment and pain. Run as far away as I can, burying everything that's happened here.

I can see Atlas's tiny face, fresh in my mind as though I just held him for the first time. His first breath, his first birthday. The moments Patrick allowed him to stay with me were brief flashes of joy in a world of torment. Moments I lost when I made a mistake, or when Patrick decided I didn't deserve them anymore.

A constriction settles deep inside me, and I close my eyes for a beat. When I open them, my thumb moves almost instinctively.

Yes.

The message blazes across the screen, each word a sharp-edged dagger cutting deeper into my resolve.

I don't care who you ask for help finding Patrick, but don't bring Atlas's name into this. If you tell anyone, Atlas will die. And since you didn't come alone, make sure your friend understands the consequences if she opens her mouth. Got it?

It feels like I've handed her a loaded weapon and turned my back. But the alternative—losing Atlas—turns my blood cold.

The space around me fades into silence as I type the only response I can.

Got it.

Whatever it takes.

Marissa whispers, "Ember, we should think about this."

"*Think about this?*" The words tear from me, sharp and jagged as they ricochet off the walls. "What the hell is there to think about, Marissa?"

Her eyes widen, and she takes a step back, her body shrinking under the weight of my rage. But I don't stop. I can't—the anger flares, hot and uncontrollable.

"She has my son—*my baby boy*—and she's not just threatening to kill him. She's *waiting* for an excuse!" I crack, the edge of fear slicing through the anger. "Do you get that? *Waiting!*"

Marissa flinches like I've struck her, her lips parting as if to speak, but the words don't come.

"You, of all people, should *understand!* You have kids, Marissa! You should know I'd burn the entire goddamn world to the ground to save him!"

Marissa's face crumples under the weight of my words, guilt flickering in her wide eyes. Still, she doesn't speak, and the heavy quiet that follows feels unbearable.

"I'd rather die trying than sit around and 'think about it' while that monster decides today's the day she takes my son's life!"

Tears sting my eyes, hot, but I blink them away, swallowing the rising wave of grief that threatens to overtake me. "He's all I have, Marissa. I can't lose him."

Tentatively, she reaches out, brushing my arm like she's testing the waters.

Her lips tremble. "I'm just scared for you, Em."

"Well, I'm *terrified* for him!" The words crack under the weight of my despair. "And I'll do whatever it takes to bring him home. *Whatever it takes.*"

Marissa exhales shakily, her shoulders slumping in defeat. "Em..." she starts.

My phone vibrates in my hand. The screen flashes.

> I'm glad to hear that. I hate hurting an innocent child, but I want what I want. Keep this phone hidden. As soon as you have my husband and proof that he's alive, I'll send you a drop-off location. Do you understand?

My fingers shake as I type, my vision blurred by the tears that threaten to spill.

> Yes, I understand.

Another vibration.

Here's a photo of your son for motivation. I hope to see you soon, Ember.

The image floods the screen. Atlas, huddled in a corner. Bruises in the shape of hands mar his fragile arms, and his favorite bear is smudged with dirt in his grasp.

A choked sound escapes me, sharp and raw, tears spilling freely as I clutch the phone close. The image sears itself into my mind, every detail a cruel reminder of what's at stake. Fury burns, blinding and hot, drowning out everything else.

"They'll pay for this," I hiss, the words escaping like a vow. "They'll regret the moment they took him."

"Em?" Her hand lands on my shoulder, but I flinch away, my grip tightening on the phone as if it's my only tether to Atlas. "Ember, you can't do this alone. Please, just let me—"

"No!" I cut her off, spinning to face her. My voice is raw, trembling with desperation and panic. "Swear to me, Marissa. Swear you won't tell anyone. If you do, Atlas will die."

Marissa stares at me, wide-eyed, her keys jangling faintly in her trembling hand. "Ember..." she starts, but freezes. "You're going to get yourself killed. Please, listen to me—"

I step closer, my hands shaking, my voice low and venomous. "I don't care if you hate me for this. I don't care if you leave and never speak to me again. My son comes first. *He always comes first.* So keep your damn mouth shut."

Her face pales, her lips trembling as she takes a cautious step back. Whatever she sees in me—wildness and desperation—silences her. "I'll help you, Em. But we have to do this together. You can't push me away."

CHAPTER 18

Krystal

The screeching on the other end of the phone is enough to split my skull in two. Every whimper from that woman, every pathetic sob from her cracked voice, is like sandpaper scraping my brain.

"Help! Mommy! Scared!" The brat's screaming carries through the house, slicing through the air like glass. I slam the phone down so hard the table rattles, wishing I could shove her voice straight through the receiver and back into her throat.

That little gremlin she calls a son is why my life has become a disaster circus. He's a constant, screaming, flailing reminder of everything Patrick ruined. And yet she has the nerve to cry like she's the one who's suffered most. Give me a break.

Patrick—my supposed husband, my once-prince-charming—turned into a walking, breathing stain. He traded me for her like I was a clearance item past its return window. She thinks I'm clinging to him out of love? No. I want him six feet under with a cement lid.

But that little redheaded parasite doesn't get it. She thinks I want Patrick back. She thinks this is some twisted love triangle. What a joke. She has no idea I'm the one who lit the match on this whole thing. I don't want him back—I want him gone. Permanently.

Keeping the boy locked up is a pain, yes, but it's also leverage. And if that leverage comes with tantrums and ear-splitting shrieks, so be it.

My father will throw a fit when he finds out, but it won't matter. The terms were simple: any child Patrick fathered outside our marriage could contest the inheritance. And I didn't crawl through years of his filth and humiliation to let *them* touch a dime of what should be mine.

I was the perfect wife. I played the role. I smiled at his clients, I cooked his meals, I kept quiet while he brought broken women into our home like stray animals. I waited for the moment he'd finally give me what I was owed.

Then *she* showed up. Perfect. Soft. Ruined everything. He looked at her like she was made of starlight. She gave him a baby, and suddenly, he's bringing her warm meals and soft blankets while I'm left in the hallway, trying not to vomit from the stench of betrayal.

He didn't break her. He babied her. He broke *me* instead.

Now? She gets to feel it. Every bit of what I lived with. Let her sob. Let her beg. Let her bleed.

I storm down the hall, each step heavier than the last. The brat's wailing gets louder. Of course it does. He's got lungs like a damn siren. My hands curl into fists, nails carving crescents into my skin. I can barely hear my own thoughts over his screeching.

I slam the door open with enough force to rattle the hinges. The sound shuts him up for a heartbeat. Just long enough for me to step into the room.

And then he runs at me. Like, I'm not the one feeding him, keeping him alive. The little beast barrels into my legs with the rage of a toddler tornado, fists pounding like they could do damage.

"Stop it, you little monster!" I hiss. He looks up at me, face a mess of snot and tears, trembling from head to toe. He tries to shove past me, his hands slipping off my legs.

I grab his arms. Too hard? Probably. Do I care? Not even a little. I drag him back, toss him into the corner like the tantrum-throwing doll he's acting like. He crashes onto the floor and curls up, whimpering.

I stare at him. The crying, the noise—it's designed to drive me mad. And it's working.

"Be quiet, just once!" I shout, crossing the room in three furious strides. I yank him upright again, shaking him, trying to rattle the noise out of him. His jaw goes slack. Silence. Finally.

And that's when I see it.

His face. His mouth. His eyes.

Patrick.

It's like watching a ghost form in front of me. Every feature that made me scream into pillows at night now sits on this child's terrified little face.

My stomach twists.

My grip falters.

I release him, stumbling a step back.

He shrinks, arms wrapping tight around himself. I stand there, staring at the kid like he's just risen from the grave.

"You don't get it, do you?" I say, my voice scraping low. "None of this is your fault. You didn't ask for any of it. But you wear his face. You carry his name. And that makes you mine to deal with."

The kid doesn't answer. Of course, he doesn't. He's five. Maybe six. Or four. I don't know. I don't care. I just know I'm crumbling, and he's sitting there, breathing, reminding me of the one man I want to see buried.

I pace away from him, my heels clicking like gunshots against the hardwood. I shove my fingers into my hair and pull.

"Your mother will come," I mutter, half to him, half to myself. "Just stay still. Stay quiet. Make this easier."

He stares, wide-eyed. Doesn't blink.

Good. Let him be scared. Let him feel it like I did, every day, for ten years. Maybe then the cycle can finally snap in half.

But deep down, I know I've already lost.

Because I see it now—he's not just his father's son. He's a child. Fragile. Terrified. He didn't choose any of this.

And still, here he is—my prisoner.

The house falls quiet. Outside, the sun sinks lower, dragging shadows across the floor.

I wanted revenge. I wanted justice. I wanted to take back what was mine.

Instead, I got this.

A cage I built with my own hands.

A boy staring up at me with Patrick's eyes.
And no way out.

PART TWO

Found

My darling, Be patient with yourself,
healing takes time, healing implies kindness,
healing means changes, becoming is not easy.
Be patient with yourself,
you are gardening your soul.
Some flowers are meant to bloom later.

- Alexandra Vasiliu

CHAPTER 19

Asher

Weeks dragged on, each day stretching into the next without hinting at Rose's whereabouts. Patrick sits in his cell, silent or smirking, spinning tales about Rose like she's still alive, like any moment, she'd wander through the front door. None of us knows how to handle a monster that refuses to crack.

Killian leans against the wall, his hands fisted, and his skin pulled tight till it's ghostly white. His eyes are red from sleepless nights; he glares at the space before him, like staring it down might force answers into the open. "I don't know how much more I can handle this… Why's he talking about her like she's still here?" His voice is worn thin by nights without rest; the anger inside him is feverish. "We know… we *know* she's gone—dumped into an unmarked grave like garbage." Killian smashes his fist into the drywall, dust pluming out as cracks spread like a spider's web. "She mattered, Ash!" he yells. "She fucking mattered!"

Blood drips from the fresh wound, splattering against the floor. The red gash stains the wall; the mosaic exemplifies the pain Patrick keeps tearing open with his words. "Let J take over, Kill," I say quietly, schooling my voice to be calm. "You're exhausted. You're not helping like this."

Killian stares at the dented wall, anger vibrating through every tendon. "I need to bring her home, Ash," he whispers so quietly I almost miss it. His eyes are distant, haunted by the same images that taunt us all. "I can't sleep until we find her." He exhales, posture dipping. "Do you... think she suffered?"

Did she suffer? Of course, she suffered, but how do I tell him that? I step closer to him, my hand settling on his shoulder. He's taut like a drawn bow. All we have is Patrick's maddening, disgusting stories—and the truth that Rose's body is still nowhere to be found.

"If Patrick's telling the truth," I begin cautiously, each word tasting like that bitter paste you put on kids' nails to get them to stop biting their nails, "she was in pain for a long time."

His head bows. "N-not Rose... I mean the girl we took to the hospital. D'you think she suffered like Rosie did?" The words crack inside me. For all his rough edges, Killian has the softest heart out of the three of us. Where Jake and I used violence and control to protect ourselves, he consoled Rose's tears, offering comfort we never could.

I open my mouth to respond when Jake cuts in, his tone quivering with restrained anger. "Let's get back in there." He storms past us, heading for our converted basement.

The stench hits like a physical blow: metal, copper—blood and piss, rancid and puke-inducing. Patrick St. John slumps in the metal chair; blood crusted on his split lips. And yet, he gives us a twisted smile that reminds me of the Cheshire Cat from *Alice in Wonderland*.

"Oh, good," he rasps. "My favorite visitors."

"Tell us where you buried her," Killian demands, his words teetering on desperation.

His laugh is like broken glass—shattered, sharp, and promising pain in return. The sound of a man who knows he's dug himself into a hole but refuses to help. His eyes gleam with sick thrill. "You're all so stupid. Haven't you figured it out yet?"

Ice floods my veins. *What's happening?* I step forward. "Figured what out?"

A blood-smeared grin stretches across Patrick's swollen lips. "Didn't you recognize my sweet kitten? I mean, I know she looks a little different now. She lost all those delicious curves, but she couldn't be trusted. I mean, look what she did to me." His eyes dart down to the angry, pinkish skin stretched across his arm, red and warped like melted wax.

"What do you mean?"

"Wow, you aren't the brightest bulbs, are you? But, I guess it did take you five years to get me." The room shrinks, Patrick's words ricocheting against the walls. It's absurd and twisted. I lock eyes with Killian and see sheer panic blazing in their depths. "She never did give up on someone saving her, you know. Always sleeping with that stupid, tattered jacket like it could save her." *No...* realization dawns. Jake stands stiff, his fists shaking at his sides.

"No," Jake snarls, lethal. "You're lying." He lunges at Patrick, seizing him by the shirt and jerking him upright with such force that it rattles the chair.

Patrick's lips curve into a vile grin, the triumph in his eyes. "Oh, it is," he purrs, reveling in our disbelief. "Didn't you recognize her? *My* sweet little kitten. Her body... made *just* for me—"

Jake snaps. The words are spilling from Patrick's mouth when Jake shoves him backward, and Patrick's skull cracks against the floor with a jarring *thud*. The sick impact echoes off the concrete, followed by silence. Time freezes, Jake's breathing heavily as Patrick slumps over, his head lolling to the side. Unconscious.

"That was her?... No, that was..." Killian sputters, the color draining from his face. The quiet despair twists my stomach. "We left her at that hospital. *Alone*. She woke up alone." His tone cracks with every syllable. "How did we not see it?"

I don't have an answer. The weight of what we missed—who we missed—crushes me.

"She's not that fifteen-year-old girl anymore, Kill," the words scrape out of me in a rough whisper. "We sure as hell didn't recognize her as the twenty-five-year-old at the races."

My hand drags across my temple in an attempt to stop the throbbing ache that's building behind my eyes. "Let's go," I say, pushing off the wall.

"Where?" Killian seizes my arm, his grip bruising. "Where are you going?"

"To get her."

"What if she doesn't forgive us?"

I WRENCH FREE, meeting his terrified gaze with a hollow look of my own.

"Right now, we don't fucking deserve it," I snap, turning on my heel and taking the stairs two at a time. "But I'm willing to beg."

Jake and Killian follow, their footsteps echoing in the cramped passageway as we leave the basement behind. My mind reels, replaying his mocking words about what he's done to her. He dies... I don't care when, but he dies for what he's done to our Rose.

We're coming, Sweet Girl. My every step is fueled by the memory of what we left behind. "Please... don't give up on us yet."

CHAPTER 20

Jake

Killian's hands clench at the edge of the nurse's station, his knuckles whitening against the sterile countertop. The harsh fluorescent lights cast sharp shadows over his tense frame, his chest rising and falling with barely contained fury. The distant beeping of heart monitors and the faint shuffle of footsteps down the hall do nothing to soften the storm brewing in his eyes—vivid green, dark with an emotion too fierce to name. "What do you *mean* she isn't here?" The question rumbles out of him, and though he's trying to keep it together, there is an undercurrent of desperation. Pens rattle in their plastic holder under his grip.

"Sir," the nurse warns, her tone firm, "I'm going to need you to calm down. Otherwise, I'll have to call security." Despite her measured words, a brief shadow of uncertainty crosses her features. She can sense there's more at play than simple frustration.

Killian drags a hand over his face, exhaling hard. His eyes cut to me, the silent plea begging for help. He's on the brink of losing it, and we both know it.

I step in, placing a steadying palm on Killian's shoulder. "Kill," I whisper, leaning close, "let me do the talking." He huffs, stepping aside.

"I'm really sorry about all this," I tell the nurse gently, offering my most placating smile. She gives me a wary once-over, her lips pursed in caution. "But you've gotta understand... we've spent so long searching for this girl—*our* girl. We practically grew up together in foster care. We thought she was dead. Then we found out she might be alive—here—and now she's just... gone again. It's killing us."

Mention of foster care pulls her up short. I see the shift in her expression, sympathy creeping into her eyes. "Your friend was a foster kid?" she asks, her tone softening. "And you... Knew her from back then?"

"Yes," I answer, and Killian nods at my side. The nurse watches him, noticing the rawness in his gaze. "We lost her once," I continue, swallowing hard, "and I honestly thought I'd never see her again. We only found out she was brought here by chance. Now she's vanished." My voice catches. "Please, you have to help us."

She exhales, her face etched with compassion but tempered by caution. "Look, I get you're worried, but I can't just hand out patient information—especially if she left alone. There are privacy laws." She hesitates.

Killian inhales sharply. "She's not just some random patient to us; we grew up together. We... we lost her for five fucking years. She was kidnapped and tortured. We need to make sure she's safe."

The nurse's hand wavers on the computer mouse, her gaze flicking between us, weighing what to do. "I'm not supposed to—"

"Please," I say, lowering my voice and leaning in, letting every bit of urgency bleed into my words. "She was missing. You can imagine how devastating that would be for her, especially after everything she's been through. We never stopped looking for her. We finally got a lead and found out she was here, and now she's gone again. We... we can't lose her again."

Her shoulders sag. "She was so scared," she admits in a hushed tone, as though remembering the girl's haunted eyes. "If she really has no one else, maybe..." She trails off, peering down the hall to ensure no one's listening. "Give me a moment. The police came," she murmurs, her lips tight. "She told them about... about the kidnapping. They didn't believe her." She shakes her head, disapproval flashing in her gaze. "She left not long after. I'm worried she doesn't have anyone."

We wait. Killian's foot taps on the linoleum, and I can practically hear the frantic thrum of his pulse. The nurse types on the computer before standing and rifling through files. An eternity passes before she quietly returns, a single sheet of paper clutched in her hand.

Looking around to ensure no prying eyes, she slides it across the counter. "I shouldn't be doing this," she says. "But... she gave us an address. That's all we have. I hope you're telling the truth—I hope you know her and want to ensure she's safe."

Killian's eyes gloss with relief as he snatches the paper, nearly crushing it in his hand. "Thank you," he breathes, voice rough. "I swear we're not here to hurt her—she's family."

"Thank you," I manage, folding the paper carefully. "You have no idea how much you've helped."

"Just find her," she whispers, meeting our eyes with concern. "She deserves better than what she's gotten. Promise me."

"On my life," Killian says, his palms flat on the counter in a solemn vow. "We'll bring her home."

I give the nurse a tight smile, gratitude warring with the tension that still grips me. I follow him, every step fueled by the memory of our missing girl's face—the faint, desperate hope that we can finally set things right.

Killian snatches the paper, thrusting it in Ash's face without a word. his brow furrows the instant he scans the text.

"What's this?" he mutters, lifting the sheet for me to see. I shrug as I try to make sense of it. "It's the address Rose gave before she checked out," I say, tension curling through my gut. "Why?"

Killian nabs it back, his frown deepening until it carves harsh lines across his features. "Then who the hell is Ember Abbott?" he spits, words clipped and bristling.

The name knocks the air from me. I yank the note from his hand, my gaze snagging on the unfamiliar scrawl:

Ember Abbott
100 W 57th St
New York, NY 10019

“What the fuck?” I growl, whirling toward the nurse’s station, ready to unleash my questions. But Ash clamps a hand on my arm, halting me mid-step.

“Wait,” he says quietly, drawing the paper from my grasp. He studies it again, the crease in his forehead deepening. “Remember why we called her Rose?”

Killian crosses his arms, vexation rippling through him. “That was her name,” he snaps. Killian holds the slip of paper between his thumb and forefinger like it’s a live wire. His eyes jump from the hurried handwriting to Ash’s set jaw, shifting to me, searching for confirmation that what’s written makes sense. It doesn’t. Not after all this time.

He lets out a frustrated hiss. “Ember Abbott,” he reads aloud, voice stiff. “Not Rose Carson. Then who the hell is Ember Abbott?”

A sick heaviness fills the space between us. My gaze snags on the folded sheet, the letters smudged at the edges as if the nurse wrote them in a hurry. The lines blur when I blink—like the truth itself is distorting.

Ash carefully eases the paper from Killian’s hand. “Remember,” he says, soft but urgent, “we never verified her legal name. Every record from the foster system listed ‘Rose Carson,’ but Rose said she hated that name. And we never saw her birth certificate, no adoption papers... nothing.”

Killian’s hands curl into fists at his sides, knuckles taut and white. “But the state’s documentation said Rose Carson,” he snaps, razor-sharp. “That’s what the fosters told us. Why would we doubt it?”

I rake a hand through my hair, feeling the pulse of an oncoming headache. “She told us her name was Rose, sure—but we never asked if it was a nickname, if it was something the system pinned on her. Maybe she was born Ember. Maybe the fosters changed it. Maybe she changed it herself after we... lost her.” My stomach churns with guilt at those words, after we lost her, because it feels like a hollow explanation for everything that went wrong.

Ash nods, his brow furrowing as he turns the paper over, as though some hidden clue might appear on the blank side. “So we’ve been scouring every database, every missing person’s site for ‘Rose Carson.’”

He lifts his gaze, meeting Killian's tortured stare. "But she might've lived—legally—under another name this whole time."

Killian's teeth clamp together so hard I hear a squeak, like bone on bone. "All these years," he mutters, "we pored over dead ends and false sightings... because we never had the right name."

The words hang in the sterile hospital corridor. Outside, someone's pushing a squeaky cart of supplies; the faint chatter of a nurse on the phone filters through. But here, the three of us stand locked in a standoff.

"Look," I say finally, swallowing past the lump. "This address is for 'Ember Abbott.' That might be Rose—maybe she changed her name—or it might be some stranger who just walked out of here. But..." I hesitate, exhaling. "We've got no other leads."

Killian shoots me a questioning look. I shrug, feeling the weight of it all. "Maybe it's the same person," I murmur. "Hell, maybe we're chasing ghosts. But after everything, I'm not taking any chances."

Ash nods, folding the paper carefully. "We only found out she'd been in this hospital because of the nurse who recognized her injuries—injuries like..." His words falter, haunted by the memory. "And now she's gone. Disappeared again."

Killian scrubs a hand over his face. "Damn it," he growls, "we were so close. Why didn't we—" He breaks off, too many regrets colliding behind his eyes. Then he looks at me, jaw set. "It's the only address we've got. Let's go."

Outside, the breeze is too warm, thick with the city's polluted air. Killian practically jogs to his bike, mounting it without waiting for us. I turn to Ash, and he's already heading for the car.

"This might not be her," he mutters, more to himself than to me, as we hurry across the lot. "Ember Abbott could be anyone. But—"

"But we have to try," I finish, a wild mixture of dread and hope surging through me. If this lead falls flat, we're back to zero. If it's true... if Ember Abbott is Rose or the girl from Patrick's basement... My thoughts spin at the possibility. *God, please let this be her.*

Neither of us speaks. Ash guns the engine and peel out of the parking area. The city lights smear across the windshield. In the rearview mirror, Killian's headlight follows close.

Between us and that slip of paper, we hold onto a fragile thread of faith. Whether it's Rose or someone else, it's our only path. And we owe it to the girl who might be our Rose, our sweet, haunted girl.

CHAPTER 21

Jake

A solid knock echoes down the immaculate hallway, the polished floors sending the sound bouncing back at us. I take a half step backward. The overhead lights hum, and a faint residue of bleach hangs in the air, the telltale sign of a well-maintained building. Good upkeep, sure—but a single buzz from a careless tenant would let three strangers sneak in.

Footsteps shuffle inside, stirring my anxiety higher. Each muffled sound makes my stomach clench until at last the lock clicks and the door creaks open.

A petite blonde appears, long hair falling in effortless waves around her shoulders. She sizes us up with a skeptical arch of her brow. Making a decision, she props her forearm against the doorframe and quirks a smirk—equal parts challenge and amusement.

"Okay... how many of you does it take to deliver a pizza?" she quips, crossing one ankle over the other. "Sounds like the start of a terrible pickup line, doesn't it?" The dryness in her tone catches me off guard.

We exchange confused looks. Killian double-checks the apartment number, squinting like the digits might've rearranged themselves to mess with him. "Uh... what?" he mutters, his posture rigid.

The woman's smile fades, replaced by a guarded edge. "So, not the pizza guys. That explains the glaring lack of pizza." She folds her arms across her chest, scanning us in quick succession. "If you're not here with pepperoni and cheese, what do you want?"

Killian shifts, a vein pulsing in his temple. "We were told an Ember Abbott lives here," he grits out.

Her posture stiffens, that casual banter vanishing in an instant. The protective set of her jaw says everything. "And why are you looking for her?"

I step forward, raising my palms in a show of peace, hoping to lower the hackles bristling around her. "We're the ones who took her to the hospital. We wanted—" I start, attempting to soothe her worries. But I am interrupted by shattering glass from inside, sending alarm bells ringing in my head. Killian, Ash, and I tense. My hands twitch toward the concealed holster at my side; I sense Killian and Ash moving in sync.

My gaze locks onto eyes—those stormy forest depths flecked with sunlight, the same ones that have haunted every quiet moment since I lost her. A rush of recognition floods me. Killian was the only one who spoke to her at the party, and Ash only saw her once she was injured. Pressure builds inside me as I take a unsteady step forward.

"Jakey?" she whispers, the sound disturbs the hush like a ripple across still water. The name—*Jakey*—rips through me like a caged instinct breaking loose. She takes a hesitant step forward, and every part of me braces, caught between moving toward her or staying frozen in place. Her wide eyes move from Killian to Ash to me, searching for answers, for stability, for proof this isn't some cruel illusion.

Blood rushes in my ears. I open my mouth, but no words come. I only stare at the girl we've been searching for, the one I let slip through my fingers so long ago. Finally found. And yet, nothing about this moment feels simple. Nothing about it is easy. We'd long since believed she was dead, but here she is—breathing, heart pumping.

"Ember, no!" the blonde yelps, nearly toppling a nearby lamp as she scrambles for a broom. "There's glass everywhere—don't move!" Her frantic motion sends more shards skittering across the floor, the sound pinging off the baseboards.

I can't tear my eyes from her. She's here. She's alive, only... she's not the same. Her once-sunlit skin is pale and bruised, her wiry frame, swimming in an oversized shirt and sweatpants, hangs limp on her body.

My eyes drop to the floor as she shuffles her feet, leaving a faint smear of red. "You've cut yourself," I murmur, stepping over the threshold with caution. I half-expect her to flinch away, but she lets me approach. Stopping in front of her, I attempt the barest hint of a smile, my insides knotting at how small she appears now. The memory of the vibrant, fearless girl clashes violently with this frail figure.

Dropping to one knee, I tap her ankle. She hesitates, her muscles flinch, but she allows me to lift her foot onto my thigh. A shard of glass, embedded just below her heel, reflects in the overhead light. My fingers quake as I take hold of it, slowly tugging it free.

Her hiss of pain guts me. I jerk my eyes up to meet hers. "I'm sorry," I say, voice low. "I don't want to hurt you."

Confusion pools in the depths of golden earth and shadowed jade as she shakes her head. For a second, it seems like she might speak. Instead, she stumbles back, arms wrapped around herself. "I'm sorry," she cries, tears slipping down her cheeks. "I'm so sorry! I didn't mean to, please don't be mad."

She huddles close to the wall as if trying to disappear into it. Behind me, Killian lets out a low growl. "What the hell is she apologizing for?"

She isn't looking at me, but keeps looking at my thigh. "I'm sorry," she sniffles, and I catch the sight of smeared blood on the worn denim. "I'm sorry."

"My jeans can be replaced, Rosie," I say, raising my hand to invite her closer. I keep my attention on her, noting how her fingers fidget. She doesn't move, but the air feels fragile, like the moment might break if I push too hard. "But you?... You're irreplaceable."

The room quiets. We all watch as she tugs at the edge of her sweatshirt. Her eyes move across the room, never settling, like she's searching for solid ground. "I-I waited for you, but... you never came," she blurts out. She analyzes Killian and Ash before returning to me as if she's trying to find the truth.

My throat aches, and I barely manage to speak. *She waited?* My thoughts scramble for a response. We left her. We didn't get there fast enough. And now she's broken in ways I can't fix.

The woman with the broom mutters under her breath as she sweeps glass into the dustpan, the tinkling mingling with Rosie's ragged breathing. Slowly, I rise to my feet, stepping closer.

"No—," I start, voice ragged, but she fixes me with a look so intense it roots me in place.

"You didn't want me anymore." A part of me contracts at the unspoken accusation—at the bitter betrayal carved into her expression.

Killian steps up beside me, his expression gentler than I've seen in years. "We've been searching for you since you left, Rosie," he murmurs.

Her chest rises sharply. She nibbles her bottom lip, gauging whether the confession is genuine. "You... never came though. Why would you be looking for me?" she repeats.

Ash's control frays. "I know," he growls, his tone brokering no argument. "Jake failed you, yes, but you still left. You're the one who ran away before we could get to you!"

The impact of that sentence is immediate. Her face crumples, and she turns, huddling into the petite woman's chest, who meets Ash's glare with one of her own. "Please," her friend growls, "she doesn't need this stress right now. You can leave if you want to cause her more pain. She's been through enough."

Rose's next word catches me off guard. "No," she begs, inhaling before turning her attention on us. "I waited until you turned eighteen, and when none of you came, I figured you had abandoned me. I didn't want to leave you. I just... I didn't think you still cared, so I left. Marissa came with me."

The admission sinks beneath my skin, a fresh wave of guilt mingling with relief. She wanted us. She waited. Yet I wasn't there.

Ash closes the distance between them in a few steps. "We would never abandon you, Rose," he says, his tone softening despite the fervor in his eyes. "Though our actions have not proven that, we will do what we can to make up for our failures."

A thin stream of tears trails down the already-formed tracks. The distance feels like a chasm, and I want to close the space, but a faint glimmer stirs in her eyes, like the last ember clinging to life in a bed of dying ashes.

Her silhouette wavers, as if caught between worlds. My body strains with the need to be near her, to close the gap, but I hold back, afraid that even the slightest movement might make her retreat further into herself. "We aren't going anywhere, Red. We're here, we finally found you."

Her gaze meets mine, and I can see the scars in her eyes–the bruises from the years that have shaped her into someone I barely recognize.

Fresh tears fill her eyes, and my every breath stalls at the sight. A heavy thud reverberates inside me, words crowding my mind but refusing to form. She moves, crossing the room until she collides with me. A ragged sob breaks free as she collapses into me, clutching my shirt in tight fists, as though she's afraid I'll disappear if she doesn't hold on.

Her cries are hollow waves that course through her petite frame, and all I can do is hold her. My arms wrap around her, fingers brushing against her back as I try to calm her tremors. A fierce protectiveness roars to life within me, leaving no room for anything else.

I rest my chin atop her head, feeling her tears soak into my shirt. Her scent—faint antiseptic from the hospital, mingled with the subtle warmth that's unmistakably her. I close my eyes, savoring the smell. I want to tell her a thousand things, to promise safety or absolution, but the lump in my throat won't let the words out.

So I say nothing. I hold her, letting her sobs rock through us, wishing I could take every bit of her pain and lock it away where it'll never hurt her again.

"I think you all might want to give her a little breathing room." Marissa stands nearby, her posture rigid, one hand resting on the small of Rose's back. "She's been through a lot, and it's only been two days since she got out of the hospital. I really hoped that finding you would help, but..." She trails off, offering a faint, apologetic smile. "I'm sorry. Maybe it's too soon, and this is overwhelming her a little."

She pulls Rosie from my arms, ushering her toward a plush armchair near a lamp, the small circle of light illuminates the haunted shadows in Rose's eyes. Marissa drapes a soft blanket around her shoulders, tucking it beneath her chin like a mother might with a feverish child. The tenderness tugs at my insides; she isn't angry at us—she's worried sick about her.

Guilt gnaws at me as I stand there, helpless, while Marissa tends to the woman who owns my heart. The three of us—me, Killian, and Ash —watch, sidelined by our regrets. I manage to find my voice, though it comes out forced. "I'm sorry," I say, with a hand raised in a gesture of surrender. "We didn't mean to overwhelm her. We've been searching for so long... and seeing her now... It's a lot to handle for all of us. We thought she was dead and have just recently learned differently."

Rosie peeks at me from behind Marissa's arm, her eyes wary, but not entirely closed off. Still, she doesn't speak—doesn't address us directly.

"Mare," she murmurs, her gaze darting from Killian to Ash before landing on me. "Don't make them leave. I—I owe them an explanation, I deserve an explanation. And they have every right to be upset with me." She straightens her shoulders, as though drawing on some leftover scrap of courage. "I was fifteen—young, impulsive. I never expected... I never understood what my choices would cause. Don't blame them for what I did."

Marissa's hand stills on her shoulder, and her gaze meets mine with uncertainty. I notice how carefully she weighs Rose's words, trying to figure out the best way to protect her while respecting what she's asking for.

Across the small living room, Ash stands rooted in place, as if physically unable to leave. His rumpled suit and disheveled hair betray the turmoil he's feeling. Finally, he breaks his silence, voice rough. "It tore us apart when you disappeared," he says, his stare trained on her like he can't look anywhere else. "We built everything just to find you. We —" His voice hitches, anger and sorrow twisting together. "We corrupted systems, bribed and threatened our way into leads. And when that failed..." He forces a short, humorless laugh. "We killed for you."

A hush settles, so heavy it feels like it might crush us. Marissa's eyes go wide, alarm flaring, but she doesn't say anything, clearly debating whether to intervene. Rose's face pales. Ash crosses the room in a few quick strides until he's standing in front of her. "I'd do it all again," he says, dropping to a crouch so he's at eye-level, "a hundred times over, just to see you breathing in front of me."

Rose's lip quivers, and another tear slips down her cheek. She takes a breath, pouncing from the chair and landing in his arms. Ash stumbles, wrapping her up as a broken laugh escapes him. "I thought you were gone," he whispers, his face sinking into her hair. "Really gone."

Her fingers dig into the lapels of his wrinkled suit. Despite my feelings, I manage the faintest smile because I know how much staying put together and perfect means to him, and how little he cares about it now that she's in his arms.

Buried in his embrace. "I thought I was going to die. If... if you hadn't—if you didn't—he would've killed me."

A furious noise comes from Killian. He spins on his heel, storming out to the narrow balcony and slamming the French doors behind him. Beneath all our relief, we're a mess of anger and shame. We had her—then we lost her. And while she was trapped in hell, we mourned a grave that didn't exist.

Rose startles at the sound, withdrawing from Ash just enough to peer over his shoulder. "Did I say something wrong?" she whispers, worry etched into her expression.

Marissa lays a hand on her arm. "Don't mind him," she says, voice gentle as she tucks the blanket more securely around Rose's shoulders. "You've been through enough, Ember. You need to rest, to focus on your recovery. Don't worry about him."

Confusion courses through me—Ember. I turn my head, dragging a hand through my hair. *Rosie.* She's always *Rosie* to me. "She's right," I force out, swallowing the emotion threatening to drown me. "Your body's barely recovered. And..." I falter, "We still need to talk about—"

Rose shakes her head with a sudden, rigid motion. "Don't," she says, stopping me mid-sentence. Whatever that name is—Patrick or another, she refuses to hear—it's still too painful. Marissa places a calming hand on her shoulder.

The tension in the room is thick. I will myself to speak again, but Marissa beats me to it. "We have pizza on the way," she offers, abrasive as ever. "You must be starving." She levels a meaningful look on Rosie, adding softly, "And you've lost too much weight... come on, you need to eat."

As if on cue, a knock at the door makes Rose jump. She draws closer to Ash, eyes flashing with fear. "Probably just the delivery," Marissa assures, squeezing her arm.

“I’ll grab it,” I say, stepping toward the door. The guy on the other side does a double-take at the sight of me—my blood-stained pants, the rigid lines on my face—but hands over the boxes anyway, leaving in a hurry once I hand him some cash.

“Pizza’s here!” I call loudly toward the balcony in case Killian wants to come in. “We can leave if you two want some space.” The words feel heavy because the last thing I want is to walk away again.

Ash tenses, shooting me a glare, but Rosie is quicker. “No! Please... don’t go,” she says, meeting my gaze. Her eyes brim with too many questions, too many horrors still unspoken. “You’re right... We have so much to talk about..”

And so we stay, bound by the past, by the pain, by her. No one moves. No one dares to walk away—not when she’s finally looking at us like we belong. She is the reason we’re here, the reason we keep fighting. And if she asks us to stay, we will. Always.

CHAPTER 22

Killian

I study the cramped apartment, half-expecting the walls to close in on us. The silence is palpable—broken only by the faint sounds of chewing and the rustle of paper plates. The overhead light casts our shadows long across the cluttered floor. I'm on my third slice, but I'm not tasting it.

Rosie sits with Marissa glued to her side on the small loveseat, whispering in hushed tones that I can't decipher. My gaze flicks to Ash on my left—pristine suit, neat hair, and visibly uncomfortable on the floor. Even hunched over, he brings tension to the room. Yet, there's a neatness to him, a care in how he holds his pizza by the edge of the crust, like he's afraid of a single drop of sauce tainting his immaculate jacket. The tension in his jaw suggests he'd rather be elsewhere than engage in this "uncivilized" ritual.

Jake, on my right, picks at his pizza in stony silence. I can practically feel his judgment aimed at my sauce-stained fingers.

The three of us crowd around a low-standing coffee table that barely accommodates our plates, let alone our sprawling legs. Another pang of guilt hits me because, as uneasy as we are, Rosie looks more rattled by our presence. She fidgets, her gaze flitting from one of us to the next, eyes darting away whenever I try to catch them.

A throat clears, loud in the hush. "So, um," Marissa begins from her spot on the loveseat. She pauses, lips pulling into a thin line, then turns slightly and murmurs into Rosie's ear. I can't make out the words, but the way Rosie's shoulders go rigid tells me it's about us.

Jake shifts, his knee brushing mine. An undercurrent of tension vibrates through his body. He sets down his half-eaten pizza, wiping his fingers on a napkin with the meticulousness I recognize. It's how he copes when he's on edge.

I take another bite—mostly to fill the silence—my thoughts churning. We spent years looking for Rosie, shaping our entire lives around finding her, mourning her in the only way we knew how to. Now, here we are, a sardine-can gathering in her tiny apartment, pretending to be normal. The weight of everything that's happened looms over us. We barely fit on her floor. We barely fit into her life anymore.

I swallow hard, my mouth dry despite the grease of the pizza. We came here for answers—to convince ourselves she's alive, to atone for failing her. Instead, we sit hunched like outsiders, picking at cold pieces of pepperoni while the person we shattered seeks comfort in someone else.

Marissa's eyes dart across our faces—Jake's rigid posture, Ash's brooding scowl, my anxious chewing—trying to figure out how to ease the tension. It's a futile attempt. The room is too small to hold all our regrets. But at least she's not angry or hostile anymore; she's being protective. She cares for Rosie in a way I wish we could.

I take a slow breath and set my pizza aside. We can't keep doing this—circling the silence, letting it stretch between us. We have to talk to break the tension. But when I part my lips to speak, the words twist and knot before they escape. Instead, I clear my throat, steeling myself for whatever comes next.

Jake shoots me a look—one of those quick, wordless glances that says, *Don't even start.* I shrug, popping another pepperoni into my mouth. Across the room, Rosie half-hides behind her slice, her lips pursing as she tries to stifle a smile, which only makes her shoulders shake with laughter.

"S-sorry," Marissa snorts, gesturing at the three of us. "It's just... y'all look like three linebackers trying to squeeze into a clown car." Her laughter bubbles up, and for a moment, Rosie can't help but join in, a quiet smile curving her lips.

"Do you find this funny, Princess?" I tease, arching my brows suggestively. The old nickname slips out before I can think, and her eyes widen, a faint flush creeping across her cheeks.

"Oh... I... um..." She fumbles for a response and ends up letting out a breathy sound. "Yes," she admits, "I guess I should've let two of you take the couch."

"No point," Jake interjects. He still has that restless air about him—like he's ready to jump into action at the slightest hint of trouble—but there's a gentleness in his eyes whenever they focus on Rosie. He discards his napkin in one of the empty boxes with a toss. "We wouldn't have let you sit on the floor."

The dusting of color on her face deepens. She sets aside her half-eaten pizza, wiping her hands on a napkin. We'd been encouraging her to eat more—her fragility is tough to ignore—but she stops after just one slice. I exchange a look with Ash on my right. "Let me help you clean up," Marissa whispers, leaning closer to Rosie and speaking softly.

Rosie shakes her head, a soft smile forming despite the shadows in her eyes. "No, you need to get home to your kids," she says, taking Marissa's hands. "Thank you for being here. I really didn't want to be alone. And... bring your kids and husband over soon."

Marissa's gaze warms, and she squeezes Rosie's hands before letting go. I notice how Jake, still perched against the far wall, keeps moving his eyes between them, as if he's trying to measure if Rosie is safe. His shoulders remain tense, but there's relief etched around his eyes. In his Jake-like way, he's searching for a sign that we're all still welcome here... that *she* wants us to stay.

Marissa's voice drops, concern threading through every word. "Of course, I will. But please be careful," she says. "Please take it easy tonight, I'm not sure you're strong enough to stand for that long in the shower, maybe take a bath?" She casts a look at the three of us huddled together. Then, in a whisper meant for Rosie but loud enough for us to hear, she adds, "Do you want them to go?"

Rosie's eyes flick to us, uncertain. "No," she answers, her tone gentle. "They can stay... if they want."

Jake uncurls himself from the floor. "We'll stay as long as you'd like," he says, stretching out a kink in his back. I watch him, feeling a pull of gratitude that we're all here—that we still have this chance to be near her.

Marissa hesitates, gaze darting between Rosie and the rest of us. "If you hurt her," she warns with the weight of a promise, "I'll kill you. And trust me, my ex's family is... well, let's say they're important, and they'd be more than willing to help."

Ash scoffs, smoothing a hand down his rumpled dress shirt in a vain attempt to straighten the wrinkles. "We're not going to hurt her," he mutters, failing to hide the flash of annoyance in his eyes. "That's not why we came."

From my place on the floor—my back resting against the cold window—I nod in agreement, wishing I could find the right words to reassure her. But Rosie beats me to it, placing a hand on Marissa's arm. "It's okay, Mare," she murmurs, guiding her friend closer to the door. "They wouldn't be here if they wanted to hurt me."

Marissa exhales. "Call me tomorrow, okay? Or tonight if you need anything." Her tone laced with genuine concern as she wraps Rosie in a hug. "Keep your door locked. And maybe on Friday, we can have dinner? I'll bring the boys, and we can order something... a little less greasy."

She looks our way, a hint of challenge crossing her expression. It softens as quickly as she bends slightly to whisper into Rosie's ear. Rosie nods, a faint, appreciative smile brushing her lips. Marissa slips out, the lock clicking into place, leaving behind a quiet stillness.

For a moment, no one moves. The faint hum of the city drifts through the window behind me, and I'm acutely aware of Rosie standing only a few feet away, still wrapped in the blanket. She looks fragile, and the shift in her expression suggests Marissa's exit gave her a moment to breathe.

At last, I push myself upright, the cold touch of the windowpane against my back helping me stay grounded. I don't know what to say or do—none of us do. But we're here, in the soft glow of her small apartment's living room, even if every breath carries the weight of everything left unspoken.

I watch her turn away, her shirt rising slightly with the motion. Her shoulders draw in, and her fingers fidget with the frayed hem. A dull ache stirs inside me—she never used to do that. The way she moves feels unfamiliar. Wrong.

"I... um... I should probably go take a—" she begins.

"Do you have a concussion?" Ash cuts in, stepping closer.

His abrupt question makes her brows knit in confusion as she tilts her head, clearly not expecting that. "I did. Y... yes, why?"

"You shouldn't be alone," Ash continues. "Concussions can be serious. Did the hospital give you discharge papers? I should read over them. We can set alarms and take turns checking on you—whatever it takes. But we can't leave you by yourself." Ash is strung tight, and he's looking for any excuse to stay near her.

Her lips part, but no sound follows. Her eyes dart, unfocused, as if the weight of his concern is drowning her, too heavy to bear. Her fingers twitch at her sides, her shoulders bracing for impact. Even without moving, I can feel the silent recoil and the urge to disappear.

"Ash," I snap, pushing off the window. "You're freaking her out."

She looks at me, her eyes locking onto mine. God, they have a hollowness—an echo of the girl I used to know. Her focus drops, tracing the changes in me. I'm broader now, taller, my shoulders built from years of training. A faint flush creeps into her cheeks as she takes it in, and regret stirs in my chest. I've become a weapon, and I can't help but wonder if she finds that threatening instead of safe.

"Come here," I whisper. She hesitates, caught between caution and an emotion I can't quite name. Slowly, she moves closer, her hair slipping over one shoulder, revealing bruises along her neck—faded yellows that churn my stomach with fury.

How did I not see her for who she was at that race? How could I have missed those eyes? Was it the haunted stare, the way her fingers twitched ever so slightly, that made her so unrecognizable? She's a shadow of the girl she used to be, every inch of her telling the story of neglect under Saint John's cruelty.

I cup her cheek slowly, my palm large against her delicate skin. She gasps, a soft sound that hits me like a punch to the gut, leaning into my hand. The tension in her posture melts away for a heartbeat, like she's drawing comfort from my touch. If only she knew the things these hands have done—what I became—to find her. She doesn't recoil, even after Ash confesses how far we went.

"Marissa said you should take a bath. Can I help you get it ready?" I murmur, low enough that Jake and Ash can't overhear.

She hesitates, my name slipping from her lips in a fragile whisper. "Killian." Hearing her speak that name again is like a blade cutting through me. A vice grips my ribs, squeezing so tight it aches. Her lashes flutter, tears clinging to the edges, waiting to spill. "I don't want you to see me like this. I'm not ready."

"I can help get the water ready, then I'll stay outside the door, just in case you need anything." A deep ache settles in me at the vulnerability. Years ago, she was fearless, recklessly brave in ways that awed me. Now, she's almost crumpling before my eyes, ashamed of scars that aren't her fault. I shake my head, leaning closer. "And you're still you, Princess. Doesn't matter what he did. You're still everything you ever were—and more."

A tear slips down her cheek, and I catch it with my thumb, my other hand sliding around her waist. She shudders in my hold, letting out a shaky exhale.

"I'm sorry," she says again, and I feel her beginning to fold in on herself.

"Don't be," I whisper, lowering my head until our foreheads touch. Her presence steadies me, anchoring us in the quiet space between. "Not now, not ever."

In that moment, her guard drops—just enough for me to sense the old Rosie still flickering inside. A mix of relief and sorrow washes over me. We're here; she's alive. But how much have we lost in the process?

I cradle her face in both hands, guiding her chin until our eyes connect. She tries to look anywhere else, but I won't let her avoid me. "Hey, Princess," I murmur, my voice soft as she nibbles her bottom lip, each shaky breath betraying her nerves. I reach for her hand, grounding us both. "It doesn't matter to me how you look. What matters is that you're here—alive, breathing—with me."

She exhales a shaky "O-okay," her hands sliding to cover mine. A part of me eases at that touch, a fraction of the guilt lifting. "I never could say no to you," she adds, a tiny, timid smile curving her lips.

A smirk tugs at my mouth. I brush my thumb across her cheek, catching a stray tear. Gently, I pull her, intending to lead her away from the tension boiling in the main room from my so-called brothers.

"Where are you going?" Jake demands. His stare bores into my back.

"None of your fucking business," I toss over my shoulder, ignoring the low rumbles of protest that erupt from him and Ash.

She falters, looking between them, her eyes flicking with concern. "Are they okay?" she whispers.

"They're fine, Princess," I say, lowering my voice just for her. "Just being their usual overbearing selves." Her brow furrows, so I arch a brow in response, watching as she looks away, too quickly. Her reaction holds a familiar trace—an innocence that sharpens my instincts, stirring the urge to shield her from everything that might steal it away.

I guide her out of the living room, closing the door with a soft click. The apartment is cramped, so it's only a few steps to the tiny bathroom. When I turn around, I catch her fiddling with her oversized T-shirt, knuckles going white as she clenches the fabric. My stomach twists—*Should I be doing this?*

I say nothing for a moment, letting her work through her jitters and move to the tub. I test the faucet, adjusting it until the water runs hot but does not scald. Steam rises in a gentle curl. With that done, I shift my gaze back to her. "Rosie?" I murmur, keeping my tone soft.

She peers up at me from under those long lashes. "C-can you turn around?" Her voice is tiny, so unlike the girl she used to be.

A tight knot forms inside me, guilt and tenderness colliding. "Yeah," I manage, turning away and placing my forehead against the door. The cool wood grounds me, but regret claws its way in. *Why did I think this was a good idea?* A rush of images—what Saint John might've done, the nightmares she must've endured—flashes through my mind. I'm practically asking her to bare herself, physically and emotionally, and I'm not sure I deserve that trust.

I can't stand the thought of her discomfort. Yet, I keep my back turned, silent, trying to steady my breathing. *She needs care,* I remind myself. *She needs to feel safe.* Maybe a bath will help wash away some of that ache. Perhaps it'll remind her she's not alone. But the doubt gnaws at me: *Am I helping, or hurting more?*

Behind me, I can hear the soft rustle of fabric, her hesitant motions. Each small sound drives home just how vulnerable she is. Still, she's letting me stay and see this new, wounded version of her—a fierce protectiveness courses through me. If I need to, I'll stand guard all night, checking the water every ten minutes. I'll do anything to make her feel safe.

I open my mouth, ready to tell her this whole thing was a mistake—that I'll give her privacy—when she stops me with a soft voice. "D-done," she manages. Slowly, I turn, bracing myself. The sight before me sends a jolt of pain through me, a visceral ache that threatens to knock the air from my essence.

Bruises line her arms and torso, faint outlines of scars crisscrossing in places that no one should ever have to bear. She's kept on a plain bra and simple cotton panties, both hanging loose on her too-thin frame. A low growl escapes my throat before I can stop it, and my fists clench at my sides, an old rage flickering. I want to find Saint John and finish what I started—finish him, for the damage he did.

"Killian?" she whispers, small, uncertain. A hand rests against my ribs, light but cautious. I flinch, the contact sharp against the thin fabric of my shirt, a reminder that she's too close. "S...sorry," she stammers, pulling her hand away as if scorched, curling it against herself. I rake a hand through my hair, forcing my eyes to meet hers, trying not to let them drift over her bruised skin again.

"No, I'm sorry," I manage, swallowing back anger that builds like acid. "I—I just wasn't prepared to see the..." My words trail off, the reality of her condition clamping my stomach in a vise.

She peeks down, biting her bottom lip. "The damage... the ugliness?" she murmurs.

"No!" The word bursts out more forcefully than I intend, and she jerks back, eyes wide with fear. My stomach clenches, and I turn off the water to keep busy, to focus on anything but her reaction. "Sorry," I mutter, extending a hand for her to hold, though it's hard to keep it still.

"You can wait outside." Her cool fingers slipping between mine. Her skin is damp, and I squeeze gently, guiding her step over the tub's edge. I support her until she's settled into the sudsy water. A faint moan escapes her lips as she lowers herself deeper.

"Is it warm enough?" I ask. She sighs, eyes fluttering closed, a small smile playing on her lip.

"Yes," she breathes, sinking into the bubbles so they crest below her chin.

"I'll be right outside if you need me, okay?"

"Stay. Please? I don't want to be alone," she begs.

"Of course, Princess."

I study the cramped bathroom, searching for some body wash or soap to help her, only to freeze when my eyes land on the edge of the sink. A small bottle of sage and cedarwood cologne sits next to two Old Spice body washes perched in the shower caddy.

A lump forms, my stomach churning. The idea of anyone else's scent here, especially after what she's been through, sends a wave of nausea rolling through me.

I force a slow breath. *She's here. She's not there anymore. And she needs me to be steady.*

"Do you need anything?" I manage, my voice raw. She peeks up at me with half-lidded eyes.

"Just... stay," she whispers.

I nod, swallowing hard. Rosie moves in the water, her body restless. "Killian?" she asks quietly, pulling my focus back. The way she says my name—it's like a ghost from the past, a sound I never thought I'd hear again.

"Did you... have a boyfriend before you...?" The words taste bitter, and I hate how unsure they sound. I nod toward the sink, my eyes landing on the cologne and body washes. "The cologne. The body wash," I clarify

A blush creeps over her cheeks, coloring the tips of her ears. She sinks deeper, letting the bubbles shield most of her face. "No," she mumbles through the froth.

I lean over the tub's edge, the ceramic edge cool beneath my arm, and gently tilt her chin toward me. "Rosie?"

"It... It's the stuff you all used before," she whispers. I pull back, studying the bottles. Recognition flickers—Jake's old scent, the body washes Ash and I used.

"Why do you have those?" I ask.

Her lashes flutter, and I catch the hint of a shy smile. "I'd use the products when I m-missed you," she confesses. A small laugh escapes me.

"You did?" I smirk, grabbing the brand of body wash I favored back then. The possessive need to have her smell like *me* again spikes inside me. She watches as I squeeze too much onto a rag, and I kneel beside the tub, swirling the cloth in the water until it's laden with suds.

She flinches a little when I swipe the soapy rag across her shoulder; water darkens the straps of her bra to a dusty gray. "Should I leave?" I ask softly, pulling back just enough to meet her gaze. The question feels heavier than it should; I don't want to crowd her if she's not ready.

Her eyelids flutter shut, and she breathes out a shaky apology. "N-No, I-I'm sorry," she stammers, voice catching on every word. "He... when he..."

My fingers clench around the fabric, the memory of him sparking a flicker of rage beneath my skin. "It's okay," I say quickly, slicing through her words before they can drag us back. The last thing I want is for her to wade through that pain again. "You don't have to push yourself into anything that hurts."

She nods, and I glide the cloth over her shoulder again, softer this time, letting the water and the faint trace of old memories settle between us.

"Please don't leave," she pleads, tears clinging to her lashes. "I can do this... I need to do this." There's a fierce resolve behind her words. Walking away now would break a part of her.

"All right," I whisper, letting out a slow breath. I study her face, searching for any sign of hesitation. When she sinks deeper into the tub, I clear my throat, trying to think of a way to ease her nerves. "How about I tell you where I'm washing first?" Another nod. Her muscles remain tense as I reach to turn on the tap, letting fresh hot water swirl in to keep her warm.

"I'm going to start with your right arm," I say, gently lifting her hand from the water. The rag moves over her skin in slow strokes, my focus locked on the motion rather than the bruises and scars catching the light. "Now you're back," I continue, guiding her forward just enough to reach her shoulders and spine. I move the cloth in careful circles. Steam curls between us, and the scent of soap lingers in the air. A quiet resolve settles in me—if I can leave a piece of myself here, something steady may help soften what came before.

"I'll do your left arm now," I murmur, easing her back against the tub. Gently, I lift her other hand, turning it over. A constricting weight settles deep inside me at the sight of the thin scars etched along her forearm. I bite back a curse.

She drifts off, her breathing evens out, head tipping until it rests on the edge. The small lines on her forehead smooth, and I smile. "I'm going to wash your legs now, okay?"

"Mhm," she mumbles, eyes closed, shoulders loosening as she sinks into the heat. The water moves in slow, constant currents around her.

Carefully, I lift her foot, mindful of every bruise mottling her skin. I wash her calf and knee with slow, measured strokes, moving to the other side. Each scar, each discolored patch, ignites a spark of fury deep in my gut. I focus on her comfort, watching closely so she doesn't slip beneath the water.

Her lips part in a barely audible sigh as I finish. "I'm going to wash your hair now," I say softly, moving to the head of the tub. She mumbles a reply I can't quite catch, her words blurred by the haze of half-sleep.

A chuckle escapes me when I notice the mix of men's hair products on the ledge. *She bought our old brands.* Grabbing the shampoo that smells like Ash, I let out a low snort. The man of habit has been using the same products for as long as I can remember. *I wonder if he will recognize the scent.*

I settle on my knees behind her, filling a plastic cup from the tap. The water cascades over her copper hair, darkening it to a deeper hue. She stirs, a soft moan escaping. Gently, I work the shampoo into her hair, fingers sliding through tangles and knots. In her sleep, she lets out a slight, contented sound between a purr and a sigh.

The click of the door behind me sends a protective jolt through my system. My first reflex is to shield Rosie's body as Jake stands in the doorway, concern etched across his face.

"How is she?" he whispers, settling beside me on the tiled floor. His eyes drift over Rosie's sleeping form.

I swallow hard, wiping a stray bubble from my hand. "One hundred and twenty-three," I mutter, voice tight. "She has one hundred and fucking twenty-three scars and bruises, J."

He exhales sharply, running a hand through his blond hair. "Fuck," he breathes, a single word dense with regret. "At least she's finally resting," he murmurs, more to himself than to me.

I trail my fingers through Rosie's hair, the suds from the conditioner working smoothly into the strands. "She uses our old products."

Jake arches a brow. "What do you mean?"

I nod at the bottles. "She bought the brands we used to wear—yours, Ash's, mine. She wanted to smell like us." A wry laugh escapes me as I rinse the last of the conditioner from her hair, carefully shielding her eyes from the water. The sight of her drifting in a quiet doze tugs at my insides. Her soft snores fill the cramped bathroom, the occasional splash of water punctuating the silence.

Jake's gaze traces her bruised arms and the pale shadows beneath her eyes. He crosses his arms, as though physically holding himself together. *I've blamed him for so long. And maybe I still do.*

Clearing his throat, Jake stands, straightening the creases in his shirt—a habit that used to annoy me, but now only reminds me how different everything is. "I'll let you finish up. Ash and I are setting up some sleeping areas in the living room. It'll be tight, but..." He shrugs, trailing off. Neither of us needs to say it: *We're not leaving her alone.*

I nod, focusing on the last of the conditioner in her hair. "Thanks," I offer, voice gruff, unsure what else to say. Jake gives a curt nod and slips out, the door closing with a gentle click.

The silence returns, broken only by Rosie's slow breaths. I lean down, smoothing the bubbles off her neck. Her hair gleams as I rinse it, her coppery strands dark from the water. *We're here. We found her. She's safe...*

"Wake up," I murmur, my lips near her ear. Her eyes snap open. She jerks away with a sharp gasp, scrambling to the far side of the tub. Water sloshes over the edge, soaking my pants and the tile floor.

"Rosie," I say quickly, both hands raised to show I mean no harm. "You're okay. You're safe." She draws rapid, shallow gasps with wild eyes as if searching for an exit or an attacker. "It's me. It's Killian."

"K-Killian?" She takes another look at the bathroom—a small, cluttered space lined with a few worn towels and half-finished toiletries—before sagging back into the water. Tears slip free, silent at first, wracking her shoulders with quiet, broken sobs.

She pulls her knees up, hugging them as sobs wracked her body, broken and hollow, echoing against the porcelain. "Oh, Sweet Girl," I whisper, shifting closer along the side of the tub. A thousand instincts scream at me to pull her into my arms, but how she curls in on herself stops me. Instead, I settle for staying near—close enough to let her know I'm here, but not so close that I crowd her.

My voice lowers, rough with emotion. "What can I do?" I ask the question, ripping at my insides. "How can I help you?" My tears slip free, hot trails down my cheeks.

She can't answer; she shakes her head, burying her face in her arms. I sit there, helpless, drowning in my anger and guilt—anger for what was done to her, shame that I couldn't save her from it sooner. Still, I stay. I stay because leaving her at this moment would be unforgivable. Because after everything that's happened, she deserves to know that I'm never going anywhere again.

CHAPTER 23

Ember Rose

"How can I help you?" Such a simple question, yet trying to answer feels like wrestling with shadows. Killian's voice barely carries above a hush, his words brushing the air like a feather. Five years —five endless years—I screamed and begged for someone, anyone, to save me. No one came. My nails dig into my palms, and the sharp ache reminds me I'm still here, fighting to reclaim what's left of me.

Memories churn in my mind: the cold of that cell, the brief flicker of hope Atlas gave me—the only light in those endless days. I fought for him as much as for myself, swearing he'd never grow up knowing only cruelty. And now he's still trapped with that bastard. I swallow the urge to spill everything to Killian—the truth that Jake is Atlas's father, that my son is the living proof of a bond between me and the men standing just beyond this bathroom door. But these aren't the same men who once rescued me from a hellish foster home. And I'm not the same girl they left behind, and I'm not sure I can trust them with this secret yet.

I lift my eyes and find Killian studying me. I want to let him in, but the words tangle on my tongue. Instead of trying to explain, I extend my hand toward him. "Take my hand," I say, wiggling my fingers in invitation. His callused palm slips into mine, and he rises to his full height. I stumble over my thoughts—he's so tall, all broad shoulders and pent-up energy. Yet the way the muted bathroom light falls over him, I can almost picture an angelic glow. No... not an angel. None of them are. They're all beautiful demons in their own way.

He draws me to my feet, and the cool air prickles against my wet skin. Bubbles cling to my arms and stomach, sliding away in little rivulets. In the quiet hush, I'm painfully aware of how closely he watches me, his gaze tracing every bruise, every scar..

"Help me out?" I whisper, my voice wobbling as I look anywhere but at his face. He gives the slightest nod, guiding me carefully as I step over the tub's edge. My foot catches on the porcelain, and I stumble forward, crashing into his chest with a soft gasp. Strong arms circle my waist, holding me upright. He doesn't let go. His thumbs brush lightly against my sides, sending awareness through my body. My cheeks flame, and I keep my eyes on the damp floor.

"Rosie?" he murmurs, and I almost flinch at the old nickname. Slowly, he coaxes my chin up with one hand, guiding my gaze to his. I see the question there—he's desperate for any answer I can give. But I can't explain that my loyalty now lies with a small boy who needs me more than anyone else. I can't tell him I'd walk through fire again if it meant saving Atlas.

So I stay quiet, letting the silence stretch between us. The steady drip from the faucet taps against the tile, too loud in the stillness. I want to believe he could understand that I could reach for him and be met with more than disappointment. But the painful truth is—I don't know if he can.

I stay in his arms a moment longer, eyes locked on his, hoping he sees her—the broken girl he once swore to protect, and the mother who's willing to do anything to keep her son safe.

"Can you get me a towel?" The name Rose still rings in my head—a name buried in dust and time. Hearing Killian speak so casually pulls at a part of me I thought I'd buried. Ember. Rosie. Red. None of them feels right anymore.

He releases my hand and wraps a towel around me. The soft fabric brushes my battered skin, and I flinch, heat rushing up my spine at the sting.

"Rosie... please," he murmurs, the edge in his words cracking under the weight of it. His hands stay at his sides, curled tight.

I breathe out slowly, forcing myself to meet his eyes. "Help me to my room?" I ask, the words barely above a whisper. I'm not ready to face what comes next, not when every option feels like a trap. I can't bring myself to tell him the truth—not yet. Not if there's a chance he'll see my son and think of Patrick.

For now, I ask for the smallest thing: not walking alone.

He hesitates, gently sliding his fingers between mine. A sharp shiver runs through me when he gives my hand a slight squeeze. Wordlessly, he leads me out into the hallway.

Three large beds sprawl across my tiny living area, crowding the space. I blink, surprised by the makeshift campsite. Jake steps forward, casting a glance at my towel-clad body before looking away. A wave of embarrassment makes me clutch the towel, reminded of how little I am now—small, bruised, and not the carefree teen they once knew. But there's an echo of that younger me inside, still wanting their approval.

"I hope this is alright?" Jake asks, gesturing at the rearranged furniture. I nod, noticing the tension around his eyes, the way he can't quite settle his gaze on me.

"Uh, yes," I mumble, disentangling my hand from Killian's. My eyes drift to my bed, tucked in a cramped alcove. I never thought I'd sleep there again, not after everything.

Stepping forward, I yank open the top drawer of the dresser. The worn wood grates on its rails, the sound reminding me of quieter mornings, rummaging for an outfit that didn't matter. My fingertips graze the familiar fabric of my favorite T-shirt, and a wave of memories floods me. Mornings in a different lifetime, filled with trivial worries—like which would tease me first or who'd snag the last piece of toast.

Footsteps sound behind me, and I tense, instincts bracing for a threat. But instead, a familiar scent wafts over me—an unspoken presence in a room too still. My hand stays in the drawer, fingers skimming over a foreign past.

It feels wrong to touch these clothes as if I can slip into them and pretend I'm not scarred—physically and otherwise. My stomach twists at the realization I might have to return to that hell, all for my son's sake.

I sense Ash close in, his presence overwhelming. But he doesn't force me to turn around. He doesn't say a word. He just... exists there, letting me wrestle with the memories folded neatly in this drawer. A shaky sigh slips out before I manage to hold it in check. Because no matter how broken I feel, I can't let them see my desperation. Not yet.

I hover between what I was and what I've become, fingers ghosting over a shirt from a life that ended the night I was taken. Ash's voice barely registers, quiet and uncertain. "Are you alright?" He's close, his heat sinking into my back. I ignore the pull to lean into it, to let it steady me. Atlas's face flickers in my mind—his laughter, light and unguarded. The idea of laughing now, without him, feels like a betrayal.

I shake my head, my lips pulling into a forced smile as I peek over my shoulder at Ash. "No," I admit, my voice barely audible. My gaze drops to the open drawer and the familiar clothes I once wore so easily. "These... belong to the girl I used to be." The words are bitter on my tongue, but I force them out. "She was pure, innocent. And now..." I trail off, biting my cheek to keep the tears from falling. "I'm just broken."

Ash exhales sharply, his breath skimming the back of my neck, setting my nerves on edge. "Then don't wear them," he murmurs. The ghost of his breath sends a shiver down my spine.

He tries to turn in the cramped space between the bed and the dresser, his arm brushing against mine. The faint contact startles me. Now facing me, his piercing blue-gray eyes study my face, searching for a response I'm not sure I can give.

"What am I supposed to wear then?" I ask, my voice tinged with frustration.

Ash's hands move to the buttons of his shirt, and a wave of shock ripples through me as I watch his fingers work methodically. He doesn't rush, each button undone with care. The fabric parts slowly, revealing muscle and the lean strength of his torso. He slips the shirt off his shoulders with a fluid motion, his muscles flexing. My lips part in a quiet gasp, and I quickly look away, heat rushing to my cheeks.

"It's already wrinkled," he grumbles, disrupting the tension as he holds the shirt out to me. His words are mundane, yet they break through the awkwardness like a lifeline.

"Are you sure?" I whisper as I observe the shirt, before returning my focus to him.

He doesn't answer immediately. Instead, he steps closer, draping the shirt gently over my shoulders. His fingers brush against my arms as he helps me thread them through the sleeves. The gesture is so careful and tender that it feels like I'm being wrapped in more than just fabric —it's safety.

I huff quietly as he fumbles with the buttons, his brow furrowing in concentration as he tries not to touch me more than necessary. The towel beneath the shirt keeps a barrier between us, but the lack of direct contact feels like a loss. I crave the normalcy of his touch, the reassurance that I'm not as broken as I think. But I can't ask him for that—not now. Not when we're both still navigating this fragile reunion.

"There," he says finally. He releases the towel from beneath the shirt, dropping it to the floor with a quiet thud. I leave the damp circle, feeling exposed even though I'm covered. Turning away from him, I strip off my bra and panties from beneath the shirt, the oversized fabric offering just enough modesty.

A low rumble—almost like a growl—pulls my attention back to Ash. His jaw tenses, muscles flexing beneath his skin, before he turns sharply on his heel and stalks out. Each step smacks against the floor, the sound fading quickly, leaving behind a silence that crushes in. His disappointment settles over me like a cold that won't shake loose.

"Rose?" Jake's voice breaks the silence. He's leaning casually against the wall, one shoulder propped up as his sharp eyes take me in. His gaze flicks over my oversized shirt before meeting my eyes.

"Jakey?" I whisper, my voice uncertain as I catch the hardened look in his eyes. His lip curls, and I shrink under his gaze, unsure of what I've done to bring out the edge in him. I study myself, dwarfed by Ash's oversized shirt, the hem brushing against my thighs. Jake blinks, snapping out of whatever thoughts had gripped him. His expression softens, though the tension in his shoulders remains. "We've set up a rotation to check on you through the night," he says, steady but subdued. "If you need anything, we'll be right out here."

I nod, clutching the bottom of the shirt like a lifeline, twisting the fabric in my hands. My voice wavers as I ask, "You promise you won't leave?" I don't mean to sound so desperate, but the thought of being alone again terrifies me.

Jake exhales, the sound weighted in the small space. He pushes off the wall and crosses the distance in a few strides. His hands grasp my face as his thumbs wipe away the tears tracking down my cheeks. His hands are broad and familiar—not rough like Killian's or refined like Ash's, but they've always been capable, always there when I had nothing left.

I lean into his touch, closing my eyes and letting the heat of his hands chase away the chill creeping into my bones. "We're not going anywhere, Red," he murmurs, a soft kiss brushing my forehead, so brief and tender it unlocks a flood of memories I thought I'd buried.

"Get some sleep," he whispers as he pulls back, his hands dropping to his sides. "We'll be here in the morning."

I nod again, watching him retreat toward the living room. The sight of him leaving stirs a feeling deep inside me, but I swallow the lump in my throat and turn toward the bed. The blankets are tucked neatly against the mattress, the familiar comfort of the cotton sheets calling to me. I slip beneath them, sinking into the softness with a sigh. It's strange, lying here again after so many years. The mattress feels unfamiliar against my body, like it no longer belongs to me, but I shift and wiggle until I find a position that feels right.

The ticking clock above my bed fills the silence, each sound marking another moment I'm here, alive, free—though freedom feels like a tenuous thread at best. I stare at the dark ceiling, listening to the low murmur of voices from the living room. Their words are muffled and indistinct, but their tones' cadence—their familiarity—wraps around me like a lullaby.

The lights click off one by one, the apartment descending into quiet darkness. My breathing evens out, the faint hum of their presence lulling me toward sleep. It's not the peaceful oblivion I used to know, but it's enough. For now, it's enough.

The stench hits me first—foul and overwhelming, invading my senses and making my stomach lurch. I gag, bile rising in my throat. The sour, acrid smell of rot clings to the air, mingling with unwashed fabric and sweat. My head pounds with every throb, the pain making it impossible to think.

The light above blares harshly, stabbing through my eyelids and dragging a groan from my lips. My cheek rests against a damp, scratchy surface, coarse against my skin. As my vision clears, I recognize the mattress beneath me—stained and filthy, a grim reminder of whoever had been trapped here before. The sight sends a shiver down my spine.

I try to move, to push myself up, but my arms are wrenched behind my back, bound tight with a coarse rope that bites into my skin. Panic sets in as I roll onto my side, then my back, writhing against the restraints. The mattress shifts beneath me, its springs creaking with each frantic movement.

"Where do you think you're going, Little Pet?" The voice slithers out of the shadows, low and amused. A tremor ripples through me as my eyes dart toward the sound. A man steps forward, the dim light catching on his sharp features as he sits in a metal folding chair, his silhouette hidden in the shadows beyond the pool of light surrounding the mattress.

"Where...?" My voice is muffled, my lips sealed by the sticky tape plastered across my mouth. I pull harder against the ropes, my wrists burning as they strain. The man leans forward, his face coming into view, and my stomach drops. His eyes glint with dark amusement, his smile twisted, predatory.

"Well, aren't you feisty?" he murmurs, rising with an unnerving grace. He straightens his suit jacket, the casual adjustment at odds with the malice radiating from him. "I couldn't resist, Pet. When he told me about the stunning redhead he'd acquired, I had to see for myself. And now..." He steps closer, crouching at the edge of the mattress, "Now, you're mine."

I flinch as his hand darts out, ripping the tape from my mouth in one brutal motion. A pained gasp escapes me, my lips stinging from the sudden exposure. "Where the fuck am I?" I snap, the words raw, desperate. I tug at the ropes again, twisting my arms against the binds. If I can just get one hand free...

His slap lands like a thunderclap, snapping my head to the side and sending a sharp sting across my cheek. The filthy mattress absorbs the impact as I collapse against it, a whimper escaping unbidden. He grabs my chin, forcing my face toward his, his grip bruising. "I won't tolerate that tone," he hisses. "You'll learn soon enough, Pet. I always break them."

He forces his mouth onto mine, his lips crushing against mine with violent fervor. I clamp my lips shut, but he bites down, his teeth scraping against my skin until I cry out. His tongue invades my mouth, the taste of him making me gag. Tears spill down my cheeks, mixing with the salty tang of blood from my bitten lip.

"Such a good girl," he murmurs, pulling away with a satisfied sneer. He stands, unfastening his belt, the metallic clank echoing in the small, suffocating room.

"No, please—" My voice cracks, but he cuts me off with a knife against the rope binding my ankles. The blade cuts through, and I instinctively shuffle back, ready to run. His laughter chills me to the core.

"You're not going anywhere." His hand slams against my torso, shoving me back onto the mattress. The rancid stench overwhelms me again, making my stomach lurch. I thrash beneath him, my screams echoing in the room, but his weight pins me down. The sound of fabric tearing cuts through the air, and my heart plummets as he rips away the last barrier protecting me.

The cold kiss of the blade digs into my neck, halting my struggle. "Now," he growls, dripping with cruel satisfaction, "be a good little pet."

The pain hits—sharp, unbearable, a brutal intrusion that sends waves of agony rippling through me. My cries fill the air, but they only fuel his depravity. He holds me down, his grip unrelenting as he takes everything from me, the vile words he whispers in my ear branding themselves into my soul.

The world blurs, my tears falling faster than I can wipe them away. My mind screams for escape, but there's nowhere to go. The light above burns into my vision, its harsh glare the only witness to my shattered world.

The sound of my name, sharp and urgent, cuts through the thick, suffocating haze. "Rose!" The shout yanks me from the darkness. My body jerks awake, aftershocks of the nightmare still coursing through my limbs. The bed shifts as someone sits beside me, the faint dip of the mattress anchoring me to the present. Gentle fingers brush damp strands of hair from my face.

"Come on, Red," a familiar voice pleads, soft but urgent. "Open those gorgeous eyes for me."

I freeze, the darkness clinging to me like a second skin. The prison in my mind feels too close. *What if I open my eyes and I'm still there?*

"Jakey?" The word scrapes out, rough and dry. I force my eyes open, blinking away the shadows until his face comes into focus. Dark chocolate eyes meet mine, filled with concern, his features etched in worry. Relief crashes over me like a tidal wave, loosening a part of me I didn't realize had been clenched tight.

"There she is," Jake murmurs, his lips tugging into a bittersweet smile. He brushes his thumbs across my damp cheeks, wiping away the tears that keep spilling despite my efforts to hold them back.

I choke on a sob, the noise tearing from within without warning. Everything I've been holding in—the fear, the shame, the pain—rushes out. I want to hide, to bury myself away, but Jake's hands remain steady.

Without thinking, I reach up, wrapping my hands around his. I pull his hands from my face, fisting them to my lap. I cling to him like a drowning woman, the feel of his solid presence grounding me in a way nothing else can. Jake doesn't move, doesn't flinch. He lets me hold on. He doesn't speak, and for that, I'm grateful. I'm not ready for words yet.

A soft murmur breaks the fragile bubble surrounding us. "How is she?"

I flinch at the sound, my body curling in on itself instinctively. Peering over the crumpled blankets, I see Killian and Ash standing at the foot of my bed. Their eyes read the wreckage I've become.

Jake doesn't release me. His hands remain steady beneath mine, his thumb brushing a soothing circle over the back of my hand. "I... I'm okay," I rasp, though the tremor in my voice betrays me.

Killian steps forward, a bottle of water in his hand. I force myself to sit up, the cold wall at my back comforting. Taking the bottle, I twist off the cap and drain it greedily, desperate to erase the ache.

Ash moves to the other side of the bed. He takes the empty bottle from my grasp and sets it on the nightstand before sitting beside me. The weight of their eyes is heavy but not unwelcome. I pull my knees close, wrapping my arms around them like a shield. "I... I'm sorry," I whisper. "I didn't mean to wake you."

Killian's eyes narrow. "You have nothing to be sorry for," he mutters. He leans closer, his green eyes locking onto mine. The panic inside me recedes, bit by bit, under his steady gaze.

"You were screaming," Jake says. He observes, his eyes focusing on the crescent-shaped scars etched into my palms. My hands curl, hiding the evidence, and I drop them to my lap.

Ash's voice is a quiet ripple in the tense air. "What were you dreaming about?"

The question rips through me, and I suck in a sharp breath. My pulse pounds in my ears, drowning out the words I want to say. "Rose," Ash says again, softer this time, his hand reaching for mine. His fingers brush against my clenched fist, prying it open with patience. His presence coaxes me out of my silence. "What was your dream about?"

I shake my head, tears slipping free again. The words sit heavy on my tongue, too jagged to speak. The weight of their gaze, their concern, threatens to shatter the fragile walls I've built around my pain. I can't tell them—not yet. Not while the pieces of me are still barely holding together.

Tears blur my vision as I bite down on my bottom lip, the sting a fleeting relief. A shudder rolls through me, my composure fracturing as I grasp Ash's hand. "I-It was the first time..." My voice falters, cracking on the words. "The first time he hurt me."

"Here." Jake's words break through the fog. I look up as he steps forward, holding out a small object. Moonlight glints off the polished surface—it's a knife. A cold rush of panic spreads through me as our eyes meet.

"I can see the anger in you, Red. You've been holding it in for too long. I want you to let it out."

My fingers curl around the handle, the cool metal firm in my grip. Turning it, I catch the faint outline of words engraved along the blade.

For the one I couldn't save.

I blink, my brows furrowing as I trace the words with my thumb. My voice comes out as a fragile whisper. "Who couldn't you save?"

His lips purse, his throat bobbing. "You."

The word slams into me, shattering the fragile composure I barely held together. My fingers clamp around the knife, the handle biting into my palm as I stare at him, pulse pounding in my ears. Before I can force out a response, Killian moves. He steps forward, then lowers himself into a crouch. His hands find the edge of the bed, fingers splayed against the fabric as his sharp gaze locks onto mine.

"You've been carrying this pain alone, Rosie," he murmurs. "You don't have to anymore. Let it out. All of it. We're here." His forehead rests against mine briefly, the touch grounding me, before stepping back.

I raise the knife, staring at its blade. Anger, grief, and a deep, aching betrayal boil over, impossible to contain. A scream rips from me, raw and guttural, and I plunge the knife into the mattress. Feathers burst into the air as I tear through the fabric, sobs wracking through my body with every violent slash.

The springs creak and groan as I rip through layer after layer, the physical act of destruction feeding a release I hadn't known I needed. The sharp edge bites into my hands, but the sting is drowned out by the storm of emotions pouring from me. My screams echo in the small room, filled with years of anger, pain, and helplessness, finally unleashed.

A pillow appears in front of me, handed silently by Ash, and I tear into it with the same ferocity, sending feathers flying like a chaotic snowstorm. Each stab feels like shedding a piece of the weight I've carried for so long, a piece of the girl I used to be—the girl I'll never be again.

I stumble off the ruined bed when the last shred of fabric falls away. Drawers slam open, and clothes fly into the air as I hurl them onto the pile of destruction. The blade flashes again and again, cutting through memories and symbols of a life that no longer fits me.

Finally, my body gives out. The knife slips from my fingers, landing with a soft thud among the wreckage. My knees hit the floor, and I sob into my hands. Strong arms wrap around me, pulling me close, holding me together as I fall apart. Killian's voice rumbles. "We've got you, Rosie. We've got you."

And in the ashes of my anger, I feel it—a tiny spark of clarity. A trace of what I thought I'd lost forever—the faint glow of hope.

CHAPTER 24

Killian

The room is in chaos. Feathers hang suspended in the air, slowly drifting down like ash after an explosion. Rose—no, Ember—is in the center of it all. The mattress is torn open, the guts of it spilling onto the floor, shreds of fabric and foam scattered like debris. Her movements are wild, frantic, as if ripping apart her small space could erase the pain etched into her soul.

Her screams pierce the air, stabbing through me, each one sharper than the last. My hands curl into fists at my sides, nails biting into my palms as I fight the urge to pull her into my arms. Jake's jaw is tight, his hands flexing as if he's ready to catch her if she falls, and Ash stands frozen, his eyes locked on her with a mixture of horror and helplessness.

When she finally collapses, the knife clatters from her grip, spinning across the floor until it comes to rest at my feet. Her chest heaves as it curls in on itself like she's trying to become as small as possible. The sobs wrack through her and I can't take it anymore.

I step forward, the weight of my boots crunching against the remnants of her destroyed life. I wrap her in my arms, aching to hold all her broken pieces together. "We've got you, Rosie. We've got you." Her tears glisten in the moonlight filtering through the window.

"Patrick broke me," she whispers, voice trembling like glass on the edge of breaking, her gaze distant, as if the pain has pulled her somewhere far beyond the room. "I pretended he didn't, but he did. I couldn't protect myself, I couldn't protect those other girls... I couldn't protect Atlas." Her words crumble into a wail.

Jake moves first. "Who's Atlas, Rose?" he asks like he's afraid the wrong tone will shatter her further.

"Stop calling me that!" she screams, launching herself at him. Jake catches her easily, his arms wrapping around her waist as she pounds her fists against his torso. Her hits are weak, drained of the ferocity from earlier.

"I'm not that girl anymore!" she cries, splintering under her anguish. Her fists fall away, body crumpling as sobs overtake her. "She died ten years ago when you left me to suffer."

Jake holds her, his hands rubbing soothing circles on her back. "What do you want us to call you?"

She hesitates, letting her head drop against him. "I... I don't know, I don't know who I am anymore." Her words are a knife in my gut, twisting as she slumps in his arms, her sobs finally quieting.

Jake shifts her carefully, cradling her. Her fingers clutch at his shirt, and for a moment, she looks so small, so vulnerable. I glance at Ash, his face as pale as mine, before I turn away, the pressure unbearable.

"Fuck!" I hiss, slamming my fist into the nearest wall. Pain shoots up my arm as the drywall gives way, but it's nothing compared to the rage boiling inside me. "Fuck!" I roar, shaking out my hand as blood drips from my knuckles. I don't care. None of it matters—not my hand, not the wall, nothing but her.

"She mentioned an Atlas... did we find anything about Patrick taking anyone by that name?" Jake asks, shifting her, brushing a strand of hair from her face as she sleeps. Ash sits on the edge of the coffee table, his hands clasped in front of him.

"We don't know who all was with her?" Ash murmurs, barely above a whisper. "Saint John never kept men around that we could find. So, who is Atlas?"

I swallow hard, my jaw clenching. "I don't know," I admit, my voice raw. My fists curl at my sides as I watch Jake cradle her trembling frame while she shatters in his arms. She looks so damn small like this, her body curled into him, her fingers clutching his shirt. But I know better. I know what haunts her when she closes her eyes.

My teeth grind as I yank on my jacket, the leather groaning beneath my grip. A deep pressure builds in my chest, tight and unforgiving. I need to move, need to act before I lose my goddamn mind.

"But I'm going to find out," I growl, my voice cutting through the heavy silence. I don't look back as I slam the door behind me.

The engine snarls to life, the vibration thrumming through my bones as I tear down the street. Streetlights streak past in a blur, but my mind is locked on one thing. One name.

Patrick Saint John.

The bastard who stole her. Who broke her.

I grip the handlebars so tight my knuckles burn, fury rolling through me in waves.

He's the only one who deserves my rage. And tonight, I'll make sure he feels every goddamn bit of it.

THE BIKE ENGINE rumbles to a halt as I pull up in front of the old brick building, its weathered exterior catching the faint glow of streetlights. I yank my helmet off, letting it dangle from the handlebars where it swings lazily, tapping metal against metal. The familiar sight of the place wraps around me like an invisible vice, squeezing tighter with each passing second. I tilt my head back, taking in the tall windows and wrought-iron balconies. This building was supposed to be our haven, a home for all of us, *including her.*

We'd bought it together after chasing a lead that felt like it might finally bring us to her. It hadn't. But we'd still hoped, still prepared. There's a room upstairs, untouched, waiting for her to claim it as her own. She's never even seen it, and yet I can't bring myself to give up on the idea that one day she will. One day.

The door swings open as I push inside, slamming against the wall like it always does, echoing through the spacious entryway. The smell of spices and garlic wafts out to greet me.

"Hey, man," Jaxson calls from the kitchen. "Didn't expect you back so soon. I thought you were chasing down that lead I sent."

I kick off my boots, sending them skidding across the floor, and shrug out of my jacket. "Yeah, we checked it out," I say, striding into the kitchen. Jaxson stands by the stove, stirring a pot that smells incredible. "Just needed to handle a few things before heading back out." I keep my tone even, though everything inside me is churning. I can't bring myself to say the words yet—not to him or anyone beyond the three of us.

Jaxson raises a brow, glancing over his shoulder. "What's cooking?" I ask, grinning as I lean over to peek into the pot. The rich aroma of spicy sausage and kale soup makes my stomach growl, though I don't know if I could stomach food right now.

"Your favorite," he mutters, rolling his eyes. "Grab a bowl. I needed a 2AM snack."

I hesitate for a moment, then decide I'd risk it for the creamy goodness in the pot. I grab a clean bowl from the dishwasher and hold it like a kid waiting for candy. Jaxson smirks, filling it with a generous ladleful of soup.

I settle at the counter, the food chasing away the chill of the night air. "Damn, you should make this more often," I say around a mouthful, savoring the heat and spice.

He chuckles, shaking his head. "You have the table manners of a feral animal."

We eat silently for a moment, broken only by spoons clinking against bowls. Eventually, Jaxson speaks up. "How's the search going?"

My spoon freezes halfway to my mouth. I set the bowl down, staring into the swirling broth. My hands clench the edge of the counter. "She's alive."

The words tumble out, and I don't dare look at him.

"What?" Jaxson's bowl clatters onto the counter as he turns to face me fully.

"She's alive." My voice cracks, and I grind my teeth, forcing myself to meet his gaze. "She's been alive this whole time."

His face twists. "How long?"

"Five years." The words taste like ash on my tongue. My fingers dig into the counter, the unforgiving edge digging into my palms until a dull ache radiates up my arms. “Five years, Jax." My voice is raw, strained, barely holding back the fury boiling beneath my skin. "She’s been under his control for five fucking years." The weight of it sinks into the silence between us.

Jaxson exhales sharply, running a hand through his hair as he paces the small kitchen. “Jesus Christ. Is she—no, she can’t be okay. Fuck.” He stops, staring at me with wide eyes. “What now? What are you going to do?”

I shake my head, the anger simmering beneath the surface threatening to boil over. “She’s not okay, Jax. She’s a fucking mess, and I don’t know how to fix it. She had a nightmare about what happened—she didn’t want to tell us, but Ash insisted. You know how persistent he can be, and she just exploded.”

Jaxson’s brow furrows. “Exploded?”

“She destroyed her entire room,” I snap, my voice rising. “Ripped apart the mattress, shredded her clothes, even tore through the damn drywall. She has nothing left but the shirt Ash gave her.”

Jaxson blinks, his lips twitching like he’s about to smirk. “Wait, Ash’s shirt?”

“That’s what you’re focusing on?” I growl, spinning to glare at him. His grin is infuriatingly smug, and I shake my head in exasperation. “You’re an asshole.”

He chuckles, leaning back against the counter. “Just saying, it’s interesting. Ash doesn’t share. Ever.”

I sigh, running a hand down my face. “You’ll understand when you meet her.”

“Not gonna happen,” Jaxson says with a shrug. “Deal’s a deal. I help you find her; I get to crash here rent-free. You found her, so I’m out.”

I stare at him, the weight of everything weighing down on me. “You don’t have to move out,” I mutter.

Jaxson shakes his head, already heading for the door. “That was the deal, Kill. I’ll finish the soup and pack my shit. Good luck.”

And just like that, he’s gone, leaving me alone in the kitchen with a bowl of cold soup.

CHAPTER 25

Ember Rose

A sense of dread knots my stomach as memories from last night flood back—feathers flying, screams echoing in my mind. Embarrassment washes over me, and I groan, burying my face deeper into the pillow. Tensing, I realize my pillow isn't just a pillow when it chuckles and shakes beneath me.

"You okay, Red?" Jake's rough voice sends a shiver down my spine, the tingling rippling through my back. I feign sleep, keeping my eyes firmly shut, hoping he won't push further. But Jake isn't one to let things slide. His fingers gently grip my chin, lifting my face toward his. "Open your eyes, Ro-Ember." I shake my head, squeezing them shut.

"Why?" His breath is warm against my cheek, and the sensation makes a faint shudder flitter through my body, goosebumps rising along my skin. The air rushes out of my lungs as his feather-soft lips brush against my cheek. "I-I'm mortified about last night," I squeak, despite leaning into him for comfort.

"You have nothing to be embarrassed about, Ember." I open my eyes, wincing as the sunlight blinds me through the open windows. Damn, I'll need to replace those curtains eventually. It's not like I sleep much as it is, but it would be nice to have the option.

Oh god... I destroyed everything I owned. A whimper slips from my lips as tears well up in my eyes. "I just ruined everything I have, and now I'm left with nothing."

Jake pulls me closer, his lips ghosting against my forehead. I inhale deeply, his scent grounding me. "You'll never have to worry about having nothing; we'd never let you go without." I give him a sad smile, letting my head rest against him, seeking comfort in his presence.

"I'll take you out today, Sweetheart," Ash chimes in, leaning casually against the back of the couch, adjusting his baby blue shirt. It must have magically appeared since I'm still wearing his white button-down from yesterday. "We'll get you some new clothes and a bed set."

"No, you can't buy everything for me!" I protest, trying to sit up, but my hand slams into Jake's stomach. He lets out a loud grunt, and I squeak in surprise, tumbling off his lap with a thud. Pain radiates through me as I hit the floor.

"I'm sorry... I'm so sorry!" I scramble backward across the floor, only to bump into a solid form. When I turn, Killian's sleepy eyes meet mine.

"Good morning, Princess," he mumbles, just as I open my mouth to speak. But before I can, his arm shoots out from under the blanket, wrapping around my waist and pulling me beneath it. After a bit of awkward repositioning, I end up facing Killian, his arm snug around me.

"Let's go back to sleep," he whines, burying his face in my neck. A soft smile pulls at my lips as I run my fingers through his hair. He exhales against my skin, his lips brushing a lazy kiss beneath my jaw.

"Let her up, Kill," Jake growls, yanking the covers away. The cool air hits my skin, and I peek at Jake over Killian's head. Killian groans, nuzzling closer.

"No, let us stay in bed."

"We need to take her shopping. Don't you want to help pick out some clothes for her?"

Killian goes still, his muscles drawing tight. For a second, I think he's going to ignore the suggestion. But then his lips twitch, a slow grin forming. "Shopping?" he asks, low and hesitant, like he's testing the word.

"Yeah... don't you want to pick clothes for her? Things she'll feel good in?"

He doesn't answer right away. His brows pinch slightly, as if weighing the idea. Then it clicks—his posture eases, his eyes brighten, and a wide, boyish grin spreads across his face. It's a look that pulls me straight back to simpler days.

"Shopping," he repeats, the word filled with growing enthusiasm. His smile widens, and his whole demeanor shifts. He lets out a low, rumbling laugh that builds until it echoes through the room. Before I can react, he grabs me by the cheeks and blows a ridiculous, wet raspberry against my face, the sound loud and obnoxious.

"Killian!" I sputter, laughing despite myself as I wipe at my cheek.

"Let's go!" he shouts, springing to his feet with surprising energy, like a kid hyped up on too much sugar. His excitement is contagious, and I smile as he bounces on the balls of his feet, clapping his hands once for good measure.

"Calm down," I tease, but there's no stopping him now. Killian is a freight train of enthusiasm, and I know there's no way he will let this idea go.

A startled squeal escapes my lips as I try to follow Killian's burst of energy, but the heavy blanket tangled around my legs has other plans. I wrestle with it, twisting and tugging, only to lose my balance entirely. My arms flail instinctively, bracing for the inevitable impact of the floor.

It doesn't come.

Instead, a strong arm snakes around my waist, pulling me against a chest. My body goes still, a ripple of surprise running through me as I lift my head and meet Ash's piercing blue eyes. His expression remains calm, but a depth behind it sends warmth rushing to my cheeks.

I catch my bottom lip between my teeth nervously, and his eyes drop to the movement, flaring before meeting mine again. His fingers tighten around my waist, a fleeting anchor before they ease away, leaving behind the ghost of his touch. The moment passes as he shifts, steadying me, his hold light, guiding me back to solid ground."Are you alright, Sweetheart?" His tone is smooth, but there's an edge of concern.

"Y-yeah," I stammer, feeling my cheeks burn as I steady myself.

He steps back just enough to give me space, but his touch makes my skin tingle. His lips quirk into a slight smirk, and he tilts his head, surveying me with an almost playful expression. "Let's find something a bit more appropriate for you to wear today," he suggests, his tone teasing. His gaze flickers toward my oversized shirt—Ash's—and his smirk deepens.

"Hopefully," he adds with a wink that flips my stomach, "you didn't shred everything."

I laugh softly, my embarrassment fading under his presence. "I think I left a few things intact," I reply, trying to match his teasing tone. But his eyes leave me feeling breathless, like the air between us has grown thinner.

"Food first," Jake snaps. My body tenses instinctively, but his grip on my hands is so gentle, it coaxes me to follow him into the kitchen. He leads me to the counter, his movements confident. Before I can protest, his strong hands grip my waist, effortlessly lifting me onto the surface. The sudden closeness burns my cheeks, his fingers digging into my hips. I choke back a noise, forcing myself to push the memories clawing at the edges of my mind away.

"But—" I start, glancing back at Ash, who's still surveying the wreckage of my bedroom with a look of resigned frustration.

"No buts, Red," Jake mutters, cutting me off with a glance. He grabs a plate from Killian, piled high with eggs, bacon, and toast. The aroma is intoxicating, and my stomach betrays me with a loud growl, cramping with hunger. Jake's smirk deepens as he steps back toward me, the plate balanced expertly in one hand as he stands between my legs, closer than necessary.

"Eat," he orders, holding the plate in front of me like a challenge.

I stare at the mound of food, my eyes wide. "I can't eat all of this," I squeak, glancing up at him, half-expecting him to relent.

"Then share," he counters, words low, a smirk tugging at his lips. It's maddening, and yet I can't look away. His eyes—deep, achingly familiar—stir guilt and a far more dangerous feeling, rising quietly inside me like a wave I can't stop.

I hesitate, fingers closing around a strip of bacon, its crisp edges rough against my fingertips. The grease slicks my grip, the familiar scent curling into the air. "Fine," I murmur, lifting it toward him. His lips part, and I place the bacon gently into his mouth. He chews slowly, and I catch myself watching the flex of his jaw, transfixed by the movement.

"Eat, Red," he whispers, his tone thick with emotion I can't quite name. The sound sends a shiver down my spine.

I take a bite, the salty crunch exploding on my tongue. My eyes flutter closed as an involuntary moan escapes. "Oh my god," I groan, savoring the flavor. "That's so good." Reaching for another piece, I barely have time to react before it's snatched from my hand.

"Hey!" I squeak, watching as Killian quickly devours the bacon, a smug grin on his face as he chews.

Killian doesn't flinch under my pout. Instead, he tosses the now-empty pan onto the stove, spinning back toward me with exaggerated drama. "Don't cry, Princess," he says, his cocky tone melting when he notices the way my lip quivers. Panic flashes across his face. He scrambles to the stove, piling more bacon onto my plate with the urgency of a man trying to appease a goddess. "Here! Ten more slices!" he exclaims, holding the plate out like a peace offering.

I sigh happily, grabbing another piece and stuffing it into my mouth. Wiggling on the counter, I savor the flavor, the sheer joy of the taste bubbling out of me in little hums of contentment.

"Whatcha doing, Sweetheart?" Ash asks, laced with amusement as he leans casually against the doorframe, watching the scene unfold. My mouth is too full to answer, so I tilt my head at him, raising a brow in challenge.

"Are you... dancing, Princess?" Killian teases, playful, his eyes fixed on me.

Heat creeps up my neck, and I quickly swallow, clearing my throat. "It's just good, okay?" I mumble, unable to meet their teasing gazes.

"She has a happy food dance," Jake chuckles, stepping closer, his presence filling the small space between us. "How fucking cute is that?"

Before I can form a snappy retort, his thighs intwining with mine, the unexpected contact pulls a sharp inhale from my lips, my fingers gripping the counter's edge for support.

"Are you going to share any more?" Jake asks, low and teasing as his eyes flick to the last piece of bacon on the plate. His closeness and the intensity of his stare make it nearly impossible to focus, but I hesitate, unwilling to give up the last bite.

"Shit, man. Don't make her cry; I can't handle it if she cries," Killian groans, tinged with panic as he glances between me and Jake. His pleading gaze locks onto mine. "I'll make you more, Princess. Just don't cry, okay?"

I hesitate, clutching the piece of bacon in my hand. A tightness settles deep inside me, but I swallow my selfish thoughts and offer it to Jake. His lips part as he takes a small bite, his fingers brushing mine for a moment. The light touch sends a ripple through me.

"Thanks, Red, but I think I'm full," Jake murmurs, his smile soft but shadowed with emotion I can't quite place. He shifts backward, giving me space, and I manage a faint smile before popping the rest of the bacon into my mouth. The salty flavor pulls my focus, and I wiggle in my seat, savoring it.

"There she goes again," Killian laughs, his grin broad as he scoops the plate from my lap. "Food clearly makes you happy, Princess."

"Come on, Sweetheart. Let's get you some clothes, shall we?" Ash says, motioning toward me. I pause for a second, then step forward, letting him help me down from the counter, his hold sure and careful.

As my feet touch the ground, the oversized shirt rides up, barely covering the tops of my thighs. Warmth crawls up my neck, but before I can tug it down, Jake moves behind me. I brush against him briefly, and my heart kicks up. His warmth spreads across my skin, and I swallow against the rising tension, the quiet realization sinking in—these men could destroy me all over again, and I might let them.

"Oh!" I blurt, an idea sparking to life. I pull away from Ash and dart past Jake, bare feet padding quickly across the floor. "Wait here!" I call, dropping to my knees and diving under the bed.

"What the hell is she doing now?" Jake mutters, exasperation trailing in his wake. I hear the scuff of his boots approaching.

"I'm getting something," I call back, my words muffled as I wriggle deeper into the shadows. The space closes in around me, and I reach until my palm hits the loose floorboard I've been searching for. Just as I lift it free, the bed dips beside me, and I scream as Killian's broad frame wedges in next to mine.

The bedframe groans under his weight, lifting from the floor. "What are we doing, Killer? Are we hiding? Because you're not exactly blending in here," he teases, his grin evident in his tone.

I bite back a laugh, shaking my head. "No, I stashed an emergency fund under here," I explain, pulling out a small shoebox and cradling it in my hands. "Just in case."

The oversized shirt rises even higher as I shimmy backward, baring far more than I intended. Killian's laughter stops abruptly, and the sudden groans behind me make my stomach drop.

"Everything okay back there?" Killian quips, pushing himself out from under the bed. "Oh, shit."

Frowning, I glance down, and my cheeks burn as I realize the shirt has bunched around my waist. Quickly, I tug it back down, covering myself. "Sorry," I mumble, avoiding their eyes as I sit back on my heels, cradling the shoebox. My stomach churns with embarrassment, but I force myself to focus on the box in my hands.

Lifting the lid, I smile at the neat stack of cash inside. "I can replace everything now!" I announce, my excitement bubbling over.

But Ash's sharp tone cuts through the moment. "You're not using your own money to replace anything," he snaps, stepping forward and snatching the cash from my hands. His blue eyes lock onto mine, his jaw tight with resolve.

"Ash—" I begin, but he cuts me off, placing the money firmly back in the box.

"No." His tone softens, but the determination doesn't waver. "I'm buying you a whole new wardrobe, Sweetheart. I'm going to spoil you and make up for all the lost time." His lips curve into a teasing smirk as his gaze drops briefly. "Do you understand?"

The burning in my cheeks spreads like wildfire, and I duck my head, biting back a shy smile. "We'll see," I mumble, clutching the shoebox, trying to ground myself as Ash's smirk deepens. "You need a new shirt since I ruined yours," I add, my voice barely above a whisper. "And I need to find something to wear from that mess." I gesture toward the scraps of material scattered across my destroyed bed.

He nods toward the nightstand, where a neatly folded pile of clothes sits. "Already taken care of," he says, his tone nonchalant, but the glint in his eyes tells another story.

Curious, I grab the bundle and slip into the bathroom, closing the door with a soft click. A heavy thrum shakes me as I lean against the sink, staring at the unfamiliar fabric in my hands. The clothes don't look like anything I've owned before. Frowning, I let Ash's borrowed shirt fall to the floor, peeling off the rest of my tattered undergarments with slow, hesitant movements.

Holding up a pair of black lace panties, my frown deepens. These definitely aren't mine. The delicate material feels soft between my fingers, and I wonder, *Did Marissa leave these here?* That's the only explanation that makes sense.

Sliding the lace up my legs, I'm surprised at how perfectly they fit, hugging curves I'd forgotten I had. Next, I hold up a pair of ripped jeans, the distressed fabric strategically torn at the thighs, knees, and calves. Slipping one leg in, followed by the other, I wiggle them over my hips, the snug fit shaping me in ways that make me feel... human again. I stare at the jeans in the mirror for a moment before picking up the bralette. Black lace, matching the panties. No way this is going to fit. But when I slip it on, the soft fabric molds to me like it was made just for my body.

I smile—just a little—and reach for the tank top, a simple razorback design that feels like home. Finally, I shrug on the emerald green leather jacket. Its buttery softness glides over my arms as I glance at myself in the full-length mirror. I pause, taking in the sight. For the first time in forever, I don't feel like the broken shell of a girl. The clothes fit so perfectly, it's almost eerie, and my grin widens as I knot the shirt at my waist.

Did someone plan this? I wonder, the thought making my chest flutter.

"Ready, Princess?" Killian's voice comes through the door, his tone laced with impatience. "I want to help pick out your clothes, too."

A laugh escapes me as I swing the door open, stepping into the room. "Ash," I begin, tilting my head. "Did you... Did you buy these for me?" My fingers fidget with the knotted shirt, waiting for a response.

But none of them answer. Instead, they stare. All three of them—Ash, Jake, and Killian—are frozen, their gazes fixed on me. The silence stretches, and the heavy silence clogs my airway. "What?" I whisper, tugging at the shirt's hem. Embarrassment creeps in, fast and suffocating. *They must think I look ridiculous.* My stomach twists, and tears prick at the corners of my eyes.

"Hey, Sweetheart," Ash's voice breaks through the haze, soft and concerned. He steps closer, his blue eyes locked on mine. "What just happened?" His brows furrow as he watches the tears spill over. I shake my head, trying to turn away, but his hands are quick, gently gripping my shoulders as he tucks me close to him.

"No, no, no," he murmurs, a calming balm against my frayed nerves. "Tell me."

"I must look silly in these clothes," I sob, the words tumbling out despite my attempts to hold them back. Ash's arms circling me, his embrace anchoring me in the moment.

"No," he says firmly, tipping my chin up so I have no choice but to meet his gaze. "You look gorgeous, Sweetheart. We were just... caught off guard. You're breathtaking." His lips brush against my hair, and the sincerity makes the words get lost on the edge of my tongue.

"Really?" My voice comes out uneven as I search his eyes, desperate for truth.

"Really," he says, his expression shifting—an unusual crack in his usual composure. His hand grips my arm for a fleeting moment before releasing me, the loss of contact colder than expected. He steps back, shadows moving across his features, and whatever he's holding back is unreadable.

"Alright," he says, tone lighter now. "Let's get out of here. I think Killian's ready to raid an entire mall." A grin tugs at his mouth, the easy humor lifting the weight in the room just enough to breathe again.

Still, unease churns in my chest as I face what I've been trying to ignore: no matter how much time has passed, no matter how fractured I feel, my feelings for these men—for Ash, for all of them—remain as strong as ever.

CHAPTER 26

Ember Rose

I haven't stepped outside my apartment since I went to the house with Maissa, and the musty, humid air feels suffocating. People are bustling down the street, bumping into and jostling me around. A hand rests against my lower back, guiding me through the crowd as I scan the vehicles lining the street, trying to figure out which one might belong to the guys. But in New York, everyone has a black SUV, so there's no surprise when the lights on a sleek black Chevy Tahoe flash.

"Over here, Princess," Killian practically skips toward the vehicle with tinted windows, definitely darker than is legal. The sight of his happiness sends butterflies fluttering around again. *God, will you guys settle down? You act like we haven't seen an attractive man in our lives.* But, I guess these guys are different; I've only ever gotten butterflies around them.

A smile tugs at my lips as I watch Killian crawl across Jake's lap to get into the back seat, apparently too impatient to walk around. "Up front, Sweetheart," Ash whispers in my ear, opening the door for me. He grabs my waist and lifts me into the vehicle. Funny how, just five years ago, I would have been mortified, convinced I was too heavy for that. But now, all I want to do is shrink away from the reality that I'm nothing more than skin and bones—a hollow, fragile skeleton of the girl I used to be.

Drawing on that little voice inside me that insists on shoving problems aside for another day, I inhale deeply. The intoxicating blend of tobacco, vanilla, and something earthy swirls around me—so good, I want to bottle it up and turn it into a candle. I sink deeper into the leather seat, my body relaxing as Ash leans over, clicking my seatbelt into place.

The crisp air bites my skin, but I barely register it. Ash slides into the driver's seat, his fingers finding mine with practiced ease. He rests our joined hands on his thigh, the contact calming—familiar.

And just like that, those damn butterflies are back, fluttering wildly.

Ash's thumb sweeps across the top of my hand, tingling, skittering down my spine, goosebumps rising across my arms—you never realize how starved you can be for touch until someone willingly gives it to you. Logically, I know I shouldn't enjoy their touch as much as I do. When the doctors took my vitals, I'd flinched away, and even with Marissa, touch had been difficult, to say the least. But with them, it's different. Their touch doesn't scare me; it feels like home. It always felt like home.

Fingers dance across the space between my neck and shoulder, and I know whose hands they are by that simple touch. Grabby...the name for Killian that had been a joke, a way to tell them apart, but oh, how the name fits him perfectly.

A faint smile tugs at my lips, the memory flashing like sunlight on chrome—fast cars blurring past, quick kisses in stolen moments, laughter sharp and quick like sparks. But all of it fades in the shadow of the truck, where the world had shrunk to a single point: my son, a speck on the horizon of everything that mattered.

"Getting lost in your head again, Red?" Jake's voice cuts through, low and teasing, with just enough of a lilt to drag me back.

Heat blooms across my cheeks. I glance down, caught, and try to pull my hand free from Ash's. His fingers are like iron shackles. There's no hesitation, no slack—just an unrelenting hold that anchors me in place.

I dart a look at him, my pulse stuttering under the weight of his silent defiance. His striking blue eyes meet mine for a moment—steady and far too telling.

Ash's fingers twitch around mine, the subtle motion drawing my attention back to him. He shakes his head, a silent answer to a question I didn't dare voice. My lips purse, but a soft hum escapes me as I approach the window.

The city blurs past in streaks of steel and glass, the light catching on the edges of buildings like fleeting memories. I breathe in slowly, the cool air brushing against my skin doing little to steady the thrum of my pulse or the ache deep inside me.

A storm brews, memories surging like relentless waves—harsh words slicing through the air, the crack of fists meeting skin, and pain so sharp it steals breath. My nails dig into the seat, the faint texture beneath my fingers anchoring me to the present. I force the memories back, burying them where they can't reach me. Not now. Not when Atlas is out there, waiting for me.

My gaze lifts, catching brown eyes in the rearview mirror—deep and familiar. His face softens under my stare, the sharp edges smoothing as a small smile tugs at the corner of his lips.

The words lodge in my throat, aching to break free. *Tell him,* they whisper. *Tell him the truth.* That out there, somewhere, is a boy he doesn't know—a boy who looks like him—*our son.*

I bite down on the urge, swallowing the words before they escape. They'd only complicate things, disrupt this fragile moment, and leave it in pieces. Would they believe me? Would they understand? Guilt and longing pull at me from within, rising fast, but I force it down. Not now.

He smiles as if sensing the weight of what I'm holding back. I look away first, my gaze returning to the city streaking past the window.

"Everything okay?"

"Fine," I say, the word brittle on my tongue. I force a shrug, hoping it's enough to convince him. "Just tired from last night."

He doesn't press, but the following silence feels heavier, charged with all the things left unsaid. Ash's ever-seeing eyes flick from me to the rear view mirror before returning to the road, his hands gripping the wheel, knuckles brushing against the worn leather.

I rest my forehead against the glass, the cold biting into my skin like a grounding touch. The tension winds inside me, like a rope pulling taut with no sign of loosening. *The police will find him,* I tell myself again. They have the report. They have the details. They'll find him... won't they?

My stomach churns with doubt, and the hollow ache of helplessness creeps in. I mentally tack it onto the growing list that stretches endlessly ahead of me: "Check with the local police for an update."

Replace the clothes I shredded in a fit of rage. Replace the bedroom furniture I destroyed because I couldn't control my emotions like a sane person. *Find Atlas.*

At least I'm working on one thing on the list, though it feels like I'm chasing shadows.

A heavy sigh escapes me as I close my eyes, the rhythm of the city flashing past lulling me into momentary quiet. But it doesn't last. The pressure builds, a silent scream trapped under guilt and frustration.

I glance down at my hands, resting limp in my lap. My knuckles are still raw, faint bruises reminding me how far I've unraveled. I ball them into fists, the familiar sting reassuring in its own way.

Focus—one thing at a time. Keep moving forward.

The truck shifts as we slow for a light, and I catch Ash's gaze flickering toward me again, just briefly, before returning to the road. He doesn't say anything, doesn't need to. The quiet tension hanging between us speaks louder than words.

Just don't fall apart now, I tell myself, forcing my spine straighter. There's no room for weakness. Not when Atlas is out there, waiting for me to bring him home.

"Okay, what stores are we hitting? What does our girl need?" I blink rapidly, attempting to steady myself while Killian's words ring in my head. My nails dig into my palms, fists clenched enough that the slight sting grounds me. *Our girl...* In all my wildest teenage dreams, I never expected they would call me theirs. But I'm not that little girl anymore with silly hopes and dreams. They're only here because they feel guilty, trying to ease their conscience for reporting me to CPS. My insides burn with the realization that I am back to where I was twenty-five years ago. Wrapped up in their magnetic pull, completely enthralled by them. Nothing more.

"Princess?" Killian's breath tickles my cheek, and I whip my head around to look at him. My nose brushes against his, and I pull back, but there's nowhere to escape.

"W-what?" My voice squeaks, and I struggle to clear my throat from the growing emotions.

"Where would you like to go?"

"Oh... um... I'm not sure. I used to shop at thrift stores or second-hand consignment shops. They were cheaper and easier for me to afford. But I haven't gone shopping in a while, so what are the 'it' places to shop right now?"

Ash's hand squeezes, the leather crunching under the grip, drawing my attention to him. His knuckles are so white, I worry the steering wheel will snap under the pressure. His brows draw together, a crease forming between them as his mouth settles into a tight line. The corners of his lips dip, an unspoken weight etched into the curve of his expression.

His jaw clenches enough to make the muscle there flicker, the tension rolling off him in quiet waves. Even without a word, the concern is apparent, written in the downward tilt of his lips and the shadows that darken his gaze. "Call BethAnn, tell her to shut down the shop, and that we'll be there in five. We can do all our shopping there; it'll be less crowded."

Killian rests his chin on my shoulder, the hairs pricking me through my thin top, the light from his phone shines in the corner of my eye. Air brushes across my cheek as he hums softly, inhaling deeply, turning his face into my neck.

I choke down a giggle when his breath tickles my neck. "Hey, it's me. Yeah, we'll be there in less than five. Close it down and send everyone home." I turn my head, my cheek brushing against his. The stubble on his cheek scrapes my skin, making me want to rub against him like a cat and purr loudly. "Thanks, babe. That's why you're our favorite," he says, and I hear the distinct sound of a woman laughing over the phone.

A rock forms in my gut, and a bitter taste creeps into my mouth, making it difficult to swallow. Jealousy flares up, turning the pesky butterflies into wasps stinging my insides. I try to push the jealousy away, knowing I have no claim to any of the three men in the car, but my heart still clings to a future that doesn't— won't exist.

The buildings inch past us, their facades blurring together in the suffocating crawl of New York traffic. One...two...three... I count them under my breath, each number a small tether to the present, pulling me away from the spiraling darkness that gnaws at my thoughts. Eight... nine...ten... The rhythm steadies me, even as my chest feels like it's caving in.

I force my mind to shift, to focus on Atlas—his laugh, his small hands gripping mine. But the memory turns cold, hollowing out as reality takes hold. I'm going to need help. Mentally, I put a big fat star next to the police. My thoughts drift to Marissa, who offered her assistance, but the guys... they might have access to things. They got to Patrick, can they get to Atlas too?

But would they help? Would Atlas be as big of a priority to them as he is for me? How long before they decide I'm a waste of their time and resources? Fear slithers into my gut. I want to pout at the taste of betrayal before it even happens.

Finding Patrick's house was the easy part. It was the only place I could think to start. So, now what do I do?

My imagination claws at me, conjuring shadows of what they could be doing to him—hurting him, breaking him in ways I can't stop. Tears sting my eyes, blurring the city outside the window. My hands curl into fists against my lap. I can't protect him, not like this.

"Ember?"

The soft sound of my name pulls me from the edge. I blink and turn, finding Ash's blue eyes fixed on me, his brow creased in worry.

"Hmm?" The sound barely escapes my lips as I sit straighter under the weight of his gaze.

"You okay?" His eyes searching mine.

"Sorry... just in my head." I try to smile, but I know it comes off as more of a grimace. "Are we here?" I look out the window and see a massive storefront with designer names and brands listed in the window. "No, no, no, no. I'm not getting designer clothes!"

I gasp as the car door flies open, a firm grip dragging me out. My front collides with a solid chest before my back meets the cold metal of the car. My fingers brush against tense muscles before my gaze locks onto Jake's. "Let us spoil you, Red," he murmurs, his lips grazing my cheek. Those butterflies dance, but I shove them aside. The girl I used to be might have loved these men without question, but she doesn't exist anymore.

I let out an exaggerated sigh, rolling my eyes as the word slips past my lips. "Fine."

Jake's lips curve upward, revealing one of his rare smiles. A quiet sound escapes as my lungs momentarily forget their purpose. It's the first time I've truly seen him since we were reunited, and the sight sends a jolt straight through me.

That smile—it's Atlas's smile. The resemblance cuts through me, sharp and sudden, pulling a flood of memories in its wake. My hand moves without permission, fingers brushing against the curve of his lips as if I could hold on to the moment.

Jake inhales sharply, the sound soft but startling in the quiet. His lips part against my fingertips, and his expression is unreadable when my gaze lifts to his. Heat blooms in my cheeks, and I jerk my hand away like I'd been burned.

Before I can say anything, movement catches my attention. A woman bursts from the shop, her heels clicking against the pavement as she rushes forward. She throws her arms around Killian's neck, clinging to him like she's been waiting for this moment forever.

I flinch, nearly stumbling back, as she smacks her lips against his with an eager familiarity that makes my stomach twist.

"I thought you'd never show up!" The woman pulls back just enough to look up at him.

My mind struggles to process the scene, a heavy pressure building inside me. I can't look away, can't unsee her lips on his—on Killian. *My* Killian.

No, I remind myself bitterly, *not mine.* But that knowledge does nothing to stop the jealous ache clawing its way up.

Killian laughs, the sound strained and uneven, as he gently pushes her back a step. "Hi, BethAnn," he mutters, his eyes flicking to mine for a fleeting moment before darting away.

Her pout is instant, exaggerated as she threads her fingers through the back of his hair with practiced ease. "You never come to visit me anymore," she complains, her tone syrupy and sweet in a way that sets my teeth on edge.

A slow-burning fire unfurls within me, licking at my senses with every passing second. My fists curl at my sides, nails digging into skin as jealousy threads through me—hot, relentless, and venomous. It feels vile, like a wildfire ripping through my veins, swallowing every trace of reason. The urge to seize whatever's within reach—to wipe that smug smile off her face—simmers just beneath the surface, dangerously close to breaking free.

"I've... um... been busy," Killian stammers, his gaze darting back to me, staying long enough to make my stomach twist. I tug at a strand of hair, twisting it around my fingers, my thoughts spinning in a thousand directions.

I should leave, I tell myself, the words circling like a mantra. I should go home. Focus on Atlas. They're a distraction, pulling me further from what matters. But the weight of their presence, the way Killian looks at me—it holds me here, tethered against my better judgment.

"Who's this?" Her eyes narrow, hostility flashing like a blade, as she grabs at Killian.

Before I can muster a response, Ash steps forward, his broad frame blocking her from view. "That is none of your concern, BethAnn," he growls, edged with warning. "I thought we made it clear to send everyone home. Or did you think we didn't mean you, too?"

The shift in her demeanor is instant. She flinches, her confidence faltering as her eyes dart nervously toward Killian. I bite my lip to stifle the laugh bubbling up, the sight of her discomfort oddly satisfying. *Jesus, what's wrong with me?*

"I—I thought..." she stammers, shrinking back as though she can hide behind Killian.

But Killian shrugs her hand off like it's nothing more than an annoyance. The move is casual, dismissive, and when he steps toward me, my instinct is to retreat, to hide behind Jake and Ash's protective wall.

Killian doesn't allow it. His hands grip my waist as he pulls me closer. His touch halts the tremor, even as he turns me to face her.

"No, you assumed," he says, calm but final. "Go home. We don't need you here."

His grip guides me toward the shop, his presence radiating control. I glance back over my shoulder, catching a glimpse of BethAnn standing alone on the street. Her lips purse, and her eyes burn with hatred as she watches us disappear inside.

CHAPTER 27

Ember Rose

Needles shoot through the bottoms of my feet with each step I take through the giant department store, the boys have dragged me through every section this place has, and now we're here… in the intimates department.

Killian shows no shame as he holds up a pair of black lace boy shorts, his bottom lip jutting out, "But, Princess, don't you think you'd look amazing in these?"

I let out a long sigh, folding my arms as Killian pulls another pair of underwear from the rack. "I don't need any more underwear, Kill."

He barely acknowledges me, choosing to scan the display, grabbing handfuls of every color as if he's stocking up for a lifetime.

Across the aisle, Jake and Ash exchange a look, their eyes narrowing in unison. Jake's jaw clicks, and Ash crosses his arms, both glaring at Killian as if willing him to stop.

Killian, of course, doesn't notice—or doesn't care. He tosses another set into the growing pile in his hand, his lips twitching with amusement.

"Killian, I don't need that many pairs of underwear!" I protest, my voice rising as I watch him gleefully grab yet another lacey pair from the rack.

He shoots me a wicked grin, his green eyes sparkling with mischief. He tosses the latest selection into Ash's overflowing arms without missing a beat.

"We need *all* the new underwear!" he declares, his excitement bubbling over like a kid let loose in a candy store.

Ash groans, shifting the mountain of lace in his arms and glaring at Killian. "Do you even hear yourself right now?"

Killian ignores him, plucking a fiery red pair from the display and holding it up with mock seriousness. "This one's a must."

My palm smacks into my forehead, torn between laughing and throwing the nearest hanger at him.

Jake sinks to his knees in front of me, his hands sliding over my calves with practiced ease. His thumbs massage the sore muscles, and a low groan slips from my lips before I can stop it. The tension melts under his touch, and I close my eyes briefly, savoring the relief.

"Just let him do what he wants," Jake says casually, his fingers working magic as he glances up at me. "You know there's no point in telling him no."

Across the store, Killian continues his one-man mission, casually adding matching bras to the pile of panties in Ash's arms.

I glance at the growing mountain of lace and silk, pouting. "Between the three of you, I'm going to need a bigger closet," I mutter, shaking my head.

Killian smirks without even looking back. "You're welcome," he says, tossing another bra on top with a flick of his wrist.

I roll my eyes but can't summon the energy to argue. "None of you ever take no for an answer," I grumble, leaning back as Jake's thumb digs into a particularly sore spot. My body quivers, my shoulders sagging. "Jesus, your hands are incredible."

Jake chuckles, the sound low as if taking pride in every bit of tension he's unraveling.

Ash gestures toward the growing pile. "Killian, she doesn't need a matching thong for every set. This is getting ridiculous."

I barely hear him. My gaze flicks to the mountain of clothes that now includes eight pairs of jeans in varying shades, three leather jackets

—black, gray, and red—and fifteen shirts in every imaginable style. Add to that nearly thirty pairs of underwear and fifteen bras, each carefully selected by Killian.

It's too much.

Heavy pressure settles over me, squeezing like a vice. My stomach churns, and panic claws its way up. My breathing turns shallow and uneven, and my pulse roars in my ears. The edges of my vision blur, darkening with each frantic beat of my heart.

"Shit, what did I do?" Killian's voice cuts through the chaos, sharp with worry.

Callused hands cup my cheeks, tilting my face upward with a gentleness that steadies me just enough to focus. His green eyes lock onto mine, his gaze intense but soothing.

"Breathe, baby, breathe," he murmurs, low and calming. He takes a breath, his body rising and falling with it, as if willing me to follow.

I try to match him, dragging air into my lungs in shaky bursts. The pressure begins to ease, the haze lifting just enough for me to see him.

"There we go, Princess," he says softly, his lips curving into a reassuring smile. "Deep breaths. That's it."

As my breathing steadies, shame burns hot inside me. I quickly look away, my vision blurring with unshed tears. Anger and embarrassment churn together, twisting like a storm inside me. *Of course,* I had to break down in front of them. After last night, they probably think I'm completely unhinged.

A shift beside me pulls my attention, and Jake releases my leg to crouch at my side. He takes my hand, his thumb brushing slow, soothing circles over my knuckles.

"What happened?" he whispers, so gently it feels like it could shatter me.

I shake my head, unable to meet his eyes.

"O-overwhelmed," I stammer as I fight to keep my composure. "Just overwhelmed. Everything's hitting me all at once, and it's... it's hard to process. It just feels like too much."

Tears prick my eyes, and I curse myself for the weakness. I blink rapidly, but one escapes, slipping down my cheek. Killian catches it with his fingers. He stares at it, his brows knitting together as if the tiny drop holds all the answers he's searching for.

"We can stop," he whispers, soft but firm as he leans in, resting his forehead against mine. "Do you want us to stop?"

I sniffle, struggling to keep the dam from breaking. "I appreciate everything you're trying to do," I say, the words rushing out before I can stop them, "but all these clothes won't even fit in my closet or my apartment—"

Killian shushes me with a finger to my lips, silencing my rambling. His eyes hold mine, anchoring me in the moment.

"Why don't you take a moment in the dressing room and try some stuff?" Ash's voice cuts through the quiet, his tone even and reassuring. He steps closer, extending a hand.

Killian steps back, giving me space, and I slip my hand into Ash's, his grip solid but gentle. He leads me to the dressing room, pulling aside the curtain to reveal a space overflowing with the clothes they'd chosen.

"Take as much time as you need," Ash says like he's trying to soothe a skittish animal. "We'll only get what you absolutely want."

I nod, offering him a tight smile. "Thank you."

Sliding the curtain closed behind me, I let out a slow breath. Relief washes over me as I note the absence of a door—just fabric separating me from the rest of the world. The thought of being confined in a closed space still sends a shiver down my spine.

I carefully peel off my clothes, folding them into a neat pile in the corner. My gaze drifts to the mirror, and I hesitate. It's been so long since I've let myself look, and now, faced with the truth, I wish I hadn't.

Scars stretch across my skin, jagged and unforgiving, each one a cruel reminder. Bruises bloom in shades of yellow and purple, fading but still painfully vivid. My hair hangs limp and tangled, lifeless against my shoulders.

I swallow hard and turn away, grabbing a pair of distressed denim from the pile. The material feels rough in my hands, but I cling to the distraction, focusing on the task instead of the reflection.

The sudden sound of the curtain being yanked open causes me to whirl around.

BethAnn stands in the doorway, her expression sharp and full of disdain.

"W-what are you doing here?" I manage, hating how my voice wavers, betraying the strength I desperately want to project. "H-how did you get in here? Where are the guys?"

BethAnn smirks, her lips curling as she cocks a hip, her eyes raking over me with thinly veiled disdain. The urge to shield myself rises, but I force my hands to stay at my sides. I won't give her the satisfaction. Still, her gaze sears through me, laying me bare.

"God, what do they see in you?" she sneers, stepping closer. Her tone dripping with venom, each word a dagger aimed straight at my chest.

Instinctively, I step back, my pulse pounding in my ears until my shoulders hit the dressing room wall.

She's barely a foot away now, her presence suffocating.

"Are you a whore?"

My stomach drops. "E-excuse me?"

She laughs cruelly, the sound sharp and cutting. "Well, you're not too bright, so you must be a whore to catch their attention."

The insult lands like a slap, and I wince, my face burning as I turn away from her.

"You are, aren't you? Ha, I knew it!" Her mocking laughter echoes in the small space, and my vision blurs as tears threaten to spill.

"I-I'm not," I manage, the words barely audible.

Before I can react, her hand cracks across my cheek, the sting radiates through my skin, and I gasp, clutching my face as she grabs a fistful of my hair.

She yanks me forward, her breath bitter against my skin as her eyes blaze with fury. "Don't lie to me, you slut!" she screams, piercing the small space.

Another slap sends me sprawling to the floor, my cheek throbbing as the taste of copper blooms in my mouth. Panic rises as I open my mouth to scream, but she's gone.

"What did you fucking call her?"

Jake's voice rumbles through the air, low and dangerous. My eyes dart up to see him gripping BethAnn's neck, his fingers digging into her skin as he drags her backward out of the dressing room. Her feet kick wildly, barely brushing the ground, and her hands claw at his arms in desperation.

"J-Jake," she gasps, her bloodshot eyes rolling back.

"Jake, stop!" I rasp, forcing myself upright on shaky legs.

He doesn't let go. His gaze burns with unrelenting fury, his jaw clenched tight as he slams her against the wall: her body sags, terror gripping me.

I step forward, placing a hand on his back. His muscles are rigid under my touch. "Jakey," I whisper, my voice shaking as I press my cheek against him. "If you kill her, I'll lose you. I can't lose you. We just found each other."

His grip falters, the tension in his hands loosening as BethAnn gasps, drawing in deep, ragged breaths.

"Fuck," he growls, shoving her aside. She collapses to the floor, coughing and clutching her neck as tears stream down her face.

Jake spins, his arms wrapping around me in a crushing embrace. He lifts me off the ground like I weigh nothing, carrying me out of the dressing room.

He sits heavily in one of the small waiting chairs, pulling me onto his lap until I'm straddling him. His face buries into my neck, his breath hot against my skin.

"Shit, Baby, I'm sorry, Killian and I went to go look at something for you, Ash was supposed to be here," he murmurs as his hands grip my waist. "I thought you were safe, if I thought—I'm so fucking sorry."

I rest my hands on his shoulders, my fingers brushing against the tension knotted there. "I'm okay," I whisper, though my voice wavers. "We're okay."

"What the fuck happened?" Killian growls as he storms into the dressing room, his green eyes scanning the chaos. His gaze lands on BethAnn, crumpled in the corner, clutching at her neck.

She scrambles to her feet, tears streaming down her face as she rushes toward him. "Killian!" she cries, throwing herself into his arms. "He tried to kill me!"

Killian's body stiffens, his jaw ticking as he looks at her. His tone is icy, a low growl laced with fury. "Jake wouldn't attack someone without cause. So what did you do?"

BethAnn freezes, her eyes darting to mine for a split second before her mask of innocence slips. "Nothing! I did nothing!" she shrieks.

Too late. Killian's hands come up, pushing her back with enough force to send her crashing to the floor.

Ash bursts through the door next, his brows furrowing as he takes in the chaos. Jake holds me close, his lips brushing against my temple as his growl rumbles against my skin. "And where the fuck were you?"

Ash's gaze sharpens, but he doesn't immediately respond. "I had to take a call for a moment," he says as he looks between BethAnn and Jake. "What happened?"

BethAnn points a shaky finger at Jake. "He tried to kill me, Ash! He—"

I roll my eyes, the sound of her whining grating on my nerves. It's funny how I only feel strong when they're with me. Without them, I'm weak, useless—a shadow of who I want to be.

Jake doesn't bother acknowledging her. Instead, he gently shifts me into Killian's arms. I cling to him instinctively, burying my face in his shoulder, my tears dampening his shirt.

"She attacked Red," Jake growls with rage held on a leash. "You left her alone, and she got attacked!"

Jake's fist colliding with flesh reverberates through the room, a sickening thud that sends my stomach plummeting. My head snaps up just in time to see Ash stumbling back, blood streaking from his nose. Jake doesn't stop, advancing on him like a storm. Another punch lands, sending Ash staggering.

"Jake!" I scream, thrashing in Killian's arms. "Killian, let me go! Make him stop!" My voice cracks with desperation as I claw at his hands, trying to break free.

Killian's arms go rigid around me. "Jake, stop!" I cry out, sobs pouring from me as each impact digs deeper into a place I can't protect. "Please, stop. Please!"

Ash slumps against the wall, breath ragged, his frame rising and falling with effort. "Let her go, Killian," he says, the strain in his words barely held back.

Killian lets me go without protest, and I collapse to the floor, crawling toward Ash. He catches me, arms strong despite the blood smeared across his face. "It's okay, Sweetheart," he whispers near my ear. "I'm sorry. I shouldn't have left you."

I pull away just far enough to stare down at Jake, lungs working fast and uneven. "Never again," I snap, the words low, trembling with emotion. "If you ever touch either of them, you'll regret it. I-I mean it!"

Jake goes still, eyes widening. Then, to my surprise, the edge of his mouth tugs into a faint, almost defiant smirk. He stays silent, shifting his focus to BethAnn, still curled up on the floor, her tear-streaked face pale and hollow.

"Well then," Jake mutters, icy and composed. "What to do with you?"

BethAnn trembles, mascara running in jagged streaks, giving her the look of a raccoon frozen in panic. "Jake, plea—"

"Leave," he snaps, cutting her off. "Get out of the state. Move. Disappear. Don't come back." His expression hardens. "Because if I see you again, I won't hold back from killing you."

She nods frantically as she scrambles to her feet. Without another word, she darts out of the room, her heels clicking wildly against the floor until the sound fades.

Silence settles over the room, thick and suffocating.

"So?" I mutter, breaking it hesitantly.

Three pairs of eyes turn toward me in unison. My cheeks heat as I remember I'm standing there in nothing but my bra and underwear. I cross my arms, but it does little to help.

"Move in with us," Killian says abruptly, his tone firm.

My eyes widen as I stare at him. "W-what?" I squeak.

"Killian..." Jake growls, the sound low and warning. The vibration sends an involuntary shiver down my spine.

Killian ignores him, stepping closer until he's right in front of me. He cups my face in his hands, his green eyes searching mine. "Move in with us," he repeats, softer this time but just as insistent.

"I can't," I stammer, shaking my head as a frantic beat drums in my ears.

"Why not?" he grumbles, his brows drawing together in frustration.

I swallow hard, my words spilling out as tears streak down my cheeks. "Because one day, you'll all realize I'm not worth all this trouble. If I move in with you, you'll feel stuck with me, and you wouldn't be able to kick me out because you'd feel guilty. I can't handle it if you ended up hating me for saying yes."

Killian lets go. His expression shifts, but the silence between us speaks the loudest—full of hurt, disbelief, and a sense of betrayal I don't know how to fix. He doesn't yell, doesn't ask questions. He just looks at me like he doesn't recognize what's in front of him. Then he turns and walks out, leaving the weight of everything unsaid behind him.

"Let's take you home," Ash says gently, pulling me away from the space where Killian had been.

I let him guide me to the pile of clothes, a tightness gripping me as I glance toward the door. "He just needs to blow off some steam," Ash says softly, offering me a small smile. "Let's get you dressed, and I'll take you back to your apartment."

Outside, Jake loads the bags of clothes into the truck. But there's no sign of Killian.

I hesitate, a band of tension pulling tight inside me as I turn to Ash. "I didn't mean to upset him," I murmur, my voice cracking.

Ash sighs, resting a hand on my shoulder. "I know, Sweetheart," he says quietly. "But sometimes Killian takes things harder than he should. He'll come around. He always does."

He helps me into the vehicle, his hand on mine for a moment longer than necessary. When he doesn't move to close the door, I glance up, my brows furrowing in confusion.

His icy eyes meet mine, a storm of emotions swirling in their depths —raw and unreadable. The intensity causes a shiver to wrack my body, and I grip the edge of the seat to steady myself.

He leans in before I can say anything, his breath ghosting against my skin. His lips sweep my cheek, sending butterflies through me, knocking the air from my lungs.

"And you're right," he murmurs, each word laced with a quiet intensity. "We'd never kick you out. It's not about guilt or wanting you gone." He pauses, his breath ghosting over my skin. "We'd never let you leave again. You'd own us completely."

Before I can respond, he pulls back and slams the door shut, the sound vibrating the space around me.

The words weigh on me as we pull up to my building. I stare out the window, my thoughts tangled and frayed, his promise looping endlessly in my head.

You'd own us completely.

It feels like a vow, unshakable and terrifyingly final.

CHAPTER 28

Ember Rose

"Good job keeping it together, Em," I grumble, yanking all the bedding off my bed in frustration. My hands shake as I wrestle with the tangled sheets, fighting the urge to give the whole mess a big "fuck you" and set it on fire.

It had taken *ages* to put away all the things the guys bought me, and just when I thought I could finally collapse onto my demolished mattress for some reprieve, a sharp-ass spring jabbed me in the back like some cruel joke.

I toss the wadded sheets onto the floor and run my hands through my hair, pulling at the tangled strands. My gaze falls on the pile of clothes I didn't have room for.

I need a new bed, I think bitterly. Grabbing my mental list and scrawling the words in bold, angry letters in my head. *And, for fuck's sake, Atlas.*

The thought hits, and I move—no time to dwell. I shove my feet into the nearest shoes. The apartment feels smaller with every breath, the air too thin, the walls too close. I need to get out. Now. Before my thoughts catch up. Before I fall apart.

The police station.

The idea hits me like a lightning bolt, jolting me into motion. I grab my coat from the back of the chair, my movements quick and jerky as I throw it on. They haven't called—not that they would since they work for Krystal. But again, I don't have a phone except for the one from Krystal, so how can they?

The walk to the station is brisk, the cold air biting my skin. My air puffs in front of me in short bursts. The looming building comes into view, its fluorescent lights buzzing as I push through the heavy glass doors.

The smell of stale coffee and disinfectant hits me—officers mill about, their voices a low hum. My palms are slick as I approach the front desk, where a tired-looking officer glances at me.

"Can I help you?" she asks, her tone neutral but polite.

"I'm here to check on the status of my son's case," I say, trying to keep the waver out of my voice.

Her brows furrow as she reaches for her keyboard. "Name?"

"Atlas," I whisper, the word catching. "Atlas Abbott."

She types, her eyes scanning the screen. I feel my stomach churn as the seconds stretch, each click of her keyboard like a drumbeat in my ears.

"We don't have any new updates yet," she says, her tone softening. "But I can check with the detective handling the case. Can you wait a moment?"

I nod, my fingers gripping the counter's edge until they ache.

As she disappears down the hallway, I try to steady my thoughts, forcing myself to focus. I came here hoping for clarity, for a next step that might feel like progress. Instead, doubt creeps in, whispering that none of this will ever be enough. The helplessness isn't loud but constant—a quiet weight I can't reason away, no matter how badly I want to believe I'm moving forward.

When she returns, her expression is apologetic. "Detective Reed says they're following a few leads, but that you should reach out to Krystal if you have any questions."

"Um, I would rather talk to a different detective, i-if possible, could I do that?"

"Of course." Her eyebrow rises, watching me. "Let me see who I can talk to."

"Thank you." *There have been no updates, no progress, nothing. Maybe*

Marissa was right... the police should be able to help me. Krystal can't control them all.

Then my phone vibrates.

Strike One, Ember.

Do you even care about your son?

My eyes squeeze shut. *Fuck!*

I suggest you leave now before anything happens to poor Atlas.

My eyes dance around the space, looking for any sign that someone could see my distress, but all the officers are scattered. A few huddled together, looking at computer screens.

Now, Ember.

I'm leaving.

The police station doors swing shut behind me as I rush from the space.

Good.

Don't make another mistake, Ember.

Your son is the one who will pay the price.

The walk back to my apartment feels longer than it should, the weight of disappointment dragging at my every step. My mental list buzzes in the back of my mind: *Bed. Atlas. Safe Place.* Each item closes in on me more than the last, a constant reminder of how far I am from fixing anything.

As I approach my door, the faint glow of the hallway light reveals a figure slumped against the wall. A jolt runs through me when I recognize him—Killian.

He's sitting on the ground, his legs stretched out in front of him and his head tipped back against my door. His eyes are closed, but his posture isn't relaxed; tension radiates from him even in stillness. A half-empty bottle of whiskey rests loosely in his hand.

"Killian?" I call softly, my voice breaking the quiet hum of the hallway.

His eyes flutter open, and they're glassy and unfocused for a moment. But when they lock onto mine, he sits up straighter, his expression unreadable as he lets out a low sigh.

"What are you doing here?" I ask, taking a hesitant step closer.

He chuckles dryly, though it's devoid of humor. "Guess I'm waiting for you," he mutters, hoarse. He looks down at the bottle, shaking his head before setting it beside him.

"Killian..." I trail off, unsure of what to say. Seeing him like this, so vulnerable, hurts me.

"You wouldn't answer the door," he says, cutting me off before I can speak. "And after what happened earlier, I couldn't just... leave it like that."

I swallow hard, my fingers gripping the strap of my bag as I shift uncomfortably. "I wasn't ignoring you. I just... I had to go to the station, check on—" I catch myself, the words snagging like barbed wire. Panic creeps in like a shadow, wrapping around me, but I force myself to inhale deeply, to steady my voice. "Check on something."

Killian's brows draw together, his expression flickering between concern and suspicion. "The station?" he repeats, his tone laced with curiosity. "What's going on, Princess?"

The nickname softens the moment, but doesn't ease the weight on my lungs. I can feel the truth bubbling under the surface, clawing to get out.

"It's nothing," I say quickly, trying to sound casual. "Just... tying up some loose ends."

His green eyes search mine, and I can tell he doesn't buy it. Sighing, he rakes a hand through his disheveled hair.

"Em, you've got to let me in," he says, so gentle it nearly breaks me. "Whatever it is, you don't have to carry it alone."

My stomach churns, the weight of his words wrapping around me like a vice. *You don't know the half of it,* I think bitterly, but I force a small smile, even if it feels hollow.

"I'm fine," I manage to say, though my voice wavers. "Really."

Killian studies me for a long moment, his lips pursed as if holding back whatever he wants to say. Finally, he steps aside, gesturing toward my door. "Fine," he mutters. "But this isn't over."

I nod, brushing past him as I unlock the door and step inside. The familiar scent of my apartment greets me. I glance back at Killian, who leans against the doorframe, watching me like he's afraid I'll disappear if he looks away.

"I should go," he says, though he doesn't move.

"Killian..." I start, my voice faltering. I want to tell him to let it all spill out. About Atlas, about everything I've kept locked away. But the words stick, tangled in fear. Krystal is watching me, and I can't afford to slip up again.

"Yeah?" he prompts, his tone softening as he looks at me with a mix of patience and concern.

I open my mouth, but nothing comes out. The silence stretches, heavy and unbearable. Finally, I shake my head. "Never mind," I say quietly, the words heavy in the thick silence. "Thanks for checking on me. Do you... do you want to come in?"

His lips pinch into a thin line, and he shakes his head. "No," he says. He glances down, pulling a small black box from his jacket and pushing it toward me.

I frown, looking between him and the box. "What's this?"

"Before you say anything," he begins, his tone firm but edged with hesitation, "I want you to have this. I need to know where you are at all times."

His words hang as I take the box, my hands brushing his briefly. The box feels heavier than it should as I flip open the lid. Nestled inside is a sleek, matte black iPhone, its surface smooth and reflective under the dim light.

"Killian, this is... this is too much," I murmur, pulling the phone from the packaging. The screen lights up in my hand.

An old photo fills the display—four kids, faces streaked with mud, grinning ear to ear. The memory rushes back like a flood: the park after a rainstorm, a makeshift slide turning into a full-on mud fest. A kind woman had stopped to capture the moment, her laughter mingling with ours as she snapped the picture. It had been on my nightstand when we were kids. I'd left it behind when I left.

I stare at the screen. The image fades to black, and the tears I've held back spill over, hot and unrelenting.

Killian shifts on his feet. "Did I mess up again?"

I look up to see his hand on the door handle, his shoulders slumping as he turns away.

He pauses, glancing back over his shoulder. "Please keep it," he says, his eyes meeting mine. "It has a tracker that will help me find you if anything ever happens."

The weight of his words strikes me like a punch to the stomach, and panic washes through me as he heads toward the door.

"W-where are you going?" I reach out, grabbing his arm before he can leave. His skin's hot under my fingertips, sending a shock through my system.

He stops, his eyes widening, but he doesn't pull away.

"Don't leave," The words spill out, desperate. "Please."

His gaze softens, the tension in his shoulders easing as he studies me. I know how I must sound—needy, clinging—but I can't bring myself to care. The apartment felt full and alive, with all of them here. Now, it feels cold, empty, suffocating.

Killian's hand covers mine, his grip firm but gentle. "Okay," he says after a long moment. "I won't go anywhere."

"Why did you think I'd want you to leave?"

Killian exhales, his shoulders rising and falling as he leans forward. Without a word, he slips his arms around my waist and lifts me. A surprised squeak escapes my lips, his steps echo in the space, and he collapses into the soft cushions of the couch, and before I know it, I'm straddling his lap. His hands grip my hips like he's afraid I'll pull away.

He buries his face into my shoulder, air fans against my skin as he inhales deeply. His chest deflates against mine when he exhales, the sound more like a shudder than a sigh. Unbidden, a shiver runs through me, and I instinctively run my fingers through the hair at the nape of his neck, my thumb grazing the edge of his ear.

The tension in his body softens under my touch, but I can feel the weight he's carrying. My mind pulls me back to when he'd hold me in the quiet. Back then, he'd sneak into my room after a night of drinking, the scent of cheap perfume clinging to him. He'd collapse beside me, broken in ways Jake and Ash couldn't fix, murmuring apologies.

"I'm a screw-up," he'd say, over and over. I'd try to argue, but he'd bury his face in my neck and refuse to listen.

Now, he tilts his head, his lips brushing against the hollow of my collarbone as he murmurs, "You'd hate me if you knew the things I've done since you've been gone."

Each word tears at a part of me I've tried to keep hidden. I frown, threading my fingers through his hair and giving a gentle tug, hoping he'll look at me. He doesn't. His head remains bowed, and the heat of his exhale brushes against my skin.

"I shouldn't be here," he continues, his tone barely audible, "but I can't stay away."

I take a shaky breath, my fingers brushing against his jaw. "If you knew everything that happened to me..." My voice breaks, and I force the words out. "Everything I let happen to me, Kill, you'd be disgusted just having your hands on me."

His fingers dig into my hips, the pressure almost painful, but I don't pull away.

"I'm disgusted with myself," I whisper, my voice cracking. "And there are things that happened I can't tell you about. But I hope I can one day."

His head lifts, his lips parting like he wants to say something, but the words don't come. "Ember, I—"

Briiing-bzzz. A sharp chime echoes through the entry with a faint electronic hum, vibrating through the air. *Briiing-bzzz.*

My head snaps toward the door, my pulse racing.

"Are you expecting anyone, Princess?" Killian asks, a wary edge in his tone as his hands remain steady on my hips.

I shake my head, the tension making it hard to breathe.

Killian shifts, lifting me off his lap with surprising ease, considering how empty that bottle was, setting me gently on the couch. His movements are calm, but there's an edge to his posture—a sharpness that sends a chill down my spine.

When he straightens, his hand moves to his back. My stomach drops as he pulls out a gun, the metallic gleam catching the dim light. The soft click of the safety disengaging makes me freeze.

"Killian!" I whisper as fear twists inside me.

He shushes me with a finger to his lips, his green eyes narrowing as he moves toward the door. "Stay there," he growls, low and firm, leaving no room for argument.

I grip the edge of the couch, frozen in place as he peeks through the peephole. His shoulders remain tense, his grip on the gun steady as he unlocks the chain and cracks the door open.

The muted sound of voices filters through the gap, too low for me to make out the conversation. Killian's gun rests against the edge of the door, ready, until the exchange ends. He tucks the weapon into the back of his jeans with a swift motion.

"Hey, Princess," he says, glancing over his shoulder. "Come here."

I approach cautiously, my body tense as I slide up beside him. The door opens wider, revealing a deliveryman holding a clipboard.

"Hello?" My voice wavers.

"Are you Ember Abbott?" the man asks, his tone polite but all business.

"Um, yes?" I glance at Killian, who places a hand on the small of my back.

"Please sign by the red 'X,' and we can start bringing in the furniture," the delivery man says, handing me the clipboard.

I take it with shaky hands, quickly scribbling my name before returning it to him as he leaves. "Excuse me," I call after him. "What furniture?"

He glances down at the invoice in his hand. "Let's see," he says, flipping a page. "Full bedroom set. That includes a bed frame, queen mattress, pillows, dresser, two side tables, sheets, and bedding."

"I... I didn't order that," I squeak.

Killian steps closer, his chest brushing against my back as he pulls me against him. His lips lower to my ear, leaving a trail of heat as he murmurs, "I think we both know who did, Princess. Did you think Ash wouldn't replace your stuff?"

I open my mouth to argue, but he moves me aside just as the delivery crew begins hauling in large boxes.

"Killian," I groan, watching the boxes pile up in my small living room. "I just finished putting away all those clothes—now I'll have to move them again!"

His laughter rumbles behind me as he brushes a kiss on my head.

His lips curl into a mischievous grin. "I'll help you unpack your panties."

My cheeks flush instantly, and I swat at his chest. "You keep your hands out of my underwear drawer, Sir," I warn, trying to sound firm.

The moment the word leaves my mouth, his eyes darken, playful fire flickering in their depths. He tugs me closer, his lips brushing against my cheek.

"You call me 'Sir' again," he growls, "and we're gonna have a whole other issue to deal with."

I falter, the words lost on the edge of my tongue as I look wide-eyed at him. His wicked and knowing smirk deepens as he begins walking me backward toward my room.

"Let's get those drawers emptied, Princess," he murmurs, his tone dripping with mock seriousness. "I don't want anyone's hands in your panties but mine."

I shake my head, exasperated but unable to suppress the flutter. "You're insane, Killian."

THREE HOURS LATER, the delivery guys are *finally* gone, leaving behind an apartment that looks like a department store exploded. Clothes are everywhere. I sigh loudly, glaring at the mess.

Killian, of course, had thought it was a great idea to dump all my drawers on the floor in the name of efficiency. "Quicker," he'd said with a grin as if that made it acceptable. At least he'd had the decency to stash my underwear in the bathroom so the delivery guys wouldn't see it.

Still, I find myself smiling despite the chaos, my thoughts circling back to his teasing.

Killian's footsteps pull me from my thoughts, and I glance up just in time to see him march out of the bathroom, grinning like a kid with a secret.

"What now?" I ask, raising an eyebrow.

He doesn't answer, strides to the bed, and spreads my underwear out in neat, colorful rows. My jaw drops.

"Killian!"

Ignoring me, he pulls out his phone and snaps a picture, his fingers flying across the screen.

"What are you doing?" I demand, crossing my arms and giving him my best glare.

He winks, slipping his phone into his back pocket. "Just exacting a little revenge on the guys," he smirks.

I groan, shaking my head as I go back to folding clothes. "You're impossible."

Behind me, I hear him chuckle. His arms flex around my waist, pulling me close. He kisses my head before speaking.

"Are you hungry, baby?" he asks.

I nod, leaning back despite myself. Every small gesture chips away at the walls I've built, stirring that long-buried crush I've tried so hard to ignore.

Killian is a freefall waiting to happen—too effortless to resist, too lethal in the way his gaze locks onto me, as if I'm the only thing keeping his world from shattering.

And that's what scares me most.

"What are you in the mood for?" he murmurs, nuzzling his face into the curve of my neck.

"Italian?" I say, my voice perking up.

He chuckles softly, the sound vibrating through me as I lean back to catch his amused expression. "We had pizza yesterday, Princess."

"Yeah, I'm aware, but that was pizza," I giggle, tilting my head to meet his gaze, "and I had it the day before too."

He shakes his head at me, the corners of his mouth twitching into a grin. "Then it's Italian."

He kisses my forehead, and the feel of his lips is like a ghost as he gives me space to finish folding.

Thirty minutes later, I've got all the clothes tucked back into their drawers... again. Who wants to fold laundry twice in one day? Gross. Somehow, I've ended up with extra space, even with all the new additions. Having enough room to spare brings a small, hopeful smile to my lips. I'll have enough room for Atlas's things. I picture his tiny shirts folded alongside mine, his laughter filling the empty corners of the apartment.

But, what if I never see him again? The thought is unbearable. I push it down, replacing it with determination. I need to call Marissa to see if she has any ideas on how to proceed. Going out alone isn't an option, but I don't want to pull the guys into this mess yet; they've already done so much for me.

"You're thinking pretty loudly over there, Princess," Killian's voice rumbles behind me, pulling me back. His heat spreads across my back as he steps closer, his presence grounding. "The food's here."

"Already?" I ask, surprised.

"Yep. Let's feed you," he says, his hand brushing against my arm, "then you can curl up in your new bed."

"Okay," I say, a soft smile tugging at my lips as I follow him into the living room.

WE SETTLE on the floor again, the glow of the TV casting soft shadows across the room. The movie plays on, some action flick I barely register, but I know it's another one of Killian's "essentials," just like the furniture. He'd claimed it was non-negotiable, like a TV was the missing piece to my chaotic life.

I sink into his side. It's reckless, this ease—the way it tempts me to believe in things that were never mine to have. My mind wanders, conjuring a life that doesn't exist. A life where I could've had them and Atlas, where we could've been complete, unbroken.

But that's just me being selfish. What makes me so special that the three guys I crushed on years ago—guys who could have *anyone*—would want me? The thought makes me scoff. Even after all these years, they probably still see me as their little foster sister.

Except for that one night.

The memory creeps in, unbidden but sharp. The race, the adrenaline, and how Jake looked at me like I wasn't just some kid tagging along. For one night, I'd been someone else. What happened between us had been everything to me for five long years—a thread I'd clung to, replaying it over and over again.

But now? Now, we're strangers, orbiting each other with nothing tethering us but fractured memories and unspoken words.

My eyes grow heavy, the room fading in and out as I fight to stay awake.

"Let's get you to bed, Princess," Killian whispers.

Before I can protest, he effortlessly lifts me into his arms. My cheek rests against him, and I inhale the familiar scent of him—diesel and darkness, uniquely Killian. I let myself melt into his embrace, cuddling into his side.

"Keep doing that, Princess," he murmurs, teasing, "and I won't be able to let you sleep in that big new bed alone."

Heat blooms in my cheeks as I realize how much I've nuzzled into him, like a cat seeking warmth. A loud yawn escapes me, and I startle as he lowers me onto the bed, the soft bedding cradling me.

"Sorry," I mumble, burying my face into the feathery pillows. I curl into a ball, the weight of exhaustion pulling at me as a contented sigh slips from my lips.

Darkness tugs at me, but before sleep fully claims me, I feel the lightest brush of his lips on my cheek.

"Good night, Princess," he whispers.

CHAPTER 29

Ember Rose

A gasp escapes me, and I jolt upright. The room is dark, unfamiliar in the hush before dawn. My heart thunders, the nightmare still clinging to me. I rub a hand over my face, willing the fear to fade, but it remains—sharp and breathless.

I can't sit in this silence. Not alone.

Marissa won't answer since it's almost 2 AM, and I don't want to wake her. So I scroll through my contacts, and my finger hesitates over one name.

Ash.

I shouldn't. But I do.

The phone rings once. Twice. Then—

"Em?"

His tone is warm, soft with sleep, almost sweet. "Everything okay?"

I exhale slowly, trying to steady my nerves. "Sorry... I didn't mean to wake you."

"Don't be ridiculous," he says, already more awake. "I'm glad you called. I was thinking about you."

His tone is flirtatious, easy. But it grazes a bruise buried deep. I don't want charm. I want the truth.

"Ash..." I pause, throat tightening. "Can I ask you something kind of serious?"

"Yeah. Of course. What's going on?"

My fingers tighten around the phone. "Have you ever thought about having a kid? Like... not someday. But now."

A pause. Longer than I expected. I can practically hear the shift in his posture—like he's sitting up, trying to read between the lines.

"Now?" he repeats carefully. "Is there something you're trying to say?"

I purse my lips together. "Not exactly. It's just... hypothetical. But maybe not entirely. I don't know."

Another beat of silence. "Okay... Well, if I found out I had a kid out there somewhere, I'd want to know. But that's... a lot to drop on someone in the middle of the night."

"I know," I say quickly. "I'm not saying you do. Or that I do. Just—" I falter, the words catching in my throat. "I've been thinking about what it means to be responsible for someone. To protect someone. Even if it wasn't your plan."

Ash exhales, the sound sharp. "What is this, Em? You're scaring me a little."

"I'm not trying to." I glance into my living room. "It's just... some people don't get the luxury of waiting for the right time."

His tone shifts, edge sharpening. "Are you saying *you* have a kid? Is that what this is?"

My chest tightens. "I'm saying... if I did, would it change things?"

A long silence. Too long.

"Jesus, Ember." His tone becomes clipped. "That's not something you hint at like it's some kind of test."

"It's not a test." My voice cracks. "It's just not something I can say out loud."

"You either do or you don't. There's no middle ground here."

I stare down at the sheets, bile rising. "Forget I said anything."

"No, don't do that. You can't drop something like that and then shut down—"

"I just needed to know how you'd react," I whisper. "That's all."

"Well, now you know," he snaps. "If this is some game, Ember—"

"It's not a game." My voice is barely audible now. "Goodnight, Ash."

"Wait—Ember, don't hang up—"

My thumb trembles as I hit the red button, ending the call. The silence in the room is louder than Ash's rejection, more suffocating than the dream I woke from. My stomach twists so tightly I think I might be sick. I should've never said anything. Stupid. So stupid.

The phone slips from my hand onto the blanket. I can't move. Can't breathe. Every word replays in my head, each one sharper than the last.

His words rattle inside me like a cruel echo, but before I can even begin to fall apart, my phone buzzes against the sheets.

Unknown number.

My pulse stutters.

I don't need to open it to know who it is.

But I do.

Strike Two.

Another buzz.

You're getting reckless, Ember.

That little heart-to-heart just earned you a warning.

I sit up straight, eyes wide, panic surging like ice in my veins. My fingers fumble over the screen.

Please… I didn't say anything. He doesn't know. I was careful.

The reply comes fast.

Careful? You must think I'm stupid. I know exactly what you were doing.

Hinting that you might have a kid?

Tsk.

You're not as clever as you think.

Another message blinks in before I can respond.

You would risk your son's life? For what?

Maybe you need a reminder of how real he is.

A photo appears. Blurry. Dimly lit.

Atlas's silhouette curled up on a thin mattress, a single bare bulb casting harsh shadows across his tiny frame. His stuffed fox is nowhere in sight.

I slap a hand over my mouth to muffle the sob.

No. Please. I wasn't trying to say anything. I was lonely. That's all. I won't do it again. Just don't hurt him.

Three dots appear. Vanish. Reappear.

You won't do it again.

Because next time I won't send a photo.

I'll send a piece of him.

My fingers curl tight around the phone, knuckles white, and I shut my eyes, trying to keep the tears from spilling.

Okay. I understand. I'll follow the rules.

I won't speak. I'll stay in line. Just keep him safe.

There's no reply.

No sick emoji.

Nothing.

Just silence.

And it's somehow worse.

TEN DAYS. Ten suffocating, soul-crushing days. Every lead has been a whisper in the wind, every shadow another dead end. The void where Patrick should be looms with each passing day, a constant weight on me, stealing the wind from my frame. Hope? It's a ghost in the wind now, flickering before vanishing altogether.

Krystal's messages are the worst of it. Each one a jagged knife to my soul. Photos of my son—his face frozen in innocence—arrive daily under the guise of "motivation." They aren't motivating; they are a poison, a slow drip reminding me how little time I have.

Alone. That word has never felt so... quiet. Marissa—my last thread of connection—is spending time with her family for a couple of days after being glued to my side since my return. I told myself I couldn't blame her, not after everything she's done for me since I got back.

But still, the feeling of bitterness simmers. She, of all people, should understand. A decade I'd spent in the same kind of nightmare I was trying to save my son from—how could she turn her back on a kid? How could she not *feel* this?

But maybe it's me. Perhaps it's the weight of what I've carried alone for so long, the walls I've built to protect the little control I've had. I tell myself I don't need her help, that I don't need anyone. I've been reckless, shutting people out, shutting *her* out. And yet, deep down, I know the truth. I can't do this on my own.

The phone in my hand feels heavy as I type out a message to Krystal.

We're getting nowhere. I need help.

Her response is quick.

What kind of help?

My fingers hover over the keys, hesitating for only a second before I can respond.

I know some people who can find him. But I need to talk to them.

The silence that follows stretches. When her reply finally comes, it's ice-cold.

No.

The word slaps me in the face.

Why not?!

They don't need to know why I'm looking. They can think I want to go back for all I care. But we need help, Krystal.

There's another pause. Longer this time. A heavy thrum of anxiety courses through me as memories of their faces swirl in my mind.

Who are they exactly?

Their names taste like ash in my mouth, my fingers refusing to type out the words.

Jake. Asher. Killian. They're the ones who got me out.

Another pause.

Hmm. Interesting. Fine. Talk to them. But they get nothing. No details.

I let out a shaky breath.

Okay.

The words feel like a surrender, but I wasn't sure to whom. I know what to do, but the thought churns my stomach. After all this time, facing them feels like stepping into a den of wolves with no way out. For days, I've avoided their names, their voices, their memories—haunted not by anger, but by the fear of their judgment, their betrayal, or worse, their refusal to help. Now, I have to do the unthinkable. I have to convince them that everything they fought for, everything they sacrificed to free me, was for nothing. That I *want* to go back.

How do you look into the eyes of the men who pulled you from hell, who saw your brokenness and stitched you back together, and tell them you'd rather crawl back into the fire? How do you weave a lie so vile it might shatter the fragile bridge between you? Each imagined word feels heavier than the last, each false plea like a twisting blade.

But none of it matters. I swallow the bile rising in my throat. Atlas's life hangs in the balance, and there's no room for hesitation, no space for self-pity.

I brace myself, knowing that I'll have to reopen old wounds. Knowing I'll have to walk into the storm of their anger, knowing that when this is over, they might never look at me the same way again.

But for Atlas, I'll endure it all. I'll burn every bridge, tear every thread of trust, and betray every bond if it means getting him back because some lies are worth telling. And some wounds are worth reopening.

THAT EVENING, the apartment feels colder and smaller as I sit alone in the dim light of a single lamp. The silence closes in, broken only by the faint hum of the refrigerator. My phone sits heavy in my hand, Jake's name glowing on the screen, taunting me. My thumb hovers over the call button, trembling with hesitation.

I hit the button, each ring echoing in my ears. When Jake finally picks up, it's like a balm I don't deserve. "Hey. It's been a while. Are you okay?"

That simple kindness threatens to undo me. And for a fleeting moment, I want to hang up. But I can't. I force myself to speak, my voice shaking. "Jake... I need your help."

"What's going on?" he asks, his tone sharpening with concern. "Where are you?"

"I—" I squeeze my eyes shut, dragging in a shaky breath. "I need you to help me find someone."

"Okay? Who?"

"It's Patrick."

The name lands like a bomb. Jake's silence is deafening, and his confusion cuts through the phone when he finally speaks. "Patrick? Why the fuck would you ever want to find him?"

The lie rises, bitter and acidic, but I shove it past my lips. "I... I want to go back."

For a moment, all I can hear is his breathing. "What?" The disbelief is like a slap. "Are you *serious*? After everything he did?"

"I know," I whisper. "I know how it sounds, but I can't explain it. I just... I can't stay away."

"*Why*?" His anger is sharp. "What could you possibly have to say to that bastard?"

"I need to make things right," I say, hating how the words taste, hating myself for uttering them. "Can you please just help me? I need to go back, Jake."

"This is insane." He spits the words, his anger barely restrained. "Why would I help you go back to that... monster?"

"Please, Jake." My voice cracks, and I grip the phone, my knuckles whitening. "I can't do this alone. I need your help."

He's been quiet for so long, I wonder if he's hung up. "Jake?" His sigh is weighted like it's being ripped from his chest. "Alright," he says, his tone reluctant, almost resigned. "But I'm telling you right now, Asher and Killian aren't going to like this. Hell, I don't like this."

"I know," I say softly, my relief tinged with guilt. "Thank you."

When the call ends, I lower the phone to my lap, staring at it as if it might turn to ash in my hands. A cold wave of nausea rolls through me, and my hand closes over my mouth as I try to fight the bile rising.

The wheels are turning, and there's no stopping them.

CHAPTER 30

Killian

The phone sits heavy in my hand, the screen glaring up at me, a silent reminder of how long it's been. Ten days. Ten fucking days since I last saw her. Touched her. Breathed her in. Every second stretches an eternity, gnawing at my sanity. I clench the phone, my thumb hovering over the tracking app. The pull to open it is almost as bad as the guilt that follows every time I give in.

She knows about the GPS—I told her when I handed her the phone. She agreed to it. She can't be too pissed. Right? Still, the thought of checking her location makes my stomach churn. What if she's back there? What if she went willingly to that house—the one we risked everything to breach? Would she do that?

Was she taken again? The thought hits like a fist to the gut. My mind tries to reason with the panic, but it's like screaming into a hurricane. Saint John is locked in the basement. He can't have her. I made damn sure of that. But she doesn't know. She has no idea he's rotting down there. So why go back?

Rage boils over before I can stop it. With a snarl, I hurl the phone at the wall, the screen shattering into a web of jagged cracks. The pieces hit the floor in a quiet symphony of destruction. Glass and metal crunching under my boots as I stalk forward.

"What the fuck was that?" Ash strolls into the room, arms crossed, wearing that smug, unaffected expression I want to wipe off his face.

"Why won't she talk to me? To us?"

Ash raises a brow, glancing at the mess of my phone on the ground. "Did you break your phone again?" His tone is so casual, so irritatingly indifferent, that I take a step toward him before I can stop myself.

He sighs, shoving his hands into his pockets. "She needs space," he says, like it explains everything. "We can't force her to come back, Killian. You know that."

The words are a cold slap, and I turn away from him, my gaze landing on the shattered phone. Without it, I can't track her at all times, unless I want to carry my fucking laptop with me. I don't know if she's safe or... panic rises like a tide, crashing against my ribs as I snatch up the broken pieces and shove them into the trash. My voice cracks when I finally speak. "Does she even want anything to do with us anymore?"

Ash sighs again, softer this time, almost like he pities me. "Why don't you take it out on Saint John instead? Before you do something you'll regret?"

His suggestion brings a grim smile to my face. Saint John. Jake and Ash don't get it. They think I should've finished him off already, ended the nightmare once and for all. But they don't understand. Saint John isn't mine to kill. He's *hers*.

When she's ready—if she's ready—he'll be waiting. Until then, I'll keep him alive.

I push past Ash, my shoulder brushing his as I mutter, "Nah, I'm going for a ride. And I need to replace my phone—again."

He barely glances up, shrugging as he drops onto the couch. "Whatever you say." His hand reaches for the book on the table, and within moments, he's gone, lost in another world, like reality doesn't matter.

The way he can detach, shut it all out so cleanly, sometimes makes me want to punch him. Perfect posture, perfect control, constantly fucking perfect. Yet, the subtle set of his jaw, the way his fingers curl around the book, betrays him.

Ash is a fortress, impenetrable to most. Ember had been the exception, her presence chipping away at the walls he's spent a lifetime building. But now she's gone, and the walls have slammed shut again, leaving all of us on the outside—even me.

We used to be brothers. Once. The kind that had each other's backs no matter what. But cracks had formed long before Ember disappeared, and now, those fractures run deep, jagged edges threatening to shatter everything.

A sharp knock at the door jerks me out of my spiral. My head snaps up, and I catch Ash's gaze. His book stills mid-page, and his brow twitches as if he's just as caught off guard. Neither of us moves at first, waiting, listening when the knock comes again.

Ash places his book down, his movements calm, calculated. I reach behind me, fingers wrapping around the grip of the gun tucked into my waistband. My steps are silent as I approach the door. No one knocks here. They either have a key or don't belong.

I unlock it, easing the knob to keep it from making a sound, and crack the door open. Hazel-green eyes meet mine, wide and uncertain, and my breath catches.

"Um... hi?" She shifts nervously, her tongue darting out to wet her lips before she catches her bottom lip between her teeth. A tiny flutter stirs, too light to be anger, too painful to be relief.

I lean against the doorframe, crossing my arms as my gaze sweeps over her. I check for injuries first—old habits die hard—but find none. Instead, I see the changes. Ten days have softened her edges, though dark circles are under her eyes. Black jeans hug her slim legs, accentuating her thighs, the rips on the knees teasing glimpses of pale skin. The sweatshirt and leather jacket hang loose on her frame. *Food, she needs food. I wonder if Jax would make her soup.*

"Who is it?" Jake's voice snaps from behind, his heavy footsteps pounding down the stairs. The trance breaks, and I swing the door wider, stepping back to reveal her.

Jake's disheveled hair and wild beard look rougher compared to her fresh glow. I smirk, catching the flicker of surprise in his eyes as he takes her in.

"Hi," she says. Her lips curve into a shy smile as her gaze flicks between us. "Can I come in?"

I step back, leaving the door open for her.

"Of course," Ash says, coming up behind me.

She brushes past me, and the faint scent of rose and sandalwood envelops me. My breath stumbles, caught between inhaling her presence and grappling with the heat it sparks. My fingers tug at my shirt collar as though the fabric is strangling me, and I can't stop the low sound that escapes me.

"Killian?"

"I'm fine," I manage, though the words scrape my throat like gravel. I take a step back, stumbling into the hallway. "Excuse me."

The bathroom door clicks shut behind me, and I lean heavily against it, the cold wood grounding me for a moment. My palms lay flat against the surface, the handle digging into my spine. My lungs scream as I try to steady my racing heart, to shake the flush that's spread through my body like wildfire.

"Get it together," I growl at my reflection. The man staring back at me is a mess—eyes wild, jaw clenched, beads of sweat tracing paths along his temples.

But her image won't leave me. I love the fullness of her cheeks, the softness returned to her face, and her flushed and inviting lips. I also love how her tongue brushes against her bottom lip, catching it in her teeth like it's second nature.

She isn't yours. The thought tears through me like a whip, sharp and unforgiving. My breathing grows heavier, and each inhale struggles under the weight.

A knock breaks the spiral.

"You good in there?" Jake's voice filters through, muffled but firm.

"Yeah, I'm fine," I bite out, though the strain in my voice betrays me. My fingers fumble for the sink, twisting the faucet on. Cold water spills into my cupped hands, and I splash it over my face, hoping it will dull the heat thrumming under my skin. It doesn't.

"I'll be right out," I snap, louder than I intend.

I brace myself against the counter, closing my eyes.

The door crashes open, ricocheting off the wall as Jake storms in, his face a mask of restrained fury. The heat of his rage hits me a split second before his hand clamps around my neck. I barely register the movement before I'm slammed against the wall, the breath forced from within my bones in a ragged gasp.

"Jake," I choke, my voice rasping, "what the fuck?"

He leans in, his face inches from mine, and I can feel the heat of his breath, "I don't know what you were doing, but get it, the fuck, together."

Shame floods me instantly, spreading like wildfire, burning my skin from the inside out. I look away, but it doesn't matter that I didn't do anything—his anger pierces my defenses.

"Don't even think about touching her," he snarls, his eyes burning with a fury that could incinerate me on the spot. "She ignored us because of Ash's bullshit. I'm not losing one more second with her because *you* can't control yourself."

He shoves me harder into the wall, and I stumble forward, coughing and rubbing at my neck as he stalks away, muttering curses under his breath.

"Shit," I hiss, following him into the living room, my steps heavy with embarrassment. My voice comes out rougher than I intend as I mutter, "And for the record, I didn't do anything."

My gaze snaps to Ember the second I enter, and the chaos inside me quiets, just for a beat. Her hazel-green eyes meet mine before she looks away, her cheeks darkening with a flush. She tugs at the hem of her jacket, the nervous motion drawing my attention to her trembling hands.

"She wanted to talk to all of us," Jake says sharply, his tone clipped as he glances at me, then shifts his focus back to her.

"Oh... um... yes," Ember stammers, shifting on her feet, smoothing the fabric of her jacket as if the motion might steady her. Her eyes dart toward me briefly before returning to Ash and Jake.

"You're probably upset I haven't reached out sooner," she begins, her words tumbling out before she pauses, straightening her shoulders like she's forcing herself to stand taller. "I needed to take care of a few things before I could work on fixing this." She gestures vaguely between us. "What happened that night... when I destroyed my room." Her gaze turns distant as her brow furrows. "It was humiliating, and I still don't know what came over me. But I needed to figure out how to stand on my own first."

Jake moves closer, his steps slow, as he gently cups her cheek. When he finally speaks, it's in a hush that feels almost foreign—gentle, hesitant. "Hey. You don't *ever* need to explain yourself to us."

Her lips tremble, but she smiles faintly, leaning into his touch. "There are things I wish I could've said." Her tone is steadier now, though quiet, as she looks up at Jake. He nods, giving her space, and she steps back.

Taking a deep breath, she slips her hands into the front pocket of her sweatshirt, her shoulders pulling tight as she speaks. "First, I think it's time to reintroduce myself properly," she says. "My name is Ember Rose Abbott. But please, just call me Ember. Rose... Rose is someone from my past, someone I needed to let go of to figure out who I really am."

The confession crushes me, unforgiving, but I stay silent, letting her finish.

"I don't blame you for what happened," she continues before swallowing. "It was wrong of me to put my feelings on you and make things so *uncomfortable*." Her body is tense, her hands gripping the edges of her sweatshirt so tightly her knuckles whiten.

The words hang heavy in the air, and I can't hold back anymore. "How did you make us uncomfortable, Ember?" I ask, stepping forward, my voice softer than I expect. Her shoulders tense at the question, and her gaze drops to the floor. Confusion churns inside me. How could she think this was her fault? We were the ones who pushed her away, not the other way around.

She hesitates. "I k-kissed you... all of you." The words barely make it past her lips. "That's what broke us." Her chest rises sharply as if the admission took all the air from her lungs. "It was wrong, and I'm so sorry for how it ruined things between us. You didn't owe me anything—didn't have to feel what I felt. I know why you called the social worker and reported me for inappropriate behavior." The shame radiating from her is palpable.

"Stop." The word comes out as a growl before I realize it, and I push off the wall, closing the distance between us. Her eyes widen as I tilt her chin with two fingers, forcing her to meet my gaze. Blazing defiance flash in her eyes for a fleeting second, but it's gone before I can grasp it, replaced by that guarded uncertainty she always hides behind.

Doesn't she see how much she means to me? How much I feel for her?

"What the hell are you talking about, Princess?" My voice drops low, steady but edged with disbelief. "What do you mean we reported you?"

Her eyes dart up to mine, round and glassy with unshed tears. "The s-social worker said I make you uncomfortable with my f-feelings," she stammers, cracking on the last syllable.

The room narrows, fire roaring as fury rushes through me. My fist moves before I can stop it, slamming into the wall beside her head. The drywall cracks with a sickening crunch, and her startled gasp cuts through the blaze in my mind.

"Killian, that's enough," Jake demands.

"No!" I snap, spinning to face him. "Whether you admit it or not, she's ours, and I won't lose her again because she thinks we sent her away." My glare dares him to contradict me. "You might be too fucking stubborn to realize what happened, but I know what I want."

"Killian?"

I turn, my fury faltering at the sight of her biting her lip. Without thinking, I reach out and gently free it with my thumb. Her eyes lock on mine, wide and unguarded.

"I would never send you away," I say, my thumb brushing against her cheek, my voice low but steady.

"Killian..."

"No," I interrupt. "Let me finish, okay?"

She nods, her gaze searching mine as I cradle her face.

"I kissed you back," I admit. "Because I'm selfish. I needed to feel you, even though I know it's wrong. I shouldn't have wanted you the way I do—but I do." I take a steadying breath, watching her eyes shimmer with unshed tears, her lips parting as if to speak, but no words come. "And after? It scared me. Scared me enough to push you away." A deep, aching pressure settles in my ribs, but I continue. "But I would never, ever send you away."

A tear slips down her cheek, and I gently wipe it away with my thumb.

"Now that you're here, though," I murmur, my voice soft but full of conviction, "all I want is to kiss you again."

Her eyes gleam, and her lips tremble as she fights back tears. I lean in, my voice dropping to a whisper meant only for her. "You mean more to me than the air I breathe, Princess."

I inch closer, stopping shy of her lips, the space between us electric. She has to choose this—I won't take it from her. Too much has been stolen from her already. The seconds drag on like lifetimes until I feel her kiss—a feather-light touch against my lips.

A low, strangled groan escapes me as I slide my hand to the back of her neck, pulling her closer, desperate to feel her against me. The kiss deepens, and the rest of the world fades away. But then, pain explodes in my scalp as someone yanks me backward by the hair.

Snarling, I whirl around, my fist colliding with Jake's face before I even register what's happening. The force of the punch sends him stumbling, blood trickling from his nose.

A guttural scream tears from me. "What the hell is wrong with you?" I roar, advancing on him with fists clenched so tight they ache.

"What the hell do you think you're doing?" Jake growls, his face twisting with rage as he steps forward, his fists clenching and unclenching like he's barely holding himself back.

"Stop!" Ember's voice cuts through the tension, sharp and desperate. "Please, just stop!" Her breaths come fast as she glares at us, her anger barely masking the pain in her eyes.

"Em," I plead.

She thrusts her hands out. "I'm not doing this again," she cries, grabbing her bag and heading for the door.

"Ember!" Jake yells, turning to follow, but I grab him by the collar, yanking him back. He staggers, cursing, as I sprint after her.

"Stop running!" I hiss as I catch up, wrapping my arms around her waist as she turns. I press her against the wall, my grip firm but gentle, my breathing ragged. Her body tenses, but I cup her face, my thumbs brushing away the tears that streak her cheeks. Her angry, tear-filled eyes meet mine, and my chest constricts.

"Please, don't cry, Princess," I whisper, my forehead resting against hers. Her pain is unbearable, every tear a reminder of how badly I've failed her. I never want to see her cry again.

She shakes her head, "I shouldn't have come. I should've stayed away." Her lashes glisten as she looks at me. "This was a dumb idea. You shouldn't have let me in."

"Why?"

"Because I'm doing the same thing again!" she snaps, shoving me back a step. "I did it once before, and I can't do it again."

I step forward, cornering her against the wall, my body caging hers in. She's cradled against me, her palms flat against my chest. "Don't fight me," I growl, and the tension between us shifts as she stills. "Let me tell you something."

"We're not the same men we were fifteen years ago. We've become your worst nightmare—the monsters that stalk the night and prey on the weak. No, we're not the same, because your disappearance broke us. It tore out our hearts and crushed them. Our jagged edges are sharp because we've been to the pits of hell, and we'd go back a million more times to save you, even if it meant destroying ourselves."

Her lips part as if to speak, but no words come.

"Well, isn't this interesting?" a familiar voice drawls from the doorway, breaking the moment like glass shattering on the floor.

I groan, turning toward the smirking figure leaning casually against the doorframe.

"Welcome home, Jax."

CHAPTER 31

Ember Rose

"What?" The word barely escapes me, high and breathless, as I stare at Killian. I pretend not to notice the figure looming behind him, focusing on the man I already know.

Killian's voice is almost apologetic. "Princess, meet our other roommate, Jaxson." His lips twitch into a ghost of a smile. "He's... well, let's say, if you're ever looking for someone—or something—he's the guy you want."

The name pricks my curiosity. *Jaxson.* The sound of it hangs in the air. My gaze slides past Killian, and the room tilts as my eyes land on him.

My breath catches like I've run headlong into a wall. My pulse races, each beat hammering loud as I drink him in. *This* man. This rugged, impossible man. It feels like the world's gone claustrophobic because of his presence.

His ink-black hair is tousled, a haphazard mess that suggests he either doesn't care or does it on purpose. Dark stubble frames a jaw so sharp it'd cut through steel, and storm eyes boring into me as if they've already uncovered my secrets. A leather jacket clings to his broad shoulders, unzipped just enough to reveal the snug black shirt beneath. The fabric stretches across his chest, and when my eyes flick lower, the way his jeans hang on his hips sparks heat that I'm not ready to face.

"Hi." The word is a whisper, slipping out before I can stop it.

The moment is shattered by a deep, guttural sound—like a growl. My head snaps around to find Jake standing in the doorway, his glare sharp enough to cut through steel.

Ash moves, his arms crossed. His eyes locked on Jaxson, burning with fire. Killian moves in closer, his body taut, shielding me against the wall.

"What is going on?" My voice wavers as I look between them, a growing unease clawing at the edges of my mind.

Jaxson's smirk hints at more. "Seems your boyfriends don't like how you looked at me, Little One." He steps further into the room, his boots heavy on the floor.

"Boyfriends?"

Killian stiffens against me, his fingers digging into my hips like he's anchoring himself.

"Oh, you heard me." Jaxson's grin widens, all teeth and mockery. "Don't care what these idiots say." His eyes flick briefly to Killian, Jake, and Ash, ready to pounce. "It's written all over them."

My heart stumbles over itself as I follow Jaxson's gaze. Jake, glaring from the doorway, fists clenched at his sides. Ash, silent and brooding, his lips curled in a faint sneer. And Killian, who looks ready to tear Jaxson apart with his bare hands.

"They're not my—"

Jaxson cuts me off, his gaze locking onto mine. "Are you sure about that, Little One? Because before I walked in, we were good—practically brothers. Now?" He chuckles, low and menacing. "They look ready to bury me six feet under."

Jaxson tilts his head, watching me with a smirk that feels like a dare. "Like I said," he murmurs, "boyfriends."

"Emmy?" Killian's emerald eyes lock onto mine, holding me in place.

"Don't leave," he murmurs, his lips brushing my cheek. "Tell me you won't leave... that you won't leave me again."

My breath falters as his lips ghost over my skin, each touch sending a jolt through me. My grasp strangles his shirt, holding on like it's the only thing keeping me here.

It's too much. Killian doesn't scare me like others have. Panic rises, clawing its way up my throat as I fight to ignore the threats that could swallow me whole.

My fingers grip his shirt, a soft whimper escaping. He doesn't react —or maybe he does—but stays buried in my neck, his kisses growing deeper, more demanding. His hands slide from my hips, anchoring me to him like he's trying to make me fit.

"Killian," I whisper, barely a breath. I try to push him away, but memories hit hard—flashes of helplessness, fear, and the sting of being powerless crash into me.

A cry tears from me as my knees turn to jelly, and Killian's weight disappears, replaced by the sound of a body colliding with a wall.

"Fuck!" Killian's voice is harsh, and I hear him groan as he slumps back. "What the hell was that for?"

"You were causing her to have a fucking panic attack, asshole," Jaxson growls, rough and furious. My gaze flickers to him, my body instinctively shrinking back as he approaches. He stops short, crouching down to meet my eyes.

"It's okay, Kitten." His tone softens, but the familiar nickname sends a wince rippling through me. My back fuses with the wall, my body begging for escape, for distance.

Jaxson freezes, watching me with a mixture of anger and concern. The scowl darkens his face as he turns to the others. "What the fuck did you do to her?" he snarls like a rabid dog.

My eyes dart around the room, searching for a way out, a place to hide before the cracks in me become visible. I can't let them see me like this—not again. The walls feel like they're closing in, and I fight to hold myself together.

"Ember." Jake's voice calls. His dark eyes meet mine, filled with what looks like longing. "Tell me how to help you."

I shake my head, the words caught inside me. My gaze falls to Killian, who slumps down against the wall, guilt etched into his face. He rakes a hand through his hair before slamming his head back with a thud.

The sound echoes through the room once, twice, three times, each impact vibrating through me, pulling me further from my fragile grip on myself.

"Stop!" My voice cracks as I lunge forward, sliding across the floor. My hands find the back of Killian's head just before it can slam into the wall again. His body stills beneath my touch, his breath hitching as he looks up at me, startled. I lean over him, shielding him with my body, a rapid thrum of urgency coursing through me.

"Please," I whisper. "Please don't hurt yourself... not because of me. Never because of me." Tears blur my vision as I lean into him, forehead to forehead, the ache I've buried for so long ripping free, messy and uncontrollable.

Killian's eyes close slowly, and his exhalation is a soft caress of heat against my lips. "I didn't know," he murmurs, the words heavy with regret. His throat bobs with the words as tears streak his face. "I swear, I didn't know."

The sight of him—this once strong man now crumbling—hits me like a punch to the stomach. My hands slide to his face, cupping his cheeks as his tears soak into my skin.

"You didn't mean to," I whisper, my voice shaky as I lean into him, my body seeking his for comfort. Killian's arms come around me, wrapping me in an embrace that feels like an anchor and a release. For the first time in what feels like forever, I take a deep, steadying breath, letting his familiar scent of diesel and cedar fill my lungs.

"I thought I could fix it myself," I admit, my voice muffled against his shoulder. "I thought I didn't need anyone. That I didn't need *you.* But I do..."

Killian pulls back, his eyes searching mine, the guilt still fresh and laid bare. Over his shoulder, I catch sight of Jake. He stands rigid, his hands clenching and unclenching at his sides, his eyes darting anywhere but to Killian or me.

Killian's fingers brush my cheek, pulling my attention back to him. His gaze is soft but full of conviction. "I want to help you," he says quietly, resolute. "Tell me how."

I don't answer right away. Instead, I lift a hand to smooth the deep lines furrowing his brow, catching a fleeting glimpse of the boy I once knew. A faint smile tugs at my lips, though it doesn't quite reach my eyes.

"I'm damaged, Kill." My voice is barely above a whisper. "What happened to me in that place... it broke something in me, changed me."

His brows knit together, the stubbornness I know so well flashing in his expression. "Then let me help you put it back together."

I glance over at Jaxson, standing near the doorway. Gathering my courage, I rise, but Killian's arms hold tight like he's afraid I'll disappear.

"You want to help me?" I murmur, placing a kiss on his cheek. "Then trust me, Killian. I'm not going anywhere."

Reluctantly, he loosens his hold, and I cross the cold floor to where Jaxson waits. I stop a few feet from him; my shoulders squared, though my hands fidget at my sides. When I look up, his stormy eyes meet mine, dancing with mixed emotions—anger, fear... anguish?

"Will you help me?" My voice wavers, the question barely out before I brace for rejection.

"With what?"

I blink, my hands twisting together. My gaze darts back to the others, watching us with wary eyes, returning to Jaxson. He clears his throat, his intense gaze pinning me in place.

"I-I need you to find someone for me," I stammer, forcing the words out.

Jaxson tilts his head, one brow lifting in silent question. I steady myself, preparing for the storm I'm sure is about to come, "Yes."

I never expected this—a person who could help me locate Patrick, who'd be living under the same roof, the kind of man who could find the impossible. A tightness settles in my body as I push the words out. "I... I can't pay you," I brace myself for the rejection, the possibility that they might turn me away because of what I can't offer. Still, a part of me clings to hope—hope they'll understand and be patient while I hold on to the secrets I can't yet share.

Jaxson's eyes soften. "Anything for you, Little One," he says, the words wrapping around me like a promise.

My gaze flicks over my shoulder, landing on Ash. His steady blue eyes meet mine, and he gives me a slight nod. Jake must not have told him—told any of them. Before I can catch Killian's eye, a low grunt escapes him. His agreement is gruff and wordless, but it's there.

I don't look at Jake. I can't. From here, I can feel the weight of his anger and how his silence cuts sharper than words. He hates this—hates that I'm even asking.

A shaky breath escapes me, and I turn back to Jaxson, forcing myself to stand tall even as my insides twist with anxiety.

Jaxson tilts his head, studying me with those stormy eyes, and I know this next part will change everything. The words sit heavy on my tongue, threatening to choke me, but I push them out.

"I need you to find Patrick Saint John."

The room feels like it freezes, the air heavy with the weight of his name. Jaxson doesn't move, but fury blazes in his expression—a glint of recognition or perhaps just the understanding of how much this means. Behind me, I hear Killian's intake of breath.

No one speaks.

CHAPTER 32

Ember Rose

Jake's boots pound against the floor like he's auditioning for a one-man stampede. His muttering is low, mostly garbled, but I instantly wish I hadn't caught the name "Patrick Saint John" in there.

Before I can ask, he storms out.

And of course, because the universe hates me, he storms right back in. No break. No pause. Just rage and testosterone slamming into the walls like they're to blame.

My jaw clenches so tight it might snap. "Can you sit your ass down already?" I bark as he stalks through the living room again.

Across the room, Jaxson lets out a low snort—mocking, of course. Because *he* never misses a chance to poke the bear.

My head snaps in his direction. "And you," I hiss, stabbing a finger toward him, "stop making everything worse just because you're bored and pretty."

Jax's smirk grows. No remorse. No shame. If anything, he looks proud.

Ash stays rooted in the corner, a perfect statue of smug silence. His only response is the faint quirk of a brow—barely there but enough to make me want to scream.

"And you," I growl, turning on him, "stop acting like you're in a silent film. Say *something* before I lose it."

Nobody moves. Nobody breathes.

The energy is thick. Uncomfortable. They're all standing there like I might break if they blink too hard, and I *hate* it.

Jake's hand snaps out and grabs my chin, tilting my face toward his. His fingers are rough, but the brush of his thumb is... softer. Confusing.

"Watch your damn mouth," he snaps.

"Look who's talking," I mutter, swatting his hand away as I shove myself up from the couch. "All bark, no brain."

He steps back, scowling, while I march toward the kitchen.

"Stupid boys and their stupid pride," I grumble, each word sharper than the last. "Like I'm the problem."

The counter meets my hands with a jolt, and I grip the edge like it might hold me together. I try to breathe—but the air feels wrong. Too still. Too full of unsaid things.

Footsteps behind me.

Clean linen.

Ash.

Of course.

His presence washes over me like a cold front with too many memories tangled inside it. For a second, I almost brace myself.

Then I don't.

"We're sorry, Sweet Girl," he murmurs, his fingers skimming the small of my back like he's touching a wound instead of a woman. Careful. Like I'll shatter if he holds on too long.

He used to be my anchor.

Now, he feels more like a lifeline, and I don't know how to grab it without drowning first.

His hands settle at my waist, turning me to face him. The contact is gentle, but cages me between him and the counter.

His expression is all guilt and effort. "We don't know what to do," he says, frustration creeping in. "Every one of us has a plan. None of us agrees. And we all think we're right."

"Maybe," I snap, "instead of playing war behind closed doors, you could try talking to the one person this affects."

His brow furrows.

I tear my eyes away from him.

"You keep seeing me like I'm that girl you left behind. Like I need to be handled. That girl's dead."

"Don't say that," Killian cuts in, his voice rough and quiet as he moves closer.

"It's the truth," I say, stepping around Ash. He stumbles slightly and collides with Killian behind him.

"She died the first time he locked me in a room without food because I talked back." My hands curl into fists. "She died the first time he hit me hard enough to make me forget my name. She died the first time he—" My throat closes. "The first time he climbed on top of me, and I screamed until my voice went hoarse."

Ash flinches.

I shove him.

Then again.

Killian reaches out, but I slap his hands away.

"She died screaming for someone to save her. No one came."

My fists slam into Ash's chest, useless but angry. "You *left* me!"

I swing again. And again.

Then I feel it—arms wrapping around me from behind, strong and unyielding, pulling me back before I can do more damage. My legs kick—my hands claw. I can't stop.

"Let go!" I scream, nails digging into skin. "Let me go!"

"Settle, Little One."

The words are low. Firm. Jaxson.

My body crumbles.

My knees give out.

I sag against him, sobs tearing through me like a storm that won't end. "If I can't find him," I choke, barely forming the words, "it was all for nothing. Everything I survived—everything I lost—none of it mattered."

Jaxson holds me tighter, but I panic as his arms begin to ease.

"No." I clutch at his forearms. "Don't. Don't let go."

His lips graze the top of my head. "Not happening."

His arms close around me like a vow made of steel.

"I've got you, Baby Girl," he murmurs. "You're not going anywhere. And neither am I."

CHAPTER 33

Jaxson

Her body heat radiates through the thin fabric of her shirt, soaking into my hands and sending an involuntary shiver up my spine. My thumbs glide over the curve of her sides, and the subtle tremble that ripples through her doesn't go unnoticed. Killian's sharp eyes flick between us, his confusion palpable. I know they're all wondering what the hell I'm doing. Hell, even I'm wondering. Comforting someone, let alone a woman, has never been part of my nature. Yet, here I am, drawn in by the haunting terror locked in her striking golden-green eyes.

Her rigid frame softens by degrees, leaning into me as a heavy sigh escapes her lips. A tightness seizes me, a rapid, almost painful thrum rising within me. "I'm sorry," she murmurs, the words so soft they barely rise above the roar of blood in my ears. Her hands clutch my wrists, her nails biting into my skin—a grounding contrast to the intoxicating heat of her body against mine.

Instinctively, I lower my head, brushing my cheek against her hair. "You don't need to apologize, Kitten." At the word, she stiffens, her relaxed body going taut. The chill of the air rushes in as her hands fall away, leaving my skin aching for the warmth of her touch. She tries to retreat, but I refuse to let her slip from my hold.

Leaning down, I let my lips hover near her ear. "Hey… what just happened?" My voice is soft and coaxing, but her reaction is anything but. She raises her head, but the pain in her expression is a shadow that doesn't quite meet the light. She nibbles nervously on her bottom lip, the slight movement holding my insides hostage.

"Don't call me that," she whispers, fragile but firm.

I tilt her face toward mine, my brow furrowing. "Call you what? Little One?"

She jerks her head, a sharp shake that denies the name even before I finish saying it. She pushes against me, a weak attempt to escape, but I refuse to let her go. "What shouldn't I call you?" I demand gently, heat rushing through me as I try to understand.

Her palms lay flat against my chest, and I'm sure she can feel the frantic rhythm beneath her fingers. Rising on her toes, she leans in, barely audible. "Kitten," she whispers. "I don't like to be called Kitten."

The words hit harder than I expect, and I pull her closer, as though sheer proximity could erase the hollowness creeping into her gaze. That vibrant golden fire dulls, leaving her eyes shadowed and distant. Tears well, but don't fall. It's a look that carves me deep, leaving me feeling helpless and raw.

"Why?" I ask again, my voice quieter, more desperate. I need to pull her back, see that fire reignite, and feel her push away my ache.

Her lips tremble before she forces out the words. "H-He used to call me that when I was good." Pain flashes across her face before it vanishes into an eerie emptiness. "It wasn't as bad when I was good... I liked being good." She drops her gaze, her fingers twisting the hem of her shirt, a sad smile ghosting her lips before it's gone. For a brief moment, sadness and longing flicker in her expression before she looks away, leaving me staring at the void she's become. A lead weight settles in my gut, heavy and sickening. How could she still feel anything but hatred for that monster?

Jake's voice interrupts my spiraling thoughts. "You never told us why you're looking for Saint John." His words hit like a thunderclap, drawing every pair of eyes to her, mine included. My arm cinches around her, a silent barricade against the weight of his question, as if holding her closer could soften the blow of whatever truth comes next. "After everything he did to you, why would you want to find him?"

Her fingers clutch my shirt, pulling the fabric taut as she moves closer, seeking refuge in the space between us. "I couldn't explain it in a way that wouldn't make you hate me."

I study her, watching every subtle shift of her face. There's more to this—something she isn't saying.

Ash's voice cuts through the fragile calm like a blade. "Do you love him?"

The question strikes her like a blow. Her eyes squeeze shut, her body curling in on itself as she fights to hold back her emotions. "H-He has something that I love," she murmurs. *What are you hiding?*

The tension in the room spikes as the others exchange looks of disbelief, anger simmering just below the surface. Jake steps forward, his tone low and menacing. "What did he give you?" His hand brushes along her back, a gesture meant to soothe her, but she flinches as if it burns. She turns, her walls so firmly in place she's shut us all out. "What could he have given you that makes you want to go back?" Jake barks, his frustration leaking into his tone.

Her head snaps up, anger igniting. "Since you're so eager to know," she growls, laced with venom, "I want to see him. I just have to go back." The words crack like a whip, splintering under the weight of the truth she's forcing herself to speak. Her eyes glisten, but her chin juts out defiantly.

Jake's fury boils over. "What!" His roar is explosive as he lunges forward, his hands gripping her arms with bruising force. She shrieks, panic spilling from her lips, and I move without thinking, shoving him back into Killian's grip.

"Back off!" I snap, stepping between them as Ember crumples to the floor, huddling into the corner of the cabinets. Her small frame trembles, her arms curling protectively around herself as she whimpers, shrinking further from Jake's reach.

Jake's expression crumples into horror, his rage instantly replaced by guilt. "Ember? Damn... My Red, I'm so sorry." His hand extends toward her, but she recoils, burying her face against her knees, her entire body vibrating with fear.

I slam a hand on Jake's shoulder, gripping hard. "Walk away, man.

You're making this worse." My voice is low and dangerous, daring him to defy me.

Jake hesitates, his body quaking with restrained emotion. "I... Ember?" He calls her name, but she doesn't look up. He wrenches himself free from Killian's hold, his movements jerky and desperate as he stumbles out of the kitchen, one hand fisted in his hair, the other clenched at his side.

As his retreating footsteps fade, I crouch down, careful not to touch her. "Little One..." I whisper, the nickname slipping out instinctively. She doesn't respond, her sobs muffled against her knees, and the ache deepens. Whatever battle she's fighting, she's fighting it alone—and I don't know how to pull her out.

Ash's fingers clamp around my arm, his grip firm but not rough, and he pulls me toward the door. "Jax, we need to talk... in private," he mutters, his tone urgent, eyes darting toward Ember.

I glance back, catching Ember's slight, hesitant nod. Her hands rest limply on her lap, her gaze tracking us as if to ensure I'm coming back. "Y-yeah," I exhale, reluctant to leave her but following Ash anyway. A knot of emotion pulls tight inside me at the sight of Killian kneeling in front of her, his posture protective. She leans toward him, her shoulders still tense but not as rigid. Killian's got this. They all do. She's been the only thing they could talk about for the past four years, and a part of me feels the need to protect her as fiercely as they do.

In the office, the heavy wooden door clicks shut behind me. I lean against it, crossing my arms. The rich mahogany and deep green tones of the Victorian-style room feel stifling, though they usually feel grounding. "What's so important?"

Ash turns, adjusting his tie out of habit, his jaw tight. "We know where he is."

The words slam into me, sharp and unexpected. "Well, that was quick." I push off the door, my hand already reaching for the knob. "Why didn't you tell her?"

Ash steps between me and the exit, his hand resting lightly against my sternum. "We need to understand why she wants to return so badly first." His tone lowers, dashing away his usual composure. "You didn't see her when we found her. You didn't see what he did to her. How can she even think about going back? It doesn't make sense unless..." He hesitates, his eyes narrowing. "Unless she still feels something for him or she's hiding something."

The idea makes my stomach churn. "Stockholm syndrome?" I mutter, more to myself than him: my mind races, flipping through every look she's given, every word she's said. "You heard her, Ash. She's furious about what he did to her. Why would she want to return?" My fists clench at my sides as my thoughts spiral. The urge to eliminate Saint John, to ensure she never has to face him again, blazes through me like an unchecked wildfire. Her desperation lingers—the look in her eyes when she talks about finding him. What's driving her?

Ash adjusts his cuffs, and his movements are practiced, almost like rituals, to mask his unease. "That's why we're not telling her yet. He's already here."

I freeze, the words sinking in like ice through my veins. "What?"

Ash's voice hardens, his resolve unshakable. "He's chained up in the basement. For now, she doesn't need to know."

A knot forms, twisting painfully. "You're serious? Do you think keeping this from her is a good idea? We promised to help her, Ash. You're breaking that promise."

His lips purse, but his gaze doesn't waver. "If we can convince her to stay, to see that she doesn't need him, then maybe—just maybe—we can protect her from whatever hold he still has on her."

I shake my head, anger and disbelief swirling inside me. "And if she finds out you've been hiding this from her? She'll hate you for it, Ash. All of you. Are you ready to risk losing her?"

His jaw ticks—doubt, maybe, or regret. The hesitation vanishes, replaced by a cold determination. "If it means keeping her safe, yeah. I'll risk it."

His words hang thick in the air, weighing me down—I push past him, frustration crackling beneath my skin. But the moment I step into the kitchen, the scene before me slams into me like a wall of ice, stopping me cold.

Killian has Ember perched on the counter, his broad frame standing between her legs, his hands resting on her hips. She's smiling up at him, a faint blush dusting her cheeks as he leans in. He whispers in her ear, causing her to laugh. The sound is light, a stark contrast to the fear she carried moments ago.

My fingers twitch with the urge to drag her away from him, to hold her in my arms instead. The logical part of me knows better—she needs all of us, not just me—but the need to protect her burns too fiercely to ignore.

Her soft voice cuts through my thoughts. "Jaxson?" Her eyes peek over Killian's shoulder, locking on mine. They're wide and uncertain, a hint of fear swimming beneath the surface. "Are you all right?"

Clearing my throat, I plaster my usual smirk, a shield to mask the storm inside. "Of course, Little One." My voice is smooth and casual, but her frown deepens, her brows knitting together as if she can see through me. "Whatever could be wrong?"

Her eyes question, but she doesn't say more. Still, the look she gives me feels like an ache, a reminder of everything I can't say and might lose.

"N-nothing, I suppose," she murmurs, barely audible, her hesitancy clear in how her gaze drops to the floor. The faint tremble sends a ripple of unease through me. That frown—it's my fault. I know it is. I put it there because I've kept my distance, telling myself I shouldn't care. She's not mine to protect. So why does the sight of her looking so unsure twist my gut?

"Don't be an ass, Jax," Killian quips, his lips curling into a smirk. He leans in, resting his forehead against her shoulder, his face burying into the crook of her neck like it's the most natural thing in the world. Her soft laugh follows, the sound making something inside me ache.

"I'm always an ass, Kill," I shoot back, my tone flat. Killian laughs, his deep chuckle vibrating through the room, and she giggles in response, a light, melodic sound that shouldn't sting as much as it does.

"Killian, that tickles," she protests, pushing him away with a playful shove. She smiles as he pouts dramatically, batting his lashes like some lovesick fool.

I stand frozen, watching their interaction. The image of Killian—easily the most fearsome of us all—reduced to a pile of mush for her is unsettling. But what's worse is how much I get it. I feel the same damn way about her.

The flare of anger bubbling inside me is too much to swallow down. "I gotta go," I snap, my voice sharper than I intended. Her head jerks toward me, startled, but I don't stop. I storm across the kitchen, grabbing my leather jacket from the back of a chair, the urge to get out overwhelming.

"Jaxson, wait!" The sound halts me mid-step, my jaw clenching as I feel her rushing to close the distance. Her hand brushes my arm, gentle but enough to send a jolt through me. "I'm sorry if I upset you," she says, small, almost trembling.

"Stop," I bark, my frustration leaking despite my effort to hold it back. The tears in her eyes hit me like a punch to the gut. She blinks rapidly, trying to hold them back, but a few slip free, carving silent paths down her cheeks. Damn it. I'm the reason for those tears, too. "You don't need to apologize," I add quickly, the words tumbling out. "I'm—" I falter, searching for a response. "I'm going out to try to find Patrick."

Her eyes widen, hope flaring like a spark reigniting in her. "Already? Can I come with?" She fidgets, her hands twisting nervously in her jacket pockets as her teeth find her lower lip again. The sight of her so eager, so desperate to help, tears at me.

"Um... you want to come with?" I ask, her request catching me off guard.

Before she can answer, Jake rounds the corner, his presence a storm ready to strike. His gaze locks onto me, blazing with anger. "You're not going anywhere," he growls, low and dangerous.

I shift my stance, squaring up instinctively, bracing for the confrontation brewing in his eyes. His tension is electric, his fury palpable. Great. It looks like I might be thrown out before I can leave on my terms.

CHAPTER 34

Ember Rose

Jake's face hardens, the weight of his frustration bearing down on me like a thunderstorm. His jaw ticks as I glare at him, my voice low and sharp. "Why not?" The words break the tension. "You don't get to decide what I do."

His broad shoulders shift as he steps closer, the familiar protective edge in his eyes flickering like a warning light. I don't flinch. My feet stay planted, even as a restless energy pours into my chest. This is Jake—my Jake, who used to shield me from everything. But those days are gone, and so is the girl he remembers. Determination floods my chest, pushing back the fear that once defined me. I can't back down, not this time. Not when I know what's at stake.

He growls, a sound that could have frozen me in place once. "We're not done with this conversation, Red."

My lips twist into a sardonic smile as I cross my arms, not bothering to mask the exaggerated roll of my eyes. "Oh, for crying out loud—"

Jake's voice drops, low and gravelly, vibrating with authority. "Did you just roll your eyes at me, Red?"

The shift in his tone sparks an involuntary shiver down my spine. I narrow my eyes at him, trying to mask his effect on me. "Why does that even matter?"

"Because the next time you roll those beautiful green eyes, I'll put you over my knee," he growls, leaning in just enough for his words to send a jolt of shock through me.

My breath catches. "E-excuse me?"

His lips curve into a wicked smirk, his tone a velvet threat in my ear. "You heard me. Go ahead, roll them again."

I blink, stunned and silent, until the faint sound of someone clearing their throat snaps me out of the haze. Whipping around, I find Jaxson standing nearby, arms crossed, one eyebrow raised. His expression holds a challenge as he tips his head toward the door.

"You coming, or what?" he asks casually, but the tension radiates off him.

Before I can answer, Jake steps closer, his growl practically a command. "No."

"Yes!" I snap back, the word tumbling out following Jake's refusal. His growl deepens, but I spin away, seizing Jaxson's arm like a lifeline.

"Jake, I'm going, and you're not stopping me," I say firmly, dragging Jaxson toward the sleek motorcycle parked just outside.

Jake's voice booms behind me, thick with warning. "Red, don't you dare. Get your ass back here before I throw you over my shoulder and haul you inside."

I glance at Jaxson, who hands me a helmet with a knowing smirk. My stomach twists, and I feel a strange cocktail of nerves and thrill.

"Ember!" Jake's furious shout cuts through the air, each syllable laced with authority and desperation. Jaxson swings his leg over the motorcycle with an effortless grace, his piercing gaze locking onto mine. His raised brow silently asks the question hanging between us—*Are you ready to do this? Ready to defy Jake?*

A fierce pounding takes over, but the answer is clear. Yes. This isn't about rebellion or recklessness, but taking control of my life.

I mimic Jaxson's fluid motion, swinging my leg over the bike just as the engine roars to life, its deep, guttural purr vibrating through me. Jake's voice grows faint behind us, drowned out by the machine's growl beneath us. Before he can close the distance, Jaxson twists the throttle, and we launch forward, the tires peeling away from the curb.

A startled squeal escapes me as the sudden rush of speed sends adrenaline coursing through my veins. My arms instinctively wrap around Jaxson's solid frame, holding tight as the wind whips past us. His deep laughter rumbles through his chest, muffled but unmistakable, and I bury the front of my helmet against the cool leather of his jacket, seeking steady ground in the whirlwind of the moment.

Jake's angry shouts dissolve into the distance, but the sense of liberation rushing through me is deafening. My hair flies wild and free, tangling in the wind, as the world blurs into streaks of light and motion around us. I've never felt so untethered, so alive. For the first time in forever, the weight of fear and control feels lighter, stripped away by the exhilarating roar of rebellion.

The motorcycle's roar fades as Jaxson cuts the engine, leaving a tense quiet in its wake. The air smells like rust and neglect, matching the house before us. Its peeling paint clings stubbornly to sagging window frames, and crumbling bricks scatter at the base like casualties of time. Weeds push through cracks in the sidewalk, an army of green reclaiming what was once theirs. Each breath is shallow as I fight to steady myself.

Jaxson swings off the bike. "We need to start somewhere," he says as his stare remains fixed on the dilapidated structure. He turns to me, a hint of a smirk tugging at his lips. "And call me Jax, Little One."

I climb off the bike, my eyes fixed on the house. The grimy curtains flutter, causing my skin to crawl.

"Jax?" My voice comes out quieter than I intend.

"Yeah?"

"Does someone live here?"

His hand finds the small of my back, firm and guiding. His touch burns against my skin, a stark contrast to the biting chill that clings to the night air. "Shouldn't be," he murmurs, his tone sharp. "But he's been dodging me. That ends now." His breath brushes my cheek, sending an involuntary shiver down my spine. "Do me a favor."

I glance at him warily. "What?"

"Don't provoke him. He's... unpredictable."

I lift my chin, the edge of defiance surfacing. "I've dealt with worse, Jax."

He halts. "Ember." His tone is soft but commanding, pulling my gaze to him. His eyes burn with unspoken questions, a tempest waiting to be unleashed.

"Tell me," he encourages, his hand brushing my cheek. The touch is gentle, grounding. "Why do you really need to find him so badly?"

The words catch. No one had asked before—not like this. Not with this intensity. I shake my head, the weight of unspoken truths too heavy. "I can't. Not yet. But it's important."

He studies me. Before I can say more, my phone vibrates, causing me to jump. I step back, pulling it from my pocket. My heart stutters as Atlas's face fills the screen. Another photo. Another taunt.

I swallow hard, shoving the phone in my pocket as Jaxson's eyes narrow. "What just happened?" he demands, his presence closing the distance between us.

"Nothing," I lie, masking my turmoil. He doesn't push, but his frown deepens as he strides past me toward the house.

"Kyle," Jaxson calls out mockingly as we step inside. "Come out, come out, wherever you are."

The interior holds echoes of grandeur, now dulled by time and decay. Water-stained walls frame shattered furniture. Above, a sweeping staircase cuts through the space like a broken monument. A creak from upstairs sends a rush of adrenaline through me.

Jaxson closes in behind me, his breath ghosting over my ear. "Scared, Baby Girl?"

I stiffen, heat rising to my cheeks. "N-no," I stammer, the word barely audible.

His low chuckle vibrates through me, playful but dark. "You should be."

The space he occupied feels hollow as he moves away, his absence as sharp as a blade. Shadows stretch across his back as he strides toward the staircase, the glint of metal catching in the dim light as he draws a gun from his waistband. Whatever's waiting inside, I'm not sure I'm ready to face it.

CHAPTER 35

Jaxson

"Kyle!" My voice snaps through the decaying stillness of the room. "Get down here before I drag your sorry ass out myself." The gun in my hand feels solid, a grim promise as I flip the safety off and gesture toward a rickety dining chair.

Ember hesitates, her weight shifting between one foot and the other. When she finally sinks into the seat, she does so with a wariness that makes the fragile chair creak beneath her. Her fingers hover over the splintered edge of the table, her gaze darting to the shadowed hallway.

"Jax." Her voice, soft but urgent, draws my attention. Her eyes widen, locked on the dim archway leading to the kitchen. "Someone's there."

My fingers dig into the gun's grip as my jaw locks. My eyes track her gaze, then a flicker of movement. Kyle's greasy head slips into view for a heartbeat before retreating into the shadows. A slow burn ignites in my chest, my patience unraveling thread by thread, ready to snap.

"Kyle, now!" My words echo against peeling wallpaper. When silence answers, my teeth grind. One step, followed by another, and I reach behind the doorframe, gripping his shirt and yanking him out like a cornered rat.

He stumbles into the room, scrawny and twitching, wiping the remnants of his addiction from his nose. The chair groans under his weight as I shove him down, half hoping the decrepit thing gives out beneath him. I step behind Ember, resting a hand on her shoulder, grounding her—or maybe myself. The fabric between us is thin, a fragile barrier against the heat of her body like an ember buried beneath ash—dangerous if stirred.

Kyle glances between us, his paranoia a palpable stink. "You weren't supposed to bring anyone."

I smirk, cold and sharp, circling the table. "And you weren't supposed to waste my time. Guess neither of us gets what we want." My fingers curl around the grip of the gun as his eyes flick nervously between me and her.

"What do you need now?" He leans back, taking a swig from a bottle that looks like it's more grime than water. "Thought we were done. I was supposed to never see your face again."

I let the silence stretch, the weight of it holding me down as I study him. His nerves crack first, his fingers twitching toward the table's edge.

"We're done when I say we're done." My voice cuts through the stale air, a quiet menace that has him flinching.

He sighs, scrubbing a hand over his face. "What is it this time? And who the hell is she?" He jerks his chin toward her, careless and invasive.

"That's not your concern." I step closer to her, protective without meaning to be. "Saint John. Where is he?"

Kyle snorts, the sound bitter. "Lost him already?"

Before I can answer, she cuts in, quieter than before but no less sure. "He wasn't at his house." Her hands twist in the hem of her sweatshirt, the motion nervous, like she's holding back more than fear. "The furniture's gone. The place is trashed."

My eyes snap to her, narrowing. "And you know this how?"

She meets my gaze, tilting her chin just enough to hold her ground, though her smile is sad, almost resigned. "Because it's the first place I checked."

The unspoken hangs heavy between us, a truth I can't drag out of her yet. But Kyle's time is running out, and I can't afford to lose focus. Later, I'll ask her to tell me everything. For now, I ground her again before returning my attention to Kyle.

Kyle leans back, his impatience radiating from how he taps his fingers on the table. "The last person I sent you after was Tristan Devereux. Did you check with him?"

"He's dead." The words hit the air with a cold finality, and Ember's head snaps up, her wide eyes locking onto mine. She doesn't say anything, but her silence screams louder than words.

Kyle shrugs as though the revelation means nothing, propping his feet on the table like he's settling for a casual conversation. "Well, there's been no talk about Patrick in the underground market. He's gone —vanished a few weeks ago."

Ember turns sharply, urgency evident. "He disappeared?"

Kyle barely looks at her as he speaks. "Yeah, poof, gone. No one's heard from him. It's weird—he's usually sniffing around the market for new girls, but he's been silent."

The shift in Ember is instant. Once resting on the table, her hands ball into fists, her knuckles whitening. "You helped him get girls?"

Kyle rolls his eyes, his nonchalance almost mocking. "Yeah, that's part of what I do, ma'am."

I don't miss how her nails dig into her palms, leaving small crescent moons in her skin. Fire flashes in her eyes, and I step closer, lowering myself to her level. My hand brushes her knee, and she glances at me before returning to Kyle.

"Do you think he deserves to live?" My words are a murmur against her cheek, soft enough to be intimate but heavy enough to make her freeze. Her lips part, and she bites her bottom lip nervously, her uncertainty bare.

I wait, watching her process. Killing someone isn't a decision you can undo—it leaves a stain that never thoroughly washes away. I should be protecting her from this, from its weight, but when I look into her eyes, I see the darkness already there. Not wild and out of control, but simmering. Waiting. She needs to learn to harness it before it consumes her.

She tilts her head toward me, "N-no."

Her answer is a whisper, but it's enough to make the room feel smaller, the air heavier. Kyle narrows his eyes at us. "What are you two whispering about?" he asks, suspicion lacing his tone.

I straighten, my hand sliding to the small of my back. The silenced 9mm feels like a brick in my hand as I pass it into her trembling hand. She startles, her wide eyes darting to mine, but I don't let go.

"You upset my girl, Kyle," I say evenly, squeezing her thigh to steady her.

Her wide eyes dart to mine. "Your girl?" she whispers.

I don't meet her gaze, keeping my focus locked on Kyle. "That's right," I say, daring her to question it further. My hand squeezes her thigh, steadying the tremor that ripples through her.

She blinks, her lips parting as though she wants to say more but can't find the words.

Kyle snorts, his laugh grating as he tosses an empty water bottle. "Like I give a shit."

Her hand quivers as she raises the gun, the barrel shaking as it aims at his face. "Maybe you should care," she says, fragile but growing stronger. "How many girls?"

I let my hand slide down her arm, steadying hers. The tremor in her body lessens, but her breaths remain shallow, each one a struggle.

Kyle leans back in his chair, smirking like he's invincible. "Get your girl in line, J," he says, cocky and careless.

I flick off the safety with a click, and his smirk evaporates. "Answer the question, Kyle," I say, leaning closer to her, letting her feel my presence beside her.

His back stiffens, his bravado cracking as his gaze flits between the gun and my face. "W-what was the question?"

"She asked how many girls you've sold." I let my chin rest on her shoulder, keeping her hand steady.

Kyle's eyes dart wildly, his fear finally overtaking him. "Shit, man, I don't know... probably close to a hundred."

Ember sucks in a sharp breath, her fingers clenching around the gun as if it's the only thing keeping her upright. "A hundred? You've condemned a hundred girls to the same hell you threw me into?"

Kyle stammers, his gaze darting between us. "Y-yeah, at least a hundred."

Her trembling worsens, tears pooling in her eyes as what she's about to do weighs down on her. "It's okay if you can't do this, Little One," I whisper, but she shakes her head, resolute.

"I have to," she whispers back. The tears sliding down her cheeks glisten in the dim light, but her resolve remains. She's trembling, yes, but in this moment, she's stronger than I've ever seen her. "I need to do this."

I place a feather-light kiss on her cheek, the contact grounding us both. "It's okay if you can't," I murmur again, but her tear-brimmed eyes lift to meet mine. In her gaze, I see the damage he's left behind, scars she's desperate to erase. And yet, the question gnaws at me—why is she so hell-bent on finding him? Why hasn't she told us everything?

Kyle's voice breaks the fragile silence, a grating interruption. "Come on, man. You can't do this. People will come looking for me."

I don't even look at him. "The only person who ever comes looking for you is me, Kyle. No one else cares about you."

Her finger hesitates, easing off the trigger. I move closer, placing my hand over hers, steadying the shaking weapon. "Let me do this for us, Little One," I murmur, brushing a kiss against her temple. Her hand steadies under mine, the tremor easing as I count softly. "Three." She draws in a deep breath, her back straightening. "Two." Her exhalation is slow and measured, and her resolve is solidifying. "One."

The muffled crack of the shot echoes through the room. Kyle's scream pierces the air as he leaps from his chair, spinning to stare at the hole in the wall behind him. "Jesus Christ! You fucking shot at me!" He growls, his hand diving into his waistband and pulling out a gun.

Time slows. My instincts take over, and in one swift motion, I yank the gun from Ember's hands and fire. The silencer hisses as the bullet rips through Kyle's skull. His body crumples to the floor, lifeless, and the room falls into an oppressive silence.

Ember stumbles back, her knees giving out as she drops to the floor. Her hands fly to her mouth, muffling a choked gasp. "You killed him... he's dead."

I'm beside her in an instant, scooping her into my arms. "Hey," I whisper, carrying her out of the room and into the dim light of the kitchen. Gently, I set her on the counter, holding her close as her fingers grip the fabric of my jacket, her face buried in my neck. "I need you to look at me, Little One. Tell me you're okay."

Her head tilts up, her lashes wet with tears, her expression a storm of confusion and guilt. "I don't feel bad... but I should've been strong enough to do it. For me, for us. He deserved to die, and I couldn't do it." Her voice cracks, and her gaze flits toward the dining room, panic flickering across her face. "What are we going to do with the body, Jax?"

"Hush, Little One," I murmur, smoothing a hand down her back. "I'll take care of it. I need to know if you're okay."

Her nod is shaky, uncertain. "I don't know. I feel fine, but maybe it's just the adrenaline." Her trembling hands drop to her lap as she stares at them. "Maybe I'm not okay. I just watched you kill someone. I shouldn't be okay with that, right?"

I clasp her hands, placing them against my frame, letting her feel the rhythm of my heartbeat. "I can't decide that for you," I say gently. "Just breathe with me, okay?"

She nods, the tension in her shoulders slowly easing. "That's it," I murmur, brushing a stray tear from her cheek. "Good girl. Let's get you back to the guys."

She whispers a soft "okay" as I lift her off the counter. Her legs wrap instinctively around my waist as she buries her face against my shoulder, shielding her from the sight of the body as I carry her toward the door.

This was too much. I should've stopped it, should've shielded her from it. But some part of me knows she needed to face the darkness that's been drowning her for so long. There's more to this, more that she hasn't told us. Tied to the nightmares she's lived through. And I'm going to find out what it is.

CHAPTER 36

Ember Rose

The scene replays in vivid flashes as we wind down the dark road back to the house. Jaxson's gun, the echo of the shot, and the way the man's head snapped back—all of it pounds in my skull like a relentless drum. My arms cinch around Jaxson's waist, fingers digging into the fabric of his jacket as the steady growl of the motorcycle vibrates through my body. My helmet rests against his back, the scent of leather and wind clinging to him, grounding me as the world blurs past in streaks of headlights and asphalt.

One of his hands drifts from the handlebars to my thigh, his palm firm against my skin, solid. He rubs gently, giving it a firm squeeze, trying to reassure me without saying a word.

As the house looms closer, I force my eyes open and brace myself. Jake is waiting. His wrath feels inevitable, a storm on the horizon. *What if he finds out about Kyle? Oh, God... he'll kill Jaxson.*

Jaxson's bike whips past their house. "J-Jax?"

"I'm not ready to deal with Jake yet, are you?" His fingers dig into my thigh, and a part of me I didn't know was worried relaxes.

"He's going to be upset."

"He's already upset, might as well do something fun before we head back."

"What are we going to do?"

"How do you feel about learning to ride a motorcycle?" My heart skips a beat, and a giddy feeling rises. I've always wanted to learn. Killian was supposed to teach me before it all fell apart.

"I'd love to."

Jaxson lets out a soft chuckle, the sound vibrating through his back and into my chest like a private secret. He pulls off onto a dirt road shrouded in trees, the darkness swallowing us whole as the headlight cuts a golden path through the night. Gravel crunches beneath the tires as he slows the bike to a stop in a small, hidden clearing.

He kills the engine, and silence rushes in—thick, heavy, and laced with the scent of pine and motor oil. The only sound is the ticking of the cooling engine and the chirp of distant crickets.

"You sure about this?" he asks, glancing back at me with a grin of boyish mischief.

"I'm sure." My voice comes out steadier than I expect.

He swings off the bike and holds out his hand. I take it, sliding off behind him, my legs a little shaky, not just from the ride. His touch never leaves mine. He holds me there for a second, his fingers curled around mine, eyes searching my face.

"Still shaking," he murmurs, thumb brushing over my knuckles. "You want to talk about it?"

"No," I whisper, eyes dropping. "Not yet."

His nod is small but understanding. There is no pressure, no judgment, just Jax being Jax—the solid wall of calm in the chaos.

"Alright," he says gently, then turns and straddles the bike again. "Hop on."

I hesitate. "Wait... You're not getting off?"

He grins. "Nope. I said *learn,* not *ride alone.* You're not ready for that yet. Trust me, you'll thank me later."

I raise a brow but swing my leg over the seat behind him again, this time with a curious, lighter energy.

His hands reach behind him, guiding mine to the handlebars in front of him. "These are yours now. I'll control the balance and speed. All you've got to do is feel it. Get used to the engine's pull, the lean of the turns."

I nod, nerves and excitement dancing in my chest like fireflies.

His tone drops lower, teasing. "Keep your hands where I put them, or I might think you're getting handsy."

I smack his shoulder, laughing despite myself. The sound surprises me. *God, I needed that.*

We take off again, slowly this time, his body moving with mine as I follow his motions, our movements syncing. The road is uneven, but the trust between us—so quiet and unspoken—makes it feel like flying.

For a few blissful moments, I forget about Jake. About the blood. About Kyle.

It's just Jaxson, the night, and the promise of a possible future.

And I don't feel afraid for the first time in a long time.

JAXSON'S HANDS slide over mine, his touch firm yet gentle as he guides my fingers around the handlebars. "Here," he murmurs, positioning my grip. "The throttle's on the right—twist it toward you to speed up, away to slow down." I bite my lip, forcing myself to focus on his words instead of the dominance radiating from him.

His fingers brush mine as he points to the front brake lever. "This one's for the front brake," he says, crouching to wrap his hand around my ankle, guiding my foot to the rear brake lever. "And this? The rear brake."

I nod, swallowing hard. The mechanics swirl in my head like an untamed storm, but it's a welcome distraction—a welcome escape.

Jaxson's breath ghosts against my cheek as he taps the clutch lever. "This is the clutch. You'll need it to shift gears." He moves my left foot to another lever. "And here's the shift lever—work them together."

"Right," I murmur, nodding even though the concepts tangle.

A soft chuckle vibrates against my skin, and I smile when he leans in, forehead resting against my shoulder. "You have no idea what I just said, do you?"

"Not even a little," I admit, grinning at him. "But I'm ready."

Jaxson groans, shaking his head. "This is such a bad idea."

I nudge him off my shoulder, eyes bright. "You promised."

Sighing, he points to the ignition switch. "Turn it on." I do, fingers trembling.

"This one?" I ask, glancing at him for confirmation.

He nods, and I flip the switch. The bike hums to life beneath me, and a startled squeal escapes my lips.

"Now shift to neutral," he says, guiding me through each step. "Squeeze the clutch and press the starter."

The engine roars, and its vibration beneath me sends a rush of adrenaline through my veins. I fight the urge to clap my hands and instead grip the handlebars.

Jaxson adjusts my helmet, fingers grasping my chin before he swings onto the seat behind me, his chest fusing to my back. "We're taking it slow. I'm not letting anything happen to you today, Little One."

As we take off, the bike wobbles beneath me, sending my heart into my throat. Jaxson's hands are steadying over mine, guiding me.

"You've got this," he reassures me through the intercom, his touch firm but comforting. He helps me shift through the gears, and soon, we're soaring down the road, the wind rushing past in a blur of freedom. His laughter crackles through my earpiece, and I join in, the thrill of speed making me feel alive in a way I haven't in so long.

Then his hands lift from mine.

"Don't let go," I plead.

"I'm right here," he promises, his hands settling on my thighs instead, a silent reassurance. "I've got you."

The tension in my shoulders eases, and I push the throttle harder, the speedometer climbing. The world becomes a blur of asphalt and endless sky, and for once, nothing else matters.

"Let's pull over," Jaxson's voice breaks through my thoughts, his hands sliding back over mine, easing us to a stop. "I think I've pushed your limits enough for today."

When the bike stops, I yank off my helmet and twist around in the seat. My fingers tangle in his hair as I pull him in, crushing my lips to his before he can say a word. A low growl rumbles through him as his hands grip my hips, lifting me effortlessly until I'm straddling him.

"Thank you," I whisper against his lips, holding him close.

His forehead rests against mine, breath heavy. “Anything for you, Baby Girl.”

Reluctantly, I sigh. “Let’s go home.”

The ride back feels different—just as exhilarating, but with a heavy reminder waiting at the end of the road. As we pull into the garage, the weight of everything I tried to outrun crashes back down. Patrick is still missing. Atlas is gone. Jake is distant and cold, while Killian and Ash are content sharing me in a way that leaves me breathless and overwhelmed. And Jax... Jaxson is new and kind of exciting.

I swing my leg off the bike, and Jaxson steadies me, pulling my helmet free. My hair tumbles around my shoulders, and I exhale slowly.

Reality might be waiting, but for now, I hold onto this moment—this feeling—just a little longer.

“Where the fuck were you?” Jake’s voice is a low, dangerous growl, his hands gripping my shoulders—not painfully, but enough to hold me in place. His dark eyes simmer with barely contained fury, his words trembling with emotion. “Where the hell were you, Ember?”

Before I can answer, he pulls me into a tight embrace, his arms locking around me as if I might vanish if he lets go.

Jaxson snorts behind us, the sound cutting through the tension. “I wouldn’t hurt her,” he mutters, shrugging off his leather jacket and stowing it under the seat.

Jake’s head snaps up, his anger latching onto the interruption. “Don’t even talk to me right now. That was reckless, and she could’ve gotten hurt!” His tone sharpens with every word, and before I can protest, he lifts me like I weigh nothing, my legs instinctively wrapping around his waist. He carries me inside like a child, his protective grip comforting.

“Jakey,” I whisper, cupping his face with trembling hands. “I’m fine.” I force him to meet my gaze, searching his stormy eyes for the calm beneath. But instead, I see cracks—fractures that reveal how deep his fear runs.

“You’re not fine,” he mutters. His hands move to my arms, checking for injuries, tugging at my jacket.

“Jake, I’m not hurt!” I try to laugh it off, but his anger irritates me.

“She isn’t injured,” Jaxson cuts in from the doorway, his tone maddeningly casual. "Though she did point a gun at my source. But, I killed him."

Jake freezes, his fingers curling into fists. He turns slowly, his jaw clenched so tight I hear the grind of his teeth. "She did what?" His tone is low, the quiet that makes your blood run cold. "Did you make her do that?"

Jaxson shrugs, leaning lazily against the frame. "She asked me to."

The truth stabs through me like a blade. I had asked. I wanted Kyle dead for what he'd done. I needed him dead.

"Bullshit!" Jake explodes, lunging for Jaxson. I throw myself in front of him, my hands grabbing his raised fist. His knuckles hover inches from my face, shaking with barely restrained fury.

"Move, Ember," he commands.

"No." My voice is small but firm. "He's right. I asked him to."

Jake's eyes widen, his anger momentarily eclipsed by disbelief. "Why, Red?"

Tears blur my vision, but I force myself to meet his gaze. "Because Kyle was part of it. He helped sell them—hundreds of girls. I had to stop him. I couldn't save them before, but I could do this."

Jake's hand drops slowly, his fingers brushing mine. "Who?" he asks, softer now, laced with pain.

Killian's voice cuts through the heavy silence, his figure leaning casually in the doorway. "Who, Princess?"

I swallow hard, my fingers curling around Jake's hand, holding on like he's the only solid thing in a world threatening to slip away. "Chrissy and Katy," I whisper, my voice cracking. "They were twins. He said they'd be punished for my disobedience, and every time he took them, they came back... more broken. More bruised. I wouldn't listen until I did. By then, it was too late."

Jake's free hand cups my face, his thumb brushing away a tear as it slips down my cheek. I stare up at him, desperate for him to see the truth in my words. For him to understand. But the cracks in his soul mirror mine, and I know we're both barely holding on.

Heat seeps through my shirt as a steady presence anchors me in place. The scent of diesel drifts in as Killian steps closer.

"What did he do to them?" The weight of the question punches through me. I lean into him, letting his presence hold me upright.

"The first time they came back..." My words falter as memories claw their way to the surface. A tightness grips me, but I push on. "The insides of their legs were covered in blood. I knew." A sob bursts from me, my body rattling under the force of it. "They cried all night, screaming for help, and I couldn't do anything." The tears come harder, searing down my cheeks. "They were only twelve years old."

My legs give out as the weight of the confession crushes me. Before I hit the ground, Jake's arms sweep around me, catching me effortlessly. "Shh, baby, I've got you," he murmurs, his gravelly voice cutting through the chaos in my mind. It wraps around me, pulling me back from the edge.

I cling to him, burying my face in his chest as my cries wrack through me. "Jake, I couldn't save them. Twenty little girls... I couldn't save a single one." The words scrape from my throat as though they're ripping my heart apart.

He pulls me close, his face buried in my hair. "You didn't fail them," he whispers fiercely. "You're here, and I've got you. I'm not letting you go." His arms lift me easily, and I wrap my legs around his waist, clutching him as if he's the only thing keeping me from shattering completely.

He carries me upstairs, and I bury my face in the curve of his neck, the rhythmic sound of his heartbeat drowning out my hiccupped sobs. A door slams somewhere ahead, and I glance up in time to see Jaxson disappear into a room, the door closing with a resounding bang.

"He's not mad at you, Red," Jake says softly, his arms circling protectively.

"He looked mad," I mumble, shifting. "Maybe I should talk to him—"

"Nope." Jake cuts me off, his tone leaving no room for argument. "You're staying with me right now." He nudges open a door with his foot and steps inside, kicking it closed behind us.

The room is all masculine charm: dark grays and navy, clothes scattered on the floor, and a bed that's only half made. Jake sets me down gently against the pillows, his gaze flicking around the room before landing on me. He scratches the back of his neck, his lips quirking in a nervous smile. "If I'd known you'd end up in here, I would've cleaned up."

"It's perfect," I say, wiping at my tear-streaked face. I smile faintly and reach for one of the pillows, pulling it close. Inhaling deeply, I catch his scent—clean and intoxicating. It settles my frayed nerves.

Jake's eyebrows shoot up. "Are you... smelling my pillow?"

Heat floods my face, and I hide behind the pillow. "No," I mumble, voice muffled by the fabric. "That would be weird."

"Sure looked like it to me." He smirks, plucking the pillow from my hands and tossing it aside. Crawling onto the bed, he moves toward me. My breath catches, the space between us growing smaller with every inch he closes. His dark eyes gleam with mischief as his hand trails up my knee, his lips brushing against the inside of my calf.

"Do you like how I smell, Red?" His tone drops into a teasing growl.

My lips go dry, words fumbling from my mouth. "I-I... uh..."

"Say it." His smirk deepens, his gaze locked on mine.

"Y-yes," I finally manage, the word tumbling out in a hoarse whisper. His laughter flickers in his eyes, and I realize too late that he's enjoying this far too much.

"That wasn't cool, Jakey!" I protest, kicking my foot out. He yelps as he tumbles off the bed, landing with a loud thud on the floor. My laughter bubbles up unbidden, a rare moment of levity breaking through the tension.

The door bursts open, and Killian strides in, his gaze scanning the room. His eyes land on me and shift to Jake sprawled on the floor, arching his brow in confusion.

"What the hell happened to you?" he asks, a mix of amusement and exasperation.

Jake pushes himself up from the floor, brushing off his jeans with a low chuckle. "Red likes how I smell," he says, flashing a wide grin. His tone is teasing, but his look stays fixed on me.

I groan, rolling my eyes at him before flopping back against the pillows. "You're insufferable."

Killian doesn't miss a beat, sliding into Jake's vacated spot with a smirk. "Do you like how I smell, Princess?" His tone is teasing as he sprawls across me, his head landing just below my chest. His arms snake around my waist, locking me against him as he buries his face into my shirt. "Mmm, you smell good to me," he mumbles, his words muffled but dripping with mischief.

A startled squeak escapes me, and I wriggle beneath him. "Killian, that tickles!" My laughter bubbles out as I try to squirm away.

"Oh no, baby, you're not going anywhere," he murmurs with mock seriousness. "You're way too comfortable now. Guess I'm stuck here."

Jake grumbles, inaudible from the other side of the bed as he climbs in, dropping down with a soft sigh. Propping himself on his elbow, he watches us, his expression soft but amused. "He's got a point about one thing," Jake says.

"And what's that?" I ask, my voice light as I thread my fingers through Killian's messy hair.

Jake's gaze sharpens, locking with mine. "You're not going anywhere."

My breath hitches, but I force a laugh. "I have to go home eventually, you know."

Killian groans dramatically, keeping his hold on me like a petulant child. "Don't ruin this moment," he whines against my stomach. Meanwhile, Jake gently tilts my face toward him, his touch firm but tender.

"Stay here with us," Jake murmurs. I protest, but his thumb brushes over my lips, silencing me. "Hear me out. You'll end up spending most of your time here anyway. Why waste time going back and forth?"

He pulls his thumb away, his eyes searching mine as the weight of his words sinks in—my mind races. My savings have been dwindling under the weight of my apartment costs. Selling it would free me, give me the chance to move closer to the guys, and make a better life for Atlas. The thought of them in his life warms my soul, and a small smile creeps across my lips.

"What are you thinking about, Princess?" Killian's voice rumbles softly from where he's still sprawled across me.

I exhale slowly. "That you're right. I can put the money back into my savings if I sell my apartment. It makes sense."

Jake's lips twitch into a smile, relief, and gratitude flickering across his face. Killian's reaction is instant. He smacks a loud, exaggerated kiss to my cheek before rolling off the bed with a thud.

"I'm telling Ash!" he shouts, bolting for the door. Echoing down the hall, excitement spilling into every word as he hollers the news to Ash and Jaxson.

Jake locks the door, crawling back into bed with me, his hand cradling my cheek as he turns me to face him. "Thank you, Red."

"For what?" I ask softly, my fingers brushing against the edge of his beard.

"For staying," he whispers. "For making him smile. It's been... a long time."

His features soften under my touch, and for a moment, I see the Jake I used to know. The one who would sneak into my room to hold me through nightmares, who shielded me from every blow, who fought to protect me in ways I didn't always understand.

I bite my bottom lip, my thoughts tangling in the possibilities. This could bring me closer to finding St. John—and getting Atlas back. The idea of finally piecing my life together sends a rush through me. But I'll have to tread carefully. Krystal's burner phone, her cryptic messages and photos—it all needs to stay hidden. I'll make it work, though. It'll be worth it if this brings me closer to my goal.

Taking a deep breath—the first one that feels full and free since the hospital—I roll onto my side to face Jake. My grin stretches wide, the weight lifting just a little. "Plus, this will make finding Patrick easier. I'll be here for all the updates, and hopefully, we'll find him sooner."

Jake's voice erupts as he shoves off the bed. "Seriously? St. John? That's where your mind went? Is that all that matters to you?" His chest heaves, his hands trembling at his sides. "Do we mean so little to you?"

Before I can answer, he hurls an object from his dresser across the room. It smashes against the wall, shards of glass scattering everywhere. I scream, scrambling back, my hands bracing against the headboard.

"Jake, stop!" I plead, but his rage only escalates.

"Do we mean nothing to you?" he launches another object, and it slams into the drywall with a *crack*. I duck as it rains slivers of glass down on me. I flinch, hands flying to cover my face as my breathing comes in sharp, shallow gasps.

The pounding of fists echoes from the other side of the door. Killian and Ash shout, their voices muffled but frantic as they try to break in. "Jake! Open the damn door!"

But Jake bolted it shut when Killian left, and there's no way they're getting in quickly. My eyes dart wildly around the room, searching for any escape. My gaze lands on the window—a small opening just big enough for me. Not him.

Jake's back is turned, his fists clenched as he paces in furious strides. This is my chance.

I leap over the bed, my bare foot landing on a shard of glass. A sharp pain tears through me, and I bite back a cry, hobbling toward the window. My fingers fumble with the latch, desperation fueling me. I manage to wrench it open and fling myself through, my body tumbling out into the night.

The drop is farther than I anticipated. The ground slams into me, knocking the fire from my soul. My chest heaves, but no air comes, just a sharp ache that radiates through my ribs. Above me, Jake's voice booms.

"Ember!" His face appears in the window, his eyes wide with anger and panic. I force myself to my feet, every movement sending glass deeper into my foot, but I don't stop. I can't stop.

His footsteps thunder behind me as I sprint down the alley. The world blurs around me, my heartbeat drowning out everything else. Spotting a large garbage bin, I dive behind it, curling into the smallest space I can manage. My knees draw close, and I bury my face against them, tears slipping unchecked down my cheeks.

"Red?" Jake's voice echoes down the alley, softer now, almost pleading.

I stiffen, trying to stifle my sobs, but the occasional hitch in my breathing betrays me. His shadow stretches across the narrow space, blocking what little light peeks through.

"Ember, baby, I'm so sorry. Please, come out," he begs, crouching down. His hand reaches toward me, but I recoil sharply, huddling further into the corner.

"D-don't touch me!" I cry, my voice breaking as I shove myself away from him—the cold wall bites into my spine.

"Please, Red, I—" Jake's voice cuts off as more footsteps approach, heavy and hurried.

"Where is she?" Jaxson's growl is unmistakable, low, and menacing. The sharp crack of a fist meeting flesh echoes in the alley, followed by a grunt from Jake. "What the hell were you doing in there?" Jaxson's voice is icy and dangerous.

I sob quietly into my hands, tremors wracking my frame. A softer voice calls out, tentative and careful.

"Emmy, Sweetie?" Killian crouches at the edge of the gap, his tone gentle but urgent.

I jerk back instinctively, the motion slamming my head against the wall. Pain blooms at the base of my skull, and I cry out, clutching the spot.

"Oh, baby, come here," Killian coaxes, his hand reaching toward me. I jerk back, causing the metal garbage to clang, echoing down the alley.

Killian's hand stills, his expression crumbling. "Okay, shh, baby," he whispers, holding his hands up in surrender. "I'm not going to hurt you. I swear."

"D-don't touch me!" I shake my head violently. My voice rises, sharp and broken. "That's what Jake said!" I hiss, my breath hitching as anger and fear twist together. "That's what *he* said."

His words become a hollow echo, drowned out by the memory of Jake's rage and the memory of someone else's.

CHAPTER 37

Asher

Jake's voice wavers, thick with guilt, as he calls out, "Is she back there, Ember? Red?"

A faint rustle draws me behind a dented garbage can, and she crouches, trembling. Her tear-streaked face is pale, and her wide green eyes bounce between us, wild and brimming with mistrust. Shallow, uneven gasps escape her lips, and her chest rises and falls like she's trying to hold herself together by sheer will.

Jake steps forward, his desperation carving harsh lines into his face. "Don't—" I shove him back, my glare sharp. "You've done enough, Jake. Take a walk."

He stiffens, his jaw locking, fists flexing at his sides. "I just want to help," he mutters, no more than a whisper.

"You've *helped* enough," I snap, though my tone softens. "Go, Jake. I've got her."

He hesitates, his eyes fixed on her huddled form. Slowly, he crouches, leaning down to try to catch her gaze. "I'm sorry, Red," he whispers, thick with regret.

Her body flinches, her green eyes narrowing as she watches him with feral intensity. She doesn't speak, but the distrust radiating off her is palpable.

Jake's shoulders slump as he rises. "I'll go."

She jerks forward, a strangled cry tearing from her throat. Panic flashes across her face, quickly replaced by pain as she tries to move. My stomach churns when I see the dark streak of blood trailing onto the pavement.

Crouching down slowly, I make sure to keep my voice steady. "He's not leaving you, Sweetie. He's just going back to the house."

Her wide eyes snap to mine, desperately searching my face. Whatever she finds must reassure her because she gives a hesitant nod before curling back into herself, wrapping her arms around her knees.

The grime of the alley sticks to my hands as I crawl closer. "Jaxson," I say, glancing at him. "I need your help to get her out. Killian, grab the first aid kit. Jake..." My voice hardens as I glare at him. "Clean up your mess and stay out of sight for tonight."

He nods stiffly, casting one final look at her before turning and slinking down the alley, his head hanging low.

Jaxson shifts nervously beside me, his boots scraping against the asphalt. "Why me?" he asks, barely audible.

"She trusts you," I reply, locking eyes with him. "She feels safe with you for some reason."

His eyes move back to her hiding spot.

"She can't stay here all night, Jax. Will you help me?" I beg.

"Yeah, sure."

It's painstaking. Every inch she moves feels like a small victory, her fear preventing her from coming out. Jaxson and I coax her; our voices patient, each minute stretching endlessly.

When she finally stumbles out, I catch her before she can collapse. Her body shakes violently, her skin ice-cold against mine. I cradle her close, brushing tangled strands of hair from her face. "We'll get you warm, baby," I murmur. "A bath, a bed... but we need to patch up that foot first."

Her small hands clutch at my shirt. "I'm sorry," she whispers, so faint I almost don't catch it.

"For what?" I ask, adjusting my grip to hold her more securely.

"For not being able to tell you the truth," she mumbles, her head lolling back.

The unnatural angle freezes me, panic cutting up my chest. "Jaxson!" I bark as her limp form sags against me.

Jaxson steps in front of me as he steadies her head, adjusting the unnatural angle of her neck. His jaw ticks, and when he speaks, it's low but edged with frustration. "How much longer are you going to keep lying to her?"

I close my eyes, exhaling slowly. The weight of the truth sits heavier with every passing second. Her tear-streaked face is the first thing I see when I open them again. Mascara streaks down her cheeks in dark, messy trails, and even unconscious, her hands are knotted in my shirt, clinging like I'm the only thing keeping her grounded.

"As long as it takes to keep her safe and away from him," I say, my voice tight.

Jaxson scoffs, his frustration flaring. "Then why not just kill him?"

I shift her in my arms, the motion jarring my already-frayed nerves. "Because Killian won't let us," I bite out. "He says Patrick is for her—to finish when she's ready."

Jaxson's jaw clenches, his gaze flicking to her fragile, battered frame. His hand twitches like he wants to reach for her, but doesn't. Instead, he steps aside, throwing me a hard look. "Then you better make her want to stay soon. I'm not keeping this from her forever."

He spins on his heel and storms ahead, his boots scuffing against the floor as he opens the door for us. I watch him disappear down the hall, his frustration bleeding into every tense line of his body.

Inside, Jake stumbles out of the kitchen, the sour stench of alcohol hitting me before his slurred words. He grips the doorframe to steady himself, his eyes glassy as they land on her limp form in my arms.

"How is she?"

"She'll be fine," I say coldly, not breaking stride. "Go to bed."

Jake hesitates, his lips parting like he wants to argue. Nodding, he sways his way up the stairs without another word.

With my elbow, I nudge a bedroom door open and lay her carefully on the bed. Her body still trembles, even as she curls instinctively into the blankets. I grab a wet washcloth from the bathroom, returning to find her eyes fluttering open, barely focused.

"Ember, Sweetie," I whisper, sitting beside her. "I need your help, we need to get you cleaned up."

She mumbles incoherently, shifting enough to fumble with her sweatshirt. It slides off her shoulders and lands in a heap on the floor, leaving her in nothing but a black lace bra. My breath hitches as the delicate fabric stretches against her chilled skin, but the sight of her scars quickly drowns any stray thought.

Her fingers clumsily tug at her jeans, her frustration mounting with each failed attempt. Finally, she flops back with a groan, her hands covering her face. "You do it," she mumbles, muffled.

A soft chuckle escapes me as I ease her jeans down, careful not to jostle her injured foot. But any hint of humor vanishes as my eyes land on the jagged scars crisscrossing her skin. My hand hovers over a particularly deep one on her stomach, heat surging through my veins.

"He invited a friend over," she murmurs, distant, detached. "Someone who liked knives a little too much. He nearly killed me, and Patrick almost let him."

The rage threatens to boil over, but I force it down, my voice soft but firm. "Then why do you want to go back?"

"I don't want to go back," she whispers, curling into the blankets. "I just need to find him. He has something of mine."

"What does he have, baby?" I persist, and I know I've lost her to exhaustion.

I get to work, dipping the rag in warm water, wiping away the blood and grime from her foot. She moans, the sound tugging at my insides.

The door creaks open behind me, and Killian fills the room. "Did she say anything?" he asks quietly.

"Not much," I reply, wrapping her foot with a strip of gauze. "Just that she doesn't want to go back. She said he has something of hers but passed out before she could say what."

Killian nods, stripping his shirt off and tossing it at me. "She can't sleep in that. Put this on her," he says, cold and detached, before slipping back out of the room.

I stare at the door momentarily before turning back to Ember; I sigh as I carefully roll her onto her side. My fingers work quickly, unclasping her bra with my eyes shut tight before slipping Killian's shirt over her.

When I pull the blankets up, she burrows into them, a soft sigh escaping her lips. I lean close, brushing a stray strand of hair from her face. “Sleep, Sweetheart,” I murmur. “We’ll keep you safe. I promise.”

CHAPTER 38

Jake

The carpet muffles the sound of my pacing feet, worn down by my frantic movements. My fingers knot in my hair, tugging until a sting blooms, but the ache does nothing to quiet the chaos. The alcohol burns in my veins, but it can't touch the guilt, can't drown out the image looping in my mind—Ember, flinging herself from the second-story window without hesitation, without a second thought for her safety.

I froze when I found her below, her body a fragile heap on the cold ground. For one terrifying heartbeat, I'd thought she was gone. Then, with a rattling gasp, she'd sucked in air, and relief had slammed into me so hard it knocked me backward. But it was fleeting.

She'd rather risk dying than face me.

I'd done this. I'd driven her to this. And when I reached for her, desperate to fix what I'd shattered, she had flinched—her body recoiling, her wide, fearful eyes cutting through me sharper than any blade. She ran. From me. And when I finally found her huddled and trembling behind a dumpster, blood streaking her skin and tears tracking down her face, the terror that flashed in her gaze had ripped me apart.

I drag in a shuddering breath, each step feeding the gnawing churn of guilt inside me. I tell myself to sleep; maybe if I close my eyes, I'll wake up with a way to fix this. But how? How do I make her understand that my rage wasn't aimed at her? That Patrick Saint John's name lit the fire within me, not her? That every furious word, every tense moment, was because I've failed her—again and again.

My legs give out, and I collapse onto the edge of the bed, elbows digging into my knees, chin sinking into my hands. Behind closed eyelids, I see her face—pale, streaked with tears, as if I were a monster. A bitter laugh escapes me, hollow. She ran, and I can't even blame her.

I fall back against the mattress, clutching her pillow and smothering my face. Her scent is faint. It's a cruel comfort, the ghost of her slipping through my fingers. The pillow muffles my groan, but the pain doesn't go away. It never will.

Everyone is asleep now, while I let my thoughts run wild with images of what happened. I can't get it out of my head. I squeeze my eyes shut, light dancing behind my lids. "Fuck!" I growl, slamming my hands down against the mattress.

A scream—raw and broken—rips through the silence, causing me to jump. A desperate cry follows it; ice shoots into my veins. I know that cry. I used to listen to it late at night when we were in that foster home together.

Shoving to my feet, I sprint down the hall, feet pounding on the wood floors. Swinging Ember's door open, it bounces off the wall, and I stand in the doorway like a madman. Panting as I watch her curl in on herself, trembling, sweat shining on her skin. I grip the doorframe so hard my nails carve into the wood. I shouldn't be here; I should get Ash or Killian after how she responded to me... but I can't.

She whimpers—soft, broken, a sound that sinks straight through me and drags me back to the nights we spent in foster care—nights filled with whispered words and secrets.

I try to walk away, but I just can't.

Not again.

Twenty Years Ago...

A muffled noise filters through the thin walls, rousing me from the edge of sleep.

"Did you hear that?" Ash groans, his face buried under a pillow.

I sit up, listening. There it is again. A soft, broken cry curling around me like a vice. Rosie. That's what they called her when she arrived. Not that it matters much—girls like her never stay. They either get adopted or run at the first chance they get.

"Jesus, someone needs to shut her up," Ash snaps, tossing the pillow aside.

A sigh drags through me. The alcohol I downed earlier churns in my gut as I shove off the covers and swing my legs over the edge of the bed. The room tilts when I stand, my hand bracing against the wall to balance myself.

"Fuck it, I'll check."

The hallway stretches in front of me, dark and quiet. The old wood floors creak under my feet, a sound I've learned to step around over the years. When I reach her door, I don't bother knocking. The lock gives way with a quiet click, and I ease the door open, stepping inside.

She's curled into a tight ball in the center of the bed, barely a shape beneath the tangled sheets. Her small frame trembles with another muffled whimper. A familiar knot forms—one I don't know how to name.

I crouch beside her, reaching out to brush a wild curl away from her face. "Rosie?" The name feels abnormal on my tongue. It doesn't feel like a good name for her. "Rosie."

Her lashes flutter, her eyes blinking open; they're red-rimmed and glassy. She stares at me, and her face softens. "J-Jakey?" she croaks.

I don't correct her. Instead, my thumb traces the damp streak on her cheek, wiping it away. "Hey, Rosie. What's going on?"

Her eyes dart to the door. I don't need to ask—I already know. It's the same thing that has happened to many of the girls before her.

"Did he try to visit again?"

Her slight nod sends a sharp spike of anger through me, but I shove it down. There's no use in letting it out now.

"Alright, Rose. Scoot over."

Her wide eyes search mine like she's waiting for the punchline, for the catch. When none comes, she shifts, making enough space on the cramped twin bed. I cross the room, locking the door with a quiet click, testing the knob twice to make sure it holds before sliding between the covers.

She watches me like a deer in headlights, tucking her hands beneath her cheek. I close my eyes, inhaling, trying to temper the frustration boiling inside me. She fidgets beside me, restless, shifting every few seconds.

"Jakey?"

"Hmm?"

"Why did you come in here?" There was a pause, followed by a quieter response, "I know you guys hate me."

The words hit harder than they should. I keep my eyes shut, swallowing hard against the tightness building inside me. It's easier to answer in the dark. "Because... a part of me thinks. I need to protect you."

"Why, though?"

I exhale. "Just go to sleep, Rose."

She inches closer, her forehead pressing against my arm. Gradually, the tension in her small frame melts into sleep. But I stay awake, my eyes locked on the door, every creak and groan of the old house holding my focus.

I don't sleep. I just watch. Waiting.

Present...

The memory claws at the edges of my mind, but I push it down and move to the bed. Lifting the top cover, I slip in behind her. The mattress dips beneath my weight, and she stills. Banding my arm around her waist, I pull her back, drawing her closer.

A muffled whimper escapes her lips, and her fingers reach for mine, gripping tight, nails digging into my skin. The sting grounds me in the present—she's still afraid.

"Shh, Red," I murmur against the shell of her ear, my voice remaining calm despite the tightness. "I've got you. I've always got you."

Her body stiffens, and I freeze, holding my breath. The old fear, the walls she's built, are all right between us. Any second now, I expect her to pull away, to retreat into the familiar distance where I can't follow. She exhales—a slow, shaky release—and her fingers weave through mine. Relief washes over me, and a smile tugs at my lips. I tug her closer, my forehead brushing against the back of her head. The scent of roses tickles my nose.

She wiggles back against me, and I know she's awake.

"Jakey?"

"Yeah?" My thumb traces lazy circles against her stomach. My eyes flutter shut, hoping, just for a second, to hold onto this sliver of peace.

She rolls to her side to face me, her breath ghosting across my lips. "I'm sorry I ran," she whispers, and it's more than an apology—it's regret. "I just needed to get away."

I could keep my eyes closed and avoid the moment's weight, but I don't. I open them, finding hers in the dim light. Wide, searching, desperate for reassurance. "I'm not angry with you, Red," I murmur, tucking a loose strand of hair behind her ear. The way she shivers at my touch hits me hard, twisting in my chest. "I'm mad at myself for scaring you."

Her hand trembles as it rises, fingers brushing over my cheek with such tenderness it threatens to undo me. "I know you don't understand why I need to find Patrick," she says softly. "But I'm asking you to trust me. Trust that I know what I'm doing."

I swallow, the sincerity in her words cutting through the layers of doubt and frustration I've built up. I close my eyes, letting her scent fill my nose before opening them again. "I do trust you," I say, and I mean it. But the truth lodges itself inside me. "It's him I can't trust."

A ghost of a smile flashes across her lips, but it doesn't quite reach her eyes. She moves closer, her fingers tangling in the hair at the nape of my neck. Her body heat soaks into mine as I hold her flush against me.

"Just trust me, okay?" Her tone fades as sleep pulls her under.

"Of course, Red," I whisper, securing her against me like I can keep all her demons at bay. Her breathing slows, but I stay awake, my mind echoing her words.

There are cracks in her story, gaps in her past that don't fit, pieces that keep me wondering what she is hiding. She hasn't told us everything.

And yet, she asked me to trust her.

I can't bring myself to tell her the truth. That Patrick Saint John isn't some ghost she's chasing—he's closer than she could ever imagine. Beneath us, lurking in the shadows.

My hold tightens, my fingers molding to the curve of her waist. I'll shield her, even if it means burying truths beneath layers of deception and bleeding out before I let her reach him.

CHAPTER 39

Jake

Sunlight spills through the blinds, painting golden stripes across the sheets and warming my skin. I stir, groaning softly, rolling over —only to freeze when my hand brushes against... someone. My pulse stutters, and I glance down to find Ember curled into my side, her face buried against me. Her leg is draped over mine, an unconscious, possessive tangle that sends a sharp ache through my chest. I hesitate, watching her lashes flutter in sleep, her body moving closer as if she belonged there.

I lift my hand, threading my fingers into the silky strands of her hair, letting them slide between my fingers. She stirs, a soft moan slipping from her lips as she nuzzles closer, her nose brushing against my collarbone. A wave of longing crashes over me. How often have I watched her laugh with Killian, whisper secrets to Ash, and feel like an outsider in the space I should own?

Her eyes flutter open, bleary and squinting against the morning light, and for a fleeting second, I see nothing but happiness in them—before they shift, before the distance creeps in. I smile, running my thumb over her cheek, desperate to hold onto this moment. "Good morning, gorgeous," I murmur.

A slow smile spreads across her lips, sleep-drunk and sweet, nearly knocking the air out of me. "Good morning," she whispers, her fingers tracing lazy patterns against my skin. "I never have nightmares when you're beside me... just like when we were kids."

My heart lurches at the memories, the stolen nights, the way I'd sneak into her room to keep the darkness at bay for her. But now, the darkness is different. It's inside me, festering in the spaces between us. I swallow hard, forcing a chuckle. "You knew I used to sneak in?"

Her lips curve, and she bites her bottom lip in that teasing way that sends a sharp pull deep inside me, almost painful in its intensity. "Of course I knew," she murmurs, eyes dancing.

I brush my thumb over her lip, tugging it free. "All I ever wanted was to protect you," I whisper, the words escaping before I can stop them. They hang in the air between us. "And I couldn't even do that right."

She shifts, pulling back, and the loss of her weight is immediate. "What do you mean?" Her brows furrow, concern flickering in her expression, but I see it—the hesitation, the way she guards herself.

My chest constricts. "I forced you to run from us once," I say, my voice rough with guilt. "And then you were taken. How can you trust me to protect you when I failed you so badly?"

Her absence feels inevitable now, the space she'll leave behind when she finally decides we aren't enough. But instead of pulling away completely, she moves, shocking me as she swings herself onto my lap, straddling me with a weight that feels like both a blessing and a punishment. My hands instinctively find her hips, gripping tight, grounding myself in the essence of her.

"Jake Thorne," she says firmly, her hands braced on either side of my head, trapping me in. "When have I ever doubted that you could take care of me? When have any of the guys thought that?"

I open my mouth, but the fierce look in her eyes silences me. It's unshakable. And yet, there's a distance beneath it that guts me. "I've never blamed you," she continues, softer now. "Not back then, and not now. You, Killian, and Ash have always been my home—my safe space." Her tone lowers, and she leans in, the scent of her shampoo flooding my senses. "I trust you with everything I am."

The words hit deep, fracturing inside me. I should feel relief, but instead, I can only focus on how she trusts them. The way she lets Ash pull her into hugs and Killian can make her laugh with nothing more than a smirk. And me? I'm just the ghost of someone who disappointed her.

"Then why do you want to leave so badly?" The question slips out before I can stop it. Her expression falters, guilt flashing across her features before she carefully schools them.

"I don't want to leave," she whispers. It wraps around my ribs and squeezes. "But there's something I need to do."

Her eyes flick to mine, and I let go instantly, cursing myself for the desperation I can't shake.

"I can't tell you," she finally admits, tinged with regret, and before I can push, she's slipping off my lap, leaving behind nothing but cold sheets and a hollow ache.

"Jake," she calls softly from the bathroom doorway, her eyes searching mine, "you promised to trust me as I trust you."

I want to argue and demand answers, but I nod, feeling more lost than ever. The quiet shuffle of her feet draws my attention back to her. She leans down, brushing a kiss against my cheek, before disappearing behind the door.

I flop back onto the bed with a heavy sigh, dragging my hands over my face. She's messing with my head, leaving me tangled in a web of worry and guilt. And worse, she doesn't even realize it.

"Hey, Red?" My voice is rough and exhausted.

"Yeah?" she answers from behind the door, the sound of running water muffling her words.

"Killian's arranging for a company to move your stuff today. Is that still okay with you?"

The shower switches off, and her head peeks out, curls damp. "Of course! Is there anything I need to do?"

I shake my head, offering a smile I don't feel, and as she disappears again, I can't shake the feeling that she's already halfway out the door.

"No," I reply with a low chuckle, leaning back against the headboard. "Killian's got it covered." My eyes flick to her as she steps fully into view, still in yesterday's jeans and Killian's oversized T-shirt hanging loose on her frame. It shouldn't bother me, but it does. "Is there anything you want to do today?"

She shrugs, running a hand through her messy hair. "I should check in with Jax about any new leads, but other than that, I'm free."

I watch how she avoids my gaze, her focus shifting around the room like she's searching for an escape. "Well, if nothing's urgent," I say, keeping my voice casual, "would you come to the office with me? I've been neglecting the business since we found you. I need to make an appearance."

Ember's lips curl into a smirk as she steps closer, eyes alight with mischief. "I'd love to see how you afford all of this." She gestures around the room. "When did you become Mr. Daddy Warbucks?"

Daddy.

The word hits low, unexpected. Not in the way I've heard it used before—this is playful, teasing, wrapped in her laughter—but it does something to me. My breath catches for half a second, mind short-circuiting as a rush of heat coils low in my gut. She doesn't even realize what she's just said—or maybe she does. Hell if I know.

She stops in front of me, and I don't give myself time to think. I reach for her, pulling her into my lap. She gasps, soft and surprised, then laughs as she melts into me, her arms looping around my neck, her warmth slipping under my skin.

"I want to know everything about you, Jakey," she whispers, burying her face against me like I'm home. Like I'm *hers*.

And I want to be.

I close my eyes, letting her sink into me. "You feel like home," she whispers, so softly that it nearly disappears into the space between us.

I grip her, my lips brushing against her temple. "You *are* my home."

She pulls back just enough to look at me, her gaze searching, always searching—for reassurance, for truth. I let her see everything I can't put into words, everything I've been trying to show her since the day she returned.

After a long beat, I clear my throat, unwilling to break the fragile moment but knowing I have to. "Let's get some breakfast and figure out our day, yeah?"

She nods and slips off my lap, tugging my hand as she leads me out of the room.

When we step into the kitchen, she freezes. The table is spread with every one of her childhood favorites—pancakes, scrambled eggs, fresh fruit, even the syrup she always swore tasted better than any other. I don't miss how her shoulders tense and her lips part in quiet disbelief. Her eyes scan the spread before locking onto Ash. He barely has time to react before she launches at him, arms wrapping around his neck.

"Whoa, Sweetheart," he laughs, stumbling back a step but keeping hold of her. "Easy!"

She slides down, her hands gripping his arms as she looks up at him, beaming through watery eyes. "Thank you."

Ash grins, cupping her cheeks in his hands, his thumbs swiping over the hint of tears she won't let fall. "You're welcome, Sweetie. Now, are you hungry?"

A genuine laugh bubbles from her lips, and it's like hearing music I didn't know I missed until now. "I'm always hungry lately," she teases, flashing him a smile.

And just like that, it hits me—how much I've missed seeing her like this. Carefree. Happy. It's like a punch to the gut, knocking my breath out.

Beside me, Killian lounges against the wall, arms folded over his chest. But his eyes hold a quiet storm like the last traces of sunlight before the rain comes. He watches her like she's fragile. "She's breathtaking, isn't she?" he murmurs.

I swallow hard, unable to answer. My attention is locked on Ember, who laughs with Ash as he attempts to show her how to flip a pancake. It goes horribly wrong, batter splattering across the counter in a sticky mess. Ember doubles over, clutching her stomach as laughter spills from her, and Ash groans, wiping his hands on a towel, though it's obvious he doesn't care about the mess. He just cares about her.

Jaxson strides into the kitchen, stopping abruptly when he sees her. His usual calm, unreadable expression slips as he watches her like we all do, like she's the sun and we're just orbiting, caught in her gravity.

Because sharing her with my brothers—the men I've trusted my whole life—is hard enough. But Jaxson? Jaxson is the wild card. He's the one she looks at differently, the one she lets in without realizing it. I can't fight it. I can't push him away. She needs all of us in different ways, and deep down, I know I can't be the only one she leans on.

"Breakfast is ready!" Ash announces, clapping his hands and snapping us all out of whatever thoughts we were lost in.

Ember spins toward the table, eyes bright, and it feels like the air is lighter for the first time in a long while. Like she's bringing life back to my world. And even though it tears at me, watching her with them, I can't stop wanting more. From wanting *her.*

"Are you sure this is okay?" Ember's voice is soft, threaded with worry as she clings to my arm, her fingers digging in just enough to ground me. Her eyes dart around the grand lobby of *Rose Incorporated,* wide and unsure, like she's waiting for someone to call her out for stepping into a world she doesn't belong in. But she belongs—more than she knows.

I glance down at her, a small smile tugging at my lips as I guide her further inside. She hasn't noticed the name carved elegantly above the entrance yet. Anticipation coils within me, waiting for the moment it clicks—for the moment she realizes this place, this entire building, was crafted with her in mind.

"Trust me, Red," I murmur, leaning close enough for my breath to ghost over her ear. "Everything's fine. No one's going to fire me for bringing you here—who do you think funds this place?"

She attempts a faint smile, but it doesn't reach her eyes. She scans the sea of suits bustling around us, the pristine perfection of the towering space making her shift uneasily. "I'm not dressed for this," she whispers. "You didn't tell me everyone else would be in business attire. We look ridiculous."

"Hush, Red." I stop, my fingers brushing the underside of her jaw, tipping her face up to mine. Her lips part, breath hitching, and I forget where we are for a second. "No one cares what we're wearing. And even if they did, they wouldn't dare say a damn thing."

Her brows lift in challenge. "And why's that?"

I let my thumb drift across her chin, savoring how her lashes flutter at the touch. "Because I'd make sure anyone who looked at you the wrong way *regretted it.*" My voice drops lower, and the effect is immediate—a blush blooming across her cheeks, and the goosebumps rippling down her arms don't go unnoticed. "Did you like that, Red?"

Her head falls lightly against my shoulder. "Yes."

A deep, primal force stirs within me, her honesty unraveling the fragile thread of control I'm barely holding onto. My gaze sweeps the room, dark and sharp, daring anyone to so much as *breathe* in her direction. A few women hover in the corridor, eyeing Ember with barely veiled hostility, their whispers cutting through the low hum of conversation. I make a mental note of every single one of them. They'll be gone before the day ends. No one disrespects her. No one.

Once we enter the elevator, I swipe my key card, bypassing all floors to take us straight to my office. The doors slide shut. Ember stays close, her big, searching eyes locking onto mine. The air thickens between us, charged and heavy. She does it—her teeth sink into her bottom lip, her gaze dropping to my mouth for just a second too long.

"Fuck." The curse slips from my lips as I snap, spinning her and trapping her back against the cool metal wall. She gasps, her hands splaying across my chest. I brace my arms on either side of her head, caging her in. "You keep looking at me like that, Red, and I won't be able to hold back."

Her chest rises and falls rapidly, heat radiating from her skin. The soft puff of air fans across my lips, close enough to taste if I just lean in. She doesn't pull away. She doesn't *want* to.

The elevator dings, jarring us both back to reality. I step back, jaw tight, hands clenched into fists. Ember stumbles as she follows me out, her flushed cheeks and parted lips leaving a vivid mark in my mind. Her hazel-green eyes lock onto mine.

"Careful, Red," I warn, my voice rough, the edges of my restraint fraying.

"Why?" she whispers, laced with challenge.

I slowly step toward her, dipping down so my lips nearly brush her ear. "Because if you keep pushing me, I might have to punish you."

She straightens, her fingers curling into fists at her sides like she's bracing herself. But her gaze doesn't falter. "What if I want you to?"

Her words land like a spark in dry kindling, igniting the primal side of me. I feel it in my veins, pulsing, searing, twisting through me with an ache that demands action. Every muscle winds taut with the need to claim her, to stamp out every doubt about where she belongs. My voice drops, rough and edged with hunger. "Say that again."

Ember bites her lip again, a nervous, fiery blush crawling up her neck. "I don't want you to hold back."

The air crackles between us. I close the distance, my lips hovering over her ear. "Be careful what you wish for, Red." I brush a feather-light kiss against her cheek, staying just long enough to feel the shiver that runs through her.

"Mr. Thorne, you're late."

Margaret's voice breaks through the haze like a cold slap of reality. She stands stiffly near my office entrance, clipboard in hand, her sharp eyes flicking between Ember and me. "Since you've been canceling, you're booked solid today. Lunch with—oh!" Her gaze lands on Ember fully, and her entire demeanor shifts. "Should I... ask her to leave?"

My head snaps toward her, my glare darkening. "Touch her, and you'll regret it, Margaret."

Margaret's face pales. "Oh... I just assumed she was another... admirer. Like the ones after you or Killian."

"She's not just anyone." My voice is steel. I step closer, my arm instinctively curling around Ember's waist. "This is *Ember Rose.*"

Margaret's mouth falls open in shock, her clipboard slipping. "Oh my god," she breathes. Then, before either of us can react, she's lunging toward Ember, enveloping her in a hug.

Ember stiffens in my arms, her eyes wide with confusion. "Uh..."

Margaret pulls back, practically vibrating with excitement. "It's you! The one they've all been talking about for years. I thought you were some *myth!*"

Ember glances at me, eyes wide. "Years?" she murmurs.

I nod, holding her, unwilling to let go. "Years."

Margaret steps back, her sharp eyes sweeping over Ember with a smile few ever see from her. There's no pretense with Margaret—never has been. She's older, tough as nails, and one of the only people not intimidated by me or the guys.

She folds her arms, huffing in exasperation. "And why, pray tell, didn't you warn me you were bringing *her*?" Before I can respond, she smacks my arm hard.

"Jesus, Margaret!" I rub the spot, scowling at her. "You could've broken something, you old bat."

Margaret narrows her eyes, unimpressed. "Who are you calling old, *boy?*" The challenge is enough to make anyone else shrink, but Ember's lips twitch like she's trying to hide a laugh.

Margaret turns her attention back to Ember, her expression softening instantly. "Don't mind this one," she says, jerking a thumb at me. "He's all brawn, no brains." Her tone is gentle, but a glint in her eye says she's been dealing with my kind of trouble for far too long. "Come with me, Sweetheart."

Before I can get a word in, Margaret has her arm looped through Ember's, steering her down the hall with the ease of someone who's used to taking charge. Ember throws a panicked glance over her shoulder, her eyes wide, silently begging me for an escape plan.

I chuckle, shoving my hands into my pockets and offering a lazy nod. "You'll survive, Red."

Margaret waves me off without looking back. "Worry about yourself, Thorne," she calls over her shoulder. "I'll bring her back when I'm good and ready."

I watch them disappear around the corner, shaking my head with a smirk. Ember's in good hands—whether she likes it or not.

CHAPTER 40

Jake

Ember bursts into my office. A blur of red hair as she slams the door and darts straight toward me. She dives beneath my desk, huddling close to my legs, breathing in panicked puffs.

"Hide. Me." She whispers, her eyes wide as she stares at me. "She's insane."

I cock an eyebrow, leaning back to give her some extra space, though I enjoy the way she huddles close to my calf. "What are you doing down there, silly girl? What happened?"

Her hand curls around my thigh, anxiety radiating off her. "Margaret is insane, Jake. Not only has she been dragging me all over, threatening anyone who so much as *looked* at me. And then—" she dramatically lowers her tone, "—she fired someone."

A smirk tugs at the corner of my lips. "Sounds like Margaret deserves a raise to me."

She huffs, slapping my leg. "Jake, I swear—" The click of incoming heels silences her.

Ember stiffens.

Margaret strides in, a familiar gleam in her eyes. "Jake," she announces, hands on her hips, "where's Ember? She ran off on me."

I lace my fingers together, resting my elbows on the desk over

Ember's trembling form. "Lost her already, Marg? Should I be concerned?"

Margaret scoffs. "Please. She bolted after I fired some guy."

I tilt my head, eyes twinkling. "Fired someone, did you?"

Margaret lifts a brow, unapologetic. "He looked at her funny. I won't tolerate that."

I chuckle, dragging a palm over my jaw. "Remind me to send you a very generous bonus."

Margaret waves a dismissive hand. "Forget the money. Just invite me over so I can get to know her properly. She's such a timid little thing."

Ember's hand lands on my knee, her nails digging in enough to make me shudder. My hand finds hers, fingers slipping between hers in a silent comfort.

Stepping forward, Margaret knocks a file from my desk. "Oops, sorry," she laughs, bending to pick it up, causing Ember to freeze, her eyes wide, lips parting.

"Don't worry about it, Marg." I beat Margaret to it, scooping up the papers and brushing my fingers lightly against Ember's cheek. "I've got it. Why don't you go track Ember down for me?"

Margaret's eyes narrow; her lips scrunched together in thought. "Mhmm," she hums. "Your next appointment is waiting. I'll send them in."

As soon as the door clicks shut, I glance at Ember, who's peeking at a document that slipped out of the file; her name is in large font at the top of the form. Shit. I swipe the document from her fingers, pinching her chin and forcing her eyes to mine. "Nosey little thing, aren't you?"

"My name was on that, Jake. What is it?"

I brush a kiss on her forehead, inhaling her delicate, floral scent. "Behave."

She works to scramble out from beneath my desk, and her eyes widen in panic when the door swings open. I place my palm against her head, keeping her in place. She doesn't resist as I push her back down, but she shoots me a pointed glare.

"Mr. Thorne," a deep voice greets the men stepping inside with briefcases. "Glad we could finally arrange this meeting."

I plaster on a smile, ignoring how Ember's hand inches up my thigh, a not-so-subtle act of revenge for not letting her out when she had the chance. "Apologies for the delays. My family and I have been... occupied."

"Of course, I understand how demanding a family can be." I work to focus on what the owners of Jet Productions are telling me, but I am distracted by Ember's fingers toying with the fabric of my pants; I catch her wrist, holding it flat against my thigh. My eyes dart down to see her lips twist, and I fight a laugh.

"So what do you think? Would a partnership with Jet Productions benefit Rose Incorporated?" one of the men asks. I think his name is Chad.

Ember jumps, slamming her head against the underside of my desk. A muffled thud reverberates through the room, and Ember's quiet groan follows. I drag my fingers through her hair as she clutches her head, her eyes glossy.

"I think I need to bring this to my business partners, gentlemen," I massage the bump forming on her crown, trying to soothe the ache. "I'm afraid I'll need to cut this meeting short. Shall we reconvene next week?"

Chad leans forward, trying to peek over my desk. "Chad, was it?" I growl, fire blazing in my eyes. My tone dips dangerously low. "I'm going to suggest you keep your curiosity in check."

The color drains from his face as he fumbles to gather his things, mumbling his goodbyes before hurrying out.

When the door swings shut, I roll my chair out, crouching to pull Ember out of her hiding spot. I settle her into my lap, cupping her cheek, and drawing her attention to mine. "Are you alright, Red?" I murmur, my thumb grazing her jaw."You're trouble."

She gives me a watery smile. "Y-you love it."

"Yeah, I do."

Margaret reappears, her assessing eyes sweep the room, landing on Ember—her lips purse, unimpressed but professional as always.

"Marg, please show Jet Productions to the lobby; they should be in the waiting area."

She nods, her gaze darting to Ember, who's awkwardly pushing up from my lap with a blush creeping up her neck. The disapproving arch of Margaret's brow is enough to make Ember freeze mid-motion.

"You have that lunch meeting soon. Would you like me to show her where she can wait?" Margaret offers her tone perfectly polite but with an edge. *Fuck I forgot about that.*

I force a smile, "Yes, once Jet Production is gone, you can take Ember out to lunch." Ember's brows scrunch together as she looks between us. "Go and take care of that, Marg. We'll be in here."

Margaret doesn't look convinced but nods, her heels clicking in perfect rhythm as she closes the door behind her.

I exhale, closing my eyes in an attempt to enjoy the quiet. Ember spins to face me, hands on her hips, eyes blazing.

"*Rose Incorporated?*" she spits, spinning to face me, hands on her hips. "*Your* company is called *Rose Incorporated?*"

I lean back, watching how her eyes blaze with fire. "And?" She opens her mouth, ready to argue. "You don't like it, Red?" My hands circle her waist, tugging her forward so that she is standing between my legs.

A startled gasp escapes her lips as her hands land on my shoulders for balance. "I-It's... that's..." I smirk, watching as she stumbles to find an answer. Her brows knit together, frustration simmering beneath the surface, but I can feel her melt against me, the tremor in her fingers betraying her. I let my hands slide to the backs of her thighs, fingertips tracing lazy patterns along the curve of muscle.

"Why wouldn't we name it after you? You're the reason it exists."

Her lips part, confusion dancing across her face. "What are you talking about?"

My thumbs drag across her hips, the skin warm beneath my fingertips. A shiver rolls through her. "Haven't you been listening to anything Killian's told you?" I pause. "We built this empire for you, Ember. We dug our way into the darkest places we could and created connections with some of the lowest people. And we did it all just to bring you back."

Her eyes search mine. I tilt my head, pulling her closer.

"Do you know why you never have to fear the dark, Red?" I whisper.

She swallows, shaking her head. I stand, towering over her, resting my forehead against her. My lips graze hers.

"Because no one would *dare* touch you," I continue. "Not when they know you belong to us. *You are ours, Ember.* And as long as you're ours, nothing in this world can touch you unless we let it."

Her chest rises and falls in fast pants, her hands gripping my shoulders like she's afraid to let go. My gaze dips to her mouth as she bites down on her lip.

I grin, spinning her around and delivering a swift swat to her backside. She jerks, twisting around to glare at me, which does nothing to hide the pink flush creeping up her cheeks.

"Go find Margaret before she comes looking for you again," I order with a tinge of amusement.

"But—" she starts, her pout irresistible.

"Go, Red." I flick a glance toward the door. Anxiety swirling in my stomach. "Find me after lunch."

I take a breath, rubbing a hand down my face before hitting the intercom button. "Marg, is she here?"

"Not yet." Her voice crackles through the intercom.

"Head to lunch, I'll grab her when she arrives. And, Marg?"

"Yes, Boss?"

"Try to keep Ember out of trouble."

Margaret's dry chuckle makes me smile. "No promises, boss."

CHAPTER 41

Ember Rose

Rose Inc. is a whole ass company built on a foundation of love and persistence—things I hadn't fully understood until now. The weight of that realization crushes me, stealing my breath and leaving me grasping at composure. *They never stopped looking for me.* The thought rattles in my head like loose change in a jar.

Killian tried to explain it to me before, annoyingly persistent—but I'd brushed him off, convinced he was only saying what he thought I wanted to hear. I should've known better. They would never lie to me about a thing like this. After all, they're helping me find Patrick, even though they hate the idea.

The creeping need to tell them the truth tastes like acid on my tongue, bile rising in my throat that I force back down. Exhaling, I squeeze the edge of the desk. An ache flares to life in my lower back as I move, a reminder of my reckless actions from yesterday. It gnaws at me, but it is mild compared to the emotions raging inside me—emotions I can't control.

Killian's kiss tingles on my lips, a ghost taunting me with things I can't have. Then there's Jake; his heart is so guarded that nothing can penetrate it, though he holds me through my nightmares, keeping me grounded so the darkness can't creep in. And Ash… my sweet, broken

Ash, reached for me when I jumped when I thought there was no one left to catch me.

Jake wants what I can't give him; he doesn't understand I need all of them, not just him. That thought eats away at me, turning the happy moments bitter.

"Everything alright, dear?" Margaret's voice pulls me back to the present. I blink, finding her kind eyes on me with an odd expression. *Is she worried about me?*

I force a smile. "Oh, yes. Just... thinking."

She doesn't look convinced, her gaze observing. "Are you sure, Ember? Did anyone tell you that I know everything?" she teases, but it doesn't reach her eyes; they show concern for me. For a stranger.

"I'm fine. Just a little... sore from yesterday," I say, rubbing at the tender skin.

Her frown deepens, but she lets it go with a soft pat on my arm. "Alright, but don't push yourself too hard."

I nod, offering a weak smile as she pulls me forward, and my thoughts plummet into the darkness. I don't want to relive the past, but it waits beneath the surface like a crocodile. It claws at the edge of what I am trying to build to prepare for Atlas's return.

There was a time when I believed Killian, Jake, and Ash would be a part of that. But why would they choose that over their single freedom? Why would they want the broken, single-parent version of the girl they once knew?

I glance around the office, seeing perfectly put-together women. Exactly like BethAnn, only feeding the doubt. Women who probably don't have scars hidden beneath their clothing. Women who don't flinch when someone raises their voice or reaches for them too quickly.

"There are my two favorite ladies." Jake booms. I turn, colliding with his chest. The familiar scent of leather and vanilla, unmistakably his, wraps around me as his hands catch my waist. His eyes, warm like molten chocolate, hold mine, and my stomach knots.

"Margaret mentioned you were hurt."

"It's nothing," I say, looking anywhere but at him. He catches my chin in his fingers, tilting my face to look at him.

"Ember?" He warns.

"I'm fine," I murmur, my fingers curling into the fabric of his shirt. "Just...sore."

Jake's jaw tightens, his hands settling on my waist. "Sore?" His tone takes on that protective edge I used to love. He used to use that force on my bullies from middle school; it always made me giddy to see them tremble. But having it directed at me feels different. I don't like it.

I try to step back, but he doesn't let me. His grip firms, and without warning, he lifts me, wrapping my legs around his waist with ease. "Jake—" My protest dies as Margaret smirks at us before disappearing around the corner.

Jake carries me into his office, kicking the door shut behind him. He lowers me onto the couch, his fingers tracing gentle circles on my outer thigh as he lowers to his knees.

"Turn around, Red."

"What?"

"Let me see your back." There's no hiding the gentle command.

"I told you, I'm fine," I insist, my pulse racing.

Jake's lips thin as he exhales through his nose, his thumb brushing over my hip, sending a shiver rushing down my spine. "Please, Ember."

It's the plea that breaks me. He's never been good at asking for things—not when it comes to me or what he wants. But here he is on his knees, begging me to look at what is causing me pain. Unfortunately, the real pain is more than skin deep.

Squeezing my eyes shut, I ease off the couch. My movements are stiff as I turn my back to him, his stare boring into me as he slides my jacket off. The cool air brushes my skin as he raises my shirt, revealing the grotesque yellowish-purple painting marring my skin.

"Fuck, Ember..." His fingertips trace over the bruise, feather-light but hard enough to make me flinch. I brace myself against the couch. My hands fisting until my knuckles turn white.

"How bad is it?" he asks, his breath warm against my shoulder.

My mouth opens, but words won't come out. I force down the lump in my throat, my voice catching. "It's not that bad," I rasp, but the words taste like dirt. "Just... stiff."

Jake says nothing, his fingers ghosting over the bruises with such tenderness that it breaks me more than the pain ever could. He would be so good with Atlas, protective like any father should be, and when his lips touch the damage, it's soft, reverent like he's trying to take the hurt away.

Tears gather, threatening to spill. "Jake..." I whisper.

"What's going on in that head of yours, Red? Stop blocking me out."

I hesitate, my heart hammering against my ribs. The truth is a storm brewing inside me, desperate to break free. "The future," I admit, my voice barely above a whisper. "I don't know what's waiting for me. For us. There is so much I need to tell you." *Do I do this? Do I risk Atlas's life to make Jake understand?*

"Jake, dearest, you called for me?" A sultry voice rushes over me like ice water because I know that voice. It can't be.... BethAnn. "Oh, am I interrupting something?" She smirks, his eyes glinting as I pull down my shirt.

"J-Jake?"

"It's not what you think, Em." He begs, still on his knees. I stand, forcing him to lean back as I look between him and her.

"Do you want me to come back in a few?" BethAnn bats her eyelashes, big doe eyes bouncing between us. But she has the classic mean girl persona, and I can see through her.

Jake shoves himself to his feet. "I didn't invite you here, BethAnn."

Her hand flies to her chest in mock surprise, "I always visit you and Killian. Don't tell me this is because of her."

"Enough," Jake growls, "Get. Out."

"Fine, I'll give you a minute. But you promised to take me out today to apologize for hurting me." Everything stops. No. He wouldn't do that to me, right? He wouldn't see the woman whom he threatened mere days ago because she was hurting *me*.

"Whatever." Jake exhales, turning toward me. "Ember..."

"W-why is she here?" I try to get the words to come out strong, but everything inside me screams that I should leave. He steps toward me, and I step back. His eyebrow raises. "W-why, Jake?"

"It doesn't matter right now; I need to know what is confusing you about us?" Whiplash, that is what this feels like. He can't be serious. That is definitely not the most vital thing to focus on right now.

I must look like a deer caught in headlights because he approaches me like a caught animal about to run away. And he is right. Turning, I snag my jacket from the couch, rushing for the door. His arms circle me, lifting me off the ground. "Let me go, Jake," I snarl, my anger getting the better of me and turning from prey to predator.

"No, not until we finish our conversation."

"Our conversation was finished as soon as Beth-fucking-Ann walked into your office like she's been here a million times!" I scream; I don't care if the whole office can hear me. The betrayal flowing through me is like a river of lava, hot and burning everything down in its path. He lets me go, and I shove him back with all my strength. "You want to talk, Jake? Tell me why the fuck *she* is here." My voice cracks. "Why would you build all this... for me, then tarnish it with *that*?"

He laughs, "Oh, that is fucking rich coming from the girl who wants us to find fucking *St. John* because she wants to go back." My flinch back like he'd slapped me. His eyes widen, his mouth popping open. "I didn't mean that."

He takes a step toward me, and I jerk back. "No, Jake. I think you did." The tears fall, trailing down my face like raindrops on a window.

Jake's hand slides to the back of his neck. "Ember...I swear she isn't important. You are important." I bark a laugh, my face heating. My emotions are all over the place as I go from gut-wrenching betrayal to sadness to pure fucking anger. "Listen to me, I'd burn the whole damn world down if it meant keeping you safe."

His words mean nothing to me right now. I'm numb. I'd almost risked it all for him; I almost risked Atlas so he would know the importance of why I was looking for Patrick. His eyes bore into mine. "Red, talk to me."

"Fuck. You. Jake." I choke out, shaking my head as I turn back toward the door.

"Where are you going?"

The door knob rattles under my grip, "As far away from you as possible, I can't even look at you." I hiss.

"But we need to talk."

I whip around, hair slapping me in the face. "You want to fucking talk, Jake? Then tell me the truth, have you slept with her?" His face loses all its color. "That's what I thought."

"Not since before we got you back."

"But, you don't have me back, do you? No, because I want to go back to Patrick, remember?" The pain is unbearable; there are words we are unable to take back. Jake's always been difficult, but he's never hurt me like this. I've asked for his trust, but once again, he proves that although I trust him, he doesn't trust me. "You'd think that after everything I've told you, you'd know there was a reason I was looking for him."

"Tell me the reason, I am begging you to give me a reason to believe you."

"I can't!" I growl, watching as he sinks to his knees before me. "What are you doing, Jake? Get up."

"Give me anything, Red. I want to believe you, but I can't think of any possible reason why you'd be looking for him."

"Get. Up. Jake." His head shakes.

"Stay with us, Ember. I am begging you."

"There is no us." My chest tightens, and I struggle to catch my breath. "I can't choose, Jake. I need all of you."

His expression darkens, pain and frustration warring in his eyes. "Red..."

"I'm sorry," I whisper, stepping away. The sudden distance between us cuts through me like a knife. I barely register how his hands fall to his sides, the loss of his touch a cold, cruel reminder of everything I've lost.

I bolt, my legs carrying me down the hall. The elevator button clicks rapidly as I slam my palm against it until the doors slide open. "Leaving so soon, Ember?" BethAnn grins, her reflection showing in the elevator doors. "I was hoping for us to catch up, so I can tell you all about my relationship with the guys."

Her words rip through me like a rabid dog feasting on the carcass of a deer. The pain is unimaginable. I stumble into the glass box, falling to my knees before the mirror. It shows just how far I've fallen—tear-streaked, wild-eyed, lost. I pull my knees to my chest as silent sobs wrack my body and doors close, cutting off a grinning BethAnn.

I fumble for my phone, needing a lifeline. "Hello?" Marissa's voice is cautious, hesitant to answer my call.

"Marissa... I need you," I cry, squeezing my phone so tight it creaks under the pressure. It's the only thing keeping me tethered to now. "I don't know what I'm doing... what I'm supposed to do. I—" My breath hitches. "I need you."

"Oh, Emmy," she murmurs, a balm on my frayed nerves. "Where are you?"

I whisper the address as the elevator dings open to the ground floor.

Stepping out cautiously, I scan the lobby, blood ringing in my ears—no sign of Jake—just the empty, sterile quiet of the building.

"I'm getting in a cab now," Marissa says. "Stay put, okay? I'll be there soon."

My mouth opens, but a shadow falls over me, a figure stepping into my path. A hand grabs my upper arm, and panic flares hot inside me. "Let me go," I say.

"Ma'am...you need to come with me."

"No!" I yelp, instinct takes over as I duck under his arm and bolt toward the exit.

"Stop! Mr. Thorne told me," Heavy footsteps thud behind me, echoing off the marble. The building entrance thankfully empty.

I push through the revolving doors, the cold air slapping me.

"Ember?" Marissa screams through my phone. Guess I forgot to hang it up. "What the fuck is going on?"

"J-Jake had someone try to st-stop me," I pant, stumbling down the sidewalk. My head's on a swivel as I look out for Jake or that man. "He tried to stop me from leaving. I t-think I lost him." My breath comes out wheezing, my heart pounding in my chest. "I-I have to find my son, Marissa. I *have to.*"

Marissa's voice sharpens into determination. "Stay calm. Keep walking. I'm almost there."

The city lights blur, and all I can hear is Jake's voice in my head, his words chasing me down like a pack of wolves after their prey.

Stay calm. You're not alone.

It's on repeat in my head like a prayer as I force my feet to keep moving. The freezing air clings to my skin, cold and damp, as I tug my jacket closed, trying to shut out the chill. Streetlights cast jagged shadows across the pavement, each stretching long and eerie, making me glance over my shoulder for the hundredth time.

"Ember, listen to me," Marissa's voice breaks through the fog of my thoughts. "Can you get to Central Park? I want you to get as far away from that building as possible. If Jake sends someone else after you... I just want you to get away from there, okay?"

"O-okay," I whisper, though the tremble in my voice betrays me. "I just... the things he said. I almost told him, Mare. I almost risked Atlas's life."

Saying it aloud makes it real, but it doesn't stop the fear from gnawing at my insides. My breath catches as an engine hums in the distance; the pressure loosens when a cab's lights flash me. I wave my hand in the air, and the vehicle slows to a stop. The driver's face is shadowed.

I slide into the backseat, the door shutting with a dull thud. The worn leather creaks, and I can't stop my hands from shaking.

"Where to?" the driver grunts, his eyes flicking to me in the rearview mirror.

I clear my throat, forcing out the words. "Central Park. Main entrance." My fingers dig into the denim of my pants as the cab merges into the city traffic. I turn my head slightly, scanning the empty street. It doesn't feel empty, though. It feels like there's something just out of sight, lurking in the shadows, watching me.

I'm in a cab now. I should be there soon.

Good.

Hang in there, Em. We will figure this out.

I know.

Will we figure this out? A part of me has given up hope on ever finding Patrick. It feels like I am running in circles, and I can't find evidence that he is out there.

The city blurs, neon signs and streetlights flash in my peripheral vision. My pale and worn reflection stares back at me in the window, and I push down a pang of regret curling in my chest.

Running away from Jake terrifies me; it feels like tearing off a piece of myself, but I can't afford to dwell on it. He is probably having a splendid time with *BethAnn*. Gag.

CHAPTER 42

Ember Rose

The entrance to the park looms over me; the wind whips around me as the leaves crunch under my boots. Pulling out my phone, I scan the area before pulling up my texts. The little red indicator tells me there are over twenty-five notifications from Jake, and I can't bring myself to open them. Instead, pulling up Marissa's.

I'm here, where are you?

Heading for the entrance now.

Ok. See you soon.

"Ember!" she yells before wrapping me in a hug. Her scent swirls up my nose, a hint of baby powder and peppermint. It's the same smell as Atlas. It comforts my freezing limbs, and I imagine she's him momentarily.

"I'm okay, Mare," I manage as she holds me at arm's length, looking over my body. "Thank you for coming."

"Always, Em," she says with a sad smile, pulling me in for another hug. "Come on, let's get off the path. I know the perfect spot we can hide and figure this out."

She guides me through the trees, slipping into the shadows as we break between the branches of a weeping willow into a small alcove. The world quiets as the leaves drown out some of the noise. Outside felt too big, too loud, but here, under the cover of branches, it's quieter. Safer. Marissa collapses against the trunk, leaning her head back against the bark. "This is my favorite place to go when I need to go away." I drop beside her, resting my head on her shoulder.

"It's nice."

"What happened, Ember? I thought they were helping you."

"I can't tell anymore; they haven't found anything. They keep throwing me off track," I choke out. "I can't let that happen, Marissa. Atlas... he's still with her. My baby is out there somewhere, and I'm being distracted by past crushes." My voice breaks, the sheer weight of it drowning me like the rising tide.

Marissa takes my hand, her grip solid. "Let's start with what we know. Maybe there is something we missed. One thing at a time, Em."

"Yeah, okay." My phone vibrates in my pocket, stopping for a second before starting up again. Pulling it out, I glance at the name and hesitate. Jax... I want to answer, but I can't bring myself to. How can I trust any of them right now? Are they helping me? They've made it perfectly clear how they feel about my need to find Patrick. Are they distracting me?

Marissa doesn't hesitate. Snatching the phone from my hands and answering it. "What do you want?" She snaps. "If she wanted to talk to you, she would've answered."

I drag my hands down my face, pulling at the skin. Marissa's voice fills the quiet space. "No, she doesn't want to talk to you, idiot. Get. The. Message." I never noticed that Marissa can give off the same bitchy, mean girl energy that BethAnn did till now. Maybe because she's never directed it toward me. Man, I'd hate to be Jaxson right now. Her frustration crackles through the air like static, each word clipped and full of bite.

She huffs, pausing for a moment before glancing at me. Putting her hand over the speaker, she pulls the phone away. "He says he wasn't the one who upset you. I thought it was."

I peek through my fingers, my voice muffled. "He wasn't. It was Jake."

Marissa rolls her eyes, "Jake, Jax, same thing, honestly." She ends the call with a curt, "Deal with it yourself," before stuffing the phone into her pocket.

"Come on," she murmurs, nudging me gently. "Forget about them. We got this."

Her words stir my determination beneath the layers of my exhaustion. "I don't remember much from when I was rescued." I attempt, but the gaps in my memory feel more like craters. My last clear memory of Patrick is a blur of pain—him throwing me down the stairs, the world spinning, my body hitting the floor. Everything after that is a void, a blank space filled with the sterile scent of a hospital room and the hum of fluorescent lights.

Marissa's voice pulls me back. "Have you asked the guys about what happened after that?"

"Whenever I even try to bring up Patrick, they shut down. Jax is the only one who looks even a little guilty that I haven't found him. But it's almost like he wants to tell me something, but can't. And the others? They—" I press my fingers into my temples, willing the frustration away. "They look at me like I'm some puzzle they need to solve, not a person."

"What could they be hiding, you think?"

"I don't know." I push myself upright too quickly, dizziness washing over me. I brace myself against the trunk of the tree. "I just... I can't keep living like this, Marissa. I need to stop depending on them to help me. I don't know if they are willing."

She listens without interruption, her eyes holding mine. When she finally speaks, her voice is calm. "After you were taken, I started taking self-defense classes. It made me feel more... in control. I think it might help you if you learned some self-defense. Would you want to come with me?"

"Really?"

"Of course," she says, nudging me. "It'd be good for you. And I could use the motivation to keep going. Lord knows I could use the exercise."

A laugh bubbles up before I can stop it—genuine, unguarded. It feels foreign but not unwelcome. "Oh, stop; you look amazing as always. But I think that would be good for me. When is it?"

"Oh, whatever; I have yet to lose the extra mom weight from Caleb," Marissa beams, squeezing my hand. "But, it is every Wednesday night; I'll come get you."

Hope flares to life inside me, a tiny ember refusing to be snuffed out. I feel like I can breathe for the first time in a long while. Like maybe—just maybe—I don't have to do this alone anymore.

"I think that's a great idea."

I jump, my muscles stiffen, and I spin toward the sound. Jax stands a few feet away, hands buried deep in his pockets, looking every bit as miserable as I feel. The usual confidence in his stance is missing.

"Hey, Little One," he murmurs, rough. He doesn't meet my eyes, and that makes it worse.

I swallow down the wave of emotions crashing into me. "W-what are you doing here? How did you find me?"

"I was worried." His gaze moves to Marissa before returning to me. "She turned off your phone. I didn't know where you were. I needed to keep track of you."

A fresh wave of anger simmers beneath my skin. "Well, congratulations," I hiss, crossing my arms. "You found me just fine."

He clenches his jaw before stepping closer, forcing me to look up to meet his stare. "What's that supposed to mean?" he growls, dropping to that dangerous edge that makes me tingle. Tonight, it only stirs the raging storm inside me.

"Why haven't you found Patrick yet?"

His body goes still, his presence towering over me. "Why do you *want* me to find him?"

"Because it's important to me!" I yell, throwing my hands up. "Why do you think I've been asking?" I turn from him. I can't look at him right now; I'm just so angry at him... at them.

A hand grips my arm, spinning me back around. He pinches my chin, forcing me to meet his glare. "*Don't* turn away from me," he growls, his breath is warm against my face. His stormy gaze locks onto mine, searching. "Tell me why."

"Jax—"

"No," he cuts me off. "Tell me *why* you're so desperate to find the man who kidnapped you. The man who *raped* you. Who *tortured* you."

The reminders cut into me like a molten knife. My mouth opens and closes like I'm a fish out of water. What can I say to that? I can't tell him the truth. But what can I say that I haven't said a million times?

Silence follows his statement, and the weight of his accusations settles in. I sense the shift, the way strangers' conversations taper off in the distance, no doubt wondering why people are screaming at each other in the trees. My cheeks burn, not with shame, but with sheer mortification.

"Stop, Jax," I hiss, stepping into him, my voice no more than a whisper. "People are *listening*."

His upper lip curls. "Embarrassed now? Why would you want to go back to him?"

I open my mouth, but nothing comes out. The words I need—the truth I've been holding onto—sit heavy on my tongue, refusing to move. My throat feels like it's closing in on itself, trapping everything inside.

"They have her son!" Marissa yells, sending Jax stumbling away from me. Forcing herself between us, she turns her back to me. "Krystal has her son!"

The world tilts. "Mare..." I gasp, jerking back from the words like a slap on my face. She turns, wrapping her arms around my trembling frame. "You can't just... you just... how could you?"

I watch as the color drains from Jax's face, his hands dropping to his sides. "W-what did you just say?"

"You heard me. I'm not repeating it." Marissa tries to soothe my shock, running her fingers through my hair and down my back. When her hand reaches the bruises, I wince, jolting me back into my body. "I took a risk saying that. She wasn't going to tell you, but, fuck, we need someone who can help us."

Jax's eyes snap to me, the storm inside them swirling between anger and a darker edge. "Why didn't you tell us? We would've—"

"Done what?" Marissa snaps, holding me tighter. "You haven't done anything to help find him yet. Unless what Em is suspecting is true. Are you all lying to her? Do you know where Patrick is?"

Jax's throat bobs as he swallows. I didn't think he could get any paler, but I was wrong. His eyes dart to the side, confirming my thoughts. "Do you know where he is?" Every part of me is begging that what I'm thinking isn't true, that they wouldn't all betray me like that, but one thing I seem to keep forgetting is that I don't know them anymore. They are different from the men that I grew up with.

"Why is Krystal holding your son hostage?" Avoid the question much? I roll my eyes, turning back toward the tree to keep from hitting him.

"Why do you think?"

"She's being threatened." The pieces finally clicking into place.

The energy crackles around us, zipping through the air like a live wire. I meet Jax's gaze head-on and don't like what I see.

"Don't," I bark. "Don't look at me like that. I don't need or want your fucking pity, Jax. Find Patrick, help me save my fucking son."

CHAPTER 43

Krystal

The empty side of the bed taunts me, the sheets cool to the touch. Patrick's still gone. Frustration gnaws at the edges of my sanity. He wouldn't just disappear—not when I'm the one keeping the lights on, footing every damn bill because he puts all his riches into his *hobbies.*

I rake a hand through my hair, pacing the room as the realization creeps in. *Ember.*

The bitter taste of acid burns at the back of my throat. Going to her for assistance has proven useless. What should I expect, honestly? If she isn't utterly stupid, then she must know something. She has to. The thought festers, and my hand grips the coffee cup. My hands shake from the force, and I scream, throwing the ceramic. It shatters against the wall, shards flying, and the liquid splashes the wallpaper with brown sludge.

If she's hiding him from me—if she's keeping *him* from me—does she even care what's at stake?

Snagging the phone from the counter, I pull up the tracking app I use to watch her. To listen to her. Mumbling to myself, I scroll through her previous locations before switching to the unanswered messages from earlier today that stare back at me.

She hasn't moved.

My blood rushes into my ears, setting off the ringing that will ultimately lead to a migraine. Ember doesn't stay still—she hasn't since I gave her the phone. So what is she doing? She wouldn't leave the phone behind, would she? Would she risk the demon spawn's life like that?

> You seem to be falling short on your end, Ember. Perhaps it's time for me to offer some extra motivation.

I hit send and stare at the screen, waiting. Watching. *Five minutes.* Nothing.

My patience begins to fray.

> Fine. Let's see how your son feels about your performance.

The phone hits the counter with a *thwack.* I force down the spike of adrenaline coursing through me, trying to calm my nerves before I do what I need to. Inhaling, I stride down the adjoining hallway. The simple truth is that if Ember thinks she can keep Patrick hidden from me, she's sorely mistaken. Patrick's will is ironclad. The wealth, the legacy, and everything he built belong to the woman who gave him a child. *My* money. *My* security. And Ember? She's standing in my way. Not that she is aware of that.

My fingers curl around the drawer handle, yanking it open to retrieve the cold metal key. It feels heavier than usual as I make my way to the locked door at the end of the hall. I haven't seen him all day; a part of me is guilty of that, but he isn't mine, which is the problem.

The door creaks loudly, and stale air greets me. The scent of fear clings to the stillness, causing my eyes to water. I squint, scanning the shadows. "Where are you?" My voice breaks the silence, disrupting the fake peace.

A quiet sniffle draws my attention to a dark corner. There he is—Atlas. Curled in on himself, his tiny frame quaking, arms wrapped around his knees. Even now, his beauty is remarkable. *He's Ember's son, but he's also Patrick's heir.* And that means he's here to destroy everything I've worked so hard for. If only he didn't carry *his* blood—if only he weren't the reason I'd been shoved aside.

"Come here," I snap, the command causing him to flinch.

He whimpers, his wide, tear-soaked eyes locking with mine before he buries his face into his arms. My patience wears thin. I have little for disobedience.

"You're so fucking dramatic." Lifting my phone, I hit record, angling the camera to capture every sob, every tremor of fear.

"This is what happens when your mother decides you're not worth protecting." My voice drips with manufactured anger, each word calculated to cause them the most pain. The camera only shows what it needs—just him, vulnerable and alone—a tool to force Ember's hand.

Because sooner or later, she'll have to face reality.

And when she does, I'll be ready.

Atlas wails, "Mommy! Help me!" I scoff, shutting off the video.

"Oh, shut up, I didn't even touch you." His mouth snaps shut as he watches me with red-rimmed eyes. "Just...stay quiet." I sigh, closing the door behind me. With a click, the lock slides into place, and I stare at the video thumbnail—Atlas, curled in on himself, his small frame trembling in the shadows. My stomach churns, but I hit send anyway, watching the progress bar creep forward.

Sent. It's done.

An exhale slips through my lips as I watch the screen, waiting. *She'll see it. She'll realize her mistake and fix it.* It's ruthless but necessary. The weight of my actions crushes me, but I push it aside, pacing the room. The seconds crawl, dragging like chains on an abandoned ship.

Doubt creeps in, gnawing at my resolve. My mind drifts back to Atlas—the tear-streaked cheeks, the way his fingers clutched the fabric of his worn shirt. *Stop it.* I grind my teeth and shake off the intrusive thought. Feelings have no place here. I need *results*.

The phone buzzes, pulling me from my spiraling thoughts. I flip it over, and the screen lights up with an incoming message from Ember. Satisfaction swirls inside me. *Finally, she's back in my control.*

Please stop! I'm coming! Tell him I'm coming.

A victorious smile curls my lips, and a thrill rushes through me. I type a brief reply, my fingers no longer shaking.

Good. Stop wasting my time.

Dropping the phone back to the counter, I roll my shoulders, the tension ebbing just enough to breathe easier. But this isn't over. Ember needs to understand what's at stake—what I'm willing to do if she dares defy me.

Flipping the key between my fingers, the jagged edge bites into my skin. My steps are slow and measured as I head back down the hall. My shoes echo off the walls, like the ticking of a clock counting down.

I hesitate for the briefest moment before twisting the lock and pushing the door open. Atlas's wide eyes snap to mine, his thin frame flinching. "I-I'm quiet."

I step inside, kneeling before him, forcing him to look at me. "I need you to be strong," I murmur, my voice carrying an edge of gentleness. The words taste foreign on my tongue. "Your mother will be here soon. ... stay strong."

His lips tremble, and he nods, his tiny hands clutched into fists. A wave of unfamiliar feelings rushes me—guilt, doubt, regret. *No. Not now.* I shove it down and force a hollow smile, retreating before I can feel anything else.

A sigh escapes me as I lock it behind me once more, the sound reverberating down the hall.

Minutes bleed into hours, and the tightness in my shoulder doesn't ease as I watch the tracker. Anxiety claws at me, but I've come too far to let it falter now. Ember will do what's needed. And if she doesn't... I'll ensure she understands how serious this is.

This isn't just a waiting game anymore. It's a battle of endurance.

And I don't intend to lose.

CHAPTER 44

Jaxson

A kid. *She has a kid.* And we've been standing in her way, keeping her from the one thing that could bring him back. My stomach churns, a sickening weighing down, control slipping from my grasp. Whenever I think about the secrets we've buried, I feel the sharp edge of guilt slicing deeper. *We kept Patrick from her.* The realization is like a living thing, relentless and unforgiving.

Em's arms cross over her chest, her stance rigid with frustration. "So?" she snaps.

I blink, forcing a nod. "Of course, I'll help."

The tension in her shoulders eases, a visible shift, but the wariness in her eyes remains. "We'll tell the guys—"

"No!" She grabs my arm, fingers digging in, and furiously shakes her head. "They can't know anything. *She's watching me.* If they find out, she'll know."

Damn. This complicates everything. I rub a hand over my face, swallowing down the frustration. Without the guys, this will be harder—*almost impossible*. But looking at Em, at the desperation trembling just beneath the surface, I know one thing for sure. *I won't let her do this alone.*

"Alright," I say carefully. "We won't tell them. But you have to show me everything you've got. There might be a clue in there."

Her hesitation is brief, but it's there, and it stings. She turns to Marissa, who silently pulls out her phone and hands it over. I scroll through the messages, my eyes stopping cold on a photo.

A little boy. His copper curls gleam even in the dim lighting, just like Em's. He's huddled in a corner, his tiny arms wrapped around himself, dirt streaking his face. Bruises. Handprints. Fear. And those eyes—Cocoa colored eyes and filled with unshed tears. My pulse pounds in my ears.

I failed her. *We failed her.*

I exhale sharply, handing the phone back. "You have to promise me something."

Her lips part. "What?"

"You let me teach you self-defense. And when it comes time for the exchange, I go with you."

For a second, I see it—the sheer weight of everything crushing her. Her lip trembles. She nods, swallowing hard. "Yes. Anything. Just... please, help me find my baby."

Marissa watches us, arms crossed, her expression unreadable. "If you're helping her, I won't have to step in," she says, smirking.

I grab Em's hand, pulling her closer. "No one else finds out about this."

"As long as you keep your word."

Em glances over her shoulder at Marissa as I lead her away, her fingers curling around mine.

"Jax," she huffs, tugging at my arm. "Slow down. I've got little legs, remember?"

I ease up, smirking despite myself. "Better?"

She grins, leaning into my side, her touch grounding me in ways I don't deserve. "Much."

I help her onto the seat, sliding a helmet over her head. "Be a good girl and don't disappear again. You'll give Jake a heart attack."

She snorts, adjusting the helmet strap. "Jake needs to get it through his thick skull that I'm not his to control."

I hum in agreement, revving the engine. As we take off, her arms strangle my waist, and my grip tightens on her thigh. She trusts me—more than she should.

The guilt burns hotter. *And when she finds out the truth... will that trust still be there?*

The engine sputters to a stop, but neither of us moves. The townhome looms in front of us, dark and uninviting. It was always supposed to be temporary, just a place to lay low—but now, the thought of leaving her feels impossible. She's lodged herself under my skin, a part of me I never saw coming. *I'd go anywhere for her. Do anything.*

"I don't want to go in," Ember's soft voice says, almost lost to the night. She leans forward, laying the front of her helmet against my back.

"Come here," I murmur, shifting and pulling her into my lap. Her knees bracket my waist, fitting so perfectly it's as if she's always belonged there. I lift her helmet off, and her hair tumbles in wild waves, framing her face, curling around her shoulders. The ache to kiss her is overwhelming, clawing at me, but I manage to rein it in. Barely.

"What happened with Jake, Baby Girl?" My voice is gentle, but inside, my gut churns with unease.

She blinks rapidly, the sheen in her eyes catching the dim light. "I misunderstood," she whispers, her fingers fidgeting with the sleeve hem. "Instead of just talking to him, I panicked. I ran. And he... he tried to have security hold me down." Her exhalation shudders, and she releases it slowly, her shoulders slumping. "I felt like a rebellious kid. I think that's how he sees me—just a stupid, young girl with a crush."

Her lips purse into a pout, and I can't resist leaning in, nipping at her bottom lip. "You're not a fifteen-year-old, Ember," I say huskily. "You're all woman."

Her eyes go wide, her lips parting, and she drags her tongue over the spot I just teased—my pulse stutters.

"I want to kiss you," I admit, my forehead resting against hers. "So badly it hurts. You do things to me, Ember Rose. Things I can't control." My hand skims down her back, fingers flexing against her waist. "You make me want to protect you, claim you."

"Jax..." Her whisper is a plea, her gaze locked on my lips.

"May I kiss you?" I ask softly, brushing my thumb over her mouth. Her tongue flicks out, grazing my skin, and I swear I'm unraveling.

She swallows, releasing a shaky breath. "Yes."

I don't hesitate. Our lips crash together, and the world around us ceases to exist. My hand slides into her hair, tugging her closer, while my other grips her hip, dragging her flush against me. Her moan vibrates through me, and I deepen the kiss, coaxing her to meet me stroke for stroke.

"Get a room!" someone shouts, followed by laughter.

Ember jerks back, burying her face against my neck.

I chuckle, smoothing my hand down her spine. "Maybe we should head inside," I murmur, kissing her temple. She nods, her cheeks flushed as she slides off my lap.

"Let's get this over with."

Stepping inside, the silence swallows us whole. The house feels... wrong. Too still. The usual chaos—Killian's barking orders, movers hauling boxes—should be filling the space. Instead, the emptiness closes in.

Em's voice is barely above a whisper. "Where is everyone?"

I kiss her forehead quickly, murmuring, "Go to your room and lock the door."

She hesitates, but the sharp edge in my tone has her obeying. I wait, listening, until I hear the quiet click of the lock before I slide my hand under the entry table, gripping the cold weight of my gun.

I move toward the basement with measured steps, ears straining for anything out of place. The deeper I go, the fainter the cries become—until I reach the door. The unmistakable sound of pain filters through the thick wood. *Dammit.*

I push inside swiftly, shutting the door behind me before Ember can hear what's happening.

Jake stands over St. John, his shirt splattered in blood, his knuckles white around the knife he drives into the man's side. Ash and Killian stand nearby, their faces tense.

"Jake—JAKE!" My shout echoes through the space.

Jake whirls, knife poised, his eyes wild. "What?" He steps forward, digging the blade into my neck. "You shouldn't be down here, Jaxson." His breath is ragged, his body taut like a live wire.

I keep my voice even. "Ember's upstairs, Jake. You need to stop."

The knife clatters to the floor with a metallic thud. "She's here?"

Jake's face drains of color. He lunges for the door, but Killian grabs him, yanking him back.

"Let me go!" Jake snarls, throwing a punch that Killian barely dodges.

"You're covered in blood, J," Killian hisses, gripping his arm. "You can't go to her like this." He gestures at the torn fabric clinging to Jake's chest, stained crimson.

Jake stares down at himself, his chest rising and falling in shallow bursts. With a frustrated growl, he tears off his shirt, shredding it until it falls in bloody ribbons at his feet. He storms toward the shower in the corner, letting the water sluice the blood from his skin.

I watch the crimson swirls down the drain, disappearing into the darkness.

Ash exhales heavily beside me. "Follow him. Make sure he calms down before he talks to her." His tone is heavy with exhaustion.

I glance at St. John, unconscious and sprawled in a pool of his blood. "You think he's still alive?" I mutter.

Killian grabs the man's legs, dragging him across the cold floor with a grunt. The clank of handcuffs locking into place makes me wince. "You should've seen Jake when he found out she was gone," he says, running a hand through his hair. "He lost it. Completely."

Ash's eyes darken. "Hurting St. John was the only way he kept from destroying everything in his path."

I swallow hard, my mind racing ahead to what to do next. *Jake's unraveling. Ember's in the middle of it. And I'm stuck trying to hold all the pieces together before it's too late.*

I drag a hand through my hair, exhaling a long, tired sigh. *I have to check on him.* My feet feel heavy with each step I take toward the door.

"Jaxson?"

Ash's voice halts me mid-stride. I glance over my shoulder, meeting his steady gaze.

"Yeah?"

His eyes narrow. "You'd tell us if there was something we needed to know about her, right?"

A tight knot twists in my gut. I stare at him for too long, debating—

how much do they already suspect? The words come easily, but they feel like gravel. "Of course. What does she mean to me?"

The lie weighs down on me the second it leaves my mouth. That boy's face flashes in my mind—copper curls, brown eyes wide with fear, dirt streaked across his skin. The guilt gnaws at me. I push it down. *Krystal's watching.* It's not just Ember's life on the line; it's that little boy's.

Ash doesn't argue, just gives me a slow nod. I don't wait for more. Turning on my heel, I pull the basement door shut behind me and inhale deeply, trying to steady the erratic rhythm of my heart.

"Damn it," I mutter, climbing the stairs two at a time. *What the hell have I gotten myself into?*

I should check on Ember. My fingers twitch with the need to see her, to reassure myself she's okay. But Jake... *Jake needs me first.* He was there for me when I had nothing, when I was drowning, when I couldn't even look in a mirror without seeing failure. He pulled me out and gave me purpose. He was the reason I started tracking people down in the first place. But Ember? *She was different.* Finding her had become more than a job. It had become... everything. And I failed just like Jake did.

I knock lightly on Jake's door, hearing the shuffle of movement before it creaks open. He stands there, towel wrapped low around his waist, beads of water dripping from his damp hair. His eyes are dark, haunted.

"What do you want?"

I lean against the frame. "Just making sure you're good before you talk to Ember."

His jaw tenses, and he huffs a humorless laugh. "I'd never intentionally hurt her."

"I know," I say carefully. "But it doesn't mean you won't be pissed at her for running."

The muscle in his jaw jumps. "I was supposed to protect her." He sinks onto the edge of the bed, his head hanging low. "And I couldn't even find her when she needed me most." His fingers rake through his hair, frustration thick in every line of his body. "And now... she wants something from me that I can't give her. She wants more than just me."

Before I can respond, a soft knock echoes through the tense silence.

Jake's head snaps, and uncertainty flickers across his face momentarily. I open the door, and Ember stands there, her expression hesitant.

"Emmy?" Jake breathes, his relief palpable as he pulls the door open wider. "You're okay."

She nods slowly, her gaze shifting to me with a small, tentative smile. I step back, giving her space. "May I?" she whispers, eyes flicking to Jake.

The air in the room shifts, thick with unspoken emotions. How he looks at her—like she's the only thing tethering him to solid ground. And yet, the truth is undeniable, written all over her face. She doesn't just love Jake; she loves Killian and Ash too. Jake knows it, and I can see it unraveling him piece by piece.

"Of course, Red," Jake murmurs, softer than I've ever heard. "You never have to ask."

Her smile is tender, and it hits me square in the gut. I get it now—*Jake doesn't want to share her.* He wants all of her, every broken piece. But she won't choose, which he can't reconcile. *Hell, I'm not sure I can either.*

"Jax?"

I blink, meeting her gaze. "Yeah, Little One?"

"Would you mind?" She gestures to the door, and I hesitate. My gut tells me to stay, to protect her. But the look on Jake's face tells me he'd rather die than hurt her.

I nod, stepping out and closing the door quietly behind me.

The moment it clicks shut, voices rise behind it. I stand by for a second, listening to the muffled argument, but I know they need this. They have to figure out where they stand.

Sighing, I head down the hall and into my room, flopping onto the bed. Staring at the ceiling, I let out a slow breath, but my mind refuses to settle. The things I've learned today twist inside me, a secret that weighs heavier than I can carry.

This could change everything. But for now, it's mine alone to bear—*the only thread keeping me tied to her.*

"Jax," her voice haunts me even in my dreams, soft yet insistent. "Wake up."

I groan, burrowing deeper into the pillow, trying to escape the intrusion. But the pull of curiosity wins out, and when I crack open an eye, there she is—the red-haired beauty invading every corner of my mind. Her scent—roses and sandalwood—wraps around me like a blanket, filling the space.

"Good morning," she whispers, kneeling beside the bed with a too-bright smile that doesn't quite reach her eyes.

I rub the sleep from my face, reaching blindly for my phone. "What time is it?" The screen lights up, and I squint against the harsh glow—*4:30 a.m.*

A sigh escapes me, heavy and resigned.

"I know it's early," Ember says, inching closer. Her breath fans across my face, her body so close that it deepens my emotions. Then, without warning, she pulls a phone from behind her back.

I frown, but before I can speak, she places a trembling finger to my lips, her touch featherlight. The glow of the screen flashes again, and my stomach drops at the message displayed:

> You seem to be falling short on your end, Ember. Perhaps it's time for me to offer some extra motivation.

> Fine, then. Let's see how your son feels about your performance.

The attached video robs me of air. A little boy, no older than four, with familiar copper curls and wide, tear-filled chocolate eyes, stares back at me from the screen. Dirt smudges his cheeks, and his small frame trembles as a shadow looms in the background—*her son.*

Ember tucks the phone away quickly, forcing a shaky smile that doesn't belong on her face. "I wanted to start my training," she says, voice too bright, too brittle. "I was too excited to sleep."

I watch her, noticing the way her eyes glisten and how she blinks too fast as if willing the tears away. She glances around the room, taking in the mess—my mess. Clothes strewn over the chair, half-empty water bottles littering the nightstand. *I should have been more prepared.* I curse myself.

"Yeah... yeah," I mutter, swinging my legs over the edge of the bed and scrubbing a hand down my face. The weight of everything should crush her, but Ember steps forward, slipping between my knees, grounding me in the moment.

Her hands are soft as they cup my face, thumbs grazing the stubble on my jaw. I look up into those wide, troubled eyes.

"I should let you sleep," she murmurs, guilt flickering. "Jake and I probably kept you up with all the yelling."

I don't respond. Instead, I wrap my arms around her waist and pull her closer, resting my forehead against the softness of her stomach. Her scent envelops me, but the image of her son burns behind my eyelids. I swallow hard, forcing the emotion down as I find my voice. "No, it's fine. Head down to the gym. I'll be there in a few minutes."

She hesitates, searching my face, then leans down and places a quick, featherlight kiss to my cheek. "Thank you," she whispers, barely more than a breath against my ear before she slips out of the room.

The door clicks shut, and I flop back onto the mattress with a groan, staring at the ceiling.

What the hell have I gotten myself into?

CHAPTER 45

Ember Rose

Heat rises to my cheeks as I wander through the townhouse, tension building with each wrong turn. My hands skim over cool walls, searching for anything that hints at the gym's location. No one gave me a tour, so I'm left stumbling through hallways like a lost child. I even tried the basement, standing before the massive, foreboding door, but it wouldn't budge. The space beyond it seemed to stretch endlessly, shadows swallowing any hope of familiarity.

For a split second, I consider retreating to my room, waking Jake, who'd snuck into my bed last night after our fight, but the thought of his concerned questions, his relentless offers to help, makes my stomach churn. I can't handle his kindness right now.

When I finally push open the right door, my breath catches. The gym sprawls before me, impossibly large. Rows of treadmills face gleaming floor-to-ceiling mirrors, their reflection making the space even more daunting. Ellipticals hum softly in the distance, weights neatly stacked against the far wall. Some machines I don't even recognize, their hulking frames unfamiliar and menacing.

Then, I see it.

A red light blinks in the corner, rhythmic like a heartbeat—a camera.

The air in my lungs thickens, and my vision narrows to a pinpoint, my body locking up. Cold sweat pricks my skin, and the floor tilts beneath me. My knees hit the ground with a dull thud, but I barely feel it. The room fades away, and the past swallows me whole.

"Come on, Kitten," Patrick's voice is a slick purr in my ear, his jacket sliding off his shoulders, his belt whispering free of its loops. A cold shiver runs down my spine as he trails the leather down my arm, letting it drag, teasing. "You'll be good for our favorite viewers, won't you? They love hearing you scream."

Tears track down my dirty cheeks as I fumble with the waistband of my sweats, my fingers trembling. "Please, Sir. D-don't make me do this," I whisper, my voice cracking under exhaustion. My hollow stomach twists, and I long for the softness I once cursed—the curves that used to insulate me from the cold that now gnaws at my bones.

The sharp crack of the belt fills the air before the pain registers, a searing line of fire across my thighs. My knees buckle, concrete biting into fragile skin. Patrick's silhouette looms, the metal tip of his belt glinting ominously under the dim light. He watches with a sick fascination, a predator savoring the moment.

"You bleed so pretty for me, Kitten," he murmurs, dragging the cold leather down my spine, over bruised flesh. A shudder wracks my frame. "Shame you've lost those delicious curves. Guess I'll have to fatten you up again."

Another crack. I collapse, skin splitting, pain blooming like a violent flower. The chat window beside Patrick's laptop flashes with a blur of words, cruel requests scrolling too fast to catch. I refuse to read them. I refuse to let them break me.

The wall behind me is rough and grimy as I stagger to my feet, using it to hold myself upright. Infection festers beneath torn skin, a slow, creeping promise of escape, and I silently pray for it to take me away.

"Come here," Patrick snaps, fingers curling in a beckoning motion.

My body obeys before my mind can catch up, sinking back to my knees before him. My stomach churns as he undoes his belt, his dark eyes locked onto mine. "You made me hard, Pet. Take care of it."

A sob claws at my insides, but I force it down. Tears drip onto my bare knees as I part my lips, shame burning hotter than the pain.

I want to go home.

A strangled gasp rips from deep in my core as I snap back to the present. The cold gym floor sticks to my cheek, and I curl inward, shaking violently. My body feels foreign, disconnected—like it's trying to crawl away from itself.

A shadow falls over me.

"Em?" Jaxson's voice breaks through the fog, hesitant but sharp with worry. My eyes flutter open, and I see him standing in the doorway, his expression tight with concern.

Another whimper escapes me.

Without hesitation, he drops what he's holding and crashes to his knees, wrapping me in his arms. I sink into him, the tremors wracking my frame, desperate for anything to bring me back to the present.

Jaxson's arms wrap around me, his tone laced with urgency. "Little One, what happened?" His heat sinks into my skin, chasing away the chill. I bury my face in the crook of his neck, inhaling the scent of smoky bourbon and leather. For a fleeting moment, I let myself drown in the safety of his embrace, gripping onto him like he's the only thing keeping me from falling.

His lips brush against my hair. "Talk to me, honey." Gentle fingers trace slow circles down my spine, grounding me.

I swallow hard, the words thick and heavy. "Just a memory..." My voice is a brittle whisper, cracking under its weight. "From when I was being held." The confession feels like shards of glass scraping their way out of me. A shiver ripples through my body as the air conditioning hums to life, deepening the chill in my bones.

Jaxson doesn't push. He kisses my forehead. "Let's go back to bed, okay?"

The thought of retreating stirs a dark anger inside me. I jerk back, shaking my head violently, desperation clawing at my insides. "No." My voice is sharp, ragged. "I won't let him win. He's already taken enough. He can't take anything else." The tears come hot and angry, cutting down my cheeks in burning tracks. I hate that even now, he still holds this power over me.

"I need to do this," I choke out, my fingers gripping Jaxson's shirt like it's the only thing tethering me to the present. "Please... help me."

Jaxson's expression hardens, his gaze locking onto mine with unshakable resolve. He nods once, the silent promise I need. He shifts, hands firm on my hips, guiding me to my feet. "Stretch first," he instructs, clipped but calm. "Then we're testing your stamina."

My eyes flick to the treadmills, doubt creeping in. My muscles already scream in protest, but I set my jaw. Maybe I can convince him to let this go, to take me back upstairs. I already feel drained after the flashback. I part my lips to argue, but the firm shake of his head cuts me off before I can even begin.

"You want me to run?" I ask, trying to keep the hesitation from showing in my voice. "For how long?"

Jaxson's smirk is all sharp edges. "Until you can't go any further." He shrugs out of his t-shirt, and I forget how to breathe for a second: no sculpted abs, but his solid chest and broad shoulders radiate strength. My eyes stay a moment too long, and when I look up, he's already watching me, smirking.

"Something wrong, Little One?" he teases.

I snap my mouth shut. "Nope," I mutter, the word laced with false bravado. "Nothing at all." I drop to the floor, stretching through the ache beneath my skin. Every movement pulls at the scars, a constant reminder of everything I've survived.

"Enough." Jaxson demands, firm but gentle. "Don't push too hard. This isn't about breaking you but seeing where we're starting."

I nod, but my focus is elsewhere. Stepping onto the treadmill, I slowly let the rhythm settle me. My breathing steadies, the hum of the machine filling my ears. But it's not enough. I push the speed higher, the belt moving faster beneath my feet. Faster. Harder. Jaxson stands behind me, silent and watchful.

Minutes blur. My eyes lock onto my reflection in the mirror, but I don't see myself. I see Atlas. I see the future I have to fight for. Jaxson, Killian, Ash, Jake—they'll help me protect him. I'll be strong for him. Once I learn to fight and am ready, nothing will touch us again.

Killing that drug dealer was just the beginning. I'll take down Krystal and Patrick for everything they did to me. For what they're still doing to Atlas. Then, I'll hunt down everyone who looked the other way —who let me suffer, who let him suffer.

I don't realize the treadmill has slowed until I hear a voice beside me, not Jaxson's.

"How long have you been running like that?" Killian's brow furrows, his hold helping me balance as I stumble off the machine. My legs feel like they're made of jelly, refusing to hold me up.

Jaxson's voice cuts in from the doorway. "An hour." He tosses a water bottle to Killian, who uncaps it and places it into my shaking hands. I gulp it down greedily, the icy liquid burning down my throat.

"An hour?" I rasp, lungs contracting.

Jaxson leans against the doorframe, arms crossed. "Yeah." His gaze pins me in place. "You run like you're trying to outrun something."

The words hit too close, and I shift my weight, forcing a shaky smile at Killian. "I'm okay," I lie, wrapping my arms around his waist and resting my chin against him. "I was just... thinking."

"Are you sure? What were you doing up so early?" His gaze flicks to Jaxson, unspoken words passing between them.

"I'm teaching her self-defense," Jaxson answers. "She's stronger than any of us realize."

Killian's brow furrows, his grip on me firm but cautious. "How long have you been training?"

I swallow, feeling small under the weight of his scrutiny. "Today was the first day..." My voice trails off, the heat of his stare making me shift uneasily.

His eyes darken. "You ran like that on your first day?" He lets out a low whistle, shaking his head. "Damn, Killer, once we build up these muscles, you'll be unstoppable."

A grin tugs at my lips despite the ache in my legs. Pride swells within me, and I glance at Jaxson, eager for what's next. "So, what now?"

Jaxson raises an eyebrow, the corner of his mouth twitching in surprise. "You're not tired?"

I shake my head, determination crackling through me like a live wire. "Nope."

He exhales, running a hand through his hair. "Alright. Since your stamina's already impressive, let's work on your stances. Some light hand-to-hand." He shifts his gaze to Killian. "Kill, since you're here, would you mind helping with the demos? I'll assess her form while you show her how it's done."

Killian shrugs, his fingers hooking into the hem of his shirt. He pulls it over his head in one smooth motion, the fabric hitting the floor in a careless heap. My eyes betray me, tracking how his muscles ripple, the lean power beneath his skin. A part of me itches to reach down, pick up the shirt, and inhale his scent, but I catch myself.

A hand waves in front of my face, and I blink up, flustered. "W-what?"

Jaxson smirks. "Getting distracted already, Killer?"

Killian steps closer, his proximity radiating heat. "Like what you see?" His tone teasing, sending a shiver straight down my spine.

I snap back, shaking my head. "Focus," I mutter, forcing myself to turn my attention to Jaxson, but he's watching me too closely, his expression unreadable. His eyes hold a sharp, dark possessiveness. My fingers twitch at my sides, tempted to test him, to lean into Killian to see how he'd react.

Jaxson turns abruptly. "Alright, let's get started," he says, voice tight. "You'll be at a disadvantage in a fight. Your size, height, and strength aren't in your favor."

I cross my arms, pouting dramatically. "Wow, thanks for the pep talk."

Killian's lips quirk as he steps closer, his forearm across my chest, pulling me in. "Don't worry, Emmy." His breath fans against my neck as he murmurs. "I'll go easy on you."

I roll my eyes, but the glint in his eyes fuels the reckless side of me. Without thinking, I pivot, using his weight against him. In one swift motion, I hook my arm under his and flip him clean over my shoulder. The thud as he hits the mat echoes through the gym.

Killian stares up at me, blinking in stunned silence. I stand over him, crossing my arms, a smug smile tugging at my lips. "Oops. Guess you weren't ready." I flick my hair over my shoulder, savoring the moment.

Slow clapping breaks the silence. I turn to find Jaxson leaning against the wall, his dark eyes filled with pride. "There's the fire I was looking for, Baby Girl."

Killian pushes himself up, rubbing his jaw. "Channel that, and no one will ever beat you."

A knot forms inside me, his words heavier than they should be. Strength. It's not just about fighting. It's about survival. About never being at anyone's mercy again. My fingers curl into fists at my sides. I'll never be weak again. Never let them take me or Atlas.

Killian's voice pulls me back. "Where the hell did you learn that?"

I shrug, forcing a casual tone. "I had to learn a lot when I left you. Needed to protect myself... keep people away."

Killian's expression darkens as he moves toward me—instinctively, I step back. The air shifts, thickening, and my back hits solid ground. Jaxson. Trapped between them, a sharp rush of energy shoots through me.

Killian smirks, tilting his head. "Nowhere to run now, Killer."

I swallow hard, my pulse hammering against my ribs.

Killian's fingers curl around my neck, his grip firm but not yet punishing. He pulls me closer, his eyes boring into mine, searching—digging. "Did someone hurt you?"

My breath stutters, my chest rising and falling too fast. The words claw at me, thick and suffocating, but I force them out. "You mean besides Patrick and his friends?" My voice is barely a whisper.

Killian's jaw tics, tension rippling through him, but he only nods. His fingers massage deeper into my skin—a silent tether pulling me back, reminding me I'm not alone.

"No..." I say, my voice strained. "I never let anyone get close enough."

A dark hum rumbles from behind me, and Jaxson's hand ghosts over my hip, his body sinking into mine. "Good girl," he murmurs, the words sliding over my skin like silk, but they don't sink in the way they should. I try to ignore the unease stirring beneath the surface, the way my muscles twitch under his touch.

His fingers move—light, teasing strokes that send unwelcome shivers down my spine. My breath hitches, my body betraying me with a soft, involuntary tremor. The air turns dense as Killian's grip hardens—a silent command.

"Eyes on me, Ember," he orders, his tone cutting through the fog creeping into my mind. His lips crush against mine, stealing what little breath I have left. He's relentless, claiming, leaving no space for hesitation. I want to pull away—need to—but I can't.

Trapped.

I lean back against Jaxson, seeking refuge, but it only keeps me between them. Their bodies cage me in, heat and power surrounding me from both sides. Jaxson's touch trails lower, his fingers moving in slow, torturous circles. My mind spins, a mixture of panic and unwanted pleasure twisting deep in my gut.

A whimper escapes before I can stop it, and Killian's hand snaps to my chin, forcing my gaze back to his. "Focus, Ember." His tone is softer, coaxing, but it still makes my skin crawl. "You're not with him. You're here—with us."

I flinch, my body reacting on instinct, but Jaxson's grip holds me in place. My hips shift under his touch, moving against the pressure despite the rising unease clawing at my insides. Everything feels disconnected, like I'm floating somewhere outside myself, watching from a distance.

Killian's kiss is fierce and desperate—an attempt to pull me back into the moment—but inside, I'm spiraling. "Are you going to be a good girl for us?" His voice dips dangerously. "Will you let go?"

I nod. "Words, Little One. We need words."

"Y-yes." My mind is a mess of fragments—past and present blurring into one indistinguishable storm. Their hands, their heat, their words... they ground me.

Jaxson groans low behind me, the sound rumbling against my spine like thunder. His fingers slide deeper, slow and careful, curling inside me with purpose. I suck in a sharp breath, my legs trembling as I fight the instinct to close them.

"Breathe, baby," he murmurs against the shell of my ear. "Let us take care of you."

Killian's hand softens at my chin, thumb stroking beneath my bottom lip. He leans in again, but his kiss is gentler this time—less about claiming, more about offering. He gives me the space to meet him halfway.

I do.

I kiss him back—tentative at first, then deeper, letting the warmth of his mouth replace the chill still clinging to my skin.

Jaxson's pace stays steady, his free hand wrapping around my waist to hold me against him. I'm bracketed by them—safe, not trapped. My body starts to believe it even before my mind does.

"That's it," Killian breathes, lips brushing mine. "There you are."

I blink up at him, disoriented. The panic is still there, but simmers lower now, buried beneath this feeling.

Desire.

"I've got you," Jaxson says, fingers working, stroking a spot that makes my thighs clench. "You're doing so fucking good."

A sound escapes me—between a moan and a sob. I don't know what's happening to me. I feel exposed, but not broken.

Killian's mouth finds my neck, his tongue tracing a slow line just beneath my ear. "Let go, Little One. Just feel."

The nickname shouldn't comfort me, but it does. It wraps around me like a warm hand, reminding me that here, with them, I don't have to be strong.

Jaxson's fingers curl again, harder this time, and my hips buck without my permission. His thumb grazes my clit, featherlight.

"Oh—God." I shudder, gripping Killian's arms, trying to stay grounded as everything builds higher.

"There she is," Jaxson growls, his teeth scraping the back of my neck.

I can't think. I don't want to.

Killian kisses me again, catching the tremble of my lips as my body tenses. My release hits like a sudden storm—no warning, no mercy. It crashes through me in waves, dragging a cry from my throat as I fall apart in their arms.

Jaxson doesn't stop until I'm squirming. He withdraws slowly, carefully, placing a kiss between my shoulder blades.

"You did so good for us," he murmurs, lips soft against my skin.

Killian brushes the hair from my face, his expression unreadable but quiet with awe. "You're stronger than you think."

I don't speak—not yet. But I nod, chest rising and falling with the weight of everything I just gave and everything they just took with such reverent hands.

They don't ask for more. They hold me between them, until my world feels like mine again.

Jaxson watches me, his eyes dark, unreadable. He lifts his fingers to his lips, tasting me with a slow smirk. "Delicious, Ember," he murmurs. "You're incredible."

My hands shake as I force a smile, but it doesn't reach my eyes, the panic resurfacing.

"S-same time tomorrow?" The words tumble out, my voice small, uncertain. Heat creeping up my cheeks.

Jaxson leans back. "Early riser, huh?" His smirk returns, but it feels different this time.

I force a nod, wrapping my arms around myself to hide the tremors. "Yeah."

"4:30," he says. "Be ready by five."

A lump forms, and a strange mix of dread swirls in the pit of my gut. I don't know what tomorrow will bring, am I ready for it?

KILLIAN'S LAUGHTER rumbles against my ear as he guides me from the gym, his hands firm on my hips. The weight of his touch should feel reassuring, but it leaves me buzzing.

"What do you want for breakfast, Princess?" he teases, a smile tugs at my lips.

He lifts me onto the counter, and I flash back to our time in my little apartment's kitchen. A flicker of childish excitement breaks the tension. "Bacon," The simple joy of food grounds me.

He chuckles, reaching into the fridge, pulling out eggs, bacon, and fruit. The normalcy of it should calm me. But it doesn't.

Killian flips the sizzling bacon in the pan, his lips curling into that infuriatingly charming smirk. "You can't just eat bacon, Baby," he says, glancing at me over his shoulder, amusement dancing in his eyes.

I push out my bottom lip in an exaggerated pout, hoping for a crack in his resolve. "But—"

"No buts," he reprimands me like he has all the control. "You need more than just bacon."

Crossing my arms, I huff, the defiance in my tone barely masking the tiny sting of disappointment. "Fine." The word is clipped, sharp, but it holds no real weight. We both know I'll cave.

Killian chuckles, the deep sound rolling over me like a slow burn. "Good girl," he murmurs, his tone thick enough to make heat stir low in my belly. I shift on the counter, pretending it's just to get comfortable, but his words leave a mark, settling deep.

I watch him move, the way his muscles shift under his shirt. The rhythmic clatter of utensils fills the space, but my mind drifts, my gaze sliding to the empty table across the room.

I close my eyes, letting a different morning take shape in my head.

Atlas sits at the table, his small hands wrapped around a glass of juice. His wide eyes watch Ash and Jake as they work side by side, their movements easy and familiar. Ash carefully slices fruit, sneaking pieces onto Atlas's plate, while Jake nudges him with an amused huff, flipping toast onto a dish with practiced ease.

Killian stands at the stove, just like before, only now he's cooking for all of us—his movements slower, more deliberate, as if getting breakfast right actually matters. Jaxson leans against the counter, phone in hand, but his attention keeps drifting—always tracking, always watching. Ash brushes a crumb from Atlas's mouth, ruffling his hair with a small, affectionate smile. Jake steps away from the stove and crosses to me, pressing a kiss to my temple and muttering about work, his hand resting on my waist like he's not ready to go.

The scene feels warm and whole—a morning untouched by fear or regret—a life we could have, maybe.

I blink, and the vision fades, leaving only the empty table staring back at me, the reality settling in like a heavy fog.

This isn't our life.

It's just a dream—fragile, fleeting—a hope I can't afford to hold onto. Jake's voice echoes in my head, yesterday's sharp dismissal cutting through the calm. *It's not that simple, Em. It never will be.*

I bite my lip, forcing the ache down, and glance at Killian as he hums softly under his breath, completely unaware of the battle waging inside me.

I wish I could stay in the dream a little longer. But I can't.

CHAPTER 46

Killian

The sizzle of bacon crackles through the quiet kitchen, filling the air with its rich, smoky scent. Grease pops against my skin. Across the room, Emmy sits perched on the counter, her bare feet swinging idly, eyes locked onto the dining room table. Her fingers drum an uneven rhythm against the edge, and the furrow between her brows deepens with every second she spends staring at the worn wood, as if it might offer up answers she isn't ready to say out loud. I turn back to the stove, letting the rhythmic cooking motion distract me. She asked us to trust her, to give her space, so I focus on the breakfast instead, even as every part of me itches to close the distance.

Jake stumbles in, his hair sticking up at odd angles, and a scowl already carved into his features. He beelines for the coffee pot, pouring without a glance in Emmy's direction. "She had another nightmare," he mutters, lifting the mug to his lips and hissing as the scalding liquid hits his tongue. He doesn't stop drinking.

Jaxson leans against the counter, arms crossed, watching Emmy. There's no judgment, just that quiet intensity that always makes it seem like he knows more than he says, "She had a panic attack this morning."

Jake and I freeze mid-motion, our eyes snapping to Jaxson in unison. "What?" The word leaves my mouth sharper than I intend.

Jaxson shrugs, gripping his mug. "Something in the gym set her off.

Found her on the floor." He takes a measured sip, but the slight twitch in his jaw betrays the anger he's holding back.

Jake curses under his breath and crosses the kitchen in a few long strides. He steps between Emmy's legs, his hands settling on her hips, and leans his forehead against her shoulder. She stiffens for a beat before melting into him with a soft sigh, burying her face into his neck.

"Good morning, Jakey," she murmurs.

Jake exhales, his lips brushing against her temple. "Morning, Red. I don't like waking up without you." The tension eases from his shoulders.

"I'm sorry," she whispers, her fingers curling into his shirt. "I got up early to train with Jax."

Jake pulls back just enough to study her face, his brow furrowing. "Training?" His eyes flicker to Jaxson, suspicion darkening his gaze.

Jaxson doesn't flinch. "She needs to be ready," he says. "If Patrick comes for her again, she will fight back."

The spatula scrapes against the pan as I plate the bacon, pushing it onto the table with a little more force than necessary. "Alright, enough brooding." I stride over and scoop Emmy into my arms before she can protest, lifting her effortlessly off the counter.

She lets out a startled laugh, squirming in my grip. "I can walk, you know."

"Where's the fun in that?" I smirk, setting her down on the tabletop. She grabs a strip of bacon, crunching it with a satisfied hum.

Across from her, Ash strolls in, ruffling his hair and eyeing the food. "Is she... dancing?" He watches the subtle sway of her shoulders as she chews.

Jaxson tilts his head, watching with a half-smile. "It's the happy food dance," Ash explains, sliding into a chair. "Bacon's the only thing that gets her moving like that lately."

Jake settles beside Emmy, snagging a piece of fruit and holding it to her lips. "Balance, Red," he says, nudging it forward until she takes a bite, chewing with exaggerated slowness.

Jaxson grumbles under his breath—calling her "fucking adorable" —before stuffing a forkful of eggs into his mouth.

I lean back in my chair, letting my eyes linger on her as the rest of the room fades into a dull hum. Her moss-green eyes meet mine when she finally looks up, and my pulse stumbles.

"Emmy," I say, my voice low.

"Hmm?" She doesn't turn, a faint smile tugging at her lips, like she's still savoring the bacon—or maybe just lost in thought.

"Want to spend the day with me?" My voice is casual, but the thudding inside betrays me.

Emmy's gaze darts to Jaxson, a silent exchange passing between them—one that twists uneasily in my gut. She turns back, her smile soft, drawing me in like a tide I can't resist. A droplet of pineapple juice slips from the corner of her lips, trailing down her chin. Without thinking, I reach out, my thumb catching it.

Her lips parted as I brought my thumb back to her mouth. She closed around it, her tongue brushing against my skin in a slow pull that sent a shiver racing down my spine. I swallow hard, and heat curls low inside me. When she finally releases me, her tongue flicks out to catch the last trace of sweetness, and the teasing glint in her eyes has my thoughts scattering.

She leans in, the light brush of her fingers against my knee sending a jolt of electricity through me. "Where are we going? Is it to find Patrick?"

I work to keep my smirk in place, tilting closer until our noses nearly touch. "No Patrick, but it does get my blood pumping."

"O-oh okay? Um, does this place have a dress code?"

I slowly let my eyes sweep over her, savoring how she shifts under my gaze. "Everything you wear is delicious. Surprise me."

A soft flush creeps into her cheeks, and without another word, she hops down from the table, excitement buzzing in the air as she hurries out of the kitchen. My eyes follow her, unable to do anything else. The room feels colder the moment she's gone, and when I glance over, I catch Jake watching too, his jaw tight, his fists curled against the table.

The silence fractures with his low growl. "Why the hell does she feel the need to ask your permission?"

Jaxson doesn't blink, his fingers tapping lightly against his coffee mug before he takes a measured sip. "I don't know what you're talking about." He spears a piece of egg with his fork, chewing like this is just another morning.

Jake shoves his chair back, and the chair screeches against the floor. "Stay the hell away from her."

Jaxson sets his mug down, each movement controlled—but his jaw clench gives him away. "You really think dragging her around chasing ghosts will help when the real monster is right below us? She's breaking, Jake. You see it. And yet you sit here pretending everything's fine. Tell her the truth. Let her decide for herself. If she's really yours like you claim, she'll choose you."

The crack of my palm against the table echoes through the kitchen as I push to my feet. "You don't know her."

Jaxson finally meets my gaze, his expression unreadable, but his words land like a punch. "I don't think you know her at all." He steps away from the table, his movements smooth but heavy with unspoken accusations. At the doorway, he pauses, glancing over his shoulder. "Are you ready to watch her shatter when she finds out what you're hiding?"

Ash exhales slowly, folding the newspaper with deliberate precision. He sets it on the table. "We're all keeping this from her."

Jaxson's steps falter. "Excuse me?"

Ash meets his gaze head-on. "You're as much a part of this as the rest of us. Don't pretend otherwise." His tone remains steady. "You've had every chance to tell her. We all have. But you didn't. You made the same choice." His gaze hardens. "And when the truth comes out—and it will—you'll deal with the fallout just like the rest of us."

Jaxson's jaw tenses, a storm swirling in his eyes, but he doesn't argue. He studies each of us, letting the silence stretch between us like a blade, before turning and walking away, his footsteps heavier than before.

The air in the room turns heavy with the weight Jaxson left behind, like the smoke of a fire no one's willing to put out—a sharp ache blooms beneath my ribs. I dig my fingers into the pain as if I can hold it all in—hold myself together.

This isn't how I pictured it. I thought Saint John would be a gift for her, my little killer. A way to balance the scales. I imagined her hands on my tools, a quiet, calculated hunger in her eyes as she made him bleed, made him suffer the way she had. But now... now I'm not so sure. She's desperate to find him, to end this, and we're the ones standing in her way.

Doubt digs its claws into me, and my gaze shifts to Ash, searching for the steadiness I've always counted on. Before I can stop myself, the question slips out. "Is he right?"

A voice—soft and bright, cutting through the tension like sunlight through storm clouds—answers instead. "Is who right?"

Emmy bounces into the room, her presence disarming.

"No one, Sweet Girl," Ash says with a sigh, standing and running a hand through her hair. His touch is a quiet reassurance she doesn't notice. "Spending the day with Killian?"

She nods, the mild excitement showing in her movements, and Ash's lips curve into a rare smile. He leans down, sweeping a kiss across her forehead. "Have fun. Stay safe. Stick close to Killian, yeah?"

Her grin is bright, a beacon against the shadows weighing us down. "Always."

I push to my feet, forcing down the unease twisting inside me. "We should get going if we want to beat traffic." My voice is rougher than I'd like, but she doesn't notice. I busy myself with small movements—keys, jacket, anything to keep from looking too long at her, at the way she remains untouched by the storm raging inside me.

Then, she turns to Jaxson, and a knot forms in my stomach. If she's turning to him for approval, I'm not sure I can handle it. But she doesn't ask for permission.

"You'll call if you find anything?"

Hope flutters in her eyes. It's not permission she needs; it's answers—answers we keep just out of reach.

Jaxson's response is gentle, his hand cupping her cheek with a tenderness that feels out of place for him. "Of course, Little One. I'm following a few leads while you're gone. Try to enjoy yourself." His voice carries a different tone. And when he smiles—not his usual smirk—it's completely unguarded.

She trusts him. Does he understand her in ways I never could? Have I failed her?

The thought leaves me breathless, and I barely manage, "Let's go, Killer." The words come out steadier than I feel.

Her smile is instant, easy, as she slides her hand into mine. Her fingers slip between mine. I squeeze her fingers gently, hoping she can feel what I can't put into words—reassurance, maybe even regret.

"Lead the way, Kill," she teases, sinking into my side as we head toward the garage.

The moment we step inside, a sharp gasp escapes her. "Wow, look at all of these!" Her awe fills the space, eyes wide as she takes in the neat rows of trucks, motorcycles, and SUVs. She moves through the garage like she's seeing it for the first time, fingers ghosting over polished metal and leather seats.

And then, she stops.

Her eyes lock onto a point in the far corner, and I see it—how her lips part and her eyes shimmer. "Is that...?"

"Yeah, Princess. That's it."

The sleek black Harley-Davidson sits under the soft overhead lights, its frame gleaming like a memory brought back to life. She stares at it, her eyes glistening and turning from a moss green to a rich color, like the earth after rain.

I can still feel the weight of it—the promise I made to her when she was younger, that this would be hers when she turned eighteen. The same bike I wrecked when I thought she was gone for good—the one I rebuilt, piece by piece, when I refused to accept that loss.

It's more than just a machine. It's us.

Her voice is just above a whisper as she reaches toward it. "Can we take it?"

Her eyes search mine, pleading, full of hope. And at that moment, with everything holding onto me, I could only give one answer.

I nod. "Yeah, Killer. We can take it."

Her smile hits me like a punch to the gut. Without thinking, I step closer, cradling her face in my hands. My thumbs trace the wet trails on her cheeks, chasing away the tears as I tilt her chin up. When my lips find hers, the kiss is soft, almost reverent—a whisper of everything I can't put into words, a promise and an apology wrapped into one.

She exhales a shaky sigh against my mouth, her fingers curling into the edges of my jacket, gripping tight like she's afraid to let go. I pull her closer, my arms circling her waist, anchoring her to me. Her lips move beneath mine, hesitant but eager, and when her tongue flicks out to taste me, a low groan rumbles from my chest. In that moment, nothing else exists—only her touch, the quiet strength hidden beneath the soft exterior she shows the world.

"Baby," I murmur against her lips, breaking the kiss just enough to breathe, to smile as she chases after me, unwilling to let the moment end.

Her lashes flutter, and she looks up at me, lips parted, a dazed smile tugging at the corners. "Mmm, yeah... we should probably go," she whispers, but her arms stay wrapped around me, holding on like she's not ready to return to reality.

I kiss her forehead, letting it stay a beat longer than I should before finally releasing her. My fingers find hers as we turn toward the bike.

For the first time in a long time, it doesn't feel like running. It feels like home.

CHAPTER 47

Ember Rose

I rip off my bright pink helmet, shaking loose my hair as the muffled ringing in my ears fades, replaced by the roaring crowd around me. The air clings heavy with the sharp scent of oil and sweat. Shouts, whistles, and pounding music crash over me like a tidal wave. My heart beats in time with the wild energy buzzing through the room. I turn toward the chaos gathering at the center.

Before I can move, familiar hands wrap around my waist, firm and grounding. Killian.

His presence steadies me as I swing my leg down from the bike, my legs numb from the long ride and unsure beneath me. I wobble, and his hold tightens just enough to keep me upright without a word. Heat radiates from his chest, his presence both effortless and overwhelming.

"What are we doing here?" I raise my voice over the noise, moving in close. His easy grin lifts, that damnable devil-may-care smirk that once made my heart race for all the right reasons. Now, it stirs—comfort mixed with unease, a sharp reminder of how he thrives in chaos. Thrill-seeker. Rule-breaker. Always one step ahead, daring life to keep pace.

Once, that reckless energy intoxicated me. Now, it knots in my stomach, tightening with every second.

He doesn't answer; he just jerks his chin toward the press of bodies and starts moving. I have no choice but to follow.

My eyes flicker back to the bike, worry tightening in my chest. Someone could take it. But before the thought fully lands, a heavier weight settles—memory. This bike is more than metal and speed; it's a promise.

My eighteenth birthday is when he promised to surprise me with my first ride, pretending it was no big deal, though I'd been nagging for weeks. The way my heart almost burst with excitement when he'd pinky swore, grumbling about my impatience.

And then our first kiss.

That moment is etched deep in me. Spring creeps in, the air crisp, the grass damp beneath my bare feet as I wander into the garage. Jake and Ash sleep upstairs, and Killian—predictably—is elbow-deep in the sleek black car Jake dragged home from the junkyard.

Sweat clings to his skin, dark hair messy, damp curls sticking to his forehead. He sees me but stays silent, grabbing a water bottle from the mini fridge and crossing the room with that lazy stride.

I perch on the motorcycle, fingers tracing the handlebars, my heart pounding like it always does around him. I'm fifteen—too young to understand love, but old enough to feel its weight crushing my ribs whenever he looks at me. He stands between my legs, forehead resting against mine, hands settling on my hips, heavy and sure. No words come; the moment hums with unspoken promises and unshed fears.

Then his lips brush mine—soft, hesitant, tender enough to steal the breath from my lungs. This isn't the Killian I think I know—no fire, no demand—just a quiet confession of a feeling neither of us can name.

By morning, it's like it never happened. He treats me like a little sister tagging along, and I let him. I tell myself it means nothing, even though it does.

The memory clings now, a ghost I can't outrun.

Killian's arm tightens around my waist, pulling me back. "Lost in thought, Killer?"

I force a laugh, nudging him. "Just a little."

He guides me through the crowd, his touch an anchor I'm not sure I trust anymore. The room pulses around us, bodies colliding from every side, music rattling my chest like a second heartbeat. When we break through, my breath catches.

A massive cage looms at the center, metal bars gleaming under the harsh lights. Inside, a motorcyclist twists and loops in a death-defying dance, the engine roaring through the crowd's frenzy like a war cry.

Killian's arms slip around me from behind, his chin resting lightly on my shoulder. "What do you think, baby?" His breath warms my skin, sending a shiver down my spine.

I try to focus on the spectacle, letting the chaos distract me, but my mind drifts to Atlas. The ache hits like a fist to my chest—sharp and relentless. The not knowing gnaws constantly. Is he safe? Scared? Alive?

Guilt twists through my bones, a crushing weight that makes breathing hard. My son. My heart. My everything.

I swallow, forcing a smile as I lean back against Killian, letting his presence hold me together just a bit longer. Past and present pull at me, but I cling to the fragile illusion of control, just for tonight.

I turn slightly, and Killian's breath brushes my lips, our noses touching in a way that sends a tremor through me. My heart flutters, caught between the weight of now and ghosts of then. For a moment, I surrender, drowning in the memory of our first kiss—how his touch once made me feel safe, the fleeting illusion that pain could be eased by simply being near.

Tilting my head, I sweep my tongue across his lips, slow and searching. He stills beneath me, a quiet sigh escaping, arms tightening around my waist. His hold isn't just desire; it's a deeper feeling, one I can't name but crave. My tongue traces the seam of his lips—hesitant, pleading—and when he parts them, I pour everything into the kiss. Desperation. Longing. The silent plea for a solid anchor in the chaos.

He groans into me, his grip firm but trembling with restraint. Then, just as I feel myself slipping under, he pulls back, forehead resting against mine.

"Fuck, baby," he murmurs, voice thick and rough, sliding over my skin like velvet and sandpaper. "If it weren't my turn next, I'd take you somewhere we could... slow down."

A shaky laugh escapes me, hollow like a balloon filled with air. His fingers trail down my arm, grounding me for a moment before a heavy hand claps his back, shattering the moment.

"Sorry, man, but you're up," a voice cuts through the haze, and Killian's hands twitch at his sides.

His eyes lock on mine—dark, searching—as if reading the parts I won't speak aloud. Then he grabs my hand and pulls me through the crowd. "Let's go, Killer." The teasing edge is gone, replaced by softer uncertainty.

The noise fades as he leads me to a dim corner of the dressing area, air thick with sweat and motor oil. The quiet should be relief, but it sharpens the thoughts swirling in my head—thoughts I can't outrun.

I press my palms to the cool door, fighting the desperate ache clawing at my chest. Where are you, Atlas? The thought curls inside me, tightening. Are you safe? Scared? Do you know how much I love you?

A low groan pulls me from the spiral. Before I can think, Killian's arms wrap around me, solid and warm. "You've got to stop looking at me like that, baby," he murmurs, voice low, thick with an emotion I can't name.

I rest my forehead against his chest, breathing in diesel, cedar, and that faint woodsy scent always clinging to him. It wraps around me like a tether, pulling me back even as the ache refuses to fade.

"I'm sorry," I whisper, voice cracking.

He kisses my head before stepping behind a curtain to change. I sink to the floor, curling my arms around my knees, squeezing my eyes shut against the tears burning to spill. The knock comes too soon, snapping me back.

"Five minutes," a voice calls, and I force myself to stand, wiping my face hastily before Killian reappears.

Clad in dark forest green and black riding leathers hugging every line of his body, he looks every bit the reckless daredevil I once fell for. He smirks, stretching his arms overhead, and I forget how to breathe for a second.

"What do you think, Killer?"

"You look good enough to eat," I say, wrapping my arms around his waist, chin resting against his chest. His smirk lifts, and I don't miss how his hand presses firm to my back.

Another knock. "Showtime!"

Killian's grin widens, excitement radiating as he spins me toward the door, hands light but sure on my shoulders. But I can't move. My feet feel stuck, the knot in my stomach tightening.

"Killian," I whisper, barely pushing the words past the lump in my throat. Atlas's face flashes—his laughter, the feel of his small hand in mine, the way he looked at me like I was his whole world. My chest constricts. "You're about to do something crazy, aren't you? You only smile like that when you're about to pull something wild."

Killian's laugh is soft, but it doesn't reach his eyes. "You know me too well, baby."

He pulls me toward the sleek motorcycle waiting nearby, but I hesitate, heart pounding against my ribs.

"Killian, I—" My voice cracks. The worry, the fear, the gnawing ache for my son. How can I stand here pretending I'm okay when I don't know if he's alive? How do they not see it—see past my mask?

His hand cups my cheek, the pad of his thumb brushing away a tear before it falls. "What's wrong?" The question comes gentle, but the concern behind it feels real.

I swallow, shaking my head. "It's nothing." My voice shakes, betraying me. "I just... Killian, I can't stop thinking about him. About Atl—Patrick." The slip burns on my tongue, the lie heavy, suffocating. I can't tell him the truth. I won't put Atlas in more danger.

His jaw tightens, a shadow of darkness in his eyes. For a long moment, he looks at me, lips pressed into a firm line. When he speaks, his tone lowers. "We'll find him." His hand closes around mine. "I swear."

The fire in his eyes blazes, matching my determination deep inside. But determination doesn't erase fear, the gnawing doubt, the endless questions without answers.

I nod, swallowing back the sob on the edge of my voice. "I know," I whisper, and for now, I let him believe the lie.

I grip the front of Killian's jacket, my fingers trembling on the worn leather. My voice barely breaks through the tightness in my throat. "I don't know if I can handle much more, Killian." The words feel small under the weight of everything crashing down on me.

Killian wraps his arms around me. He buries his face in my hair, lips brushing my temple, and for a moment, I lean into him, seeking comfort in the warmth of his touch. "You're stronger than you realize, baby," he whispers, quiet conviction steadying me. "Stronger than anyone I've known. But right now, I need you to trust me, okay?"

I nod, but it feels empty, like a promise I can't keep. His smirk returns the second he pulls back, masking the worry that almost appears in his eyes. "Now, get in the cage, Killer," he says, nodding toward the looming steel globe ahead, its metal bars shining under the harsh lights.

I blink, thrown off. "What?"

"You heard me." His grin widens, eyes sparkling with mischief. "Get in the cage."

"Killian, I—" I start to protest, unease twisting in my stomach, but he pushes me forward, his touch light but firm.

"Do you trust me?"

I hesitate, biting my lip—the thoughts of Atlas gnaw at the edges of my mind, relentless and cruel. My pulse pounds in my ears, but when I look up at Killian, a desperate intensity in his eyes pulls me in.

I swallow and nod. "Fine," I murmur, stepping forward, frustration curling through me as I climb inside the cage.

A voice cuts through the noise before I can fully grasp the absurdity. "What the hell are you doing, Thorne?" A man strides over, irritation and disbelief written across his face as Killian wheels the bike in behind me, shutting the door with a loud clang.

"Killian, what is this?" My voice sharpens, confusion twisting inside.

Instead of answering, he comes over and cups my face, pressing a quick kiss to my lips, the taste of him washing away my questions. "Just stand still, arms up," he instructs, voice calm despite the roar of the bike's engine beneath him.

I hesitate, muscles tense, but I obey, heart hammering as the vibrations from the bike rumble through me. The cage shakes around me as he picks up speed, the metallic hum buzzing through my body. Killian moves close, the wind from his motion whipping around me.

His gloved fingers brush my side as he passes, and against all odds, a laugh escapes me—soft, hesitant, and unexpected. The rush, the thrill, the ridiculousness of it all makes my chest feel lighter, just for a moment. But then reality creeps back, slipping through cracks like smoke. My thoughts snap back to Atlas, and the fragile levity breaks. The ache returns, sharp and unforgiving, and tears sting my eyes before I can stop them.

Killian slows the bike, pulling it to a stop. He removes his helmet, grin wide and unapologetic. Before I speak, his hands find me, pulling me close, his mouth claiming mine in a kiss so deep it steals what little breath I have.

"You're incredible," he murmurs against my lips.

I close my eyes, resting my forehead on his. "I don't feel incredible," I whisper, voice cracking under the weight. "I just feel... lost."

His hands grip my hips, holding me steady. "Then let me help you find your way, baby. Even if it's only for tonight."

I want to believe him, want to lose myself in him, in this. But the ache for my son clings to me, refusing to let go. I let him hold me anyway, take some of the weight I can't carry alone. His arms lift me easily, carrying me toward the edge of the cage, and I don't resist.

The sudden slam of a door causes me to flinch, and before I can turn, Killian closes me in against the cold metal. The chill seeps through my clothes, but it's nothing compared to the heat of his hands as they roam down my body with possessive intent. His touch burns, a dangerous distraction, one I know I shouldn't give in to—but right now, it's the only thing that keeps me from breaking.

"Too many clothes," he mutters, voice rough with need, and before I can answer, my jacket disappears, tossed on the floor. His fingers trail over bare skin, igniting every nerve they touch, and I let it consume me for one fleeting moment. Let him consume me.

Because the fear, the pain, and the relentless ache, those will still wait until after this moment ends. But for now, I cling to him, to the illusion that I can feel anything but loss, even if only for a little while.

Killian's breath stutters as he pulls my shirt over my head. His eyes darken, locking onto the black lace clinging to my skin. The fierce hunger in his gaze sends a shiver down my spine, a sharp contrast to the cold air.

"Fuck, baby," he rasps, voice thick and low, like gravel and smoke. "You're trying to kill me." Before I can respond, his mouth is on me, hot and demanding, tugging the lace between his teeth. The sharp tug and wet heat of his tongue make my head hit the door with a dull thud, and a gasp escapes me, my hands threading into his hair instinctively. His touch isn't just a distraction; it's a lifeline, a solid hold amid the hollow ache gnawing at my chest.

My hips press against him, desperate friction earning a low, guttural groan as he moves up to meet me. I whimper, need clawing toward the surface. "More, Killian," I plead, voice broken and soft, begging not just for his touch but for anything to quiet the relentless chaos inside me.

With a growl, he lets go, hands trembling as they strip off his gear with frantic urgency. I fumble with my jeans, shoving them down my legs and kicking them aside before launching myself back into his arms. He catches me effortlessly, grip firm, grounding, and the world tilts as he spins us, lowering me onto a worn wooden bench with surprising gentleness.

His lips trail open-mouthed kisses along my collarbone, then downward between my breasts. Each touch feels like a claim, and I clutch him, nails digging into his skin, desperate to hold on.

"Tell me to stop, Ember," he murmurs against my skin, breath hot, voice laced with restraint unraveling thread by thread. "Because I don't think I can."

I shake my head, pulling his lips back to mine, biting his bottom lip just enough to make him groan. "Don't stop," I whisper, hands sliding down his back, slipping beneath the waistband of his jeans. The words feel strange on my tongue but liberating—mine. Patrick never let me have this. My pleasure. My own choices.

Killian freezes for a moment, then curses softly before sinking to his knees in front of me. His hands spread over my thighs, touch firm and reverent, gaze locking onto mine with an intensity that steals my breath. "Are you wet for me, baby?" he asks, voice rough, lips brushing my skin.

A sharp pang laces through me, ghosts of memories lurking in the corners of my mind, but I push them down and nod quickly. I need this. I need part of myself back.

His fingers curl into the lace of my panties, pushing them aside. The cool air hits my heated skin, making me shiver. I try to close my thighs, but he holds me open with a soft, reverent groan.

"So wet," he murmurs, dragging his thumb in slow, lazy circles over my clit. The heat of his touch sends sparks through me, and my body arches off the bench. "So perfect." His grin is wicked, and the low rumble of satisfaction in his chest makes my toes curl.

"Killian," I breathe, voice trembling when his tongue replaces his thumb, tracing a slow, torturous path through my folds. His hands grip my thighs, keeping me pinned as he devours me, a moan vibrating against my core.

My fingers tangle in his hair, pulling him closer, and he growls in approval, tongue working me into a frenzy of need that tightens more and more. The pleasure builds too fast, too much, but I chase it anyway, grinding against his mouth and begging for release.

"Killian," I cry out, my body clenching around him as his fingers slip inside, curling with relentless focus. "D-don't tease me." My voice breaks, and I hate how desperate it sounds, but I don't care.

His eyes meet mine, dark and intense. "I'd never tease you, baby," he whispers against me, his words sinking deep into my bones.

The pressure inside breaks, a scream tearing from my throat as I fall over the edge. My muscles grasp him, my body trembling as waves roll through me, leaving me breathless and weak on the bench.

Killian kisses my inner thigh, warm breath soothing my skin as he moves above me, his presence solid, protective, safe. He presses his lips to mine, his tongue tracing the seam, still tasting me, and a groan escapes my lips.

"You taste like heaven," he mutters, and I groan, hiding my face in my hands, suddenly feeling more vulnerable than I expected.

"Don't hide from me, baby," he says gently, pulling my hands away. Making my chest ache.

I shiver beneath him, his touch calming yet thrilling, but reality slips back in as warmth fades. The emptiness left by Atlas hits again, stealing the air from my lungs. My chest tightens, and I look up at him, voice shaking. "Killian..."

His hands cradle my face, eyes searching mine with a silent question. "What is it, baby?"

I swallow hard, fingers pressing against his chest. "No one's ever... put my pleasure first." My voice barely escapes, heat rushing to my cheeks. Patrick's shadow looms over me, dark against Killian's gentle touch.

His jaw hardens, a fierce spark lighting his eyes. "That changes tonight," he promises, hands moving carefully as he helps me dress. There's no rush now, only softness, and the way he pulls me close makes my throat burn.

Once I'm dressed, he kisses my forehead, and I soak in the closeness for a moment. "Let's get you home, baby," he murmurs as I look down, noticing the strain in his jeans.

"What about you?" I ask softly.

Killian's smirk is slow and lazy, full of confidence. "Tonight wasn't about me."

I bury my face against his chest, letting his words settle, but an ache remains, simmering beneath the surface, whispering that no pleasure can erase the pain of what I've lost.

His words repeat in my mind as we enter the cool night air. His hand rests on the small of my back, grounding me, but the ache inside won't quit. No promises or fleeting touches can fill the place where Atlas should be. The emptiness sits heavy, a dull ache that never fades.

The ride home hums with tension, thick and suffocating. My cheek rests against Killian's broad back, the leather of his jacket warm against my skin. My arms grip his waist like he's the only thing stopping me from falling apart. His hand slides to my thigh, fingers curling there, but it's not enough to calm the restless stirring inside.

The bike hums beneath us, but my thoughts shout—wild, relentless. I trail my fingers down his stomach, slow and teasing, feeling his muscles tighten under my touch. Lower. Testing. His breath catches, his body stiffens, and a smirk tugs at my lips. For a brief moment, I savor the control, the way I can unravel him so easily.

But reality is close behind. The bike slows, and the looming shadow of the garage swallows us. The engine's purr dies, replaced by a heavy quiet that settles between us. Before I can even take it in, Killian pulls me into his lap, hands gripping my hips with a desperate need that tightens my chest.

He removes my helmet, tossing it aside before his lips crash against mine. There's nothing gentle about it—just raw, consuming hunger, a battle of lips and teeth and silent longing. My fingers tangle in his hair, pulling him closer as I press against him, searching, needing. His groan vibrates through me, but before I can lose myself, his hands hold me still, stopping my movements.

"Stop." His words are strained, breath uneven. "You don't know how much I want you... how much I need you. But not like this."

His words hit hard, cutting through the haze with brutal clarity. I freeze, the sting of rejection sharper than I expect. His hands cup my face, thumbs brushing away tears I didn't know had fallen.

"This isn't about you," he murmurs, his green eyes heavy with frustration and a pain that runs deep. "It's about me. I can't do this, knowing you're still planning to leave." The last word falls bitter, edged with danger.

I swallow hard, chest aching. "I... I'm sorry," I whisper, voice barely louder than the soft hum of the cooling engine. The fight drains from me as I slide off his lap, cold seeping into my bones as the space between us grows vast and unfamiliar.

Killian exhales sharply, running a hand through his hair before setting the bike on its stand. "Go inside, baby," he says, voice softer now, exhaustion threading his words. "I need a cold shower before I lose my goddamn mind."

I manage a weak smile and nod, but my feet feel heavy as I step away. The house waits ahead, and I move toward it on autopilot, the ache in my chest growing heavier with every step.

Light spills from the library, warm and inviting. I pause in the doorway, drawn to the quiet refuge inside. Ash sits in an oversized chair, head bowed over a book, fingers absentmindedly tracing the worn edges of the pages. He looks up when he senses me, his eyes softening.

"Welcome home, Sweet Girl," he says, voice low and soothing. "Rough night?"

I shake my head and step inside, warmth wrapping around me. My eyes drift over towering shelves, the scent of old paper and leather embracing me like a familiar hug. "I didn't know you had a library," I murmur, voice quieter than I mean it to be.

Ash leans back, a faint smile pulling at his lips. "It's my sanctuary." His eyes scan me, thoughtful. "Did you have fun tonight?"

I hesitate before nodding, giving him a watered-down version of the evening, careful to leave out the parts that feel too raw or too tangled. He listens in his quiet way, his expression thoughtful, and his focus entirely on me.

"I'm glad," he says.

I glance at the book in his hands, raising an eyebrow. "A biography? Of course."

His lips twitch, dimples appearing. "And what would you suggest, princess?"

Spinning on my heel, I scan the shelves until my eyes land on a familiar title. I pull it down and hold it out with a grin. "Throne of Glass."

Ash studies the cover, brow furrowing. "Fae fiction?"

"Yeah." I bite my lip, excitement sparking despite the exhaustion. "It's about fairies and mythical creatures. Sarah J. Maas weaves fantasy and emotion like no other."

He flips the book over, skimming the back before handing it back. "Read it to me."

I blink, surprised. "What?"

Ash's eyes lock on mine. "Read it to me," he repeats, softer this time.

"I... I don't think—" My voice falters, but before I can back out, he reaches for my hand, touch warm and sure.

"Please," he murmurs, thumb brushing my knuckles. The way he looks at me, like I'm worth holding onto, makes my chest ache differently—softer, yet no less deep.

I swallow against the lump in my throat and settle beside him, my shoulder brushing his. His arm slips around me, grip light but steady, and for the first time in what feels like forever, I breathe out without the weight crushing me.

Opening the book, my voice trembles as I begin to read. The words wrap around us, and slowly, piece by piece, the tension inside unravels. Ash listens, his calm presence a balm against the raging turmoil.

And for a little while, just a little while, I let myself get lost in more than fear.

CHAPTER 48

Asher

"What?" Ember's voice is a whisper. She clutches the book, her fingers curling around the worn edges. She bounces on her toes—nervous energy or excitement, maybe both. She probably doesn't even realize she's doing it, but I do. And it's impossible not to want to pull her in, to still her restless movement.

I reach for her hand, my fingers curling around hers, guiding her down beside me. The couch dips as I slide an arm around her waist, pulling her close. "Read it to me."

Her brows draw together, and for a moment, I expect her to refuse. Ember knows I don't read fantasy—hell, I don't read much of anything that exciting—but the way her eyes light up when she talks about this story makes me want to hear it. To have her tell it to me.

She hesitates before opening the book; her tone is initially soft, and the words are tentative. As the story unfolds, she leans into it, her tone shifting, growing richer with every sentence. I close my eyes, the cadence pulling me in like a slow tide. Her body relaxes, her stiff posture melting away inch by inch until she rests against my arm. For a moment, everything feels... right.

Then, she moves just enough to break the spell.

"Something wrong?" I murmur, tilting my head to catch the uncertainty in her eyes.

She purses her lips, a tiny frown tugging at the corners. "I'm not comfortable," she admits, voice laced with apology.

She's already moving before I can suggest anything, standing with a newfound determination. "Lie back against that," she motions to the armrest, her tone leaving no room for argument.

I do as she says, observing her with curious eyes. She slides between my legs, her back fitting perfectly against my chest. She wiggles, adjusting until we're flush together. A sigh escapes her. Her head tilts back, eyes searching mine. "Is this okay?"

I rest my hand on her hip, fingers tracing slow circles. "Perfect," I murmur. "This is perfect; keep going." My arms circle her, pulling her in until she's all I can feel.

Ember's voice pulls me under, drawing me into the story, though all I can focus on is how she fits against me and how her body rises and falls with each breath. My thumb grazes the soft curve of her stomach, an absent motion that neither of us acknowledges. Time slips away, unnoticed, until Jake's silhouette appears in the doorway. I shake my head once, dismissing him. I'm not willing to give up my time with her just yet.

The story continues, her voice increasing in pace when it gets exciting and slowing down when it drags until she begins to waver, her head dipping forward as a yawn escapes. The book slips from her grasp, and I catch it before it falls, marking the page before setting it aside.

She murmurs words I can't catch, turning into me with her face tucked close. I bury my nose against her head, breathing in her scent. "Let's get you to bed, Sweetheart," I whisper, scooping her up.

She makes a sound similar to a protest, but she doesn't resist as I lay her down, tugging the blanket over her. I watch her, brushing a strand of hair back from her face, but as I step away, her hand catches mine, fingers quivering.

"Stay, please," she breathes, barely audible, but it's enough to root me to the spot.

The words come easily. "Anything for you."

I tug my belt off, rolling it into a tight ball before shrugging off my shirt and folding it neatly. I place them both on her dresser, smoothing out the wrinkles before sliding beneath the covers. The space between us disappears as she curls into me, and I hold her, feeling the calming rhythm of her heartbeat. There's no need for words in the quiet, in the dark.

She shifts in her sleep, a soft murmur slipping past her lips before she turns into me. Her head nestled beneath my chin, her fingers fisting into my shirt, gripping it like I might disappear if she let go. "Did you like it?" she mumbles.

I trail my hand up and down her back, letting the motion settle us. "Like what?" I whisper, my lips brushing the top of her head.

"The book," her words dissolve into the quiet as sleep tugs her under. Her body melts against me.

I stare at the ceiling, the unfamiliar shadows stretching across the room, the clock's steady tick interrupting the silence. Everything feels still, too still. This isn't my routine—this isn't the rigid schedule that's kept me sane for the past five years. An hour in the library, a workout, a shower, a podcast to drown out the noise in my head. That's my anchor. That's how I keep control.

But tonight... I don't have it. I've disrupted it for her. But how could I not? She's here, curled against me, interrupting the structure I've built with nothing more than her mere presence. And the worst part? I need it. I thought having her near me would be enough for this one time, but I can't close my eyes. The voices in my head are at war, the noise too loud to drown out.

Her breath flutters, the softest reminder of how easy it would be to let this become more permanent. The thought twists into a dangerous kind of longing I haven't allowed myself to feel before; it creeps up like a phantom. I brush my lips against her temple.

"Ash?" Her sleep-rough and uncertain voice pulls me from my spiraling thoughts. I glance down, meeting her rich, moss-green eyes, hazy with sleep.

"Did I wake you?" I ask, my voice raspy.

She blinks slowly, her brow furrowing as she studies me. "I don't think so, but have you slept?"

I shake my head, looking back at the ceiling. "No."

"Why not?"

I hesitate, swallowing down the admission. "I have a compulsive routine," I say; the words feel heavier than they should. "I can't sleep without doing it."

"Why didn't you tell me?" Her head tilts, hair brushing my skin in a way that makes it difficult to think. "What kind of routine?"

"I read for an hour, work out, shower, and listen to a podcast before sleep."

She hums quietly, her fingers tracing circles across my skin. Goose bumps scatter along my arm, a shiver running along my spine. "Did I mess up your routine? You should've told me, Ash." She scolds, teeth sinking into her bottom lip. My cock hardens, throbbing painfully against my slacks. Begging for her attention.

I brush a hand through her hair, my voice quiet. "I didn't want you to leave me alone; I've enjoyed every second with you... But I need it."

Instead of disappointment, a smile tugs at her lips. I watch Ember slide off the bed, bare feet padding across the hardwood. She stretches, arms reaching overhead, a yawn escaping before she turns to me with a glint in her eyes.

"Okay, let's do it."

I blink, propping myself up. "What?"

She claps her hands, her grin sleepy. "You won't sleep until you do your thing. So, come on, where do we start? Reading?"

I watch her, half amused, half stunned. She's serious. And the idea of her slipping so easily into the structure I've clung to is almost enough to make me laugh.

I rake a hand through my hair. "No, but I'd like to add your reading to my routine sometimes. It was very relaxing."

She stops mid-step, turning slowly, her eyes searching mine as if waiting for me to take it back. "You mean that? This isn't some joke?"

I push off the bed, closing the distance in a few strides. My hand finds her cheek, and she leans into it. My thumb brushes over her bottom lip, and a pretty flush creeps up her neck, painting her cheeks the softest shade of pink.

"Haven't you figured it out? I would do anything to keep you close," I murmur, the weight of the moment heavy. "If I can convince you to be a part of my daily routine, don't you think I would do that? Unfortunately, there are three other surly bastards I have to share you with."

Her lips quirk into a smile, her lashes fluttering before she peeks at me. "I'd be happy to read to you every night, Asher."

Her response sinks into me, dissolving the last traces of anxiety that had been clinging to me. I exhale. "Good," I brush a strand of hair behind her ear. "Because I don't think I can sleep without it now."

A giggle escapes, soft and sweet, tugging at a hidden part of me. I smile.

"So... what's next?" she asks, laced with an edge of sleepiness.

I glance at the clock. "I need to do a quick workout," I reply. "Then a shower."

She tilts her head, her lips parting, "Can I join you?"

The question knocks the air out of me. My brain stutters, and heat creeps up my neck, as images I definitely shouldn't be thinking about play through my mind. "You... want to join me?" I manage, my voice rough, betraying the usual calm I pride myself on.

"If that's okay," she says, shifting her feet, her fingers playing with the hem of her shirt. The slight bounce in her stance making her look shy.

Without thinking, I reach for her, pulling her flush against me. She gasps, her hands landing on my shoulders, and the scent of roses surrounds me—sweet, familiar. But beneath it, there's a jarring edge. It's not her. The harsh sting of gasoline and scorched rubber clings to her skin, slamming into me like a bowling ball to the dick. Mood: officially dead.

I lift her, and she wraps her legs around me, her hands gripping my shirt. "Ash? What's wrong?" she asks, tinged with concern.

"You don't smell right; need to make it better," I mutter, the words coming out harsher than I intend. I stride toward the bathroom, kicking the door open, ignoring her protests.

"Asher!" she squeaks, wriggling in my hold, but I can't let go until I get her clean. "Ahh," she screams when her legs hit the cold counter. "Fuck that's cold." Her hand pushes against my torso, trying to force me back.

"Don't move," I growl, stepping away to turn on the shower.

"Asher, stop! I refuse to be the reason you don't sleep tonight," she says, her tone brokering no argument. "Go work out first. Then we can shower."

Her words are a gut punch, and a grin spreads across my face. She doesn't realize it, but I'd let her boss me around all night if it meant having her in bed with me.

Her lips part and then close as she fidgets, chewing her bottom lip. "We?" I whisper, the pink in her cheeks deepening.

I lean in, letting my fingers brush under her chin, tilting her head back. "Are you asking if I will shower with you, Sweet Girl?" My voice is teasing, but the way her throat bobs makes my blood rush south. My pants do little to hide my arousal.

Her eyes dart down to the prominent bulge, her throat bobbing as she swallows, "I-I will... *if* you go work out first," she stammers, her hands fluttering at her sides like she's unsure what to do with them.

I can't stop the smile that pulls at my lips. "This will be the longest workout of my life," I murmur, letting my thumb trace the line of her jaw. "Careful, Princess. I might have to make you part of my nightly routine."

Her eyes widen, and she squeaks out, "O-okay."

I kiss her cheek, savoring how she shudders under my touch, before heading for the door. Every step feels like torture, and the face she is waiting for me only makes it ten times worse.

When I hit the gym, my muscles are tight with restless energy, but I push through. Sit-ups, push-ups—every rep feels like a punishment, a distraction, but it's not enough to shake the ache in my pants. *Fuck, how much longer do I have?* Checking the clock, it's only been ten minutes. I want to put my head through the wall.

My blood sings, crackling with energy, and the workout hasn't done a damn thing to quiet the voices. Every pull-up and every sprint delays what I really want right now. And I am *done* waiting.

Taking the stairs two at a time, I reach the bedroom door, but the sight that greets me halts me mid-step. Ember's sprawled across my bed, her hair spilling over my pillow like a halo, though the devilish smirk on her lips says otherwise. She's stripped down—a black tank top hugging her curves, lace peeks out, barely covering her ass, and I bet every cent in my bank account that if she spread those thick thighs, it wouldn't cover the soft, pink flesh between her legs. My throat dries.

She props herself on her elbows, legs crossed lazily at the ankle, the glint in her eyes far from innocent. "Did you have a good workout?" she purrs.

My eyes drag over her exposed skin, where the thin fabric clings, betraying the rugged peaks of her nipples. I drag my tongue across my lip, sweat clinging to my skin. "It was... unusually tough," I admit, my voice thick as I slowly approach her.

Her lips part, teasing. "Looks like you could use a reward."

My eyes lock onto hers. "Looks like you changed."

She shrugs. "I got more comfortable."

Before she can say another word, I reach for her, my hands sliding around her thighs and dragging her to the edge of the bed. She yelps, the sound melting into laughter as I scoop her up, tossing her over my shoulder.

"Asher!" she gasps between giggles as she stabilizes herself on my lower back.

I smirk, delivering a playful slap to her ass. "Keep laughing, Princess."

She's laughing as I carry her back into the bathroom, the cool counter meeting the back of her thighs when I set her down. I turn away to fiddle with the shower knobs, my fingers clumsy, distracted by the way she watches me. Her lip caught between her teeth.

"Clothes off."

"Yes, Sir," she teases, and I growl, attempting to keep my focus on getting the water to the perfect temperature. Rustling fabric fills the space, and when I glance back, her tank top is gone, revealing the delicate black lace of her bra. My fists clench at my sides, jaw tight as she reaches behind her back and unhooks it, letting the straps slide down her arms.

My breath stutters, and my control frays when she slips off the counter, revealing nothing but bare skin and temptation.

"Are you just going to stare, or are you getting in with me?"

Her fingers hook into the waistband of her panties, sliding them down inch by inch, and I swear the world stops. My boxers hit the floor a second later, and the way her eyes lower, the sharp breath she takes—it sends a rush of blood straight to my cock. It throbs for her, but then her arms lift, crossing over her stomach. Her teeth dig into her lip—not in that sexy, playful way, but with hesitation.

"I know I'm not as skinny as some of the other women you've been with," she says, no more than a whisper, shaking. "Prettier, skinner, sexier—"

"What are you talking about?" I close the space between us, cupping her face. "Look at me."

She does, and I hold her there, my thumbs sweeping across her cheeks. "They don't matter. Not like you."

Her eyes glisten, vulnerability pooling there, sending a deep ache through my heart.

"You," I murmur, "are the most breathtaking thing I've ever seen. Your curves, the softness, the way you fit against me—it's all you. And nothing compares."

She gives me a small smile and melts into me, her fingers clutching at my shirt.

"No one's ever made me feel like you do," I whisper, my voice hoarse. "You're my home, Ember. My reason for breathing."

Her hands tremble as they slide up my arms, and when she looks at me, there's no doubt left—only trust.

"Show me," she breathes, snapping the last bit of my restraint I had.

I'm on her in an instant, my hands gripping the back of her thighs as her arms wind around my neck. Her lips find mine, soft at first, growing hungrier. A low groan rumbles from inside me as she circles her legs around me.

She pulls back. "Shower. Now."

"Yes, Ma'am," She releases a breathy moan as the water cascades over her. The heat surrounds us. Droplets slide down her skin, catching in the hollows of her collarbone, and I can't resist trailing my lips along the curve of her neck, teasing, tasting.

Her fingers thread into my hair, tugging me closer, and I push her back against the tile, my mouth mapping every inch of her skin. She gasps when I nip along her jaw, and the sound fuels my primal need.

Her hips move, fusing with mine, and I groan, grinding against her opening. Her wetness coats the tip. "Fuck, Ember, Sweetheart." I bury my face into her neck as I thrust between her thighs, my cock catching on her opening and sinking in an inch before I pull out and repeat.

"Ahh, Asher, more," she begs as I trail my hands down her sides.

I lean in, my lips brushing her ear. "Careful, Sweetheart. You're making me rethink this whole routine thing."

She laughs, breathless and beautiful, and I know in this moment, I'm never going back to life before her. She is it for me.

"Ember," I rasp, my voice thick with restraint as Ember's lips move feverishly across my jaw. "Ember... Sweetheart."

"Hm?" she murmurs; her exhale is a soft caress on my hot skin, her body moving in slow, purposeful motions that make it impossible to think straight. My cock sinks inside her again, and I struggle to pull myself out.

"Fuck, we need to stop," I manage, the words strained, but she only moves closer, her nose brushing mine.

"No," she whispers, a soft plea. Her body shifts again, and whatever control I had left unwinds thread by thread.

I grip her hips, stopping her movements. "If we keep going, I won't be able to stop. Ember, I don't want to hurt you."

"You could never hurt me." Her forehead rests against mine, her eyes searching, vulnerable. "I don't want you to stop," she breathes. "I need you to remind me I'm okay. That I'm not broken. I need to feel whole again."

My hands slide up to cup her face. "Are you sure?"

She swallows, nodding. "Yes... But," she hesitates, biting her lip. "There's something I need to tell you."

I tilt my head, brushing a stray lock of wet hair from her face. "If this is about Killian," I say with a chuckle, "don't worry. He already told us everything—in fact, he bragged about it."

A flush creeps across her cheeks, and she buries her face in my neck. "It's not that," she mumbles. "It's... have never... not until...I don't know if you'll understand."

I lift her chin, forcing her to look at me. "Don't be embarrassed, Ember," I murmur, tracing the soft curve of her jaw. "We were all jealous of Killian."

Her eyes dance with humor, the tension easing. "All of you? Somehow, I doubt that."

"Oh, don't doubt it." She smiles, her wet body glides against mine as she unwraps her legs from around me and slides down to the floor. She looks at me from beneath her lashes. "What do you want, Sweetheart?"

"I want you."

I pump shampoo into my hands, massaging it through her hair as she hums, the sound vibrating through her chest. My lips twitch. "Careful. You'll wake the whole house, and I want you to myself tonight.

Her lashes flutter closed as the rich copper strands slide like silk through my fingers. They gleam under the warm light, so much more vibrant than they had been a month ago, lifeless and dull. Now, it shines —just like her.

I rinse her, shutting off the water and wrapping her in my arms. "Let's get you in bed." She clings to me as we step out, her wet skin sticking to mine, her head resting against my chest.

Grabbing a fluffy towel from the warmer, I wrap it around her. "There, nice and warm," I smirk, pulling her back against me.

"I'd rather be naked and sweaty." I choke on my spit, staring down at her as she watches me. Her lips pinch together, trying to hold back her laughter.

"Naughty, Ember," I scold, walking her backward from the bathroom. She topples over when her knees meet the mattress, and she pulls me down with her, her hands sliding up my back, nails scraping, sending shivers chasing down my spine.

Her lips find my shoulder, planting soft kisses that turn desperate as they move up my neck. My hands roam, exploring the smooth curves of her waist, hips, thighs. I settle between her legs, my cock resting against her; she shudders beneath me.

"Moan for me, Sweetheart. You moan so pretty for me, Princess," I murmur, my mouth finding the delicate peak of her breast. My tongue flicks over it, and she gasps, arching into me, her hips moving, searching for more.

"Ahh, Ash," she trembles as I flip us over, her thighs straddling me. She grinds down on me, my cock sliding between her folds. Her breath comes out in short, ragged bursts. “More, Ash,” she whimpers, her eyes heavy-lidded and pleading.

I grab her hips, slowing her desperate movements and guiding her. She drips on me, and I force myself not to thrust into her. “Lift, baby,” I murmur against her neck. “You’re going to ride me.”

She lifts onto her knees, her eyes boring down into me as my cock pushes through her entrance. Her warmth wraps around the tip. *Fuck, she feels so good.* Her breasts sway in front of me, and I snap forward, latching my teeth on one of the dusty pink nipples. Ember screams, sinking her nails into my chest. The pain flows straight to my cock. I roll my tongue over the stiff bud, soothing the ache. “Sit on me, Ember. I want to feel you wrapped around me.”

CHAPTER 49

Ember Rose

I scream as Ash sinks into me. *Fuck, he's big. I didn't think this through enough.* My movements are frantic as I roll my hips, driving him deep inside me. Sweat drips down my back as my nails drag across his chest, little trails of blood bubbling up from the wounds.

He growls, flipping us over so I'm on my back. I wrap my thighs around his waist as he plunges into me. My body starts shaking, pleasure coursing through me. My eyes roll back as I thrust up to meet him. Skin slapping against skin echoes through the room, the sound erotic and driving me closer to the edge. "Ah, Ash," my body tightens, sending me tumbling over the edge, waves of pleasure washing over me.

"I want another one, Ember. Give me one more." He growls, his teeth sinking into my breast. The pain sends pleasure sparking through me.

"I-I can't," I whine as he drives into me, his tongue rolling over the sensitive bud before repeating it on the other. "A-Ash," I grip his shoulders, letting the sensation of his cock pull at my sensitive insides.

"Yes, you can."

I cry as he drives into me repeatedly. Electricity shoots through my body, I move my hands, fisting the sheets.

Memories tunnel my vision, and I beg them to stop, but they drag me under as I squeeze my eyes shut.

"Look at you, Kitten. Begging for my cock like my good little slut." Patrick's breath is hot against my face. I squeeze my eyes shut, begging for it to be over as he pounds into my body. "So tight for me." My hands twist into the sheets, tears gathering behind my eyelids. I want to die, I can't do this.

"Open your eyes, Ember," Ash growls, pulling me from my panic. My eyes snap open to meet his. "Stay with me, baby." A whine escapes as the pleasure begins to build again. Ash pulls from me, my insides clenching around him to pull him back. "What do you need?" He asks as he sinks back into me.

"Take it away, take it all away," I beg, wrapping my arms around his shoulders and dragging him down. His lips meet mine in a searing kiss that has my toes curling; he thrusts in and out of me.

Ash pulls away from my lips, one of his hands snapping out to grab my jaw. "I want you to cum for me on the count of three and I want you to watch me while you do it. Say 'Yes, Sir. '"

My pussy clamps around his cock. "Y-yes, Sir." The words tumble from my mouth as he sinks into me at a snail's pace and pulls back out. The friction drags against my insides. More, I want more. Faster. Harder. But he continues his slow pass, keeping those stunning earthy orbs locked on me.

"Three..." He starts, rolling his hips into me. My hands grip his hips, my nails digging into his skin, trying to pull him in faster, but he keeps up his slow pace. "I am not rushing this, baby. You will know who made you cum."

I moan, lifting my hips to meet him, but he pushes me down with his torso. I can't move, can't meet his torturous movements. He rolls his hips, his cock sliding in and out of me. A moan escapes. "Two..." he groans, his face dropping down to mine. His lips trace my jaw, down my neck, before he tugs my nipple back into his mouth. My back tries to arch to meet his mouth, but he holds me in place.

He looks at me from beneath his lashes, suddenly pistoning into me. The momentum shatters me. "One..." he whispers, my body shaking violently beneath him. My pussy spasms around him, and I feel his release as it fills me.

"Ash," I scream, another orgasm ripping through me. "Ah, Fuck." He flips me over again, laying me across his chest. He lazily thrusts up into me, his fingers sending shivers down my spine. Goosebumps spread along my arms when his lips meet my temple. I cling to him, willing him to keep me afloat. "A-ash, n-no more," I whine, my hands fisting.

"I know you can, Baby," he whispers, grabbing my hips and pulling me down to meet his strokes. "One more for me."

I whine as another one courses through me, my body quaking from the aftershocks. He kisses my temple, wrapping his arms around my waist.

With his cock still buried inside me, we lie quiet in the aftermath. Our breathing ragged.

With a heavy sigh, he pulls out of me, and I can feel our releases spilling out between my legs. Rolling out of bed, he struts into the bathroom. "W-what are you doing?" Self-consciousness starts taking over, and I pull a sheet up to my chest.

Ash walks out with a swagger that throws me off. "Taking care of you. Why are you holding that sheet?" He stops at the foot of the bed, holding an object. It's wet, dripping between his fingers.

"W-what's that?"

He smirks, gripping my ankle in his hand and pulling me to the end of the bed. "I'm cleaning you up, now let go of the sheet, Sweetheart." My grip loosens, and he pulls the sheet from me, leaving me bare to him. Heat creeps up my neck. I shouldn't feel so exposed to him after what happened, but the way he looks at me sends pleasure shooting through me. "There you are," he smiles, gripping my thighs and spreading me open to him. "Mmmm, look at you. Such a mess." Using his fingers, he scoops up the mixture of our release before pushing it back inside me. "Look at how full you are of us."

My eyelids are heavy as he uses a washcloth to wipe away our mess. "Ash," I whisper, pulling his attention to me. "Thank you."

"Anytime, baby." He winks, throwing the cloth into the laundry before crawling back into bed with me. He stretches out beside me, pulling a blanket over us.

Wrapping his arms around my waist, he pulls me close. He tucks my head under his chin, and I kiss his chest.

I relax, my eyes closing as he holds me close. Tonight changed everything; I want them to know. I'm going to tell them about Atlas.

CHAPTER 50

Jake

The muffled sounds from Ash's room bleed through the thin walls, and I groan, rolling onto my side and yanking the pillow over my head. It doesn't help. Ember's moans spill through the cracks, threading into my ears and digging under my skin. Sleep is impossible when I know what Killian's done to her, too.

It's only been a day since Killian got to taste her; now Ash has her sounding like *that*. She's lived with us for a month. A month of stolen moments—flirty morning kisses and cuddling. A month of Jaxson sculpting her, pushing her through brutal training sessions until her once-soft curves grew firm, her muscles honed. She's becoming one of us, slipping deeper into our world.

Yet, despite everything, she's still chasing shadows—wild goose chases we've been feeding her, breadcrumb trails leading nowhere. Hope flickers in her eyes each time we offer a lead, only to dim when she returns empty-handed. Killian and Ash are settling in to share her, satisfied with how things are. But not me. She's mine—mine to protect, to hold, to claim. But after the office incident, I've had to face the truth after she ran from me again. She'll never be just mine.

A cry of pleasure echoes through the wall. "Ah, Ash!"

I hurl my pillow at the wall, the thud doing nothing to drown out the sounds. She's been avoiding me—maybe it's for the best. The others are circling a dangerous idea—Patrick. Letting him go, letting her find him. I won't allow it. Jaxson's silence is worse than his anger; his disgust weighs whenever he looks at me. It's only a matter of time before he breaks down and tells her the truth. Then we'll lose her for good.

I sink into the couch in the farthest corner of the house, where the silence is comforting. My body betrays me, the ache in my cock a reminder of what I can't have—what I want more than anything but can't touch.

"You're thinking too hard."

Her words rush over me, causing my pants to become even more uncomfortable. I look at her. Ember leans against the doorframe, arms crossed, lips pursed. Her sleep shorts ride high on toned legs, and the tank top clings to her, highlighting the muscles Jaxson has been carving into her body. Knives, guns, defense—she's been learning, adapting. She fits into our lives seamlessly, yet she still feels just out of reach from me.

She tilts her head, one brow raised in question. "Jake?"

I swallow, forcing my gaze away from her tempting curves, the memory of the sounds she made still buzzing in my head. "Come here, Red."

She stares at me, hesitating, before crossing the room. She sinks into my lap; her legs draped across mine as she sits sideways. My arms wrap around my waist, and I bury my face in her hair, breathing in the scent of roses and... fucking linen. Fucking Ash. Her smell is my solace; it calms my demons. It brings me peace, if only for a fleeting moment.

"I just need you for a minute," I murmur, kissing her temple.

She nods, letting me hold her for a while. "Jake?"

"Hmm?" I hum, pulling away from her.

"Are there any new leads?"

"Not since last night." She sighs, slipping from my embrace, leaving behind an ache. Leaning against the wall, she looks at me. "I-I'm sorry, red."

She exhales sharply, pushing off the wall, "Not your fault, we can't find him." *Fuck, the betrayal hurts.* The knowledge that it is my fault. "See ya, Jake," she mumbles, walking out, her disappointment hanging heavy in the air.

I rub a hand over my face. She's slipping further away, and I'm losing my grip on keeping her here. My phone feels heavier with every word as I type out a message to the guys, asking for another fake lead, just enough to keep her looking. To keep her close.

Killian and Ash see it but don't reply. They're done with the game. Jaxson, though—he usually plays along, begrudgingly, for the sake of keeping her busy. But tonight, his response comes fast.

> No.

That one word is enough to send panic coursing through me.

Killian and Ash fire off questions, but I can't focus on them. My insides twist, and my breathing gets heavy. My vision swirls with dark shadows. *Fuck!*

Jaxson knows where Patrick is. And if he's not playing along anymore, it's only a matter of time before Ember knows.

My phone vibrates with another message from Jaxson. It glares up at me from the screen, each word a punch to the gut.

> I will no longer help you lie to her. You aren't there. You don't have to hear her excited chatter during the drive, see the hope in her eyes when we arrive, or watch her fall apart when it's just another abandoned lot. She'll find him by tomorrow, Jake. Decide how you want to handle it because we all will have to face the consequences.

My heart slams against my ribs. *No. No. Damn it.* My fingers shake as I clutch the phone, the weight of his ultimatum suffocating. Panic claws its way out of me, ragged and uneven. I can't let her see me like this; if she sees me now, I won't be able to control myself if she asks me that same question again. I won't be able to hold it together. She trusts me, and I've been lying to her.

I snatch my jacket from the back of the couch, my movements jerky.

The house's walls are closing in as I bolt down the stairs, through the front door, and into the city before anyone can stop me.

Cold air slams into me, but it does nothing to cool the wildfire raging inside me. I bury my hands deep in my pockets, my shoes thudding against the concrete. Each step creates cracks in the chasm, the space between me and the truth growing. I'm a coward. My family, my brothers, my secrets—everything is spiraling out of control.

But it constantly circles back to her. Ember. She's the center of my world. The thought of her slipping away, realizing what we've done and hating me for it, gnaws at me.

I stop at the edge of a darkened park, the playground eerily still beneath the dim glow of the streetlights. The swings creak in the wind, an unsettling contrast to the chaos inside me. Leaning against a tree, I close my eyes and try to picture a different reality—one where Ember's mine, where I could hold her without fear. But the image is hazy, slipping through my fingers like grains of sand.

Footsteps crunch the leaves, pulling me from my daydream. I glance over my shoulder, spotting Ash. His face is unreadable, but I can feel the weight of his judgment. He stops a few feet away, mirroring my stance, with his hands shoved into his jacket pockets.

"You ran out pretty quickly," he says, the tightness in his shoulders giving him away, his relaxed posture.

"Needed some air," I mutter, swallowing hard and forcing my voice to stay steady.

Ash nods, but his eyes stay on me, searching for answers I'm not ready to give. "She's asking questions, Jake. We can't lie to her forever."

"I know," I growl, grinding my palms against my eyes, causing a kaleidoscope of colors to dance across my vision.

"She won't stop." Ash steps closer, placing his hand on my shoulder. "And when she finds him... what then?"

I can't answer him. I don't want to. The truth is, I've spent too long dodging the thought of what happens when Ember finds Patrick. When everything we've built—every carefully placed lie—shatters under the weight of reality. When she looks at me, she sees nothing but a liar.

Ash lets the silence stretch. "She deserves to know, Jake."

The words hit like a punch to the ribs, and I snap harsher than I mean to. “And then what? Watch her walk away? Watch everything fall apart?” My fists clench. “You think she’ll stay if we tell her the truth?”

His shoulders slump just a fraction. “No,” he admits, a bitter edge to his tone. “But we can’t keep lying to her either. We’re just pushing off the inevitable.”

I drag a hand through my hair, frustration building like a tidal wave. “So what’s your brilliant idea, Ash? We spill everything and hope she forgives us?” A humorless laugh escapes me.

“Maybe it’s time to let her make her own choices. We’ve been pulling the strings for too long.” The truth sits there, undeniable, and I hate it. I hate that he’s right. That we’ve been so consumed with protecting Ember that we’ve been controlling her instead. But letting go… letting her choose for herself, even if it means losing her—it terrifies me.

“I can’t lose her, Ash.” I croak.

“And what if you already have?”

I stagger back, the possibility sinking into my bones, wrapping around me like a vice. I’ve been so focused on holding her close—on keeping her away from Patrick, from the truth—that I never stopped to consider that I’ve already lost her.

Ash scrubs a hand through his hair, exhaling slowly. “We’re all scared, Jake. But we can’t keep pretending everything’s fine. She’s not stupid.” His eyes meet mine, holding me accountable for what I have been avoiding. “She deserves better.”

I look away, my jaw tight as a panic swells. I know he’s right. I’ve always known. But the idea of watching her walk away, of her turning her back on me after everything—my throat locks up at the thought. I don’t know if I can handle it. If I’m strong enough to let her go, even if it’s what she wants.

Ash steps back, giving me space. “I’ll give you time to figure it out. But we can’t keep this up much longer.” With that, he walks away, leaving me alone in the stillness of the park.

I lean back against a tree, eyes squeezing shut. I try to picture a future where she can be mine—where I can pull her in and hold onto her without fear. But the image won’t take hold, slipping further from reach the longer I chase it.

Pushing off the tree, I start walking, letting the day guide me. The streets are quiet, my shadow stretching out in front of me. My feet move on autopilot, and my mind is tangled in knots. I don't know how to untangle.

Every thread leads back to her—to all the moments when I could have told her the truth. Instead, I let the lies build, letting my fear win. I see her face in my mind—hopeful and trusting—shattering into betrayal. The image guts me.

I wander the streets, circling the city as the sun begins to disappear past the horizon, when I find myself standing in front of the house, the glow from the windows in contrast with the hollow feeling inside me. I hesitate at the door, staring at it like it'll burst open from an angry Ember. I'm not ready. I don't know if I'll ever be.

The house is quiet, eerily so, when I step inside. Everyone's asleep—or pretending to be. But I know Ember. She doesn't sleep when her mind is racing, when the need is gnawing at her.

My feet carry me upstairs, each step heavier than the last. I stop in front of her door, my hand hovering over the handle. *Just knock. Just go in, talk to her, tell her the truth.* But my hand shakes, and the words I need to say tangle, choking me.

But I'm a fucking coward. So, I turn away, retreating to my room. I drop onto the bed, staring at the ceiling. The bed feels too big, too empty. I got a bed to accommodate us both, but she hasn't been here since that first day. I got it after that, though she doesn't know that. I feel the crushing weight of everything I've done—the lies, the manipulation, the selfishness.

Digging my phone out of my pocket, my thumb hovers over her name in my contacts. I could text her everything. It would be easier than facing her, but Ash is right, she deserves better from us...from me. And what words could possibly fix this? I drop the phone with a sigh, staring into the dark.

Time drags, and sleep never comes. Every scenario I run through ends the same way—Ember walking away, leaving me behind with nothing but the ruins of what we never got to be.

I can't keep lying to her. I know that. But the thought of losing her? I don't know if I'd make it through.

THE EARLY MORNING hours creep in, the darkness outside thinning into a dull gray. The house is silent, but everything feels too loud inside me—my heartbeat, my thoughts, the weight on my windpipe.

Groaning, I sit on the edge of my bed, the phone heavy in my hand, my fingers hovering over the screen. My thumb hesitates, trembling, before typing the words I've been avoiding all night.

We need to tell her.

The message stares back at me, and I want to delete it. Each second stretches as my finger hovers over the send button. And then, with a sharp exhale, I hit send.

The reality of what I've done weighs me down like a stone. There's no undoing it now. No more delaying, no more running.

The screen lights up almost instantly with a response from Ash.

Let's meet in an hour.

Killian's response comes next, curt.

About time.

My fingers curl around the phone, the edges biting into my palm. Jaxson doesn't respond. His silence says everything—I can feel it. He's been ready, standing at the edge while the rest of us clung to the illusion of me, waiting for us to stop hiding behind the lies we built.

I set the phone down and stare ahead, the ticking clock on the wall deafening. The weight I've carried for so long still suffocates me, but a quiet relief stirs beneath it. A hairline fracture in the dread that's ruled me. Maybe it's knowing that, for the first time in a long while, I'm not making it worse. I'm finally doing the right thing.

But it's fleeting.

The sun filters through the blinds, painting my room in golden hues. My hour is almost up, and doubt creeps in. My mind is racing with *what-ifs* that I can't answer. *What if we've already lost her? What if she walks away? What if I never get another chance to fix this?*

I drag my hands down my face, a headache forming behind my eyes. *I fucked up...* The memories come unbidden—Ember's smile when she thinks she's getting closer, the way her face falls when the truth slips just beyond her reach. The way she looks at me with trust. That trust... I've spent so long building it, only to crush it.

Lying down feels futile; I'm just wasting time at this point. Sleep remains elusive because my time is up.

I run through every scenario and every possible way this could play out, and none end well. The image of her walking away, of turning her back on me—on all of us—burns itself into my mind, and no matter how much I try to push it away, it festers inside me.

I sigh, pushing off the bed. I guess it's time.

CHAPTER 51

Jaxson

Ember's body has grown stronger, but I can see the cracks forming daily. The light in her eyes dims more each day. Hope slips through her fingers, piece by piece, and I can't watch it happen anymore.

Tomorrow, Saint John gets out of the basement. The others can chase their shadows, but this ends in a matter of days. Ember still gets those gut-wrenching texts from Krystal—pictures of Atlas for which she pours every ounce of her strength into surviving. Since I found out about him, I've been planning every detail, every step to get her away from here with Ash and Killian while Jake's at work. She'll find Saint John exactly where I want her to—an abandoned building I've been scouting, a breadcrumb trail leading straight to him.

From there, it's simple: we take him to Krystal, get Atlas back, and ensure no one comes after us again. No loose ends. No second chances. Maybe then, we can all breathe again. At least, that's the plan.

But last night, I made a mistake—refusing Jake. And now he's been gone all day. Ember mentioned she saw him but didn't say more, avoiding him like she's been doing for weeks. She spends less time in her room, always drawn closer to Ash and Killian. It's harder to talk to her about Atlas without the stolen moments we used to have. Those pointless searches Jake sent her were a cruel gift—an excuse for us to talk and hold each other when disappointment left her in tears. I remember the way she clung to me, sobs wracking her frame, and the way Killian would slip into her room hours later, lock-picking skills in full use. He never talks about what happens there, but Ember always looks a little steadier when they emerge. And Jake? He doesn't ask, but the tension in his jaw speaks louder than words.

"Jax?" Ember's voice carries from down the hall.

"In here," I call back, lowering the weights to the floor.

She appears in the doorway, arms crossed, a playful smile curving her lips. "Of course, you're in here. Do you do anything besides work out?" The casual way she leans against the frame, dressed in leggings and a sweatshirt, shouldn't make my heart race, but it does. Her curves are soft, but training has sculpted her, given her an edge that wasn't there before.

I smirk, grabbing a towel to wipe the sweat from my face. "I fix cars and go joyriding."

She laughs, shaking her head. "Such a guy thing to say." But the laughter fades too quickly, replaced by the familiar shadow of desperation in her eyes. "Do we have any more leads?"

The air thickens between us. I shake my head, and the weight of disappointment settles over her like a heavy cloak. "Come here, Baby Girl." She doesn't hesitate, stepping into my arms and burying her face against me. Her shoulders shake, her tears wetting my shirt. I kiss her head, my voice low and soothing. "Shh, baby. I've got you."

"I'll never find him," she whispers. "I'll never get Atty back."

I tilt her chin up, wiping away the mascara smudges with my thumb. "Let's get out of here, go for a ride?" I see the doubt flicker in her gaze, but I push on.

Her brows knit together. "What?"

I grin, hoping to pull her out of the spiral. "Let's take some of the bikes from the garage. We'll keep our phones on us if the guys need us."

She hesitates, lips twitching like she wants to argue, before her shoulders drop. "You promise I'm ready? It won't kill me?"

I chuckle, brushing a strand of hair behind her ear. "I'm pretty sure you're not that easy to kill, Little One." The way her cheeks flush under my stare is a reminder that she sees more of me than I'd like to admit.

Before she can second-guess, I grab her by the hips, spinning her toward the garage. She stumbles with a surprised laugh, and I steady her, my grip staying just a second longer than it should.

"There's no need to push me, *Sir,*" she grumbles, dragging her feet dramatically as she trudges through the house, shooting me a pointed look over her shoulder.

I step in front of her, blocking her path, my eyes narrowing. "What did you just call me?" My voice cuts through the air like a blade.

She freezes, blinking up at me. "Sir?" Her bravado slipping. "It was just a joke." She swallows hard, her gaze darting to the side.

Without hesitation, I close the distance between us, my hand wrapping around her neck, pulling her in until our noses almost brush. The air between us crackles, charged and volatile. "Careful, Little One," I murmur, my thumb tracing along the delicate line of her jaw. "Call me 'Sir' again, and you'll be in my bed."

Her eyes widen, her lips parting in a silent gasp. I lean in, capturing her mouth in a teasing kiss, nipping at her lower lip just enough to make her tremble.

"O-okay," she breathes, barely above a whisper.

A slow smile spreads across my lips. "Good girl." I take her hand, leading her toward the garage. "Choose a bike, Baby Girl."

Her fingers curl around mine for a second before she lets go, stepping forward, her eyes sweeping over the rows of motorcycles lined up like soldiers. "Any bike?" she asks, soft, almost reverent.

"Any bike," I confirm, leaning against the wall, arms crossed as I watch her move through the space. She takes her time, running her hands over the chrome and leather, her gaze filled with an intensity I rarely see in her.

She stops in front of one, her fingertips tracing its sleek frame. "What's this one called?"

"That," I say, pushing off the wall and closing the distance between us, "is an MTT 420-RR."

Her fingers slide down to the seat. "Is it fast?"

A grin tugs at my lips. "Tops out at 273 miles per hour."

She exhales softly, almost in awe. "It's stunning," she murmurs, her eyes holding a spark that pulls tight at my chest. "I want to ride this one."

I arch a brow. "You sure you don't want to start with something a little less... insane?"

Her gaze snaps to mine, determination etched across her face. "This bike will make me feel free," she says. "It'll help me escape the chaos."

I toss her the keys, watching her face light up with a grin. She catches them effortlessly, circling the bike like she's already claimed it. "But," I add, "you'll need the right gear."

She tilts her head, curiosity crossing her features. "Gear?"

I nod, guiding her toward the back of the garage storage room. "Killian took care of it. Said we couldn't put you in danger again."

Pushing the door open, she's met with a mannequin dressed in sleek black leather and a vibrant pink helmet. Her eyes widen as she steps closer, running her hands along the smooth material. "Killian got this for me?"

"Yeah," I say, leaning against the doorframe, watching how she studies the gear. "After that last ride, he said he wouldn't risk it again. Too many variables, too many risks."

A soft smile plays on her lips. "Killian, always the protector of his own wild ideas," she murmurs, before looking back at me. "Now... how do I put this on without looking completely ridiculous?"

I chuckle, grabbing the leathers off the mannequin. "You? Never."

She snorts, tugging at her jeans. "Mhm, you say that now. Just wait until you see me try to squeeze into these pants. Tighter than a pair of Spanx."

I frown. "What the fuck are Spanx?"

Throwing her head back with a laugh, she struggles to shimmy into the tight leather. I try to look away, but the sound of her frustrated grunts is impossible to ignore. I glance over, just in time to see the pants stuck around her thighs, pink lace peeking out. She shoots me a pleading look, bottom lip jutting out in a perfect pout.

"Help," she whines, wiggling her hips and tugging helplessly at the stubborn fabric.

"Damn it, Baby Girl," I groan, dragging a hand down my face as I watch her struggle. "You must think I'm some kind of saint." My voice is rough with frustration, but there's a teasing edge I can't quite hide.

"Lord, give me strength," I mutter, but the smirk playing at the corners of her lips tells me she's enjoying every second of this.

"Oh, just help me, you big baby," she huffs, wobbling closer with an exaggerated pout.

I grip the sides of the leather pants, holding them steady. "Ready?"

She nods, jumps, and wiggles her hips as the tight material slowly slides into place. With one final tug, the pants snap snugly over her waist.

"Finally," she exhales, rolling her shoulders. "That was way too much effort." Sliding into the jacket, she easily zips it up before spinning in a slow circle. "So?" She strikes a playful pose, tilting her head with a cheeky grin.

A low chuckle rumbles as I hook an arm around her waist, pulling her flush against me. "You look absolutely delectable, Baby Girl."

She bats her lashes, wrapping her arms around my waist as she rises onto her tiptoes. "Thank you, Sir."

I stiffen instantly, my grip pinching her chin as she meets my gaze. "What did I say about calling me Sir?"

A nervous laugh slips past her lips. "T-that the next time I called you Sir, it would be in your bed."

I lean in, my lips grazing the corner of hers, my tongue flicking out just enough to taste her. She gasps softly, and I take the opportunity to deepen it, swallowing the soft sound that escapes her.

"And are we in my bed?" I whisper against her lips.

She shakes her head, her hands fisting the leather of my jacket.

"So why tempt me?" I murmur, sliding my tongue past her lips, and she melts into me with a moan, her body molding to mine like she belongs there.

"Well, well," Killian's voice cuts through the thick haze of desire. He strolls into the room, his lips curling in a knowing smirk. "What's happening here?"

I feel Ember tense, but she doesn't pull away, and Killian's grin widens. "I knew you'd look irresistible in those," he says, stepping behind her and resting a hand on her hip.

Ember glances over her shoulder, arching a brow. "Ah, so it wasn't *just* about my safety?"

Killian chuckles, his thumb tracing idle circles against her waist. "Your safety is always my priority, Sweetheart," he says smoothly, "but I'd be lying if I said I didn't want to see you in these skintight pants." He grinds against her like a dog in heat, causing her to gasp.

Ember groans, clutching my jacket as if to steady herself. "We'll never get out of here if you keep that up, Kill."

Killian hums in amusement, his lips brushing the side of her neck. "Maybe I could join you both?"

I let out a low growl and yank her away from him, glaring. "She's mine."

Killian steps back, hands raised in surrender, his grin smug. "Glad to see you've finally joined the harem," he teases, throwing a mock salute before sauntering out of the room.

"Harem?" Ember peeks around my arm, her expression caught between curiosity and amusement.

I roll my eyes, shaking my head. "Who knows with him?" Turning to the shelf, I grab my leathers and slip into them effortlessly.

As I zip up the jacket, I glance at Ember, leaning against the wall, eyes closed, exhaustion weighing heavily in her features. The dark circles under her eyes speak louder than any words ever could—sleep hasn't been kind to her, not since Atlas, not since all of it.

I approach slowly, placing my hands on either side of her head, my thumbs brushing lightly along her jaw. "Baby Girl?"

Her lashes flutter, and she hums softly. "Hmm?"

"Do you want to reschedule this?" My voice is gentle, a rare thing when it comes to her. "We can do this another day."

She opens her eyes, the resolve in them cutting through the fatigue. "No," she says, pushing off the wall and wrapping her arms around my waist. "I want to go out."

I nod, kissing the top of her head. "Then let's go."

Grabbing our helmets, I hand hers over before wheeling the bikes out of the garage. Ember stays close, and without hesitation, she straddles the seat with practiced ease.

I climb onto mine, and her voice comes through the intercom with a playful edge. "I'm in the mood for speed, what do you say?"

A grin tugs at my lips. "Then speed is what you'll get."

With a twist of the throttle, we roar out of the driveway, the wind whipping past us as her delighted squeal rings in my ears.

THE WORLD BLURS into streaks of shadow and light as we tear down the empty backroads, the low hum of our engines vibrating beneath us. Her laughter crackles through the helmet intercom—bright and wild, the sound of someone remembering how to live.

I glance in the mirror and catch a glimpse of her hair whipping beneath her helmet. Her posture is confident, and her body leans into every curve like she was made for this, like the weight of the world isn't clinging to her shoulders.

"You okay back there?" I ask, my voice low in her ears.

"I haven't felt this alive in forever," she breathes. "Don't you dare slow down."

That's all the encouragement I need.

I gun the throttle, weaving us along the snaking road like we're chasing freedom, peace, maybe just the feeling of being *real.* The wind claws at my jacket, tears at the edge of my restraint, but I let it. I let it take the guilt, the blood, the weight of what I did for her tonight.

We crest a hill, and the stars open above us—sharp pinpricks of light that pierce through the velvet dark. I slow just enough for her to ride up beside me. Her helmet turns toward mine, and even through the gear, I *feel* her looking at me.

She lifts a hand and signs *"thank you"* against her chest, tapping her fingers to her helmet and extending them toward me. It's soft and silent, and it damn near breaks me.

"Don't thank me, Ember," I say quietly. "You deserve a night without ghosts."

She doesn't answer; she just leans closer until our shoulders brush as we ride. And I swear the world holds its breath with us.

Eventually, I lead us to the edge of the quarry—an overlook hidden by trees, with just enough clearing to see the valley below. I kill the engine and swing off my bike, reaching for her hand as she dismounts.

She tugs off her helmet and shakes out her hair, cheeks flushed, eyes shining. "You always bring me somewhere like this."

I murmur, "Only you."

We stand there for a moment, the bikes ticking as they cool, the night pulsing with crickets and the far-off rustle of leaves.

"Do you think Atlas would like it here?" she asks suddenly, voice barely above a whisper. "Can we bring him?"

I reach out, tucking a strand of hair behind her ear. "Of course. I'll take you both to all my hiding spots."

She exhales, eyes searching mine. "I'm scared, Jaxson."

"I know," I whisper, pressing my forehead to hers. "But you're not alone anymore. You have me. And I'll burn this whole world down before I let anyone hurt you."

Her breath catches, and she nods. Then, without hesitation, she kisses me—soft at first, like a question. I answer without words, pulling her closer and pouring every unspoken promise into her lips.

And beneath the stars, with the smell of gasoline and pine between us, Ember finally lets herself fall into a moment that doesn't demand survival—only being.

CHAPTER 52

Ember Rose

The kiss lingers even after it ends. I feel it in the soft press of his forehead against mine, in the way his breath fans across my lips like a whispered vow. Jaxson doesn't rush me, doesn't speak. He just stays there—close, grounding me in that way that no one else can.

The night air curls around us, cooler now, the stars endless above the tree line. I can hear the quiet pop of the engines and the hush of wind slipping through pine needles. It's peaceful out here. It feels like a secret place we weren't supposed to find.

Maybe we weren't.

Maybe that's why it feels like ours.

I keep my eyes closed for a beat longer, memorizing the way he smells—leather, smoke, and a warmth I can never quite name. My fingers dig into his sides. I don't want to let go.

As I finally pull back, it's reluctant. Jaxson's eyes are darker now, unreadable in the shadows, but there's a tenderness in the way they roam my face—like he's searching for cracks, for a way to make it right. Maybe there are too many to fix.

"Sorry," I whisper. I don't even know why.

His brow furrows. "For what?"

I shrug, suddenly unsure. "I don't know. For kissing you. For dragging you into this mess. For... making it harder."

"Harder?" He takes my chin gently between his fingers, lifting until I have to look at him. "Baby Girl, being with you isn't the hard part. It's watching you pretend you're fine when you're not. That's what kills me."

The honesty sinks deeper than it should. I turn away, wrapping my arms around myself as I stare at the valley, the distant specks of lights from the city blinking like lazy fireflies.

"I keep waiting for him just to appear," I admit. "But every time I get disappointed. It's like—just when I can breathe, something reminds me that I'm still missing something. That they could still ruin everything for me. That I'll never be free until Atlas is back with me."

Jaxson doesn't say anything. Instead, he moves behind me, wrapping his arms around my waist and pulling me flush against his chest. I melt into him without resistance, leaning my head back until it rests against his shoulder.

"We'll get him back," he says quietly. "I promise."

A part of me wants to believe him. Wants to believe that this is real. But I've trusted wrong before. I've *loved* wrong before.

"What if I don't know how to be a proper mother?" I whisper.

His arms tighten. "We'll figure it out."

The silence between us shifts, not heavy, not uncomfortable—just thick with things we don't say. Things we're still learning to believe.

After a long pause, I speak again. "Killian said something earlier. About you joining the... 'harem.'"

Jaxson groans softly into my hair. "Don't let that idiot get in your head."

I smile, just barely. "So you're not?"

"Not what?"

"Trying to claim me like the rest of them?"

He turns me slowly in his arms so I'm facing him, his expression all fire and truth.

"I'm not trying to *claim* you," he says. "I already did. You just haven't realized it yet."

My heart skips, stumbles, then launches into a gallop.

He leans in, pressing a kiss to my temple before grabbing my hand

and tugging me gently toward the bikes. "Come on. Before I talk myself into stealing you away for the whole night."

"You wouldn't."

He throws me a smirk over his shoulder. "Try me."

And even though I know there's chaos waiting when we get back—Jake's temper, Killian's taunts, Ash's quiet watching—I follow Jaxson willingly.

Because for the first time in a long time, I feel like someone is running *with* me.

Not after me.

Not away from me.

Just... with me.

And maybe that's enough for now.

My leg meets the ground just as strong arms wrap around my waist, pulling me backward into the dimly lit storage closet. My back meets the cool wall, and Jaxson's breath is hot against my ear. "Looks like I get to help you get undressed, Baby Girl," he murmurs, sending a shiver down my spine.

I swallow hard, my pulse racing as I nod toward the mannequin outside. "We should-should put that back," I manage, my voice breathy, but Jaxson is already tugging at the zipper of my jacket, the metallic rasp filling the tight space. He slides it from my shoulders, letting it fall to the floor in a careless heap.

"I have other plans," he whispers, his lips trailing featherlight kisses along my jaw and down my neck, each touch leaving a scorching trail in its wake. My breath hitches when his fingers deftly unbutton my bottoms, and with one smooth motion, he peels them down my legs. They puddle at my ankles, and I step out of them, the air cool against my skin.

His eyes darken as they flick down to my lace panties, a wicked grin tugging at the corner of his lips. "These pretty pink panties have been driving me insane all day." His hands grip my ass firmly, squeezing before he lifts me with ease, urging my legs to wrap around his waist. The friction sends a sharp jolt of pleasure through me, and I whimper softly, my damp core resting against the stiff leather of his suit.

"God, you're such a good girl when you whine for me," he groans, rocking his hips into mine in a slow, torturous rhythm.

"Yes, Jax," I breathe, my fingers digging into his shoulders as I grind against him, desperate for more.

"Fuck, Baby Girl, say my name like that again." His tone is thick with need as his fingers curl into my panties, and with one sharp tug, the fabric gives way with a satisfying rip. The sudden coolness of the leather against my bare skin makes me gasp, and I instinctively pull back.

A teasing grin curves my lips as I sink back onto him, rolling my hips in deliberate circles. Leaning in, I let my breath ghost over his ear. "Jax," I purr, threading my fingers into his hair.

"Who's calling Daddy Jaxson's name like that?" A familiar voice drawls from the doorway, sending a bolt of irritation through me.

Jaxson groans against my shoulder, his body tensing with frustration. "Killian," he grits out, his forehead dropping against my collarbone as if gathering patience.

I peek over his shoulder, finding Killian lounging against the doorframe with a smug grin, arms crossed, one ankle lazily hooked over the other. "Oops, am I interrupting again?" he asks, eyes twinkling with mischief.

I smirk, running my fingers soothingly through Jaxson's hair. "I swear, he must have a tracking device on you," I whisper against his ear.

Jaxson mutters a muffled sound, his body shielding mine from Killian's curious eyes, not that there's much of me Killian hasn't seen before. Still, Jaxson's protectiveness stirs a flutter inside me.

"What are you two whispering about?" Killian teases, shifting his weight with an infuriating smirk.

I glance up at him, my expression all honeyed sweetness. "Killian, darling," I coo, batting my lashes.

He tilts his head, playing along. "Yes, baby?"

With a coy smile, I trail my fingers down Jaxson's chest. "Could you give us a moment?"

Killian chuckles, pushing off the doorframe with a mock bow. "Anything for you, baby." He winks before swaggering out, leaving only the echo of his laughter behind.

As soon as the door clicks shut, Jaxson sighs heavily, sliding me down his body until my feet touch the ground. "That guy ruined my moment," he grumbles, dragging a hand down his face.

I reach up, cupping his face and forcing him to meet my gaze. "We'll have our moment, Jax," I murmur, brushing my lips against his in a soft kiss. "This is just the beginning of our story."

His lips quirk into a slow smile, his eyes softening. "You're right. Just the beginning." He kisses my forehead before stepping back to strip off his leather gear, his movements still heavy with frustration.

I stifle a laugh, grabbing my discarded clothes. "Oh, stop your grumbling," I tease, tossing a shirt at him. "You're acting like a kid who didn't get their Halloween candy."

A squeal escapes me as Jaxson's arms wind around me, yanking me flush against him. His breath fans hot against my neck, sending shivers down my spine. "That's because I *am* a kid who didn't get their candy," he murmurs, releasing a low growl. His tongue traces a slow path from my shoulder to my neck, his teeth grazing the sensitive skin. "The best damn candy of my life."

A shaky laugh slips from my lips, but the burning in my core gets snuffed out when Ash's voice cuts through the moment. "Sorry to interrupt, but has anyone seen Jake since this morning?" His arms are crossed, his gaze locked on the floor.

I swallow hard, keeping my voice calm. "Oh, um, no. Is he still not back?" My eyes meet Ash's, searching his face for any hint of a deeper feeling he's too guarded to show. I know how close he is to Killian, but with Jaxson, there's always an unspoken strain. A rivalry. A push and pull.

Ash sighs, rubbing a hand over the back of his neck. "No, he's not. We've been texting and calling, but he isn't responding."

As I move toward Ash, I step away from Jaxson, the loss of him jarring. "Should we go look for him?" The concern slips into my voice before I can stop, and Ash notices. His eyes search mine, and a softness settles into his expression.

When our gazes finally lock, relief washes over me. There's no anger, no resentment, just quiet understanding. He lifts a hand, cupping my cheek with a gentle touch that steals my breath.

I turn to Jaxson, sweeping a quick kiss to his lips. His grip on my hip is possessive, reluctant to let me go. I see it in his eyes—the frustration, the jealousy, the way he hates how much Jake's absence affects me. But he doesn't say a word, and I don't explain. We both know it wouldn't change anything.

As I follow Ash out of the room, my mind spins with the weight of it all. I'm holding on too tightly to all of them. Afraid that if I let go of one, I'll lose everything. And the worst part? I don't know if I'm strong enough to make that choice.

Hey, Red. You want a coffee? Don't tell the others, though. Figured you deserved a treat.

The text notification lights up my phone, and just seeing his name sends a flutter through me. *Jake.* I glance over my shoulder and spot Ash approaching. He's out there, somewhere, thinking about me. He still contacted me even though the others haven't heard from him. I clutch the phone, fire creeping up my neck.

A part of me aches for him to be here with us. Spending time with Jaxson today reminded me how lucky I am to have them—him, Killian, Ash... and Jake. But wanting them all doesn't change the reality staring back at me. Jake doesn't share, not the way the others do. And I don't know if I can let the others go to have him.

I quickly type back, biting my lip as I focus on the screen.

How about a venti black iced tea with a splash of whole milk and four full pumps of white chocolate and brown sugar? PLZ!

His reply is instant.

What the hell is all that?

I pinch my lips together, a giggle threatening to escape as I lean back into Ash's hold. His steady heartbeat pulses against my back, a quiet rhythm that holds me in place, even as my thoughts remain tangled with Jake. Ash's head rests on my shoulder, eyes closed, but he cracks one open when he hears my quiet laugh.

"What's so funny, Princess?" he murmurs, voice laced with lazy curiosity.

I tilt my phone toward him, still grinning. "Jake doesn't like my Starbucks order."

Ash takes the phone from my hands before I can protest, his fingers moving quickly over the screen. I reach for it, but he lifts it out of my grasp with a smug grin, nipping at my nose. "Ash," I whine, narrowing my eyes. "What did you do?"

When I finally wrestle the phone back, my giggles turn into full-blown laughter.

It tastes like an oatmeal cookie. Record yourself saying the order for me, please.

I swat at Ash playfully. "You're such a menace."

His only response is a smirk as I watch the message bubble appear, my heart leaping into my throat as I wait for Jake's reply.

For fuck's sake, Red.

A smile that tugs at my lips, I can almost hear his exaggerated sigh and see his dramatic eye roll from here.

Oh, hush, this is just a little punishment for disappearing all day and making me worry.

The message flickers from delivered to read, but the screen stays silent—no typing bubbles, no response. My fingers curl around the phone, my grip turning rigid as unease slithers through me.

"He's not answering," I murmur, staring at the screen like I can will it to light up again.

Ash slides his arms around me, drawing me in. "He's not mad, Sweet Girl." A kiss lands on the side of my head. "Jake just can't say no to you."

I pout, folding my arms as I glare at my phone. "Then why isn't he texting back?"

Ash chuckles, his chest vibrating against my back. "Because he's probably ordering your creative drink."

I huff but pick up my book, flipping pages without reading them. My thoughts are stuck on Jake—his voice, his presence, the way he always manages to get under my skin in the best and worst ways.

When my phone buzzes, I jump, tossing the book aside and scrambling to open the message. A video. My pulse spikes. "Ash, I need headphones. *Now.*"

He hands over a pair without hesitation, watching with amusement as I fumble to connect them. Settling back into his arms, I hit play, anticipation thick.

Jake's voice filters through the speakers, deep and irritated, and I close my eyes for a second, letting it wash over me. God, I want him. I *always* want him. But I can't give up Killian, Jaxson, and Ash for him.

I don't know if I ever could.

I hit play on the video, and Jake's face appears on my screen, his dark eyes flicking up at the camera before he sighs, rubbing a hand over his jaw.

"I can't believe I'm doing this," he grumbles, stepping into Starbucks. The familiar hum of the store buzzes in the background, and I can't stop the small smile tugging at my lips. He's doing this for me.

"What can I get for you?" the barista chirps behind the counter.

Jake stares at the menu like it personally offended him, letting out another deep sigh. "I hope you know what I'm ordering, because this is about to get confusing." His tone is almost pouty, and I bite my lip to hold back a laugh.

"I need a... Venti black iced tea with a splash..." He pauses, his brows furrowing. "...of whole milk and four full pumps of white chocolate and brown sugar flavors?" My hands fly up to cover my mouth to stifle the giggle.

"Anything else?" the barista asks.

Jake gives her a skeptical look. "You actually understood all that?"

"Of course!" she responds, still chipper as she punches in the order. "That's a mild one compared to some of our regulars."

Jake mutters under his breath, shaking his head. "Seriously? Jesus Christ."

I grin, a slow heat unfurling in my chest like the first rays of sunlight piercing through the morning haze. He's grumpy, impossible, and yet... he's here, doing a silly thing just because I asked him to. My heart aches a little at the thought, caught between amusement and a deeper feeling I try to push aside.

"Is there anything else you'd like?" the barista asks.

Jake clears his throat, clearly eager to be done. "Yeah, a venti iced black coffee with cream." His relief is so evident that I let out a soft laugh.

I watch him step aside in the video, the screen freezing on his annoyed but begrudgingly patient expression. I trace the edge of my phone, unable to stop the smile on my lips.

Jake always shows up for me in his own way, even when he acts like he doesn't care. And that's the problem—because I care. Too much.

A soft giggle escapes me as I watch the video again. It's far too easy to fall back into this—fall back into them. The laughter, the comfort, the way they make me feel like I belong. But beneath it all, guilt gnaws at the edges of my thoughts. I'm still keeping secrets; their weight grows heavier every day. And the worst part? I didn't even tell Jax; Marissa did.

My gaze drifts to Ash beside me, his steady breathing lulling me into a calm. But the peace is short-lived. The weight of reality creeps in, pulling me under. Jake and Ash are on edge whenever Patrick's name comes up, and I have tried to reassure them that the reason I need to find Patrick is important, but I think they still doubt me.

A sharp pang stabs through me as Atlas's face flashes in my mind—his small, fragile frame marked with bruises. Every picture Krystal sends is worse than the last. His arms, his legs, his face... he's slipping further away and I can't reach him. I can't *protect him*. Not while Krystal stays one step ahead.

"Hey, Ash?"

He hums in response, his eyes skimming the pages.

I swallow hard. "Where do you think Patrick is? Why can't we find him?"

The sharp slap of his book closing makes me flinch. Ash sits up, his jaw ticking, and when he turns to face me, his eyes burn with unspoken rage.

"Tell me why you need to find him?"

I blink, startled. "What?"

His stare doesn't waver. "No more bullshit, no more veiled truths. Tell me why you are looking for him. Don't we treat you good? Is finding him worth possibly being retaken? Why are you so desperate to leave us again, especially when we've *only just found you?*"

I reach for him, but he pulls away, turning his body away from mine. The sudden distance between us feels like a chasm. "Ash, you know I can't explain everything right now," I whisper. "Why can't you just trust me? I've trusted you since I came back—why can't you do the same?"

He lets out a bitter laugh, shaking his head. "Because you *don't* trust me, Ember. I don't understand why you won't talk to us... Talk to me. You won't explain anything to me." His words hit like a punch, and before I can respond, he walks out without looking back.

The sound of the door clicking shut feels like a blow, and I sink into the couch, burying my face in the cushions. The sob comes, shaking my entire body. I always knew this search might cost me everything. I didn't expect it to hurt this much.

But I can't stop. Not when Atlas is out there. Not when I'm his only hope.

I wipe my tears, forcing myself to breathe through the ache. If I have to do this alone, I will. No matter how much it hurts or how much distance grows between me and the people I care about. Their feelings don't matter right now.

Atlas does.

CHAPTER 53

Ember Rose

A rhythmic thud vibrates the walls, pulling me out of my thoughts. I ignore it at first, brushing it off as old pipes groaning under the weight of the house. But the sound persists—three steady thumps, perfectly timed, again and again.

My skin prickles. "What the hell?" I murmur, pushing myself up from the couch. The eerie repetition pulls me toward the kitchen. Each step heightens the sound, the thuds becoming more insistent—my pulse races.

"Hello?" My voice wavers, barely filling the silent house. Is Jake back? Maybe Killian or Jax? But the garage is empty, and the absence of one of the black SUVs increases my unease.

The thudding grows louder, calling me like a siren song to the basement door. My fingers hover over the knob, hesitating. The heavy metal door feels colder than I remember. Frowning, I twist the knob. *It's locked. Why would they lock it?* They told me it was just storage—unfinished, forgotten.

A tremor runs through me, but I tense, stopping the involuntary shudder. Heart racing, I tug a bobby pin from my hair with shaky fingers and kneel. Killian's lessons filter through my mind, a phantom whisper guiding me through the motions. The lock gives with a soft click, and as the door swings open, I feel the world tilt beneath me.

Patrick lies on the floor, shackled to a rusted pipe. His face is a ruin of bruises and dried blood, his lips cracked, his eyes sunken.

"Well, look who it is," he rasps, a jagged whisper slicing through me. "Did they finally send you to finish me off?"

I stagger back, my breath hitching, the air too thick to pull in. "What...?" The word barely makes it past my lips, my mind spinning, struggling to process what was right in front of me.

Patrick shifts, grunting as he leans against the wall, the faintest smirk curving his split mouth. "They don't know you're down here, do they, Kitten?"

The nickname sends a violent shiver down my spine, dragging me back into the nightmare I thought I'd escaped. My throat tightens. "How long?" The question scrapes out, my voice raw, caught between horror and disbelief.

"What day is it?" he asks, eyes half-lidded. A predatory glint shines through those pupils.

My thoughts are slow to recall, and my answer is a whisper. "September twelfth."

He chuckles, low and brittle. "Then... just under three months."

Three months.

My knees give out, and I grip the doorframe to stay upright. Bile rises in my throat. "You've been here the whole time?" The room spins as the realization sinks its claws into me. I force myself to look at him, really look at him, and it's like staring into the darkest part of my soul.

His lips curl, savoring my reaction. "Your boyfriends didn't tell you?"

I shake my head, the motion too sharp, too frantic.

His laughter is a hollow rasp, more animal than human. "Guess you shouldn't have trusted them."

The words slam into me, knocking the air from my lungs. My chest constricts, my vision blurs, and a broken sob escapes before I can choke it back. They lied. They *all* lied. While I was tearing myself apart, trying to save Atlas, begging them for help, pleading for answers, they *hid him.* They kept him here, locked away, like a dirty little secret, all while knowing I was searching for him.

My hands tremble, covering my face as the sobs wrack through me. I can't stop them. Can't stop the weight crushing my ribs, the betrayal flooding every inch of my being. They let me drown in my desperation, in my fear, in my pain, all while holding the truth behind a locked door.

I was never free. Not really.

Time spirals, and my sluggish thoughts echo until a clear path emerges. There's only one thing to do. Steeling myself, I descend the remaining steps and approach my captor.

Patrick's voice slithers through the silence, dry and heavy with that sickening amusement I know too well. "Well, isn't that a useful little skill, *Kitten?*"

Hands trembling, I force the bobby pin to keep steady, working the lock on his chains. My teeth grind together at the nickname, the sound of it like nails down my spine.

"Shut up," I snap, finally hearing the soft click of metal surrendering under my touch. The chain falls away with a dull clank, and I step back, my pulse hammering in my ears. His wrists, still encased in handcuffs, rest limp in his lap. "I'm not taking those off," I say, my voice sharper than I feel. "I'm not taking any chances with you."

Patrick rattles the cuffs, a lazy smirk tugging at his split lip. "What? You don't trust me, Kitten?" His tone drips with mock hurt.

"Stop calling me that," I snarl, wiping my shaking hands against my jeans, trying to rid myself of the filth of him. "Get up. We're leaving."

He chuckles, a weak, pathetic sound that still manages to claw at my skin. He tries to stand but collapses back onto the mattress, groaning and curling in on himself. He's frail, his body all sharp angles and bruises, but I know better than to pity him.

"Some help would be nice," he wheezes, a ghost of his old arrogance still clinging to him like a parasite.

My jaw locks. "Yeah, well, being kidnapped and assaulted wasn't exactly a walk in the fucking park," I spit, yanking the chain between his cuffs and forcing him to his feet. He stumbles forward and uses me to balance himself. I recoil from the stench of stale sweat and decay clinging to him.

"Oh, come on," he breathes, too close. "You didn't *really* hate me. If you did, you wouldn't be setting me free." His sour breath hits my cheek, and I gag, shoving him back against the wall.

I want to hit him. I want to scream. Instead, I steel myself. "I'm freeing you because your *bitch* of an wife is holding my son hostage until I bring you back," I grit out, shoving him toward the stairs.

Patrick's laugh is empty, scraping against the walls as he leans heavily against the wall, dragging his feet. "Ah, my lovely Krystal. Always looking out for me," he muses with a pained chuckle.

I stay near, but not too close. He might look weak, but I won't be fooled.

As we pass through the kitchen, I grab a handgun from the drawer, its weight grounding me. I slide it into the waistband of my jeans, my fingers itching to pull the trigger and end him. I could end this, and he would never hurt me again. But Atlas is more important than my revenge.

In the garage, I pop the trunk of a black sedan, stepping aside and gesturing inside with a pointed stare. "Get in."

Patrick's brows lift in disbelief. "The *trunk?* Come on, I'm not a threat to you."

"Says the man who tortured me for five years." I pull the gun free, leveling it at his head with a steadiness that surprises me. "Get. In. The. Fucking. Trunk."

He mutters under his breath but crawls inside, his movements sluggish. I grab the emergency release cord and rip it free before slamming the trunk shut. Hands trembling, I secure the gun back at my waist and head to the driver's side. My pulse pounds in my throat, choking me.

Sliding into the driver's seat, I grip the steering wheel, my knuckles whitening. "You got this, Ember. You got this." Motivating myself doesn't seem to work as I stare at the garage door. "Fuck, Ember, go."

"Ahh!" I scream as the passenger door swings open, Jax slipping in. "What the fuck are you doing?"

"I'm coming with you." He states, tension pinching his brows, and his jaw ticks.

"No." I stick the barrel of the gun against his temple, my hand showing my nervousness. "*Get. Out.*"

"No." His black eyes lock on mine. "I'm not letting you do this alone."

I shake, fury bubbling over. "I've *been* doing this alone for three months!" My voice cracks, the gun shaky in my grip. "How long, Jax? How long have you known he was down there?"

His jaw tightens, and his answer cuts through me like a blade. "Since the beginning."

I choke on a sob. "You *knew.* You fucking *knew.*" My vision blurs with tears, my whole body trembling. Terrified I might pull the trigger without meaning to, I pull the gun back, pointing it at the ground.

"And Atlas... you've known about him for a *week.* A week, Jax." My voice cracks, the betrayal slicing me apart. "And you didn't tell me."

Fury blazes through me, and I slam my fist down on the steering wheel, the horn blaring in the silence.

"I didn't want to lose you," he murmurs, thick with regret. "I'd just found something that made me want to live again, and I—"

I dig the gun into his head. "You're going to lose me anyway," I whisper. "I'm leaving. I'm taking my son, and I'm *never* coming back."

Jax reaches for me, his touch hesitant. "Let me come with you. Let me make this right. I can't— I *won't* lose you." Slowly, his hand wraps around the gun, gently pulling it from my grip. "Let's go get your son, baby. Let me help you do that."

Our eyes meet, and despite everything, I want him with me. Maybe I don't have to be alone for this last trial. My breath shudders as I turn the key, and the engine roars. I grip the wheel like it's the only thing holding me together. I dial Krystal's number, and my fingers are ice cold.

She answers with a sharpness that shreds my resolve. "So, you finally found him?" The distant click of her heels echoes in the background.

"He's alive," I bite out. "Where do you want him?"

She hums, amused. "The last place you saw your son."

My stomach churns, but I force myself to respond. "Understood."

I hang up and toss the phone into the backseat, swallowing the fear threatening to consume me.

Jax's hand inches toward mine, but I jerk away, my breath ragged. "Where are we going?"

I stare ahead, my knuckles white on the wheel. "Back to their glass fucking fortress."

CHAPTER 54

Ember Rose

I skid to a stop a hundred feet from what was once my prison, the place I swore I'd never return to if I ever got us out. Yet here we are. The towering structure looms beneath the dark sky, its cold, gleaming surface reflecting the stars instead of the horror within its walls. The surrounding air is silent, the closest house miles away, their lights barely visible in the distance.

"What now?" Jax's voice is quiet with unspoken words—pain, anger, and complexities I don't have time to unravel.

Ignoring him, I shove the car door open, my heart thudding painfully. A cry pierces the night. My head snaps toward the sound. There she is—Krystal, her fingers digging into Atlas's arm, his tiny frame trembling beneath her grip.

A sob escapes me, but I bite it back. Hands shaking, I fumble with the trunk latch, and the stench that floods out makes my stomach lurch. The sick mix of piss and vomit rolls over me in a wave. Patrick lies sprawled inside, his face pale and slick with sweat, and his clothes clinging to him.

"Did you have to hit every fucking bump?" he groans, peeling himself out of the trunk and crumpling to the ground with a pathetic moan.

Jax stands behind me, gagging when the stench hits him. He recoils, covering his nose. "Jesus Christ. What the fuck?"

Patrick coughs, wiping at his sweaty face. "Yeah, yeah, I know. I smell like a fucking field of lilies." He struggles to get to his feet, swaying. His bloodshot eyes move toward the house.

I give him a moment to regain his footing before shoving him forward; my gaze stays on Atlas—his terrified face—*my baby*. My heart clenches, rage swallowing every other emotion.

"Oh, look, it's my beautiful wife," Patrick croons, stumbling up the steps. He collapses at Krystal's feet, grinning through cracked lips. "Did you miss me, Sweetheart?"

Krystal's nose wrinkles. "You forget, dear husband," she spits, eyes gleaming with venom. "I don't give a damn about you. You're only breathing because I want what's supposed to be mine."

Jax steps forward, lethal. "We'd hate to interrupt your little reunion, but you have something we want."

"I want," I snap, glaring at my reluctant partner. "He's mine."

Atlas whimpers, his body jerking forward, but Krystal yanks him back. "Mama!"

"Let him go." I take a step, but Krystal's hand flies up, halting me with cold metal - a gun aimed at my face.

Jax moves, his body warm against my back, protecting me from behind. His gun comes up over my shoulder, trained on Krystal.

"You broke the rules, Whore," she hisses, her gaze bouncing between us. "You weren't supposed to bring anyone."

My world narrows to the boy in her grasp. "Please," I whisper, my voice cracking. "Please, just let him go. I don't want anything else. Just him." Hot tears slide down my face.

Krystal's lips curl into a wicked smile, her grip squeezing Atlas until he screams. My heart shatters at the sound, but then, my eyes look past them, and I see it. A large metal cage, its bars thick, looms in the shadows.

Cold horror crashes over me, stealing the air from my lungs. My knees wobble, and I stumble back into Jax, his arms locking around my waist, holding me upright as I sag against him. The world narrows, my vision tunneling on that cage, on what it means.

She wasn't going to let us go. She just wanted me back. But why?

Krystal's voice slithers into my spiraling thoughts. "Get in the cage." Her gaze glints with sadistic delight. She tugs Atlas closer, his cries like shattered glass. "Or he dies."

"W-why?" I choke out. The word feels small, weak against the terror swelling inside me. I clutch Jax's arm, my entire body trembling as I stare at Atlas's tear-streaked face. "Just let us go. Please, Krystal." A sob breaks free. "Let us go. Or at least, let Atlas go. Please." My eyes dart to the cage again, bile rising in my throat. The thought of being locked inside it—trapped, helpless, while she hurts my baby—sends ice crawling through my veins.

Jax's grip on me tightens, making it so I can't move or breathe. I can only watch Krystal, her manic smile widening, feeding off my fear.

The cage stands as a silent threat. And I know—if I don't act or make the right choice, Atlas and Jax won't leave here either.

Jax's voice is eerily calm. "Let him go, or you die."

Krystal's laughter is sharp, cutting, and then everything blurs.

A gunshot shatters the air.

Krystal staggers back, eyes wide, blood blooming across her chest. She crumples, her hand still latched to Atlas, sending him flying back.

"No!" I break free from Jax, scrambling up the steps, my knees hitting the pavement as I gather Atlas in my arms. He's sobbing, his face buried against my neck, his tiny hands clutching at me like a lifeline.

"I've got you," I whisper, rocking him and breathing him in—baby shampoo and peppermint, a scent that relieves me. My tears soak his soft hair.

Behind me, Patrick screams, but I don't care. All I can think about is getting Atlas away from t*his place, away from them.*

I need to get him somewhere safe. Somewhere filled with love. But where?

I can't go back to them—Jake, Killian, Ash—they don't deserve to be a part of our lives, not after what they did. They lied to me.

Holding Atlas, his head tucked against my neck, I retreat, avoiding getting too close to Patrick. Jax stands at the bottom of the steps, his eyes watching the remaining threat.

"You killed her, you dumb bitch!" Patrick's voice gurgles with fury as he struggles to get to his knees, his hands grasping at nothing. "You fucking killed her!"

I freeze, turning to face him. I stare at the man who once held my life in his hands, the monster who broke me, shattered me piece by piece. And yet, through all the torment, he also kept the only thing that mattered away from me. The little boy trembling in my arms is why I'm still standing. He's the reason I fought, bled, and survived.

I shift Atlas higher on my hip, his small fingers digging into my hoodie. My grip tightens around him, and I ground myself in his warmth, in the life I refused to let slip away.

Leaning in, I lower my voice to a razor-sharp whisper. "Maybe you'll think twice before ripping someone apart next time." The weight of years—of suffering, of survival—presses into every syllable, my voice a quiet promise. My eyes burn with a fire I refuse to let him see, my rage held just beneath the surface.

"I didn't kill your wife, Patrick...You did."

His eyes blaze with hatred. "I'm going to gut you," he snarls, launching at me.

Another shot cracks through the air before he can even get to his feet.

Patrick collapses with a sickening thud, his body folding lifeless. Blood pools beneath him, spreading across the concrete like spilled oil. I watch, unblinking, a cold relief flooding through me.

Jax steps up, his hand resting against my lower back. I flinch at the contact, moving away, cradling Atlas tighter. His little body shakes with the aftershocks; I place little kisses across his head and face, "Shh, baby. Mommy's got you. I love you so much, and I'm sorry it took me so long to get to you." My fingers thread through his soft curls, sticky and damp from my tears.

"Ember."

I glance up, my eyes narrowing. "What?" The exhaustion in my voice cracks like a whip. "You can leave now. We'll be fine on *our* own."

Jax doesn't move. Instead, he steps closer, his presence wrapping around me. "I'm not leaving you."

My back hits the railing of the stairs. I meet Jax's black eyes, searching for deception, for anything I can use to push him away. But all I see is determination.

His hands come up, framing my face. The tenderness of the touch knocks the breath from me. "I am *not* leaving you."

The dam breaks, and tears fall as I stare at him. "I don't trust you," I whisper.

Jax's thumb brushes against my skin, wiping away the tears. "You don't have to trust me, Baby Girl," he murmurs. "That's something I need to earn back."

The sincerity unravels a part of me I've kept locked away. I inch toward his touch, letting myself feel his presence—the steadiness, the promise I desperately need.

"I-I don't want to be alone anymore," I admit, my voice barely above a whisper.

He leans in, placing a feather-light kiss on my forehead—a gesture so gentle it shatters me. My arms tighten around the small boy nestled against my chest, his tiny fingers fisting my clothes like he's afraid to let go.

"You'll never be alone again," Jax promises. His lips anchor me before he shifts, reaching out to ruffle Atlas's hair with a soft, affectionate touch. "It's you, me, and this little man right here... against the world."

Atlas sniffles, burrowing closer, and Jax lets his hand rest against his back.

I close my eyes, breathing him in, and for the first time in forever, I dare to believe that maybe—just maybe—I won't be alone.

CHAPTER 55

Jake

The moment I step inside, the emptiness suffocates me. Everything feels off. So fucking wrong. I've grown used to Ember's energy humming through the house, but now there's only silence and the creak of floorboards beneath my feet. I clench the drink, the thin plastic crumpling in my grip.

"Red?" I tap against her bedroom door, though she rarely spends time there. "Red, you in there?" My voice sounds loud in the quiet. When silence answers me, I knock again, harder this time. "Ember, come on, baby. I brought you your favorite drink."

Still nothing.

I fumble for my phone and send a message to the group chat, my fingers clumsy and stiff.

Is Ember with any of you?

Killian replies instantly.

Nope.

Ash follows.

No. I left her in the library.

I wait for Jax's response, but it doesn't come.

Anxiety courses through me, crushing my lungs. "I-I'm coming in," I announce as the door swings open.

My stomach drops. *No.*

The room is empty. The kind of emptiness that guts you—her clothes gone, the little things that made it *hers* wiped clean like she was never here at all.

A choked curse tears from me. "Fuck!" My fist collides with the wall, the drywall splintering under the impact. The drink flies from my hand, splattering in a mess of ice and syrup across the floor.

This can't be happening.

Desperation drives me forward. When I reach the basement, the sight of the open door slams into me like a freight train. Saint John is gone.

"No!" The roar tears from my throat. Grabbing Killian's work table, I send it crashing to the ground, the clatter of metal against concrete echoing against the walls. It's not enough. None is enough to drown out the sickening truth clawing its way to the surface. I clutch the back of my head, pacing like a caged animal. *I did this. I fucking did this. Where is she?*

The front door slams shut, followed by voices. I sprint up the stairs, hope rising to the surface. My heart sinks again when I reach the entryway and see only Killian and Ash.

Killian leans against Ash, both of them frowning at me. "Woah, J, what's wrong?" Killian asks, his signature grin fading. His eyes are glassy, his words slurring.

I swallow hard, my voice barely holding together. "Em-Ember is gone."

Ash stiffens. "What the hell do you mean she's gone?" He shoves Killian aside, sending him sprawling to the floor as he storms off to check the rest of the house. Killian groans, rubbing his face like he's trying to wake himself up from a bad dream. I ignore him, my fingers threading into my hair as I resume pacing, unable to look at Killian.

While the center of our universe packed her things and ran from us, he was getting wasted...again.

Minutes pass before Ash returns, his jaw tight, his eyes darker than obsidian. "Jax's stuff is gone too."

The words hit like a strike to the balls. I yank my phone out, dialing Jax, straight to voicemail. My hands are shaking now, but I push through it, dialing Ember next. *Please. Please, pick up Red.*

"Jake."

Her voice halts the noise in my head.

"Ember, let me explain—" My words tumble out, frantic, desperate, but Ash steps in behind me, a dark presence. Killian tries to sit up where he's slumped on the floor, muttering nonsense.

"Explain?" Ember's voice cracks like a whip, all venom and heartbreak. "You've had more than a month to come clean, Jake. A month."

My grip tightens on the phone, like I can somehow hold onto her through it. "Red—"

"Stop." The finality guts me. "I trusted you to be honest with me. And you couldn't even do that."

I squeeze my eyes shut, the weight of her words making it hard to breathe. But she doesn't hang up. I hear her breathing, uneven, and I know—she's waiting for me to speak. Anything. *Think, Jake. Tell her to come home.*

But what the fuck am I supposed to say? That I was scared? That I was trying to protect her? That I was too much of a coward to tell her the truth?

Ash watches me, waiting, too. Killian, now sitting up, groans and rubs his face. "Wait, is that my Emmy? Let me talk to her. I wanna tell her I miss her."

"Ember—" Her name is a prayer on my lips.

"I'm done, Jake." Her tone softens, but it's not in kindness. It's exhaustion. It's *final.* "Don't call me."

The line stays open like she's waiting for one last thing. I don't know what it is, and I don't know if I can give it to her.

I feel like I'm standing on the edge of a cliff—I can't help but feel like if I take a step, I will plunge to my death. I dig the heel of my hand against my forehead, feeling the weight of everything I've done—*everything I didn't do.*

Ash takes the phone from my hand. "Princess..."

Ember lets out a shaky breath. "Ash..."

"Please come back, or tell me where you are. I can fix this. I *will* fix this."

She doesn't answer, but she doesn't hang up either.

Killian stirs from his drunken haze. "Tell her... tell her I miss her."

"Now isn't the time, Kill," Ash mutters, but Killian, too far gone, pushes off from the wall and staggers to his feet. Before I can stop him, he snatches the phone from Ash's hand, his fingers fumbling over the screen.

"Killer, baby, is that you?" he coos, his lips pulling into a crooked, drunken smile as he slides back down to the floor. He cradles the phone like it's precious, but his sloppy grin falters.

"You're drunk." Ember's voice is ice-cold.

Killian chuckles, making a half-hearted kissy face at the phone. "Yesss, but I missed you." His attempt at charm falls flat, crashing into the reality of what we've done—what *he's* done, what *I've* done.

The silence draws out for a moment, and then— "I have to say, Killian, your betrayal hurt the worst. You were my best friend—the man I *loved.* But you lied to me. For a month, you held me while I cried, and you fucking lied."

Killian's face drains of color, his smile disappearing. "Ember?" His tone changes, no longer cocky, just... scared. "Baby, what are you talking about?"

"I found him, Killian. I found Patrick."

A cold shiver crawls down my spine. My jaw clenches so tight it aches.

Killian's face scrunches up like a petulant child denied a toy, his lips twisting into a deep frown. "Who told her?" he mumbles. His glassy eyes flick between me and Ash, unfocused but searching for someone to blame.

"He was supposed to be a present," he grumbles, shoulders sagging as he sways slightly. "We were supposed to torture him together." His lower lip juts out just a little like he's genuinely upset that the moment was stolen from him.

"Killian," I snap, yanking the phone from his grip before he can make it worse.

But it's too late. Ember's voice erupts through the speaker, furious. "You bastards—" she chokes. "You kept him a secret because you thought I wanted to torture him?"

A child's wail echoes through the phone. Ember's voice softens, filled with gentle guilt. "Shit, Atty, I'm sorry. Go back to sleep; Mommy's almost done."

My heart stops.

"Ember," I rasp, panic clawing up my throat. "Who's with you?"

There's a heavy silence that makes my skin crawl. "Not that you deserve an answer," Ember finally replies, "but he's why I needed to find Patrick. I have a son."

My vision blurs.

"He was being held hostage by Patrick's wife," she continues, voice tight with tears. "She threatened his life if I told anyone about him."

The room spins. I stumble backward, hitting the wall. My hands shake so bad I nearly drop the phone.

A child. A little boy.

My mind races through the past, through all the times I thought I knew what Ember needed—what she *wanted.* And all along, she was fighting for *him.*

"What's his name?" My voice catches, terror strangling me. "Is... is he Patrick's?"

Time slows, my heartbeat thumping in my ears. Ember whispers, "His name is Atlas, and no... he's yours."

The air leaves my lungs.

Mine.

I sway, the phone slipping through my fingers. It clatters to the floor, but I don't move to pick it up. My hands cover my face, but nothing stops the onslaught of guilt, of fear, of everything I should have known.

Ash swears under his breath, running a hand through his hair before picking up the phone. Killian stares at it, his drunken haze lifting like a fog clearing in the wake of a storm.

"I-I..." My throat locks up. I don't know what to say. What the fuck *can* I say?

"Jake," Ember's voice fades, and I feel her slipping away. "You should've trusted me. You should've known I wasn't doing this because I *loved* him."

I blink rapidly, swallowing down the lump in my throat. "I thought I was protecting you."

"No, Jake." She's tired, so tired. "You were protecting yourself." The call ends. I stare, unable to move past this revelation. *Mine.*

Ash clears his throat, his expression hardening. "What do we do now?"

I force my breathing to be steady. "We find her," I say, my voice no more than a whisper. "We find *them.*"

Killian wipes a hand down his face, suddenly looking wrecked. "And what do we do about Jax?"

"We'll figure it out...Together."

I stare at the phone in Ash's hand; Ember's voice echoes. *His name is Atlas, and he's yours.*

"Let's move. We've already wasted too much time. Killian, track Ember's and Jax's phones. Ash figure out where they went. I have a feeling there is a mess we need to take care of somewhere."

With every step forward, the regret compounds, threatening to drown me, but I don't have the luxury of wallowing. *I have a son.* And I've failed him before I even met him.

I won't do it again.

CHAPTER 56

Ember Rose

Jax's hands grip the wheel, his knuckles pale under the glow of the dashboard lights. He keeps his eyes forward, silent, while soft, uneven sobs come from me as I rock Atlas in my lap, my lips brushing the crown of his curly hair while I hum a broken lullaby—my voice trembling with every hiccup. His tiny fists clutch the fabric of my shirt, his tear-damp face burrowing into my chest.

"Ember?" Atlas startles, his tears starting again.

"Not now," I murmur, burying my nose into Atlas's hair, inhaling the familiar scent of baby shampoo mixed with the crisp peppermint that's uniquely his—God, I've missed it.

Jax sighs. "I know you don't want to hear this, but we need to get rid of our phones. Killian can track you, and if you don't want him to—"

"Then get rid of them." I snap, interrupting him. Exhaling slowly, I lean back, my head hitting the cold leather seat. In the rearview mirror, the darkness swallows the road behind us. Leaving behind everything that I have known and loved. *How could they do this to me? To us?*

Jax lowers the window, and the wind whips me in the face. It's cool and sharp but carries away the remnants of what once felt like home. "Just throw them out."

My fingers tremble as I lift the phone, the screen reflecting a faint ghost of my face before I let it slip through the gap in the window. It's gone in an instant, left on the side of the road, swallowed by the night. Jax rolls the window up without a word.

Atlas sniffles, shaking in my arms. "It's okay, baby," I murmur, kissing his forehead. He sighs, loosening his grip on my shirt as his breathing evens. My fingers smooth his tangled curls as my thoughts drift to what comes next—what I *have* to do next.

A fresh start. A new life.

With the bank account Ash helped me set up, I have enough to get a place, enroll Atlas in daycare so I can work, and maybe even buy a car if I can find a cheap apartment. It's a real chance to build a better life for him, for us. Jax said he's sticking around, but I know better than to get my hopes up. One day, he'll go back. Back to them. Because it's easier than staying with me, a single mother.

The serenity of having my son with me pulls me under, exhaustion weighing heavily. My eyes droop closed, and my plans for tomorrow drift off with my consciousness.

"Wake up, Little One." Jax rumbles.

I mumble incoherently, my face sinking into the familiar warmth of his shirt, soft fabric carrying traces of firewood, bourbon, and diesel. Atlas's weight is still against my chest, but I feel Jax's strength as he lifts us both, his steps careful. "I can walk."

"Hold on," he whispers. "Let me get you both settled."

I want to tell him I can manage that I don't need help, but my body isn't responding to my wants, my eyes refusing to open. The plush surface welcomes my weight, and I curl around Atlas, pressing my cheek to his hair.

Before sleep can fully claim me, warmth spreads across my back—Jax. His arm wraps around us, comforting me in a way I didn't realize I needed.

"Sleep, Little One," he murmurs. "We'll head out again in the morning."

I don't fight it. I let the steady rise and fall of his breathing lull me into the darkness, holding onto the fleeting sense of safety for as long as it lasts.

I REACH OUT, fingers brushing cold sheets where warm little limbs should be. My stomach twists. Blinking against the murky hotel room light, I sit up, frantically scanning the unfamiliar space.

"Atlas?" I croak, throwing back the covers. The bathroom door is cracked open, but there's no sound inside. I shove it open. Empty. "Atlas!" Panic claws at my throat, and I bolt into the hallway, my bare feet thudding against the carpet.

A sudden giggle bursts through my panic, followed by an excited "Mommy!"

I whip around, knees buckling as Atlas runs toward me, arms flailing, his face bright with excitement. His mismatched socks slide on the carpet as he stumbles forward, colliding into my side. I drop to my butt, wrapping him up tight. His little hands pat my cheeks, and freezing drops of water splatter my face.

"I got ice!" he announces proudly, opening his tiny fist to reveal half-melted cubes, droplets sliding down his palms.

Jax saunters up with an ice bucket and an unapologetic grin. "Figured he'd like a little adventure." I shoot him a glare over Atlas's head. "We agreed to let you sleep a little longer before hitting the road."

Atlas wiggles free, holding up his wet hands. "It's cold, Mommy! Look!"

I sigh, taking his little hands in mine and wiping them dry with the edge of my shirt. "Did Jax bring you to see the ice machine?"

"Yeah! He let me push the button, and the ice went *boom!*" He mimics the noise with a dramatic explosion of his hands.

Jax chuckles. "He's got a knack for drama."

I shake my head, ruffling Atlas's curls. "How about we trade the ice for a bubble bath?"

Atlas's eyes widen, his mouth forming an excited "O". He jumps in place, grabbing my hand and tugging me toward the room. "Bubble bath, Mommy! With bubbles!"

Laughing, I let him pull me inside. Water pours from the faucet as he turns it on full force. "Alright, alright. Let's not flood the whole place." I twist the handles so a slower stream fills the porcelain tub.

I glance back as Jax hovers in the doorway, arms crossed. "I'm not going anywhere, Baby Girl."

"Yeah, that's what you keep saying," I mumble, forcing him back by closing the door between us. I lean my forehead against the door, my breath fogging the wood. With a forced smile, I turn toward Atlas and watch as he pours a ridiculous amount of the fancy hotel bubble bath. *If Jax is paying, he can pay for the expensive bubbles.*

Atlas squirms, his little feet tapping against the tile floors. He tugs at my sleeve. "Can I get in now?"

He squeals as I scoop him up, kicking at me while I lower him into the water. He giggles as the warmth envelops him, splashing his arms and sending water cascading onto the tiles.

"Atlas!" I laugh, shielding myself.

He giggles, scooping handfuls of bubbles and piling them onto his head like a lopsided crown. "I'm a prince!"

"Yes, a very messy one." I grin, reaching for shampoo. As I work it into his tangled curls, the water turns cloudy, and I break. Months I spent without him, without being able to do the simple routine of washing his hair or sleeping next to him. I attempt to blink back tears, my hands shaking as I rinse the gray suds. His vibrant copper shines. "T-there, a-all clean."

Atlas watches me with curious eyes. "Why are you crying?"

I force a smile, cupping his chubby cheeks. "J-just so h-happy to be with you."

He seems satisfied with that, returning to his bubbles, but a quick knock at the door causes me to jump. "Everything okay in there?" Jax's voice filters through the door.

Before I respond, Atlas pipes up, "Mommy's crying!"

The door swings open, bouncing off the wall with a thud as Jax kneels beside me, his hands finding my face, thumbs brushing away the dampness that isn't from the bath.

Leaning forward, he rests our foreheads together. "What's wrong?"

I shake my head, biting my lip. "Why does it hurt so much?"

Jax exhales slowly. "Because you've been through hell and finally got your son back. It's a lot."

"Am I broken?" My voice trembles, barely more than a whisper, as I pull away.

Atlas, still captivated by the bubbles, pauses. His tiny brows knit together, his head tilting. “Mommy’s broken?”

Jax’s lips twitch into a grin despite the heaviness in the air. He ruffles Atlas’s hair before grabbing one of the towels off the warming rack and handing it to me. I reach into the tub and lift Atlas out, wrapping him up. “Nah, buddy. Your mommy’s not broken. She’s just figuring things out.” He smirks at me. “Plus, she still thinks I’m sexy.”

I roll my eyes, warmth creeping into my cheeks. “Who thinks who is sexy?” I tease, brushing past Jax with a playful pat on his chest.

Atlas squirms free from my arms, his towel slipping loose as he scampers across the carpet, leaving a trail of damp footprints in his wake.

I glance back at Jax, a smirk tugging at my lips. “Let’s get dressed and get out of here. I want to be as far from New York as possible.”

Jax watches me; his expression is soft and unreadable. “You got it, Baby Girl. Whatever you need.”

Epilogue
EMBER ROSE

Everglades City, Florida

Five Years Later...

"Atlas James, if you break that lamp, I swear on all things holy, I'm going to make you eat vegetables for a week."

He doesn't stop.

Of course, he doesn't.

His sneakers screech across the hardwood, arms flailing like he just won gold in Olympic Couch Sprints.

"Victory is mine!" he shouts, launching onto the cushions beside Jax.

Jax doesn't flinch. Just stretches one long arm along the back of the couch, baseball cap tugged low over his eyes like he's been napping through a hurricane. But his mouth twitches—barely. That's his version of laughing.

And damn if watching him play dad doesn't do something to me. Something warm and stupid and hormonal.

"You cheated," Atlas accuses, pointing like he's standing in a courtroom instead of our living room. "You weren't even *trying* until the last round."

"I don't cheat," Jax says, tossing the controller. "I just don't let children win."

Atlas scowls. "Rematch. Right now. Best of three."

"You sure you're ready for that, kid?" Jax teases, ruffling his hair.

"I'm not a kid," Atlas snaps, ducking away.

But he kind of is.

Not forever. Not for much longer. His legs don't fold neatly against me anymore. His questions have gotten harder. I haven't checked his homework in weeks, and last night he asked how babies were made—with that *tone*.

Still, in moments like this, I catch flickers of the tiny boy who used to fall asleep on my chest like I was the safest place in the world.

I watch them from the kitchen, with a dish towel in hand and my heart too full for my chest. The breeze floats through the windows, bringing salt, sand, and the distant crackle of someone's bonfire down the beach. The quiet hum of Everglades life is slow, sun-drenched, and nothing like New York.

Jax turns his head toward me, just enough to catch me staring. "You good?"

I nod. "Just waiting to see if Atlas finally snaps and throws the controller through the window."

"I'll bet he does it before round four," Jax says, deadpan.

"Mom's rooting for me," Atlas shouts.

"She *always* roots for you," Jax groans. "You two are conspiring. This whole house is rigged."

"You're just mad because I'm smarter and faster."

"And shorter," Jax fires back.

Atlas huffs and flops onto the couch. Jax smirks. I roll my eyes.

And for a moment, everything is fine.

Then someone knocks.

Not the lazy, friendly knock of a neighbor who wants to borrow sugar.

A *firm* knock. The kind that doesn't ask—it *announces*.

Atlas sits up, his body stiffening. "Mom?"

Jax rises with a casual stretch, but I catch the twitch in his jaw. "Relax, kid. It's probably the surprise I told you about."

He flashes me a wink.

That wink sets off every internal alarm I own.

"Jax." I step away from the counter, heart thudding. "What kind of surprise?"

"Just trust me, Babe." He wraps an arm around my waist, leans close enough for his stubble to scrape my cheek, and murmurs, "You're gonna want to breathe through this."

The word *surprise* hasn't felt this ominous since Marissa threw me a birthday party with strippers.

Atlas peeks through the window. "There's... three guys. Just standing there."

My stomach sinks. "Three?"

He nods. "One's leaning on the railing like he owns the place."

I reach for the doorknob. My palm is damp.

The door creaks open.

Salt-heavy wind rolls inside.

So do ghosts.

Three silhouettes stand framed by the setting sun, burned into the sky like a bad omen.

The one on the right—too quiet, too still—has eyes I used to fall asleep thinking about.

The one in the middle—always too charming for his own good—tilts his head, lips twitching with a smile that knows *exactly* how much it hurts to see him again.

And the last—tall, arms crossed, jaw clenched—doesn't move at all.

"Hello, Red," he says.

The words land like a spark in a dry field.

Atlas grabs my hand. "Mom?"

"Why don't you invite them in, Little One?" Jax's voice floats over my shoulder, light on the surface, but I know that tone. That's his *I've been waiting for this* tone.

"You knew," I whisper.

He shrugs. "They reached out. I figured you'd want the chance to throw something at them in person."

I glare. He grins.

My stare snaps back to the porch. "Why are you here?"

The one in the middle steps forward, pockets deep, chin tilted. “Easy now, Princess. We’re not here to stir the pot.”

“Really?” Jax steps beside me, arms folded. “Because your whole *vibe* screams home-wrecking chaos.”

The tall one stays near the railing, eyes fixed on Atlas.

The silent one speaks first. “We just want to talk.”

Jax scoffs. “You remember how?”

That gets him. His mouth twitches before he wipes it away.

My fingers tighten on Atlas’s shoulder. He leans closer to me, a quiet question in his eyes that I don’t have an answer for.

Not yet.

The doorway feels like a trap.

Like if I let them in, everything we built here might get knocked off the foundation.

But I can’t slam the door, either.

Not when the hollow part of my chest— the one I buried with every missed phone call and memory—won’t stop thudding.

Not when every cell in my body still knows their names.

Jake. Killian. Ash.

And not when the last thing they ever told me was a lie.

Acknowledgments

Writing this book felt like diving headfirst into a storm without a map, armed with nothing but sheer stubbornness and a questionable supply of caffeine. But thanks to an incredible crew of supporters, I not only made it through the chaos but found a spark of confidence I never thought possible. So, let's raise a glass (or a heavily caffeinated beverage) to those who made this journey not just bearable but unforgettable.

First and foremost, Grandma — my biggest cheerleader and the original muse behind my storytelling obsession. From the moment I first picked up a pen, you've listened to every wild idea with patience and unwavering support. Your dream of seeing my words in print has fueled my own, and I dedicate this book to you. Thank you for teaching me that dreams come true with a bit of perseverance and a whole lot of love.

Samantha Raffles (Author of Thicker Than Water)— you brave, beautiful soul. You plunged into the depths of my messy manuscript, emerging unscathed and with words of encouragement that kept me afloat. Your unwavering belief in my writing, even when I was drowning in self-doubt, means more than I could ever put into words. Thank you for being my constant source of motivation and for making me feel like maybe, just maybe, I'm onto something here.

Mady — you've been my rock from the moment you signed up as my first BETA reader (aka unsuspecting volunteer). You've been there through every plot twist, meltdown, and random late-night idea, offering encouragement, tough love, and the occasional reality check.

You're more than just an ALPHA/BETA/ARC reader; you're the anchor that's kept me grounded and the friend I never knew I needed. This book wouldn't exist without you; honestly, I wouldn't want it to.

To Tara, Amy, Dakota, Emma, Kristina, and Laney — thank you for taking a chance on me and stepping into the chaos with open minds and hearts. You each brought fresh eyes, honest feedback, and the kind of support that makes all the difference in a project like this. Whether it was pointing out what worked, gently highlighting what didn't, or simply cheering me on when I needed it most, your contributions helped shape this book into what it is today. I'm beyond grateful you trusted me enough to dive in and offer your time, insight, and encouragement. I couldn't have asked for a better crew to help polish this wild ride.

Finally, to the characters who hijacked my brain and the plot bunnies that refused to be tamed, thanks for making this journey one hell of an adventure.

This book is more than just words on a page; it's a testament to the friendships, love, and sheer determination that brought it to life. Here's to the end of one chapter and the thrilling start of many more.

With all my gratitude (and a sprinkle of chaos),

Harlie Kay

About the Author

Meet Harlie Kay—the author who went from dodging books to building entire worlds readers never want to leave. It all started in sixth grade when one magical story flipped a switch, igniting a love for storytelling that never faded. Since then, she's been devouring novels, crafting dark, swoon-worthy romances, and writing the kind of love that lingers long after the final page.

Her debut novel is the result of years of grit, countless late nights, and an endless loop of Smosh Games and Markiplier horror videos playing in the background. Fueled by salty snacks and sheer determination, she poured everything into a story that's as intense as it is unforgettable.

When she's not writing, Harlie's buried in a binge-worthy read, snuggling her mischievous Pembroke Welsh Corgi, or turning a homemade meal into another takeout adventure. A hopeless romantic at heart, she lives for love stories that make your pulse race—especially the ones with a few deliciously dark twists.

She's also a proud member of her local writing group, *Shut Up and Write*, where she's found her people. Their downtime? A glass of Moscato and conversations that are anything but wholesome.

One of Harlie's biggest dreams is to walk the halls of a RARE Book Signing as an attending author, sharing space with her literary idols like K.A. Knight, Jodi Ellen Malpas, and Willow Winters. Until then, she's hard at work crafting stories that will pull you in, wreck you in the best way, and leave you desperate for more.

Ready to fall in love with her world? Dive in—and enjoy the ride.

Sneak Peek At Book Two's Playlist

Scan the QR code below to get an early listen to the emotional wreckage —and the healing—that's coming next.

This playlist teases what's to come:

More heartbreak.

More groveling.

And finally... a glimpse of the happiness Ember never thought she'd earn.

You've survived the storm. Now get ready for the aftermath.

www.ingramcontent.com/pod-product-compliance
Lightning Source LLC
Chambersburg PA
CBHW070343010826
48976CB00019B/1507
9781966611035